The Viscount Can Wait

By Marie Tremayne

The Reluctant Brides

Lady in Waiting

The Viscount Can Wait

Coming Soon

Waiting for a Rogue

The Viscount Can Wait

The Reluctant Brides

Marie Tremayne

AVONIMPULSE
An Imprint of HarperCollins*Publishers*

This is a work of fiction. Names, characters, places, and incidents are products of the author's imagination or are used fictitiously and are not to be construed as real. Any resemblance to actual events, locales, organizations, or persons, living or dead, is entirely coincidental.

Digital Edition OCTOBER 2018 ISBN: 978-0-06-274737-2

Print Edition ISBN: 978-0-06-274740-2

Cover design by Patricia Barrow
Cover art by Christine Ruhnke
Cover photographs © Shutterstock (woman); © Ellya/Shutterstock (fireplace); © Michael Agaltsov/Shutterstock (flowers); © Andrey Skat/ Shutterstock (dress)

FIRST EDITION

18 19 20 21 22 HDC 10 9 8 7 6 5 4 3 2 1

With much love to my parents, Dorinda and Dave.
Thank you for being my biggest fans, both in life and in writing.

Prologue

Lawton Park
Kent, England
Summer 1841

Tick, tock. Tick, tock.

The ancient grandfather clock in the corner kept a steady cadence as Eliza stood in the open window of the drawing room. She watched in silence as the guests arrived in gleaming carriages to proceed up the front steps of her home. Not that it would be her home for much longer. Or her drawing room either, for that matter.

A light breeze flowed through the casement, toying with the golden curls that hung softly alongside her face, and she enjoyed this rare moment of peace before the evening's party when the chaos would begin. The chaos had long since started inside her head. At just sixteen years old, she was engaged to be married. It was to be officially announced tonight, and as could be expected, her thoughts were a whirling jumble of emotion. The fact that women were often married at such a young age did little to ease her anxiety, and she wondered how she could reasonably be expected to manage a change of such magnitude, even if her soon-to-be husband was a good sort of man.

The heady fragrance of honeysuckle perfumed the air, and she closed her eyes and breathed in, trying not to think about the difficult adjustments that lie ahead. The move that would take her halfway across the country and away from her family. Her new responsibilities as the mistress of a large estate. The changes she would face in becoming a man's wife.

Her father had assured her that she would grow to love Hampshire, and her fiancé had spoken kindly of the residents of the closest neighboring estate. There was even a girl who was about her age, the daughter of a duke. Eliza took an unsteady breath and placed a shaky hand over her abdomen. She hoped the girl was nice.

Eliza didn't quite feel ready—not that any young lady ever did—but her father was convinced she would find no better man. Reginald Cartwick was wealthy and smart. A landed gentleman who was accomplished and had proven himself to be valuable in matters of business. And she was fortunate. Compared to other marriageable candidates, he was relatively young.

She held no burning passion for him, but he had the makings of an excellent marriage partner. Despite the brevity of their courtship, she had already come to think of him as a friend, and perhaps that friendship could transform into love...although she knew this wasn't necessarily reasonable to expect.

Eliza's chest ached at the thought. She longed for love.

Tick, tock. Tick, tock.

A glimpse of a black-haired man below quickened her pulse. It was Thomas, Viscount Evanston, a good friend of her brother's and an unabashed rake. He was notorious in the London clubs, and notorious with the ladies too. Looking at him now, moving deftly around the small group of people who had gathered and waving ahead to someone else, she knew why. He was tall and muscular, broad-shouldered, and handsome like the devil.

Sinful like the devil too.

Eliza moved to the side of the window so she could continue to watch him undetected. At twenty-five years of age, he was a full nine years older than her, a disparity that seemed like a vast chasm of life experience that she did not possess. With his father's death and the acquisition of his title, Thomas had chosen to live his life by indulging in a few select vices: women, brandy, cards . . . in that order.

Of course, she'd heard stories from friends—cautionary tales, spoken in hushed and giggling voices—of his prowess among the *ton*. Had seen evidence of it herself at the start of this year's season. And even after it had become abundantly clear that Reginald Cartwick was her father's favored suitor, she still couldn't help but feel a curious tug of envy each time she'd watched Evanston flirting with a woman, or casting a meaningful glance at a beautiful widow as he took his leave for the night.

In a timely and accurate illustration of her thoughts, Lord Evanston greeted a female guest on the drive below. She couldn't quite make out the identity of the woman due to her elevated vantage point and the lady's oversized hat, but the fluttering hand that came to rest upon her heart indicated the lady's pleasure at his approach. Eliza supposed she was lucky that he'd never shown her the barest amount of interest, for she was half-afraid she might spontaneously catch fire if he did.

She recalled one time her father had caught her gazing a little too long in the viscount's direction, and that evening, he had been very clear regarding his feelings on the matter, feelings that were loudly echoed by her brother William. Evanston was to be seen as a family friend. Period. Anything more than that was not even a consideration. Tonight, her engagement to Mr. Cartwick would be officially announced and this was absolutely for the best. He was a good man. A responsible, well-respected man. And she was happy.

Tick, tock. Tick, tock.

There was the clock again, counting down her final minutes as the heretofore unengaged Lady Eliza Halstead. She would miss many things from this place when she left but would be glad to rid herself of that tick-tocking reminder of the impermanence of life. Was there a grandfather clock at Greystone Hall? If so, there wouldn't be for long.

A sharp knock at the door shook her out of her reverie, and she blinked in surprise. Her moment of privacy was at an end, and someone had come to collect her from her refuge in the drawing room. Eliza inhaled deeply and crossed to the door, then twisted the knob and opened it.

Lord Evanston stood before her.

She choked in surprise. "Thomas, I—er . . . wasn't expecting you."

His lips curved into a knowing smile. "But surely you knew I was invited."

"I—well, yes. I suppose I did know that," she stammered, her eyes darting past him into the hallway. Stepping backwards, she gestured for him to come inside, knowing it was the last thing she should be doing. At this point, she only hoped he wasn't seen. "I just didn't expect you to find me here."

His eyes crinkled in amused skepticism as he turned to close the door behind him. "I find that hard to believe since you were staring at me so intently from the window."

Every inch of her body flooded with mortification, and Thomas uttered a low laugh.

"Rest easy, Eliza," he said, smiling fondly. "I'm only teasing you."

She frowned. "Well, I wish you would stop."

It took whatever remained of her significantly deflated dignity to march across the room in a huff, but she managed to do it, the viscount watching in quiet contemplation. Why he was here with her now was still a mystery, but when she spun back around to face him, his expression was inquisitive.

"When did you grow into such a fearless woman?" he wondered aloud.

Now it was her turn to laugh. She'd never felt more frightened in all her life than she did right now on the brink of her engagement. "Does deciding to marry a man make me fearless . . . or somehow more of a woman?"

One dark brow raised in evaluation. "You tell me," he said.

She stared at him, mentally debating how wise it was for her to pursue this line of conversation with this particular man. "I believe you are entertaining yourself at my expense," she said instead.

With an irreverent grin, he crossed over to the sideboard and retrieved a glass. "Do you?" He shook his head. "I think I'm just now seeing a woman, where before there was only a girl. And I'm a little surprised." Removing the stopper from the crystal decanter, he raised it over his glass, then paused. Sliding out a second glass, he poured two brandies, then turned to offer one to her.

"So, you do think marriage is the measure of a woman, then," she said, unthinkingly accepting the drink. "How very old-fashioned of you. I didn't think you placed much stock in the institution."

Leaning back against the polished wood of the sideboard, he folded his arms across his chest and smiled, surveying the amber liquid in his hand. "On the contrary, I have a great appreciation for marriage. It provides me with a good many bereaved widows who end up in dire need of a living man."

She tried to swallow but her throat had suddenly gone dry. "I see," she said weakly, not sure if she should be offended or not. Taking a sip of the brandy resulted in watery eyes and a not unpleasant burn that stung all the way down her throat.

"I don't mean anything nefarious by that," he clarified offhandedly, raising his own glass for a drink. "I realize how it sounded."

Eliza scoffed. "Of course not, my lord. That would imply some kind of interest."

To her surprise, he paused, his bright eyes gazing at her from over the sparkling edge of the glass. She felt a sudden quake of apprehension, but before she was able to think on it further, he tipped back the rest of his drink and set the glass down with a bang. Similarly, she attempted to finish her brandy but ended up choking halfway through. His deep chuckle earned him a scowl and he took the glass from her hand before she could try again, placing it firmly on the sideboard.

"You should stop," he said seriously. "They might be used to it with me, but I think your father and brothers would take exception to you smelling of alcohol."

"Oh, no . . ." Eliza said, her eyes widening in horror. "Thomas—why did you have to give it to me in the first place?"

Evanston took a step closer. Too close. "I wanted to share a drink with you to celebrate your newfound womanhood," he teased, "before sending you off to the party."

She bristled. "For the last time—"

Thomas lowered his head and it shocked her into silence. He appeared to be sniffing the air between them. "Oh, you most definitely smell like brandy," he said quietly, a trace of a smile lurking on his roguish face. "What *will* people think?"

There was a shiver of alarm as she saw the way his gaze darted down to her mouth. His smile vanished and she heard a low noise in the back of his throat, as if he were wrestling with some internal conflict. Perhaps it was the fact that he was about to do something that he very much knew he shouldn't, and similarly, she found herself helpless to intervene. Although she should. She knew she should.

They stood like that, locked in a stalemate . . . the hot caress of his breath flirting with her lips, Eliza motionless in panic . . . until she broke the spell with an awkward laugh.

"No matter, I'll just stop by the kitchen and ask Mrs. Humboldt for a sprig of peppermint—"

With a decisive slide of his hands around her head, Thomas leaned down at last to press his lips against hers.

Eliza stood there, immobile, unable to even protest. The warm glide of his mouth set butterflies loose throughout her body, and although instinct begged her to pull him closer, she knew enough to keep her arms firmly planted at her sides, hands clenched into tight fists. Evanston took advantage of the moment to deepen the kiss, and she thrilled at the intimacy of his exploration even as she was filled with loathing at herself for enjoying it.

A raucous laugh could be heard through the heavy door, a necessary reminder that the oak portal was all that separated this ill-advised kiss from her family and the man she was supposed to marry. In a daze, she pushed away from him and hurried to stand near the cursed clock and far away from the viscount.

"Forgive me, Eliza," he said, smoothing a hand absently down over his cravat. "I just had to know for myself."

Her body was trembling though she struggled to conceal it. She would not give Thomas the satisfaction of seeing how he affected her. She tipped her chin up.

"Know what?" she demanded, her voice shaking.

"Whether you tasted like brandy, as well."

She stared at him in stunned outrage. Eliza would have been foolish to think that this had been motivated by anything other than his desire to toy with her. How many women had fallen prey to his charms in similar fashion?

"I see," she said with a withering stare. "And you think that makes your behavior acceptable?"

Thomas shrugged. "If you're asking whether I'm sorry I kissed you, I'm not," he replied. "You were very . . . sweet."

She had the distinct impression that to a man like him, *sweet* was probably an insult. Her cheeks grew hot. "If you've got no regrets, then you won't mind if I tell William about this, will you?"

He walked slowly across the room to approach her once more, his eyes twinkling sharply. "Feel free. But then you'll also need to tell him how you did not utter one word of protest when I did."

She scoffed. "I—"

And then she realized that it was true. She'd been too shocked to even speak until it had been too late.

Brushing past, Eliza gripped the handle and threw the door open in one swift motion.

"Get out," she snapped. "And stay away from me tonight."

Thomas strolled forwards, but his face had lost its mocking gleam. She turned her head away as he approached, unwilling to be swayed by any acts of false contrition.

"Come now, Eliza. You and I are friends, are we not?"

She felt her hesitation to provide him with an honest

answer. Finally, she gave him a tiny nod. Yes, they had been friends for years. He was almost like family, despite his questionable habits. Eliza couldn't imagine that changing even if he'd overstepped with her today . . . which he absolutely had.

"Then please accept my wishes for a happy marriage." Thomas placed a hand over his heart. "And forgive my insatiable curiosity. I do thrill at the challenge of making you blush. The women of my usual acquaintance have lost the ability, you see."

"Let me eliminate any doubt then, Thomas," she seethed. "I am not one of those women."

"Duly noted, my lady," he said with a tip of his head, staring at her a moment too long before striding past her to rejoin the gathering.

Eliza slammed the door behind him. Then she stood there, awestruck. He'd merely wished to taste her for himself before she was signed away to her husband . . . probably out of boredom. He'd done it without a thought for how it might make her feel on such a momentous night, and she hadn't even had the foresight to see it coming. Her eyes stung with tears and she willed them away.

What does it matter? She was set to be wed soon—to a man who would never be Evanston—and no one needed to learn of this kiss. It would almost be as if it had never happened, for she was sure that Evanston knew that his neck was at risk if word got out.

Eliza heard the inexorable swing of the pendulum, the monotonous ticking and tocking as if none of this truly mattered. It didn't matter who stole a kiss, and it didn't matter who she married. Not really. Even though her world would change . . . had already changed . . . time would continue to slide on without a thought for anyone or anything. And all would be well.

Throwing one last final glare at the grandfather clock in the corner, she took a shuddering breath and gathered her skirts in tense fistfuls to go join the party.

After all, there was an engagement to announce tonight.

Chapter One

Lawton Park
Spring 1846
Five years later

Thomas stretched his legs within the cramped confines of the carriage as it tilted and shuddered, heaving its way up the drive to approach Lawton Park. His friend from childhood, William, the Earl of Ashworth, stood on the front steps like some formidable sentry, appearing strangely serious as a gust of wind swept in to tease his dark blond hair.

There was the possibility that his friend's expression might be entirely benign, and he supposed it was easier to imagine yourself in trouble when you were often up to no good. Still, the look on William's face did give him the slightest amount of pause as the vehicle creaked to a taut recoil before him. Thomas elected to ignore his concern as the door flew open, and he stepped off the carriage with his hand extended.

"Ashworth, you're a welcome sight," he announced, gratified at the returning squeeze of William's hand.

"It's about time you paid a visit, Evanston," answered his friend, a smile lurking at the corner of his mouth. "I'm damned sick of your letters."

"You're lucky you even got those, my friend. As you well know, I've been busy preparing for my yearly sojourn to London."

"Yes, and as *you* well know, there are business matters that must be tended to, regardless of the season and its demands." William eyed him in annoyance. "There has been much activity with the establishment of our northern cotton mill as of late, and it's not the type of matter that I wish to discuss over scraps of parchment."

So this was the source of his irritation. Thomas grinned in irreverence at the earl's displeasure. "Absence makes the heart grow fonder, Ashworth," he answered lightly, "or so I've heard." Patting William good-naturedly on the arm, he proceeded towards the front doors. "Shall we get the dull minutiae out of the way so we are able to enjoy ourselves tonight?"

The earl halted on the gravel behind him, and Thomas likewise stopped on the stairs to turn and stare at his friend.

"Actually, I have something other than business that I wish to discuss first."

Evanston's brow lifted, and he turned to sardonically scan the landscape. "Do you wish to discuss it here on the drive? Or shall I accompany you inside the house?"

William stepped closer and lowered his voice. "Eliza is inside the house, and I do not wish to be overheard."

Eliza.

An image of William's sister, lovely and lush, invaded his thoughts. With a start, he wondered if Ashworth had finally discovered the truth about his stolen kiss those many years ago. He imagined if he had, the man wouldn't be nearly this calm.

"What is it you have to say?" he asked, his tone suddenly serious.

"You cannot hazard a guess?"

"I would rather not."

"Fine," Ashworth said with a scoff. "Let me be clear, then. Should you encounter Eliza in London this summer, you are only to treat her as a sister."

He stared at him, evaluating. "Has Eliza said something to indicate that I—"

"No. I speak simply from my own observations and my knowledge of you."

"And what are your own observations?"

"Come now," William grumbled. "Playing dumb doesn't suit you. I've seen enough questionable banter between the two of you to feel this tête-à-tête is more than justified."

There was a moment of tense silence as Thomas considered his words. Yes, he had flirted with Eliza in the past, although whether or not she had reciprocated was certainly up for debate. It had been difficult to help himself. Despite the grief of losing her husband, father and brother in a tragic carriage accident just two years before, she had somehow bloomed in the face of such overwhelming adversity. Eliza had always been a beauty, but now she possessed something else as well . . . an effortless sensuality that many women desperately tried for and never achieved. She was also highly intelligent and powerfully dedicated to ensuring her young daughter's security. Although she disliked the blinding glitter of the *ton,* Thomas knew she would endure it with the same stoic determination she'd drawn on since the accident . . . all to provide a better life for her child.

He'd never found himself lacking for ample female attention, but even distracted as he was, Thomas couldn't deny that he admired her—both as a friend and as a woman. Oddly enough, William's censure of him today was only serving to remind him of this. He guessed it was not quite the effect Ashworth had been hoping for.

Thomas dragged his eyes back up to meet William's. "You want me to act like her brother?"

"Yes."

"So . . . possessive and overbearing?" he inquired sharply.

The muscle jumped in Ashworth's jaw. "I believe you mean *protective* and *concerned.* If this annoys you, then my apprehensions are likely founded in truth." William sighed. "Look, Thomas. I revere you as a friend, but you and I both know how you are with women—"

"And you believe I would treat Eliza no better than some meaningless dalliance if given half a chance?"

"I'd like to believe the best about you, but it's the uncertainty that must be resolved before her season. And there is no chance, Evanston," he asserted meaningfully. "Half or otherwise. My sister is forbidden."

A thought suddenly occurred to Thomas. And while he immediately hated himself for it, it did hold a certain allure.

That almost sounds like a challenge . . .

Straightening, he smoothed a hand over his ebony hair and hitched his broad shoulders into a shrug. "Eliza has grown into a lovely woman, William, and I won't deny that I enjoy flirting with her. You wouldn't believe me if I did. And while we could argue for days about the blackened state of my character, it would all be for naught. She would not have me, even were I so inclined." He did, after all, remember her angry rebuke after their kiss.

Ashworth appeared to be awash in relief. "So you are not inclined?"

Rather than saying the words, Thomas merely shook his head.

"And you will behave blamelessly in London? Shall we shake on it?" William held out his hand.

Evanston nimbly reached beyond his hand and clapped him on the back before pulling him close.

"Let's drink on it instead."

Eliza sighed restlessly in her chair, scanning the ballroom while toying with her gloved fingers. She smiled at her friend Caroline, appearing charming this evening in a cornflower-blue dress ornamented with ivory lace flounces, and couldn't help but notice the mischievous smile that was tugging at the corners of Caroline's lips.

"Are you happy for a brief respite from Lord Titherton's attentions?" Caroline asked.

Eliza laughed. "My goodness, *yes*. What would I have

done without Clara?" She glanced gratefully at the Countess of Ashworth, her brother's new wife, who was currently occupying said gentleman's time with a dance. As the dark-haired beauty spun around, she affected an enthusiastic laugh for one of Titherton's comments while casting a conspiratorial wink in Eliza's direction.

Eliza's chest swelled with sisterly affection for the woman who had managed to gain the love of William, herself and Rosa—and under the guise of a housemaid, no less. She still couldn't believe the lengths the wealthy heiress had gone to in order to escape the baron who would have been her husband. She had sacrificed everything to get away from the awful man, desperate enough to go into hiding as a domestic servant at Lord Ashworth's estate. In doing so, she'd not only won the love of the earl, she'd brought him back from the brink of a dark depression that had taken root after the accident. It had earned her the tremulous fascination of the *ton* as well . . . not that she gave two figs about the *ton*. It was yet another aspect of her delightful nature.

Still smiling, Eliza heaved another sigh and glanced at the floor. There was a squeeze of Caroline's hand, reassuring and warm, upon her own.

"Why so glum?" she inquired. "Are you feeling anxious about your impending departure?"

"Are you not?" asked Eliza, turning her hand upward to return a gentle squeeze. "And if not, I'd like to learn your secret. We leave tomorrow for London, and I swear it wasn't nearly half this distressing when I was but fifteen years old being presented before Queen Victoria herself."

Caroline's amusement turned sardonic and she raised an elegant chestnut eyebrow. "Perhaps I am more at ease because I enter into this season holding no illusions of tempting a suitor tonight, or any other night." Her head swiveled back to face the crowd and she released her friend's hand to touch her coiffure, unconsciously gauging its tidiness. "But *you,* Eliza . . . I should think your return to London society will garner quite a lot of attention—"

"That is an unkind evaluation of your charms, Caroline, and not at all true."

"You are my friend, and I thank you for your charitable opinion," the girl replied with half a smile. "But you have much more to offer a prospective husband than do I. You are the sister of an earl."

"You are the daughter of a duke . . ." Eliza answered with a disbelieving stare.

"Yes, but we both know my parents have essentially deserted me. And so does the *ton,*" she added bitterly. Caroline smoothed her skirts before continuing. "You are the widow of a wealthy man who was well-respected amongst the landed gentry and aristocracy alike."

"Who just lost any claim to my late husband's lands or finances due to his heir being located."

For a solitary moment Eliza worried Caroline's temper might overshadow her manners. Her friend crossed her arms over her chest, soft gray eyes darkening to black in her fury.

"Caroline—" Eliza whispered pointedly.

"You can't expect me to accept it," she finally replied. "To turn out a widow and her child? It's barbaric," she railed in disgust.

Eliza sighed. It would not be the first time they'd had this conversation. "It is the right of first-born males to inherit the family estate," she said. "And it's the law, no more, no less. You know that."

Her friend shook her head in repudiation. "You've just finished your period of mourning, only to be booted out of your home by an *American*. If the estate had gone to a nephew, or even a cousin . . . but to go to a man whose relation to your husband was so remote it took two years to find him?" Caroline glanced away and sniffed.

Eliza was sure the man was, in fact, a cousin of some sort. Still, she could not disagree with her friend. It did seem unjust for her to lose her home, her *daughter's* home, to a man Reginald had likely never even heard of and had certainly never met. But so it was, and so it had been for countless years when no closer descendant could be found.

Caroline had not taken it well when Eliza and Rosa had found themselves ejected from the Cartwick estate and relegated to Lawton Park's Dower House. She was also likely irritated at the prospect of neighborly dealings with the new heir. Inwardly, Eliza did not envy that man, however much he had inconvenienced her.

Speaking of inconvenient men, she caught sight of Lord Evanston on the dance floor, whirling around with one of only many eager female partners here tonight. Eliza didn't know the girl well; she was pretty and petite with champagne-colored hair, and currently Thomas was smiling down at her as if she were the only woman in the world. Eliza snorted quietly to herself and turned away. It was part of his appeal, she supposed. He had the uncanny ability to make ladies feel as if they were something truly special . . . right up until he walked away to charm the next one.

"Nonsense," said Caroline lightly. "That is a situation which happens to many widows anyway and is certainly no fault of your own. You are still the sister of the Earl of Ashworth, who, I might add, has caused quite a stir by choosing the daring Clara Mayfield for his countess." Her eyes shifted back to Eliza. "And now it is expected that you shall remarry and cause an equivalent commotion."

"Hateful necessity that it is," Eliza interjected moodily. "If only London society could keep their opinions to themselves, perhaps the season would only be half as miserable." She scowled down at the blush-pink satin of her gown, gleaming and luminous, bathed in the glow from the chandeliers above. "Now I know how William felt, with the *ton* sniffing at his heels."

Caroline reclined ever so slightly in her seat to examine her friend. "I know how you have suffered, Eliza. First, losing your husband, and nearly your entire family . . . then your home. You've been through so much. But you've also been alone for a long time, and as you've discovered, a widow's situation can be unpredictable."

This was certainly true. Her world had been a nightmare of changing landscapes over the past two years, with the appearance of the next male Cartwick relation serving as the latest obstacle. As difficult as it had been to leave Reginald's family home, it was that much harder to pretend as if all was well for Rosa's sake. She still couldn't imagine marrying again, but knew that doing so would provide a sort of protection they just couldn't achieve otherwise in society. The Dower House was a temporary solution, but not something she wanted for Rosa in the long term, and Eliza would do just about anything to keep her daughter from feeling adrift ever again. She could only hope her youth had prevented her from absorbing the enormity of it all.

"Yes, it can be," she agreed softly.

Caroline glanced over at the Earl of Ashworth, who had reclaimed his bride from Titherton and was currently on his way to spending an unfashionable amount of time dancing with his wife, much to the scandalized delight of his guests.

Her gaze softening, Caroline lowered her voice. "And you don't truly wish to be alone . . . do *you?*"

Eliza sighed, and the discontent she had been trying to ignore came crashing back down around her, leaving her feeling brittle and exposed. Unhappy.

The fact was, she was scared. Reginald had turned out to be a good husband, and during their brief marriage, a warm friendship had grown between the two. At some point, she found she'd actually felt quite fortunate in the pairing, and months later, her belly had grown heavy with his child. Given time, there could have been love.

But his time had been cut short. Not only had death taken him, it had dispelled any illusion she might have had of her own security.

Caroline's brow creased. She looked worried now as she whispered, "Do you wish to be alone?"

Eliza cast her eyes towards the windows, now black with night. What she wished was to escape the maddening circus that was to become her life these next few months. But venturing to London for the season made sense for her now. And for Rosa.

Realizing she had not answered her friend, she glanced over guiltily. "No," she managed, her voice catching. "I don't want to be alone." She supposed it was the truth.

Relieved, Caroline's gaze returned to the men and women at the ball, making and receiving introductions, socializing. "And what about here, tonight. Is there any man worth knowing better?"

Staring out at the guests, Eliza observed politeness and restraint. She perceived men in their immaculate black jackets and crisp white linen shirts, and women, most younger than her, floating about the dance floor in their layered gowns of tulle and muslin. She noted a girl concealing her demure giggle as a gentleman lauded her with compliments. She witnessed proud country mamas belaboring the numerous virtues of their daughters. She watched those girls, terrified and vulnerable, perform before the stark lens of the high-society people they had painstakingly polished and primped themselves to impress.

And of course, she saw the broad shoulders and sleek black hair of Lord Evanston, turning beneath the glow of candlelit chandeliers as he danced with yet another partner.

Eliza shook her head and looked away with a frown, and

Caroline tipped her head in inquiry, searching the floor to discover what had caused her friend's upset.

"What is it?" she asked, craning her neck.

"It's nothing."

Her friend gave her a cynical glance. "I don't quite believe you." Caroline rose up slightly to gain a better view of the ballroom, and Thomas happened to pass by at that moment, aiming a sly wink in Eliza's direction as he resumed his circuit around the floor. A bloom of heat rose to her cheeks as Caroline sank back down into her seat and turned to gaze at Eliza with a wry look stamped across her pretty features.

"Oh. Him."

Eliza raised her eyebrows and nonchalantly tugged at her gloves. "I'm not sure what you mean," she replied.

"I'm sure you know exactly what I mean," Caroline said with a laugh. "You've always been a bit awkward around Lord Evanston, who is—forgive me for saying this—not a proper sort of man."

"Come now, he's not as bad as all that." Even if it was the truth, Eliza felt a distinct reaction at having Thomas insulted.

"You're right, he's worse," countered Caroline, grasping her hand tightly. "You are a beautiful woman, just twenty-one years old, with so much to offer a prospective suitor. Don't waste your time on someone like him—"

"You mistake me. I never would," Eliza answered brusquely, retrieving her hand and shifting uncomfortably in her chair. She scanned along the dance floor, but the viscount had disappeared from view. "He is not suitable in the least, and Father warned me against him when he was alive. But he has been a good friend to my family, regardless of whether you approve of his lifestyle or not. And he has been a friend to me too."

Caroline arched a slender eyebrow. "Why would your father need to warn you against him at all? Did you proclaim a preference for Evanston when you were younger?"

"*Preference* is too strong a word," she fibbed, "but Father wasn't taking any chances. Trust me, I am fully aware of the viscount's baser tendencies. I am not interested, and William would never allow it even if I were. Thomas and I are simply friends," she said, fanning her face with her hand. It had grown stiflingly hot in this ballroom, and the current topic of conversation wasn't helping.

"What if the day comes when he no longer wishes to be your friend?" Caroline asked. "What if he wishes to become your lover?" Eliza flashed a warning glance at her friend, who raised her palms in surrender. "I'm not saying he would, but a friendly conversation with that man could easily turn into seduction. Can you ever really trust a man like that?"

It was a good point, and the answer was a resounding *no*. Lord Evanston was definitely not a man to be trusted, at least not in matters of love. Or lust. And despite the increasing frequency of his flirtations with her this past year, she did not believe his feelings for her contained a scrap of anything other than friendship. As their kiss in the sitting room had proven, he was not interested in seducing her, and he was not interested in her. Not truly.

She sighed.

"No. Of course he's not to be trusted," she finally answered. "But he is still a friend and will be in London for the season, too. That makes the situation . . . complicated."

Caroline scooted her chair closer to Eliza and slipped a protective arm around her shoulders. "What if we were to find you a proper eligible husband before things become too complicated?" she suggested, gazing out towards the couples. "Come now. Are there any other men here who might tempt you?"

Eliza scoffed. "The selection in the country is woefully inadequate. This year's London season will have a more varied assortment of potential suitors." Unable to prevent a giggle from rising to her lips, she added, "And you know, of course, that the viscount is one of England's most eligible bachelors, don't you?"

Her friend smiled impishly. "Oh, did I say eligible? I meant *appropriate*."

Their laughter was interrupted by a rich baritone voice, deep and familiar.

"Which viscount?"

She froze, both at the sound of the familiar voice beside her, and at the look of surprise on Caroline's face. Both of them shot to their feet, chairs scraping loudly on the floor as they did, and Eliza raised her eyes to confirm that yes, it was Lord Evanston. He looked attractive as usual—stunning, if she was being honest—and was smiling as if he were privy to a joke that Eliza had yet to hear. It appeared that he had finished his dance and had come close enough to hear their last snippet of conversation, which was mortifying to say the least. Eliza did her best to ignore the heat of embarrassment that was spreading across her cheeks.

"Forgive me, my lord. What do you mean?"

His smile did not waver, and his blue eyes shone brightly in the golden light from above. "The viscount you were discussing—the eligible one. Surely, you couldn't mean me."

Caroline muttered something uncharitable beneath her breath and Eliza shot her a stern glance before facing Evanston once more.

"Surely we didn't."

His dark brow raised in amusement, his grin broadening. "Am I not considered eligible, then?"

"Perhaps you would be, my lord, were you not so very ineligible." She dipped into another curtsy to soften the blow, but Evanston only threw his head back into a laugh.

"Touché, Lady Eliza," he said with a chuckle. "How dare I attempt to discern the subject of your clandestine conversation."

She couldn't help a small smile in return. "Yes. How dare you."

William's footman, Matthew, passed by with champagne, and Thomas unloaded three flutes from the tray. He extended a glass in her direction and she accepted the proffered drink, her fingertips grazing his as she did, causing her to flush yet again. Evanston didn't act as if he'd noticed, and she guessed it would take a far sight more than brushed fingers to incite a reaction in him. Passing the second glass to Caroline, he glanced at Eliza with what could have been construed as compassion.

"Truth be told, I don't envy you at all. It's one thing to attend the season just for the endless varieties of entertainment. It's quite another to endure the drudgery of the marriage mart with your eye on finding a husband."

"Of course," said Caroline, "finding a husband is a tiresome business. But one can only hope Eliza will find the parties amusing."

Eliza smiled at her friend. "Well, at the very least, I will have you there to amuse me."

"Certainly, the company of a good friend will lessen the tedium," he agreed. "Although if my observations are correct, Eliza may have already secured a husband?"

Evanston's eyes shifted over to Lord Titherton. Clara, having now been reclaimed by the Earl of Ashworth, had left the man in want of a dance partner, and he was now casting furtive glances in Eliza's direction. Despite the awkwardness of the situation, she found herself relaxing and laughing with Caroline at Evanston's teasing.

"I am almost tempted to accept him merely to escape the frenzy of the season," she replied with a roll of her eyes.

"Will we be seeing you much in London, my lord?" Caroline asked with a sideways glance at Eliza.

His shoulders lifted in a shrug. "Lord Ashworth will keep me rather busy with the business of his cotton mills, I expect. But we will see."

Caroline nodded in satisfaction.

It seemed that Evanston would be too tied up with his own pursuits to cause much trouble for Eliza, something that clearly pleased Caroline, whose gaze was suddenly captured by her aunt from across the room.

"Oh, I apologize, but Lady Frances is summoning me."

Her friend hesitated for a moment as she realized that she would be leaving Eliza alone with Evanston. Then, seeing no way to avoid it, she shot her an apologetic glance and hurried off.

Eliza felt herself flush, the insidious heat spreading over her skin like a sunburn. Clearing her throat, she decided to turn the tables by facing the viscount directly.

"Funny thing," said Eliza, challenging the sultry blue spark of his gaze. "Most unmarried people attend the season to find a mate, not hunt for random bedfellows."

"Most unmarried *ladies* do, that is true," he corrected her.

She rolled her eyes. "Cotton mills and mistresses. Sounds like you've planned yourself a splendid time."

"And you as well. I'm certain you will be courted by many men."

"Are you?" she inquired with a skeptical laugh.

It was only after his ensuing silence that she looked at him more intently—noticed the way his gaze lowered to her lips. By the time their eyes met again, she no longer felt entirely in control of the conversation.

"Yes," he said thoughtfully, stepping closer to brush a fingertip across her cheek. "I am."

The gesture seemed hesitant . . . a compulsive need to touch her rather than a true show of affection. Eliza's eyes narrowed into slits. She was not the naïve sixteen-year-old girl she had once been.

"Thomas—"

"*There* you are!" came the breathless exclamation of her brother's wife. Clara floated over with a sunny smile to wrap her arms around Eliza, handily preventing any further unpleasantness. "I've been trying to find you for half an hour, but these men insist on dancing."

Eliza felt a considerable amount of relief as Evanston stepped back. She squeezed Clara in unspoken gratitude.

"By all means, stand beside me and I will fend them off on your behalf," she said with a laugh.

"Speaking of men who love to dance, I'm rather surprised the viscount has allowed himself a respite." Clara's eyes darted to the sides of the room where at least a dozen women were glancing over at him in watchful hope, shooting dark looks of envy in Eliza's direction. "Perhaps he might be willing to rescue one of those forlorn creatures?"

"Sadly, I cannot," he replied with a grin. "I made a promise to a lady tonight that I intend to keep." After draining his champagne, he set the glass on a nearby table, his eyes dancing with amusement at the shocked looks on their faces. "Lady Eliza, Lady Ashworth . . . until we meet again."

With a final bow, he departed as quickly as he had arrived, striding confidently from the ballroom. Eliza shook her head at Clara and finished her drink in silence, wondering why on earth she felt the unmistakable jab of jealousy.

Until we meet again . . .

A tiny shiver raced over her skin. She could only hope that between his cotton mills and mistresses, their next meeting wouldn't occur until after the conclusion of the season . . . and long after she'd found herself a reliable husband.

Thomas proceeded down the hallway of Lawton Park, allowing himself a small smile. Had his comment made her jealous? There was no way to know for sure, but he did find the notion strangely exciting.

He brushed the thoughts away. Her charms were more than enough to tempt even the most resolute aristocrat out of hiding, and while she was destined for a spectacular season, he knew she was not seeking one. She only sought reliability, and after all she'd been through, he couldn't blame her.

My sister is forbidden.

He couldn't blame Ashworth, either, even if his edict grated on his nerves. After all, they had grown up together despite their difference in ages, and he knew William was only looking out for Eliza.

Upon the rare visit home from Eton, or Oxford in their older years, William and Thomas could never be rid of her. Motherless as she was, the earl had asked on more than one occasion for the boys to show her great kindness . . . perhaps more than they thought an annoying little sister deserved.

So they had, and in the process the three of them had grown quite close. William's older brother, Lucas, was not nearly as present since he was often out with the earl on business, learning what was to become his way of life as a peer. A way of life that was sadly, ironically, ended before it could even begin.

Evanston's jaw ached at the remembrance of losing those loved ones—men who had been like family to him—and he gripped the polished banister to vault up the stairs. He knew what loss felt like, although his own father's death ten years earlier had not been traumatic or unexpected. Still, his life had become rather serious upon inheriting his title, and he had dealt with it in the only way he knew how . . . by refusing to be serious. Even now, this infuriated his mother to no end—an unexpected benefit, in his estimation.

Reaching the nursery at last, he shrugged off his melancholy mood to rap sharply on the door. The door creaked open, revealing the golden glow of light from within. Rosa's kindly nursemaid peered out, her eyes crinkling at the corners. "Good evening, my lord! Miss Rosa was getting rather anxious—"

"Thomas!"

Florence opened the door to allow enough space for Rosa to greet her guest, who was summarily tackled about the waist by the happy four-year-old. In the midst of his laughter, he knelt down so he could properly embrace the little girl.

"Hello, little one. Have I kept you waiting?"

He possessed no great love for children, but Rosa had established herself as the one exception to the rule. Not only were her bright moods infectious in their fun, but she was the youngest member of a family he had grown to love. Thankfully, she seemed blissfully unaware of the calamities that the last two years had wrought . . . a credit to Eliza and her constant efforts.

Rosa tried to pout, but a good-natured giggle broke through the attempt. "I was waiting and waiting . . . and the music is so nice . . . and I just want to *dance*!" Detaching from his arms, she retrieved her dolly, swinging the poppet to the faint strains of a waltz drifting up from the ballroom below.

He rose to a stand and watched Eliza's tiny daughter, face squeezed in delight, as she whirled around with her cloth partner. He had come to say good-bye, for a while at least. It would be such a small thing . . . why not give the little girl some joy?

Thomas came to a stop before her. "Would you honor me with a dance, Miss Rosa?" he asked, bowing formally and stretching out a hand.

Her eyes grew huge as saucers and she halted in place, dropping the doll in the middle of the floor. *"In the ballroom?"*

"No, no," he said, laughing warmly. "Even I sometimes have my limits. However, if you will accompany me . . ."

He reached down and took Rosa's hand. Florence fluttered around behind them, fretting about the proprieties, but Thomas simply silenced her with a finger to his lips before leading the girl into the hallway.

"Now," he said earnestly, scooping Rosa into his arms. "Where can we hear the music best?"

They both listened, venturing further down the wide corridor until reaching the top of the staircase, where the music seemed to float magically around them. It was possible they could be seen from down below if someone entered the foyer, but unlikely at this point in the evening since most guests would still be occupied in the ballroom.

"Right here," whispered his partner with shining eyes. He grinned before adopting a serious expression and tightening his hold, his right arm supporting her weight and his left extended to clasp her small hand in his.

"Are you ready?"

She beamed and nodded, her golden curls bouncing.

Thomas counted them in and they were off, whirling carefully about the confines of the hallway. Rosa tipped her head back and dissolved into giggles as they neared the nursery once again. Florence was standing, arms crossed with her back against the wall, watching them, determined to disapprove. But even the stoic nursemaid couldn't resist the mock seriousness with which he danced, and the contagious laughter of her charge. Eventually she too could be heard chuckling beneath her breath.

They continued that way for a few minutes until Rosa's excitement softened into a relaxed kind of enjoyment, her head tucked affectionately against his neck as he redirected their course when the music grew quiet, back towards the staircase. Knowing now was likely the best time to deliver his good-bye, he leaned in and planted a kiss upon her chubby cheek.

"I must leave tomorrow. I'm heading to London."

Rosa lifted her head, unworried. He'd been gone at length before, so it appeared that this alone did not concern her.

"For how long?" she asked, her eyes closing as he spun her around.

"Most of the summer, I'm afraid."

Her eyes snapped wide in disbelief. "Most of the summer? But Mama is leaving tomorrow too and . . . and . . ."

His dancing slowed as he heard the music coming to an end from downstairs. Thomas set her gently on the floor and dropped to one knee.

"I know, and it's true. But you and your uncle and Clara

will get up to all sorts of mischief while we're away, and I'll need you to tell me everything when I return."

"Will you and Mama be together?"

Thomas paused. "I—well, no. Although we may both be in London and could therefore . . . it's feasible that . . ."

A voice from the foyer below alerted him to someone's presence. Turning to identify the intruder, his gaze landed with some surprise upon the cool gray eyes of a certain woman's friend.

Lady Caroline.

Consecutive expressions of shock and revelation crossed her features, as if to say, *So this was the lady you were so determined not to disappoint this evening.*

Surprisingly, as they stared at one another, her expression turned neutral. She blinked once, tugged on her white satin glove, then gave him a quick nod and exited the foyer—and in those few seconds, he reached a certain conclusion.

Caroline was not going to reveal the truth of his secret visit to Eliza, and he wasn't sure how he felt about that.

Chapter Two

Eliza stifled a yawn with the back of her hand in a failed attempt to conceal her exhaustion, earning a snicker from Caroline and a disapproving *tut* from her friend's aunt, Lady Frances.

"A lady must never display her weariness, regardless of the demands of her social calendar," the elderly woman stated severely, sending a sideways look at Eliza. Her embroidery hoop drooped with apparent displeasure.

"Of course, Lady Frances, I apologize. How thoughtless of me," replied Eliza, smiling wanly in the direction of her friend.

It had only been two weeks, yet Eliza already craved a respite from the ceaseless dinners and parties. She had ventured out to call on Caroline this afternoon for the kind of reassurance and relief a good friend could provide. Still, she was not entirely safe from judgment, even here in her friend's drawing room. Lady Frances was a well-intentioned woman who had sacrificed much of her own life to raise her brother's child. She was like a mother to Caroline, and had certainly been more than a friend to Eliza during her time in Hampshire. Despite the woman's censure, Eliza knew that any critical remark was simply an attempt to help prepare her for the *ton* and their own bloodthirsty brand of judgment.

Caroline's gray eyes were dancing. "You must forgive her rudeness, Auntie. It's simply that she is unused to the rigors of the London season. Eliza has been tucked away in the country, has she not? You and I have profited greatly from the experience of the past two seasons and we cannot expect her to come back out into society without some small period of adjustment."

Lady Frances raised her eyebrows and resumed her embroidery, casting her gaze downward to focus on her task. "My dear, need I remind you that the ultimate profit lies in securing a husband? Why just yesterday I received a letter from your parents—"

"How odd," said Caroline in a whisper, leaning conspiratorially towards Eliza. "I received no such correspondence . . ."

"—and they urged me to ensure that you find success during this year's festivities—"

Caroline shrugged, unconcerned. "Not likely, since I'm not actively seeking success," she added under her breath.

Eliza reached out to playfully shove her friend, then adopted an expression of supreme innocence when Lady Frances glanced up suspiciously up from her needlework.

Not for the first time, she felt heartsick at her friend's

predicament. Abandoned at a young age by the Duke of Pemberton and his wife, Caroline had become accustomed to being ignored by her parents, whose capricious nature dictated their continuous travel of the continent without her. Always without her.

Eliza could never imagine treating Rosa with such unfeeling neglect. It actually took every ounce of strength she possessed to keep from leaping into her carriage and hastening the driver back to Kent, where her daughter anxiously anticipated her return. She knew Rosa was in excellent hands with her brother and Clara to watch over her, and indeed, two more protective guardians she could not have found. Their help had given Eliza the freedom to be courted by men without the process affecting her young daughter, and she was grateful for the assistance.

The stakes were high and she was determined to succeed. Could she find a man who would be a kind father to Rosa? Would he love them, and perhaps more importantly, could they grow to love him back? These questions weighed on her as she viewed the harrowing prospect of navigating the *ton*, and she reminded herself that the notion of love was a luxury, but certainly not a requirement.

"Would you care for more tea?"

Caroline's friendly inquiry interrupted her thoughts, her gaze clouded with concern. Eliza blinked and glanced around the room. Lady Frances had apparently finished her lecture on Caroline's marriage goals and was once again working on stitching the outline of a peony in varying shades of pink thread.

She was unsure how long she had spent in the midst of their company, carelessly allowing herself to daydream, but it had been long enough that her friend had noticed something was amiss.

"I . . . no, thank you. I should return home to rest before Lady Humphrey's dinner party tonight," she replied weakly, rising to a stand and smoothing her skirts, the fine satin rustling beneath her hands. "A pleasure to see you as always, Lady Frances."

"Likewise, dear Eliza."

"I'll walk with you," said Caroline, linking her arm through Eliza's and gently towing her through the drawing room doors. Once out of earshot of her aunt, she paused and turned to face her friend with an inquiring look. "Are you well? You looked upset."

Eliza enfolded Caroline in an embrace, pulling her close. She valued her company more than she could ever possibly express, especially with her temporary relocation to London and the isolation it brought. Such a curious thing, to be surrounded by people yet feel utterly alone. She had felt it for a while when she'd been in full mourning but had since been able to relearn her ease. Still, she couldn't deny that there were times when she felt overwhelmed.

Taking a breath, she stepped backwards to release Caroline. "I'm fine. Tired, but fine. Really. I just had a melancholy moment, that's all."

Caroline's eyes gleamed with compassion. "This whole, sordid endeavor must be so difficult for you. For so many reasons." Her friend squeezed Eliza's shoulders kindly. "I will see you at the party tonight. And you are welcome here any time you tire of receiving your many callers."

Eliza grinned wryly. "My callers are not nearly as interesting as you are."

"Not yet," her friend answered with a laugh.

Eliza felt much improved on the carriage ride home. It was very silly to let herself get too caught up in her thoughts. All she could do was attend these burdensome events—the luncheons, the parties, the balls—in the hopes of finding a man who could somehow be acceptable. A man Reginald would have deemed worthy.

With refreshed clarity, she decided to write Rosa another letter before departing for that night's event. Her daughter had already penned four letters—with assistance from Clara, she was sure—detailing the daily happenings in and around Lawton Park. These included matters of great import to the little girl; everything from creating a tasty new dessert with the cook to the playful scampering of her favorite woodland squirrel was discussed with the stilted phrasing and colorful language of a child. The thought of her daughter's enthusiastic retellings caused her to beam with joy, a welcome respite from the rules and seriousness of the season.

Her lips were still curved in a smile when she entered Carlton Place, the Earl of Ashworth's London residence. Slipping the fashionably beribboned bonnet from her head, Eliza hummed a tune as she reached for the tidy pile of calling cards on the silver tray in the entry hall. But the song abruptly died in her throat, her face freezing upon reading the name imprinted on the card at the top of the stack.

Viscount Evanston

She stared in disbelief, blinked, then stared some more. It appeared that Thomas had decided to seek her out after all.

Eliza chided herself for being silly. He was probably stopping by London on his way up north for business with the cotton mills, or he had chosen to pay a visit before leaving for supper at one of his clubs. Perhaps it was simply a social call.

Or perhaps he is seeking a new widow.

A frisson of alarm raced through her. Jumping to this conclusion put her in danger of flattering herself and it was most definitely untrue . . . but what if it wasn't?

Her fingers toyed with the folded corner of the card—top left corner, an indication he had visited her residence in person. Thomas's likeness stole into her mind's eye. How her heartbeat had quickened each time he'd glanced in her direction. How her pulse beat faster now with the remembrances of shared jokes, pressed hands, that singular stolen kiss. . .

Eliza bit the inside of her cheek in gentle remonstration. No, this would not do. Not when she was here to find a man who was precisely the opposite of Evanston in every way. He was a scoundrel whose penchant for women and brandy outweighed every other reasonable consideration. And if he were interested in her? It would be an interest of the most sordid kind. It would be . . . what was it he had called it the night of her engagement?

Insatiable curiosity.

Hadn't her father been clear on this before she'd been wed? And William after him? She was not to entertain the viscount during the season. As much as it irked her to be told what to do, she knew her brother meant well, and it spoke volumes of Thomas's character that his own best friend would warn her away from him. Stability, reliability, dependability . . . Thomas had proudly shunned these values many times over, and thanks to the ladies of the *ton* and their thirst for gossip, she was all too familiar with the details of his various exploits.

And Eliza refused to be exploited.

She trod unhurriedly up the carpeted steps to her bedchamber, lost in thought. If only she could hate him, or even better, feel indifferent . . . it would be much easier to maintain her distance. But Evanston had sought to be present for her family, to assist after the carriage accident as a good friend would. He had been there for her brother, and had even succeeded in lightening some of her darkest days. His attention had included her daughter, as well, which she especially appreciated given that he was not overly fond of children.

Despite this, she was no fool. Her fascination with Evanston was simply that. However, the attraction was subdued by knowing that her father was likely watching her from the afterlife, disapproval hardening his gaze, and that neither of her brothers—dead or alive—would permit Evanston to add her to his long list of delights. Even if there had been times when she'd longed to delight him.

She squeezed her eyes shut until a bloom of brightness

spread across the field of darkness, then opened them to banish him altogether. A futile undertaking. How on earth was she supposed to endure the rest of the season if he insisted upon invading her life? If only he weren't so . . .

Charming . . . Attractive . . . Clever . . .

Infuriating.

A notch formed between her brows as she ran her thumb over the smooth surface of his calling card. It was probably best if she didn't acknowledge his call, as she did not wish to encourage his visits while she was here on her own. Caroline hadn't been wrong before. When you were dealing with Thomas, a friendly conversation could easily turn into seduction.

Eliza snapped open her beaded reticule, slid the card into its hidden depths, and took a deep breath. She was ready to prepare for yet another evening's festivities and if luck was on her side, Evanston would learn to keep his distance.

"Come back here, darling."

Tugging on the bellpull, Thomas glanced over his shoulder at the woman beckoning to him from his bed, her body half-covered by the filmy drape of a sheet. As for the other half . . . well . . . it reminded him why he liked attending the season so very much.

Isabella was the widow of the unfortunate Earl of Ipswich, a man who liked to eat. Had he not enjoyed the practice so very much, perhaps he might have managed to escape the particular canapé that had done him in, or maybe he could have taken the morsel in three bites rather than the one he had attempted. At any rate, Lord Ipswich had met his maker, and his countess had met Evanston soon after, now three years in the past. She always paid him at least one visit when he was in London, and she worked diligently every time to make it worth his while.

Right now, she was being very diligent indeed, sliding the rest of the sheet aside to entice him from across the room. His eyes skimmed appreciatively over her bared skin, but he'd had all afternoon to enjoy her charms and there were other obligations to attend to this evening.

"Sorry, love," he said. "But I have a dinner party in Belgravia that I must be at soon. It's time for you to leave."

A soft rap at the door signaled the arrival of his valet, and he cracked open the door. "Draw a bath, please. And ready Lady Ipswich's carriage."

With a sharp nod, the valet was on his way. Evanston closed the door and turned to see that Isabella had taken the hint and was modestly wrapping herself with the sheet, her full lips puckered in a pout.

"You don't waste any time in getting rid of me, do you?" she complained.

Thomas smiled and crossed over to the bed, planting a kiss on the top of her caramel-colored hair. She swatted him away.

"You act as if this is something new," he replied, retrieving her undergarments from the floor where they had been tossed earlier and handing them to her. She ripped them from his hand in a fit of temper and his smile widened. "I do enjoy our time together, but all good things must come to an end."

Sliding her chemise over her head, she scoffed. "Or you could marry finally. Have you ever considered that?"

Evanston paused in the act of retrieving her dress from a nearby chair, and he rotated to view her in astonishment.

"Marry?" he asked. "Marry *you?*"

The countess raised her eyebrows defiantly but refused to meet his eyes, applying her focus to the task of tugging on her stockings. "Perhaps. Would that be so bad? I thought we rather enjoyed each other's company."

He stared at her, nonplussed, then uttered a loud and sudden laugh. Shrugging on a cobalt satin robe, he cinched the belt tightly about his waist and shook his head in amusement.

"Have you been mistaking our visits as some kind of courtship?" he asked. "Forgive me if I had a different impression altogether. I assumed any woman who would engage in a relationship that occurred solely in a bedchamber would understand exactly what was going on."

The glare she shot at him could have turned a lesser man into stone. "Of course, I understood. I was only thinking—"

"Your first mistake," he interrupted. "Your second mistake was thinking that I am even remotely interested in marriage."

They stared at each other in the dim candlelight of the bedchamber, Isabella having finally fallen silent. It was too bad, really. He had enjoyed their arrangement, but now it obviously would not continue. Thomas could forgive many things of his paramours—fits of temper, jealousy—but one thing he could not move past was the erroneous expectation of love. It was one of the reasons he preferred widows to debutantes . . . there were usually no messy emotions involved. Usually.

He moved to grasp the doorknob and stared at her in unsmiling courtesy. "I'll send a maid up to help you dress."

And with a twist of his hand, he escaped into the hallway and, more importantly, away from the needy countess.

Stepping carefully down from their carriage, Eliza and Caroline took a moment to admire the shining spectacle that was Lady Humphrey's well-appointed Belgravia town house. The evening was unseasonably warm, a balmy breeze doing little to provide relief. Eliza glanced down at her beautiful cerulean gown, made heavy by its puffed sleeves, skirts, bows and other gleaming ornamentation, then took a moment to blot her face with a lace handkerchief before joining the gathering. It was a bitter kind of irony that the season should occur in the summer months when ladies and gentlemen were expected to wear layers upon layers of their most decadent finery. Unlike some, she was rather sensitive to the warmth.

The pair journeyed forwards to pay their respects to the bedazzled hostess, swathed in silk and jewels, then made their way inside. Light cascaded down from sparkling chandeliers to illuminate the massive floral displays crowding the tables—roses, peonies and lilacs artfully arranged with bits of greenery added for contrast. She paused near a large vase, leaning forwards to inhale the luscious fragrance, then rose to smile at her friend, who was doing the same.

"The peonies are my favorite."

Caroline released a breath. "They're marvelous."

"Preferable to the smell of London in the heat, for certain," Eliza said with a laugh. Her expression changed upon noticing an unfamiliar man glancing furtively at her from the far end of the hallway. He was well dressed with a neatly trimmed moustache and light brown hair. His conversation halted as his eyes met her own. Caroline followed her gaze.

"Are you acquainted with him?"

Eliza shook her head. "Not at all," she answered. "He was staring as if he knew me, though."

"Perhaps he simply *wants* to know you."

"Nonsense," she scoffed. "Don't be silly—"

The man's conversation partner, a distinguished-looking older gentleman with graying whiskers, turned to view them, and his face lit with recognition.

"Lady Caroline! What an unexpected pleasure!" he crowed, approaching them eagerly to bow in greeting. The mysterious man followed closely behind. "I've been thinking about you. Why, I received a letter from your father just last week."

Caroline lowered into a curtsy, visibly irritated by the man's words. "Lord Latimer, perhaps you will be so kind as to tell me how the duke fares, as I've not heard from him in months." She clamped her lips shut as if she regretted the comment, but her expression gave no hint of apology.

"What she means to say," interrupted Eliza hurriedly at

seeing the surprised looks of the gentlemen, "is that it can seem like months when a cherished family member travels at length."

The older man relaxed and chuckled in agreement, while the younger smiled and eyed Eliza in keen evaluation.

"Why yes, I suppose it could seem like months," blustered the older man to her friend. "But chin up, dear girl. Nothing would bring him home faster than the announcement of your impending nuptials!" Caroline stared while he smiled and continued, ignorant of the turmoil his words had caused. "And who, pray tell, is your lovely companion?"

With a tiny sigh, Caroline composed herself and gestured politely to Eliza. "Allow me to introduce Lady Eliza Cartwick, sister to the Earl of Ashworth. Lady Eliza, this is Baron Latimer, good friend to my father."

Lord Latimer's smile faltered, then died, when he realized who Eliza was, and she felt herself tense, anticipating the familiar stumbling reaction to her family tragedy. Surely there would be some awkward attempt at conversation, perhaps a poorly phrased question regarding the deaths of her husband, father and brother. Instead, he plastered a bright smile upon his face and bowed in her direction.

"My lady, it is an honor to make your acquaintance. You look—" Latimer's gaze traveled down her form, as did the man's next to him. "Why, you look much younger than your years, I am sure!"

"I am sure I look exactly my number of years, as I am only one-and-twenty," replied Eliza evenly with a bow of her head. It was a fact of some annoyance that people often questioned her age, believing a widow with a daughter ought to be older somehow, but she was determined to remain courteous. She smiled cheerfully at the gentlemen.

The baron stared back at her in apparent dismay. "Yes, well . . . this man is Sir James Landry, my neighbor in the country." He rested his hand on the man's shoulder, and Landry tipped his head.

"I am pleased to meet you, Lady Caroline," said the man, extending his hand forwards to claim her fingers in greeting. His attention quickly shifted to Eliza. "And what a pleasure, Lady Eliza." He similarly clasped her hand in introduction, but seemed slightly more disinclined to release it. It was unnerving, but not altogether unpleasant. At last, she slid her gloved fingers from his.

"Do you both reside in Hampshire?" she asked.

"Yes," answered Landry. "Are you familiar with the area?"

"I've only recently moved away."

The baron chimed in. "Ah, I'd heard you had returned to your brother's estate in Kent."

Eliza stiffened. It was not the first reminder she'd had here in London that her life was the subject of gossip in the *ton*. As usual, she worked to show it had little to no effect on her. Some days, this apparently being one of them, took more effort than others.

"Is that what you heard? Well, I suppose your sources are well-informed." She threw a sideways glance at Caroline, who already looked prepared to bolt. "Good evening, gentlemen."

The ladies curtsied and turned to leave, but Landry

leaned forwards to touch Eliza's elbow. She glanced up at him in surprise to find inquiring, blue eyes.

"Could we speak again later?"

Eliza tipped her head. "Perhaps."

A small tug from Caroline and the pair merged into the crowd in Lady Humphrey's expansive drawing room. Her friend issued a disbelieving laugh.

"I don't think the baron was trying to offend us. Nonetheless, he was quite effective."

"He didn't even know he was doing it. I can't be offended at that." Eliza sighed. "It was terribly uncomfortable, though."

Caroline's auburn hair gleamed red in the candlelight as she surveyed the noisy gathering. "Was it the baron's remarks, or your handsome new admirer that you found so discomfiting?" she asked nonchalantly.

The corner of Eliza's mouth quirked upward in amusement. "Did you think him handsome?"

"He had a rather impressive moustache."

"Has that become the standard of an attractive man?" Eliza asked absently, her mind drifting, unwittingly recalling the strong square line of Thomas's jaw, the tempting curve of his lips. She couldn't help but think an excess of facial hair would only serve to obscure his natural appeal, although she couldn't deny that the moustache suited Landry.

Realizing her friend had yet to answer her question, Eliza brought her attention back to the present moment.

"Caroline?"

"Yes, sorry, I . . ." The girl was focused on something

across the room. After a moment's pause she asked, "You don't suppose that's your Viscount Evanston, do you?"

Eliza suddenly felt cool from head to toe, as if someone had poured ice water over her body. She couldn't be certain if it was caused by dread or excitement as she craned her neck to squint through the mass of guests.

"Surely not. Why I—"

But indeed, there he was. Impossible to miss since he was so much taller and more handsome than every other man in the room. Not to mention he was surrounded by a veritable swarm of beautiful women, as was typical. Young, old, married, unmarried . . . all of them available to him, she was sure.

Inwardly, she took a moment to curse him. He had not wasted any time inserting himself into her social affairs and she knew that his presence would be a distraction, regardless of whether he intended it to be or not.

Eliza clutched Caroline's hand in her own and forced a cheerful expression. The last thing she wanted was for either Thomas or her friend to think something was amiss. "Actually, I do believe that is Evanston, although he certainly is not *my* viscount, to which the collection of ladies besieging him can attest," she said with a tinkling laugh that she hoped sounded natural. "Shall we go make ourselves known?"

Caroline let out a delicate snort. "And add to the throng? You may if you wish, but I would rather wait for . . . Oh dear, we've been spotted."

Her gaze snapped up and a jolt of awareness seared its way through her as Lord Evanston's eyes met hers in something that resembled surprise. Perhaps he wasn't trying to meddle after all. He was immaculately dressed, his dark hair in perfect complement to his formal black-and-white attire. She watched as he politely extricated himself from the group, and once successful, made his way across the room to stand before them, a small smile playing about his mouth.

"Lady Caroline," he intoned, bowing deeply over her proffered hand. His eyes flicked to Eliza, scanning briefly over the shimmering blue satin of her dress before meeting her gaze. "Lady Eliza, I am pleased to see you. I was not expecting the pleasure." He bowed over her hand to place a kiss upon the back of her satin glove. She tried not to stare as he did it.

"Are you? With so many diversions, it's a wonder I hold any sway whatsoever," she chided gently.

His dark brows lifted ever so slightly, in direct correlation to the furious blush that crept up her neck. Eliza had no right to be jealous and knew he would mock her if he sensed it.

Evanston smiled pleasantly. "You know you do, my lady. Did you not receive my card from this afternoon's visit?"

Caroline glanced in her direction, clearly missing that piece of information. As much as she abhorred lying, Eliza knew that telling her friend about his earlier visit would only raise more questions that it would answer. Feigning ignorance here was the only course of action at this point.

"Did you call on me, my lord? I am sorry to have missed you but pleased to see you here tonight, even if it is most unexpected. Which brings me to a question of my own," she added, tilting her head. "Why are you here tonight?"

The viscount's smile grew wider and his voice lowered perceptibly. "Why, don't you know?" he asked, his eyes dancing. "I won't rest until I've scared off every last one of your suitors."

Chapter Three

Evanston observed Eliza's face, watching as her normally lustrous skin turned pale. He wasn't certain what kind of reaction he'd been expecting with his comment, but it hadn't quite been this one.

After a moment, she seemed to realize that he was joking and the color revived in her cheeks. "Of course, you aren't being serious. I should have known."

He tilted his head in evaluation, his gaze lowering to rest on her luminous green eyes. "I'm sure I could be serious if there was a need," he said blithely, reaching down to tug on the sleeve of his jacket and scanning the room, already in search of his next conquest. "Thank God there rarely ever is."

Caroline rolled her eyes and glanced away, while Eliza continued to stare at him, unsmiling.

"How very lucky for you, Lord Evanston," she said.

"What a happy existence that must be, where nothing serious ever seems to occur."

His eyes halted their progress, then jerked back to Eliza. He had just said something idiotic to a woman who had endured a lifetime of losses, and she had understandably taken exception. There was a sick slide of guilt as he realized his mistake. Regardless of their differences, he cared about Eliza deeply. In fact, she and William were probably the closest thing to family that he would ever have. He needed to remember that occasionally.

"No offense to you, of course, who has suffered greatly these past two years," he said, his voice tinged with regret. "You know what I meant."

"I'm not sure that I do, but I'll take that as your attempt at an apology."

He reached forward to take her hand and pressed it solemnly to his lips for a kiss.

"I do apologize."

When he straightened once more, he found her color had risen again. Whereas the conversation had started with her appearing ashen and pale, now the crests of her cheeks had turned undeniably pink in what could only be described as a blush.

Interesting . . .

Thomas could sense the burgeoning desire within him; could feel the same intrigue that had prompted him to briefly disregard caution those many years ago at Lawton Park. He pondered the reality of the situation. Eliza Cartwick, with her curls of spun gold, eyes of lightest green, sweet rosebud of a mouth and soft, generous curves would make any man an excellent wife.

Or she could make him an excellent paramour.

Almost as if she could read the direction of his thoughts, she tugged her hand away and took a step backwards.

The idea was outrageous, of course. It would probably cost him his relationship with her, such as it was, and it would cost him his friendship with William too. It wasn't even worth considering. But as his eyes raked across her, he could feel his arousal increasing. It wouldn't do to interfere with her husband hunting, but could they not enjoy each other's company in private? What could possibly be more satisfying than having Eliza in his bed?

Looking eager for escape, the woman in question took immediate notice of the approaching Lady Humphrey, who had begun the process of organizing guests for dinner.

"It appears we are about to dine," Eliza said hurriedly, lowering into a curtsy. "Good evening, Lord Evanston."

He inclined his head. "Good evening, my lady."

With a bow to both her and Lady Caroline, who was making a show of eyeing him distrustfully, he took his leave to join the hostess. Lady Humphrey had decided to claim him as her escort into the dining room, as her husband was away from town on business. He did not mind as it garnered him a bit of attention, and with a gentlemanly flourish, he extended his arm to her.

Dinner passed tolerably well. The constant chatter of the ladies surrounding him was the usual irritation, but one much easier to ignore when stealing tiny glimpses of Eliza, who had now thoroughly managed to capture his fascination. His observant hostess noted the direction of his gaze shortly after the first course began.

"It was most unexpected to find both you and Lady Eliza in London for the season, my lord," she said while casting a mischievous glance in his direction. "Quite frankly, it was too good to pass up, the opportunity to have such interesting guests at my residence. You, being so eligible yet so hard to pin down, and she, missing from society these past years and . . . appearing not at all how a bereaved widow ought to look."

Thomas was unsure if the lady was insinuating something less than ideal about Eliza's character. In a rare instance of pique, he found it did not sit well with him.

"And how, pray tell, ought a widow to look more than two years after the tragic event?" he snapped. "Surely London cannot expect her to live out the rest of her years in widow's weeds?"

Lady Humphrey threw back her head and laughed, her hand floating gently down to rest upon his own. "Why no, my dear. You misunderstand me entirely." Her eyes shifted to find Eliza at the opposite end of the table, smiling charmingly at a male guest who was clearly enamored with her. "She may wear whatever fine colored satins and laces she likes." The lady slid her hand off his and seized her napkin, dabbing her mouth carefully with the corner. "I know you both have become *friendly* over the years, so perhaps you do not view her in the same light as society. But indeed, she possesses such natural beauty that one would be hard-pressed to find clothing unsuited to flatter her. This, I suppose, is what the *ton* strives to understand. How a woman who has endured so much can still manage to be so ravishing." She paused. "Don't you think?"

Evanston knew she was trying to lure him into a telling response, and as much as he would endeavor to entertain her on any other day, Lady Humphrey's excessive interest in Eliza bothered him for some reason. The prattle of the other women surrounding him at the table petered out as they inclined their heads in anticipation of his answer.

"Why, I am certain there is no way for me to know what the *ton* is thinking, about her beauty or anything else, for that matter," he said with a tight smile.

Those nearby murmured placidly in agreement, though he could sense the disappointment his response had evoked in his listeners. They'd certainly been hoping for more feeling, angst . . . *something* incredibly diverting, and were probably surprised he had not delivered. It was not in line with his usual habits.

His noble hostess was not as easily dissuaded and eyed him warily, leaning back slightly to allow the footman to remove her soup bowl from the table as they moved into the next course.

"You know what I do find curious, is that as close as you two are rumored to be, you have spent far less time conversing this evening than I would have expected."

Inevitably, those nearest him glanced over at Eliza, who had indeed done an impressive job of avoiding Evanston's gaze upon their entrance to the dining room. Perhaps she really had read his mind earlier.

"Is not the purpose of a social engagement such as this to expand one's friendships and acquaintances?" he asked innocently. "It would make little sense for her to speak only to me."

"Yes, 'tis true. And Sir James Landry has occupied most of her time so far."

Taken aback, he examined the man seated next to her in closer detail. He had not recognized Landry with the addition of a moustache, and yet there he was, hanging on Eliza's every word, eyes fixed closely upon her.

"Surely all is well between you two?" asked Lady Humphrey, not missing the envious nuance of Evanston's stare.

Averse to satisfying her curiosity any more than he unwittingly had already, Thomas forced himself to relax back into his chair and raised his wineglass towards his meddling hostess, the crystal glittering in the glow of the candlelight, ending the topic of conversation with one word.

"Surely," he answered, with a smile as false as his reply.

Eliza sighed amidst the insufferable heat of the drawing room, the rapid beats of her fan only managing to circulate the stifling air about her face. The warmth was part of the problem, but she could not discount the viscount's presence this evening as also causing her some significant amount of distress.

Despite avoiding his gaze through some pleasant conversation with Sir James during dinner, the simple knowledge that Thomas was there, close enough to touch, vexing in every possible way, was enough to cause her chest to constrict. She could only hope she didn't look as pink and flushed as she felt, for she'd gotten the distinct impression that he had keenly detected the way she had responded to his nearness.

It was too early to leave the party without attracting unwanted attention, but she needed some air and a moment to quiet her chaotic thoughts. Her eyes darted around the room. Caroline was caught in conversation with a man who, for once, did not seem to annoy her, so Eliza was hesitant to interrupt. Landry was distracted at the moment as well, chatting with Lady Humphrey as she sipped on a glass of sherry. Lord Evanston she could not find, but was sure there had to be an assortment of ladies keeping him occupied. The time to break away was now.

Eliza proceeded down the hallway and found a footman en route to his next task.

"Excuse me, but is there access to the rear garden?"

With a convivial nod, he gestured for her to follow him. Soon she was stepping outside into a small but beautiful terraced garden behind the residence. Thanking the servant as he took his leave, Eliza proceeded carefully down the rock pathway. The flagstones were covered with lush green moss, masking her footsteps as she took great gulps of the air that had turned mercifully brisk at this later hour.

She sank down onto an ornately carved bench placed to advantage beneath a wooden arch thick with flowering clematis vines. A deep inhale of the perfumed air improved her mood dramatically, and she flattened her palms down beside her on the seat to ease herself back against the bench, closing her eyes in relief.

"May I join you?" asked an unexpected voice.

Eliza jerked in surprise and sat upright to face the man who had made the request. To her amazement, Sir James Landry, with whom she had conversed earlier, had followed her in her flight from the drawing room.

She was not entirely at ease. While she did like Landry and thought him to be amiable, the last thing she wanted was for another guest to come upon them together in the garden. Alone.

"I'm not certain that is wise, sir."

"I will leave, if you wish," he replied with a bow. "Although I would rather enjoy another chance to speak with you."

"As would most of the men present here tonight," declared a sardonic baritone from near the house. Lord Evanston strolled out onto the flagstones, his size appearing all the more imposing given the close surroundings. "Manners maketh man, Landry, wouldn't you agree? Or haven't you the sense to detect when a woman wishes for a moment to herself?"

Given their recent history, Eliza would not have believed Evanston capable of delivering her from a most awkward situation. Yet here he was, smoldering . . . setting her aflame while giving her new suitor a proper setdown. It was almost as if . . . but no, it wasn't possible . . .

Is he jealous? The query took root and sprouted in her mind as a distinct, although distant, possibility, soon to be followed by another thought that was definitely not a question. *He followed me outside.*

A dizzying thrill spun throughout her head, causing the world to rotate slowly, and she cursed herself for allowing these old feelings to resurface. She could not know Thomas's intent, but even if it was only to protect her from Landry's advances, he had cared enough to both watch and pursue.

Pursue? That was likely too strong a word.

"Lord Evanston. I remember you well," replied Sir James in a dry tone of voice. "What I do not remember, however, is the nature of relationship you share with Lady Eliza. How is it that you have come to speak on her behalf?"

Eliza stood and interrupted before Thomas was able to make his retort. "Lord Evanston and I were raised almost as siblings," she answered. "Any interjection on his part is surely born from his sense of obligation."

To her surprise, Thomas did not respond. Instead he stared at her with those incandescent blue eyes and listened in silence.

"Ah. Then I suppose he would have no objection to my escorting you to the theater next week," said Landry, shooting a dark look in Evanston's direction.

She glanced over at him again, and still he remained quiet. This only served to increase her curiosity. Was he here to interfere with this potential suitor for some reason, or was he truly feeling protective?

"I would be pleased to accompany you, sir," she answered, directing her attention to Landry once more before she lost her courage.

Landry's expression changed, his glowering at Thomas interrupted by her answer and transforming immediately into triumph. He approached her and lowered into a polite bow.

"You do me a great honor, my lady. I will count the hours until I see you next." Turning to depart, he paused to address Lord Evanston, who had stepped into the path to block his way. "You," he muttered quietly, "have not changed since Oxford."

Thomas eyed him with pity. "While you, I see, have tried to grow a moustache."

Sir James stiffened in offense. Worried that tempers would again escalate, Eliza shot daggers at Evanston, who finally relented and stepped aside, permitting the man to leave. When she and Thomas were alone at last, the space seemed preternaturally quiet. Her slippered feet made no sound as she stepped nearer to the clematis vine hanging over the bench, and she reached out to gently stroke an open bloom with her fingertips.

"I take it you know him?" she asked.

"I do."

"You could have been more civil, I think."

"I suppose so," he replied, with no hint of apology.

"Are you here to distract me?"

"That depends," he asked, taking a step closer. "Do you find me distracting?"

Eliza sighed, trying to ignore the racing of her pulse. "Are you here to interfere?" she asked more insistently.

"I am here to enjoy the season."

"So why are you following me?" she asked. "Our purposes are not aligned."

His brow creased. "Are you saying I shouldn't try to defend you if a man chooses to disregard propriety?"

Eliza's heart leaped. He had been trying to protect her. She quelled the foolish thought.

"Coming from a man who disregards propriety on a regular basis, I find that most ironic. Let me remind you that I am a widow, my lord. I require no chaperone . . ."

"And yet, despite your vast experience and advanced age, I would rather ensure you are not caught in a compromising position." She could see the muscle in his jaw tense as he glanced away. "Besides, William would expect it of me."

"I think William would prefer it if you left me alone," she said, bristling. "Of all the gentlemen who could place me in a questionable scenario, you are perhaps the likeliest."

Thomas didn't disagree with her. Coming closer, he took her hand.

"Eliza, I am not here to clip your wings and will be too busy with my own affairs to bother you overmuch. But all the same, I cannot stand by if your suitors behave in such a way."

Evanston was acting brotherly at the moment, but the behavior he professed to be concerned about could also come from him at any time. Indeed, she remembered an instance when it had. Eliza liked to think she'd be more prepared now to guard herself against such an event, but the sting she'd felt at his allusion to *his own affairs* was making her doubt herself more by the minute. Eliza tipped her chin up.

"You mean if they behave like *you* would?"

His eyebrows raised in surprise. "Actually, yes."

"Forgive me, but it seems you are familiar with Sir James

and have formulated your opinion already," she snapped. "I, as of yet, have no real opinion of him, and would appreciate you giving me space to create one. That is, unless you know him to be something other than a gentleman."

He released her hand at last. "Landry has always had a self-righteous air about him—"

"The man would likely say the same of you," she said with a small laugh.

"—but despite my bias against him, he is sure to be worthy," he added, shocking her into silence. "You are beautiful, Eliza, and have much to offer that these spoiled debutantes do not. Landry will not be your sole suitor; I only ask that you be careful."

Eliza stared at him in astonishment, unable to move past something he'd said.

You are beautiful.

Deep down, the part of her that longed to be close to him rejoiced at hearing the words. But the girl who had been humiliated by him in her own drawing room was not nearly as forgiving. She knew it was lunacy to believe that his acknowledging her prettiness could amount to something like love, but the question remained: Would it matter even if it did? Thinking back to her father's words and William's warnings, she knew that it wouldn't.

And he was most definitely not being serious. The viscount was rarely serious, after all.

Her heart thundered in her ears. "I will thank you to not speak of beauty, Lord Evanston, even in jest."

"In jest?" Realization dawned on his face. "Eliza—"

The door burst open and Caroline rushed onto the terraced steps. "*There* you are! My goodness, I have spent a quarter of an hour looking for you . . ." Her words faltered when she perceived that Eliza was not alone and, more importantly, who she was with. She dipped into a surprised curtsy, and Lord Evanston bowed back in kind. "I beg your pardon, my lord. All is well here, I hope?" she asked, her eyes darting to Eliza in confusion.

Eliza had to laugh. She'd come outside to seek respite, from the heat and from the viscount, and had only succeeded in perspiring further in the presence of the man she'd been hoping to evade. Snapping open her reticule, she removed her handkerchief and touched it to her forehead.

"I am overheated, I fear," she stated, perhaps more urgently than she felt. She latched the decorative vessel closed. "Do you think we will be missed if we leave now, Caroline?"

"I am happy to oblige. The only interesting man at the party was one of the first to depart," she said glumly, then winced up at Evanston. "No offense meant, of course."

"None taken, although I hope not everyone present tonight shares your sentiments."

Eliza couldn't tell if he meant that as a general comment or had directed it at her, but she had grown weary of guessing at his motives. With a decisive swish of her skirts, she traversed up the flagstone steps, pausing at the top to spin round and lower into a curtsy.

"Good evening, Lord Evanston."

Before he could make his bow or even say a parting word, she continued on her way into the residence, eager to place as much space between the two of them as possible.

Evanston waited until the door had shut behind the two ladies, then ambled to the spot where Eliza had stood. A charming bench, a carved trellis with flowering vines overhead, mossy ground cover underfoot.

A card on the flagstones, trapped in the moss.

The scrap must have fluttered out of Eliza's reticule when she'd removed her handkerchief. She had been too occupied to notice.

I only ask that you be careful.

His words to her echoed loudly in his mind, and he felt the force of his own hypocrisy. Thomas ignored his conscience on a daily basis, but that didn't mean it never voiced itself.

Lowering himself down onto the bench, he sighed, gazing up at the tiny swatch of night sky. He was astonished to discover that Eliza somehow thought herself lacking, but she had always been exceedingly modest. Tonight, though, he had said too much. And to his dismay, he was growing increasingly obsessed with the idea of having Eliza all to himself. At least for a time, until she found an actual husband. Perhaps even afterwards too if she allowed it.

Evanston knew it was beyond wrong to even attempt such a thing. That there were many female guests lingering in the drawing room who would be more than happy to distract his misguided lust. Briefly, he considered making use of one before the night was through.

Yes, he thought. Perhaps he could even find a flaxen-haired beauty with shining green eyes . . .

With a scowl, he rubbed his temples. The idea didn't hold as much excitement as it should have. And the thought of Eliza being courted by another was beginning to weigh on him in ways he hadn't expected. He wasn't certain what to make of that.

Shaking his head, he stared down at the card on the ground, leaning forwards to extract the scrap from its entanglement. It appeared to be blank.

No, not blank. There was text on the opposite side and one of the corners had been folded over. It was a calling card. He flipped it over between his fingers, expecting nothing significant, only to have his breath catch in his throat. A grin slowly spread across his face.

It was his calling card, and Eliza had dropped it.

Chapter Four

The days passed, flowing in and out of existence, each one so similar that it was difficult for Eliza to distinguish one from the other. She was called upon, and placed calls of her own. She attended concerts and balls, rode horses with Caroline in Hyde Park, and when not otherwise engaged, stayed up after dinner to play cards with Caroline's aunt. Flowers were delivered to her town house in the interest of various potential suitors, and were often courtesy of Sir James Landry. Only once had she seen Thomas during those days, riding his enviable black Arabian along Rotten Row. It had greatly displeased her to discover it had been, without a doubt, the highlight of her week, for he did cut a fine figure on his horse.

Regardless of her discontent, the evening of her outing with Sir James arrived at last. Drury Lane was a beacon—a shining spectacle in the London night—and she stood outside, gazing up at the grandeur before her. The majesty of the theater's great columned portico was unique among the neighboring structures of Catherine Street and never failed to impress. Eliza felt a tremor of excitement as they entered the bustling crowd. She was more than eager to see tonight's showing of the comic opera *L'elisir d'amore.*

She and Sir James made their way into the entry hall amidst the multitude of society's most refined patrons. Her companion had, so far, behaved as a gentleman, even extending his invitation to include Lady Caroline and her aunt. The pleasant offer had been declined by the ladies with some sadness as Lady Frances was not feeling especially well, and Caroline felt it best if she should stay home to tend to her.

An unsettled feeling gathering in Eliza's stomach. She felt guilty about concealing the truth of Thomas's call from her friend and wasn't even sure how the lie had begun. It was such a minor incidence, although she suspected her panic upon seeing the viscount's card at her town house, coupled with the knowledge that Caroline did not approve of him, had likely played the greatest parts in it. During the ride home from Lady Humphrey's dinner party, her friend had questioned her at length over not just her opinion of Thomas, but their encounter in the garden.

Nothing happened, she had reassured her, but it hadn't felt like nothing. Evanston's pursuit of her into the garden and his ensuing reaction to Sir James had felt very much like something, no matter how she tried to deny it. And Eliza spent that night fitfully tossing in her bed, trying to imagine the things he might have said to her, had they not been interrupted.

I will thank you to not speak of beauty, Lord Evanston, even in jest.

In jest? Eliza . . .

Landry showed her into his theater box with a gallant sweep of his arm, and Eliza took her seat, carefully arranging the full skirts of her evening dress. She felt the dark green gown complemented her well, with its gleaming satin bodice, low neckline and sleeves worn entirely off the shoulder. A part of her felt dreadfully exposed, while the other part of her . . . the part that had married young and lost nearly everything . . . luxuriated in the admiring glances, covertly stolen. Having spent so long hidden away in the country, she couldn't help but enjoy a bit of attention, even if it was the jackals of the *ton* that were providing it.

You are beautiful.

Eliza shook her head as if to rid herself of an annoying gnat. As usual, she scolded herself for being unwise where Lord Evanston was concerned. Inferring too much into such a meaningless conversation could lead to her straying off course and prevent her from finding a steadfast husband. Lead her to . . . distractions.

She glanced over at her companion, who was also taking his seat. Landry had shown the appropriate level of admiration upon seeing her tonight, and his attention was a compliment in itself. But she suspected, had he been present tonight, that Evanston's singular blue gaze would have scorched pathways over her body. If he truly thought her beautiful, he would not bother masking his appreciation with politeness. The thought sent a pleasant shiver of heat down through to her core.

Eliza reached up to adjust her emerald earbobs, then slid her fingertips down to linger on the strand of pearls encircling her neck. Her father had often mentioned how the necklace had been a particular favorite of her mother's. Touching it now, in this moment of reflection, she wondered what honest advice her mother might provide, were she alive to give it. Stay clear of Evanston, and all things related? That was likely the only reasonable conclusion and yet it didn't feel right with Thomas. Reprobate or not, he was a friend. And there was a pull with him that was becoming increasingly difficult to ignore, although heaven knew she had years of practice.

"We have a splendid view from my box. Wouldn't you agree?" Landry inquired in his cultured accent.

"Oh, yes. Such a lovely prospect from this location," she said, determined not to think of Thomas any longer and leaning forward to take in the sight. They were situated in a rear box on the lower tier. It was not the closest box to the stage, but quite nice all the same. She could see the orchestra practicing in the pit, their tuning cacophony sent outwards to float lazily through the air.

Her eyes swept across the theater seats below to marvel at the crowd—the ladies in their sparkling finery, the gentlemen in their dress suits and tailcoats, and the gilding on the walls illuminated by the glowing chandeliers hanging from above. Curious for a closer look, she raised her mother-of-pearl opera glasses to inspect the occupants of the other private boxes.

Eliza panned around until she reached the box on the opposite side, nearest to the stage. The inhabitants were a couple, presumably a lord and a lady of some sort, the woman wrapped in a dress of an eye-catching shade of red. Her inky black hair was swept up with an abundant mass of curls left down to frame her face. Eliza was not familiar with the beautiful woman, but she certainly appeared to feel at her ease in this environment and was, of course, seated in a prime location with her companion.

"Can you tell me, sir . . . who is the woman in the red dress?" she asked Landry, handing him her glasses. "The one in the first box. Do you know her name?"

He smiled, accepted the binoculars, and leaned in for a closer look. Silent at first, he continued to stare, muttering possible monikers under his breath. Then he went still abruptly. Reclining back in his seat, he relinquished the opera glasses and stared moodily at the stage, still concealed by its curtain.

"While I, myself, am not familiar with the lady, it appears Lord Evanston may be able to enlighten you."

Her eyes widened at the same moment the orchestra fell silent with the appearance of the conductor. The audience politely applauded as she lurched further in her chair, raising the glasses so quickly they nearly struck her in the face. Eliza needed to prove Sir James wrong, and perhaps prove to herself that Thomas wouldn't dare show himself at the theater on an evening he knew she would be in attendance while accompanied by another man. After all, he had said he would leave her alone.

Yet there he was, seated next to the alluring lady in red.

Her breath seized in her chest. Soon she was seeing red everywhere.

How had she missed him? She simply hadn't been looking. Had not expected such a violation of her trust. There was, of course, a small chance it was a coincidence, but there were also a hundred different amusements in the city at any given moment.

Her nagging instinct told her he was here to impose on her night in some way. Aside from this, she couldn't exactly explain the magnitude of her anger. Her eyes narrowed at the mystery woman beside him, the one who was so very striking. If she were being truthful, she could admit the lady was quite more than that. If she were *really* being truthful, she could also quantify her reaction as precisely what it was.

It was jealousy. And now she was going to impose on the viscount.

The orchestra began to play. The lights rose upon the stage. Landry clapped but glanced nervously at Eliza while she seethed in irritation, staring blindly down at her lap, until she finally lost the battle.

"Pray, excuse me, Sir James," she said, rising from her seat despite her best efforts against it. "I shall return shortly."

She could almost feel the movement of countless opera glasses throughout the audience, turning to focus on their box and the sudden commotion. Color rose upon Sir James' cheeks as he also detected the unwanted attention, and he stood, disbelief marking his features. Before he could change her mind, she turned and made her way to the door.

"The show has begun!" she heard him call in astonishment, but she had already exited the box, her heavy skirts rustling as she advanced through the hallways, intent on dismembering Lord Evanston.

Thomas leaned back in his seat and grinned, lacing his fingers across his abdomen as he waited for Eliza. She had spotted him much earlier than he had expected she would, and now, set on questioning him, was about to break with all decorum. He couldn't wait.

It wasn't but a moment later that he heard the door behind him opening, and Thomas twisted lazily around in disingenuous surprise. Mrs. Victoria Varnham, the woman who was his companion tonight, turned to face the intruder with an expression of offended alarm, but Eliza proceeded unperturbed, to lay her hand on Evanston's shoulder.

"A word outside if you please, my lord." Her tone was deadly.

Victoria stirred in her seat. "I beg your pardon—"

"Now," Eliza said, choosing to ignore the woman's outburst. She removed her hand and spun on her heel before any more was said, leaving the stately wooden door ajar so Evanston could join her.

Sighing in amusement, he leaned close to Mrs. Varnham and whispered his apology before standing and quietly exiting to meet Eliza.

He emerged into the corridor outside the row of private boxes to find her glaring at him with arms crossed. Softly shutting the door behind him, Evanston allowed himself a split second to admire her. It had been impossible to appreciate the curve of her waist, the naked lines of her shoulders or the creamy swells of her breasts from his vantage point across the dim theater. But here in the abandoned hallway he saw it all. The emerald satin of her gown was in perfect complement to her hair, her eyes, her skin.

Bloody hell . . .

A surge of arousal raced through him, and all too easily he could imagine Eliza in his arms, calling his name in a moment of rapture. Closing his eyes for a moment, he reminded himself that maintaining control was of paramount importance. He still wasn't exactly certain what he was after with her, but he had no desire to jeopardize whatever it was by being overly eager. Standing straighter, he met her gaze.

"May I help you?" he asked a bit too politely.

Eliza paused, then broke away with a huff of frustration. "You may begin by telling me why you are here tonight."

"I am here to see the opera." He furrowed his brow and regarded her in confusion.

"Oh, is that all? I assumed you were here to make things difficult for me."

Thomas uttered a laugh. She was correct, of course, not that he would admit it. "I daresay had you not been peering into private boxes, I would have slipped your notice entirely." He took a step closer to her. "However, I am unsure why my presence here tonight would cause you such difficulty. Perhaps you might explain it to me?"

Her luminous green eyes widened a fraction before she stiffened once more into a defensive posture. "You are a man known for causing trouble."

"Am I?" Evanston smiled, still advancing. "Why did no one tell me of this before? I would have taken great pains to do my reputation justice."

Eliza stepped back and bumped into the wall on the far side of the corridor. She glanced around her, seeming surprised that she had retreated so far, then reclaimed her step forwards and raised her gaze in defiance.

"I believe you've done quite enough to merit your status, my lord. Don't come any closer—" she added suddenly, stretching out her hand as if to ward him off.

The muffled notes of the orchestra filtered through the walls, creating an ambience of surreal solitude that only heightened his heated awareness of her. He planted his feet solidly on the carpet.

"If I am truly as wicked as you believe me to be," he said in a low voice, "would I not already be ravishing you against the wall?"

Eliza's mouth fell open in astonishment, a pretty pink blush slowly spreading across her cheeks. It took her a moment, but she finally regained the ability to formulate a sentence. By the time she had, her eyes were shooting sparks.

"For all I know, you have ravished the woman behind that door at least once already tonight," she said haughtily. "Perhaps you do not feel the need this particular moment."

He thoughtfully considered this. "Perhaps," he conceded.

Eliza's color rose even further. Dear God, she was the loveliest creature. Even here, like this, wanting to tear him to pieces. He longed to infuriate Eliza beyond her capacity to bear, then soothe the tension away with his hands, his mouth, his body . . .

Her terse voice interrupted his daydream. "Who is she?"

Yes. She had just made a pivotal mistake, one that filled him with satisfaction.

"Why do you ask?"

A flash of guilt crossed over her features. "Never mind," she said. Then added more quietly, "You are insufferable."

Thomas smothered a laugh. "I am aware. But tell me," he added, sobering. "Is it considered more or less insufferable to be untruthful to your friends?"

Her mouth dropped open in what seemed like confusion when the door to Evanston's theater box unceremoniously swung open. The music grew louder and Mrs. Varnham stood there, flushed in irritation, then stalked over to hook her hand possessively around his elbow. The spike of annoyance he felt at being interrupted quickly gave way to gratification at how Eliza's brows drew down at the sight.

"Stop wasting your time out here, darling," Mrs. Varnham insisted with a veiled glare at Eliza before gazing coquettishly back at Thomas. "You're missing the performance."

He smiled down at her. "I shall be in shortly," he replied.

She wrapped her arm more tightly around his to pull him closer. "Surely this cannot be more entertaining than—"

"I shall be in," he repeated in a still pleasant, but slightly tighter tone of voice. She knew better than to try managing him. "Shortly."

There was a momentary pause during which Mrs. Varnham realized she had just been dismissed, and the woman's eyes narrowed dangerously. Then the expression vanished, the corners of her garnet mouth pulling upwards into a smile of passive indifference.

"Of course, my lord."

Releasing him, Mrs. Varnham pivoted on her heel to return to the darkened safety of the theater box, shutting the door behind her with an annoyed pull. Glancing once more over his shoulder to ensure privacy, he brought his gaze back to Eliza, who was watching him with curiosity.

"Please, continue."

She hesitated. "I can't recall the course of the conversation."

"Allow me to assist you then," he offered. "You were about to tell me why you've been untruthful with your friends."

Her confidence flagged, and then she straightened her spine. "I'm not certain what exactly you are referring to, but I wonder what my brother, the earl, might have to say about your harassing me in London. Or your kiss on the night of my engagement."

So she remembered it too. Thomas wondered what she thought of it now that five years had passed.

"I have no fear of you informing William of anything. Not when I'm certain you've even kept the sordid details from your best friend. That little hellcat would be clawing my eyes out if she knew." He paused. "And then of course, there is the matter of my calling card."

"Wh-what are you talking about?" she asked with a voice that was not steady.

He stepped forwards, reaching into his coat pocket as he did, to retrieve the card she had dropped at Lady Humphrey's dinner party. "This should help to clarify," he replied, sliding it into her hand, resisting the urge to close his fingers around hers. He jerked back immediately. "I assumed since you felt strongly enough about it to carry it in your reticule, that you would wish it returned."

She froze, staring down blankly at it until understanding, then mortification lit behind her eyes. Eliza parted her lips, but no sound came out. At last, she managed a weak reply.

"Thomas, I can explain . . ."

Evanston silenced her with one shake of his head. It was rewarding to see some semblance of softness from her, even if it was only over a deuced calling card.

"Is your association with me so very detestable that you are not even willing to own the simple fact of my visit to Caroline?"

Eliza's gloved hands twisted together in her discomfort. "No, no. I was just unnerved—" She bit off her words and glanced awkwardly to the side.

A surge of adrenaline caused his heart to pick up speed, and Evanston slipped one fingertip beneath her chin to raise her gaze, feeling increasingly unnerved himself.

"Why?"

She shook her head, once more averting her eyes. "I don't know."

He didn't believe her. She trembled beneath his touch

and, unable to stop himself, his eyes traveled from her anxious gaze, down the pert slope of her nose, to settle on the lush raspberry flawlessness of her lips. A dissolute whisper swept through his silent ponderings.

Kiss her.

"What unnerved you?" he asked again, rendered nearly immobile by the delicious tension building between them. It was too soon to indulge in a kiss, but suddenly it was the only thing he could think about.

Kiss her.

He glanced up from her mouth and was startled to find her eyes fixed on his own lips. The worry that had consumed those peridot depths only moments before was now replaced with something much warmer, something like anticipation. And she was not struggling to free herself from his gentle hold on her chin. Rather, it seemed she was ready to melt into him at the slightest provocation . . .

In a flash, Evanston knew what had unnerved her. She did not want to resist him. Maybe she didn't think she could. It was exactly what he yearned for, but it scared the hell out of him too. Never had he thought it would be so easy to lose two of his closest friends. That's where this would end up, were he to pursue it.

Thomas released her and quickly crossed to the door of his private box. He stood with his back to her, gripping the doorknob for a few long moments to collect himself before finally turning back around to face her. This was Eliza, his best friend's sister and a friend to him in her own right. He needed to put a stop to this fantasy that had somehow taken root before it went too far. It wasn't as if he lacked for female companionship. It made no sense at all.

"We know many of the same people, Eliza," he muttered. "While I cannot guarantee to never encounter you at various engagements here in London, I can pay you the courtesy of not meddling in your affairs. I will not seek you out, nor will I ask you to dance, should we meet at a ball. If only you would, likewise, refrain from lying to me, I imagine we could coexist in peace."

Disappointment sliced through his chest, but he was relieved that he'd said the words. Did he spy a similar disappointment darkening her features?

"I'd imagine so," she whispered.

"You should return to Sir James before he sets out to find you."

Eliza's mouth twisted in a halfhearted attempt at a smile. "I don't believe he would be so improper as to leave his box during the performance."

With a quick motion, he pulled upon the heavy door.

"Well, I certainly would," he muttered under his breath, before disappearing into the gloom of the theater.

"Welcome home, my lady. I hope your evening was pleasant?"

Patterson fussed over Eliza as she divested herself of her cloak in the foyer. With a wan smile, Eliza pulled on each gloved fingertip and regarded her lady's maid.

"I'm not sure *pleasant* is the proper way of putting it, but it was diverting nonetheless."

Patterson's brown eyes grew large. "Things did not go well with Sir James, my lady?"

Eliza laughed softly. In her opinion, although many employers would disagree, Patterson's concerned candor was one of her finest traits. That, and she was staunchly loyal, having served the family since Eliza's first season, which seemed like ages ago. She had unflinchingly accompanied her young mistress into London, dried her tears on the eve of her marriage, shared the joy of her impending birth, then held her hand through the depths of hell and back. The two women were close, probably closer than most ladies and their maids. This afforded her a certain kind of comfort, particularly in the absence of family and friends.

"Things with Sir James were good," she answered.

The maid rested her palm over Eliza's discarded vestments and stared at her. "That is hardly a rousing endorsement."

"Oh, no. He is very much a gentleman," Eliza said as she mounted the staircase. "The theater was lovely, and Sir James was a fine companion. I had a marvelous time. It's just—"

"Yes, my lady?"

Eliza sighed as the pair reached the top of the stairs, turning around to face Patterson. "I can't imagine being his wife."

Patterson smiled, her eyes filled with empathy. "I suppose these things have been known to take time."

"Yes, but even with Reginald I think I could always *envision* it, regardless of how I felt about it at the time. With Sir James, I can't. Even though he is handsome and respectable. It's just that . . ."

She was having a hard time putting her finger on exactly what bothered her when the unlikely answer popped into her head.

He's not Evanston.

Not that picturing Thomas as her husband was any easier. Frowning, she shook her head and forced herself to use reason. "Landry has many admirable qualities—"

"Moustache . . ." Patterson stated succinctly, opening Eliza's chamber door.

"I am certain that the man is more than just a moustache!" she exclaimed with a chuckle, setting her reticule on the vanity table. "Why, between you and Caroline, you'd think that was all there was to him." Eliza gazed absently while unfastening the pearls from around her throat and sliding off her emerald earbobs. "His demeanor cooled as the night wore on, although I suppose I did give him some cause for complaint."

The maid laughed off her assertion. "Nonsense, my lady. What could you have possibly done?"

"Well . . . I left him alone to confront Evanston as the show was beginning." Eliza scowled down at her hands as she relinquished the jewels to Patterson, her expression darkening. "I wish to know how one man can possibly be so vexing!"

It took the maid a moment to overcome her surprise at Eliza's lack of etiquette. "I'm assuming you are referring to the viscount, and it is because he wishes to vex you, my lady." She cleared her throat and crossed to the bureau. "So, Lord Evanston was at the opera tonight?"

"He was, as a matter of fact."

The maid raised her eyebrows knowingly. "And did he deign to compliment your appearance?"

Eliza glanced sideways at her. She had not divulged the particulars of her attraction to Evanston, nor the fact of their kiss when she was younger. However, being an exceptionally perceptive person, it was possible that Patterson had managed to glean some truths regardless.

She thought back to their interaction in the hallway. "No, he did not," she replied, although Eliza had not missed the appreciative gleam in his eyes, nor the way they had lingered over her body. Still, she was reluctant to take too much comfort in the act. She had a feeling that any woman dressed nicely had a chance, to some extent, of catching his eye.

Patterson released the final hook on her dress. "I have wondered at the way he looks at you, my lady. You should be careful."

Eliza couldn't help the laugh that escaped her as she stepped out of her dress. Thomas had said the same thing to her, although whether he meant it was something she would never know. She gazed pensively at her reflection in the looking glass; a young woman clad in her corset, chemise and stockings stared back. There was something oddly appropriate about seeing herself this way while musing about Evanston's motives.

The idea of the woman in red with him tonight, in a similar state of undress, made her surprisingly envious. She had to imagine that the black-haired beauty and her catlike grace was much more to his liking than Eliza could ever be. He would want a woman who held no doubts about herself. Not one who had spent the past two years mourning in solemn celibacy. Although the mirror told a different tale, Eliza couldn't help but still feel like a little girl sometimes. After all, she had been the baby for so very long, with Thomas nine years her senior and William nearly the same.

Well, if Eliza didn't have the sense to protect herself, William would certainly do it on her behalf. And even if she had wished for Thomas to court her, could she ever imagine such a man being open to marriage? Although he'd been kind to Rosa in the past, she knew that Evanston held no love for children, and that locking him into such an arrangement would only serve to create resentment. Not to mention the bitterness she would feel when he returned to his gaming clubs, bored with her at last, in an effort to pretend she did not exist.

But had he not come perilously close to kissing her at the theater? Or had that simply been her, longing for him? If only she could know the true nature of his feelings, it would at least satisfy her irritating curiosity.

Insatiable curiosity.

Her brows furrowed. She kicked herself for dwelling on him again.

"As is the usual way of things, I suspect he's up to no good," she finally replied, shedding her corset and relishing her first deep breath in hours. The undergarments followed, quickly replaced by a plain white nightdress.

Patterson collected her crumpled garments and folded them neatly over her arm. "Knowing the viscount, it could be anything." She paused. "It could even be you."

He promised not to meddle. Told me he wouldn't even ask for a dance.

"Unlikely," Eliza countered, lowering herself into the chair before the vanity.

The maid said nothing, only approached from behind to give her shoulders a friendly squeeze. "Well, Sir James will have another opportunity to woo you at the ball this weekend. He does seem quite taken with you, my lady. I'm sure all awkwardness will be forgotten by then," she said with a smile.

"Yes, I'm sure," Eliza said with a sigh and a smile.

"Would you like me to assist with your hair before I leave?"

"No, thank you. Good night, Patterson."

"Good night, my lady."

Dipping into a low curtsy, Patterson departed the bedchamber, closing the door tightly behind her. Eliza extended her arms above her head to remove the pins holding her coiffure in place, and her hair tumbled over her shoulders, the blonde curls untwisting to finally rest in haphazard fashion against her back. She reached for her silver hairbrush, then glanced down, her hand stilling in midair.

Her beaded reticule rested on the vanity. She seized it, rummaging through the contents until she found Lord Evanston's calling card. Slowly she withdrew it, gazing at the simple rectangle. A flush of embarrassment rose as she recalled the viscount's words to her earlier that evening.

I assumed since you felt strongly enough about it to carry it in your reticule, that you would wish it returned.

Her fingers tightened around the card. She ought to throw the wretched thing into the fire and be rid of it once and for all. Instead, she found herself raising it to her nose, inhaling as her eyes drifted shut, as if she might detect some hint of the man who had given it to her. Eliza brushed her thumb gently over the surface of the card.

She glanced at the glowing fire just a few feet away.

Then hurriedly, greedily, she shoved the card back into her reticule.

Chapter Five

My dearest Rosa,

Thank you for your letter. I do love hearing how your favorite woodland friend has taken such a liking to Mrs. Humboldt's tarts, although the dear cook might be unhappy to discover so much of her hard work is being consumed by a squirrel, however adorable. I am also relieved to know the furry tart-eater has taken to meeting you nearer to the meadow instead of deep in the forest, even though that well has been covered. I know Aunt Clara is keeping close watch over your adventures, though, so I shall not worry too much.

Caroline asked me to convey her affections when next I wrote. She misses you a great deal and is eager to see you at Lawton Park when the season has concluded, only six weeks away now. Summer in London has been a whirlwind of balls, parties and dinners, which must sound thrilling to you, my sweet, but in truth is so very tiring. You will know what I mean once you have come out into society. All in good time.

You are constantly in my thoughts. I wish I were back in Kent with you already. Be a good girl until I return, mind Aunt Clara and Uncle William, and take care with Florence. Her knee still bothers her at times and I would venture to say it is not easy being nursemaid to such an active ward.

With love,
Mama

Eliza slipped the missive into an addressed envelope and sealed it with wax, then scanned fondly over Rosa's most recent letter once more, only glancing upward at the soft intrusion of a knock upon the library door.

"Yes?"

The door opened to reveal Roberts, the butler, who was a fixture exclusive to the Dower House and the London town house, when needed. Her brother, William, had so far denied the necessity of requiring such a position at Lawton Park, but Eliza had a suspicion that Clara was in the process of convincing him otherwise. Their reentry into society had increased the demands placed on his existing household staff, and given the changes, it was no longer reasonable to expect Mrs. Malone to continue on as she had. Especially if he were interested in retaining the efficient but overworked housekeeper.

Were Eliza to find a husband as planned, then Roberts would be free to join the earl at his estate. In truth, he was

William's to procure whenever he felt the need, but she knew that for now her brother was most concerned about her and Rosa being well looked after.

Roberts's posture inclined into a dignified bow, the contrast of his salt-and-pepper hair catching the candlelit illumination from the wall sconces.

"Lady Caroline has arrived, my lady."

She smiled brightly. "Excellent! Thank you, Roberts, send her in." The butler bowed once more and turned to leave, but she reached out to stop him. "Oh, and if you could please post this letter—" Eliza placed the letter into his hand "—I would be most grateful."

"As you wish, my lady," came his reply, and with another polite bow he turned crisply to exit the room. Half a minute later, Caroline entered with a swish of her skirts, only to pause abruptly, staring aghast at Eliza as she tidied up her writing materials.

"Please tell me you weren't writing a letter in your *ball gown*."

Eliza brushed a tendril of golden hair away from her face and gave Caroline a long-suffering look. "I wanted to send off a note to Rosa. No need to worry—"

"Says the lady who just smeared ink on her cheek," said Caroline in a stern voice, approaching with her handkerchief at the ready. "Please don't touch your dress . . . in fact, don't touch anything. Let me ensure you are clean." She shook her head as she tended to Eliza's face, and once clear of smudges, shifted her attention down to her fingertips. After a moment of silent scrubbing, Caroline tipped a wry grin at her friend. "I'd swear you were raised by wolves."

Eliza laughed. "Literate wolves, and yes, very nearly, since you'll remember I spent most of my childhood trailing after William and Thomas."

"Which reminds me—I've heard Evanston will be in attendance this evening."

The information had been inconspicuously delivered, but when Eliza raised her widened eyes to meet Caroline's, she saw her friend closely evaluating her reaction. Ridding herself of the appearance of emotion, she hitched her shoulders into a shrug.

"He is welcome to attend any event to which he is invited."

Caroline's gray eyes appraised her. "Yes, and yet it seems he is being invited to a disproportionate number of gatherings where you are in attendance, even going so far as to follow you into gardens."

"Well . . . perhaps," she replied with some discomfort. "But that was only because he was being protective."

Her friend scoffed. "I wonder what else he'll be forced to do in the name of protecting you."

"I'm sure it will be fine. He's even insisted he would not interfere with my suitors."

Caroline considered this, giving Eliza's fingers one last polish before replacing her handkerchief into her reticule. "I suppose we will find out tonight," she said, crossing to exit the library.

Eliza glanced up as she tugged on her gloves. "Find out what?"

Caroline's paused on her way out of the room, her sardonic gaze skewering Eliza from around the door.

"How good Lord Evanston is at keeping his word."

"Lady Eliza, how lovely to see you again."

Sir James came forwards to take Eliza's hand in his own and place a lingering kiss upon her knuckles. She was relieved at his apparent forgiveness for her behavior the other night and did not hesitate to smile at him in return. He looked, as always, sharp and perfectly pressed with every hair in its place.

"Likewise, Sir James. And you may remember my friend, Lady Caroline?" she asked, gesturing to the woman in question.

He turned to greet Caroline with a dutiful bow. "Indeed, I do."

"Sir James," Caroline replied with a small curtsy, "Lady Eliza tells me *L'elisir d'amore* was delightful. I am sorry Lady Frances and I could not accept your kind invitation."

He chuckled, and Eliza saw him glance surreptitiously in her direction. "As am I, Lady Caroline. However, I find that the more time I spend in Lady Eliza's company, the less inclined I am to sharing her with others."

They all laughed politely, but Eliza did not miss the meaning behind his reference. She was starting to dread how he might react tonight upon discovering Evanston was here at the ball.

While Sir James and Caroline shared friendly conversation, Eliza looked out casually at the guests. There was no sign of him as of yet. She reached up to nestle a pin more firmly into her hair, then glanced down at her dress. Her gown was in a fashionable style similar to the one she had worn to the theater, low-cut and off the shoulder. Luminous ivory satin was framed by decorative swaths of lace. A rose-colored bow adorned the small of her back, prettily accentuating the fullness of her skirts. With Landry having suddenly emerged as the man most interested in pursuing her, she wondered if he found the dress to his liking.

Then Eliza immediately thought of Thomas, who had repeatedly turned up and despite his insistence to the contrary, did not act entirely uninterested. Again, she looked out amongst the crowd filtering through the ballroom, and her pulse jumped upon finally locating him on the other side of the room, smiling charismatically at a timid debutante who had dared to approach with her mother.

Evanston's was the one face she eagerly sought, and it had been that way for years. At six feet and three inches he was quite tall, made all the more physically imposing by his shock of black hair and muscular build. She knew how it felt to be intimate with a man, but how many times had she imagined what it would be like with him? The memory of his illicit kiss had tormented her for years, and although it had been wrong of him to do, she yearned to know more. Like the feel of his hands on her . . . his mouth on her skin . . . his flesh against hers. Something about the way he looked at her sometimes made her think he envisioned the same things with her, and she hungered at the thought even as she worked to keep him at arm's length.

Still engaged in a pleasant exchange, Thomas's eyes flitted across the room to Eliza, returning immediately to the girl in front of him, only to lift once more upon catching Eliza gazing openly in his direction. His smile faded, conversation paused, and he held her heated stare, the connection between them as palpable as if he were touching her now.

Then it was gone. She blinked in confusion, registering that he had casually resumed his conversation, and Eliza had to wonder if she had just fallen victim to some sort of daydream. She lowered her brows in consternation.

Stupid. Stupid!

How many times could one woman be so silly over a man? No, he wasn't here for her. It was evident in the way he interacted with the ladies. Requesting the honor of a dance here, and smiling captivatingly all the while there, lavishing his attention on everyone but her. Soon, the heat she felt was nothing more than her own humiliation.

Caroline sought her gaze in what appeared to be nervous anticipation. "Lady Eliza, may I introduce someone to you?"

Eliza glanced over to find that a gentleman had joined their group, and she smiled congenially in recognition. Tall and lean, with chestnut hair, this was the man Caroline had been so taken with at Lady Humphrey's dinner party.

"I would like nothing more," she replied, extending her hand to him.

He took her gloved fingers and bowed politely. "Lord Braxton, my lady."

"A pleasure to make your acquaintance, sir."

Her eyes danced merrily over to Caroline, who looked a bit flushed, something unusual for her friend, who was typically so jaded about male suitors and the notion of love. Eliza suspected that given the proper man, her resistance might crumble regardless of how much she wished to oppose her parents and their hopes for her marriage.

To her right, Sir James cleared his throat. "I see Lord Evanston has seen fit to grace us with his presence again," he muttered beneath his breath.

Eliza tried to act nonchalant, although every nerve ending in her body caught fire at the mere mention of him. "He is bound to show at some of the same events," she said with a dismissive toss of her head. She smiled at him. "It doesn't matter."

"No, I suppose it doesn't," replied Landry with a slow smile, seemingly reassured. He extended his hand out to her. "Might I request the honor of a dance?"

She curtsied and took his hand. "Certainly, sir."

They took their position on the floor. Eliza studiously fixed her eyes on Landry's cravat, unwilling to stray off course for fear of being distracted by the roguish viscount.

Thomas guided his partner into a waltz, narrowing his eyes as Landry led Eliza in similar fashion. Tension caused him to squeeze the girl in his arms and she tittered nervously, glancing up at him in modest inquiry. Loosening his hold, he murmured an apology, then resumed scowling discreetly at Sir James behind his back.

They had known each other at Oxford. Not well, of course. Landry and Evanston had very little in common, save their ages and income. It had always seemed that Landry had resented him, but for what, he didn't know. What he *did* know was that with each passing minute, he could feel his subtle dislike for the man growing into outright animosity. He had clearly succeeded in gaining Eliza's regard, and it even appeared she was enjoying herself in his company. Thomas could only watch her twirl around in Landry's arms for so long before he had to close his eyes against it and look away.

The dance concluded, and Thomas was relieved when she was joined by a different man for the second dance, and perturbed once more when Sir James claimed her for the third. It was generally considered a breach of etiquette for a man to focus excessively on one woman during the course of a ball. Thomas was not normally a stickler for rules, but at this ball, with this woman, he was finding it difficult to forgive the additional attention. Two dances could be considered tolerable, but should Landry request her for a third . . .

Evanston could not think on it without his blood boiling. Even had Eliza wished to refuse Landry, which remained unclear at this point, she would not risk potentially insulting her suitor. He had expected difficulties in observing her actions from afar, but he had not anticipated that his feigned affect of indifference would melt away so quickly after watching Sir James monopolizing her time.

Sir James must have known how his preference for Eliza had shown, for he found himself new partners for the next few sets, and Thomas was cautiously optimistic. The night wore on, and Evanston stoically endured it with women of no consequence while glancing surreptitiously in Eliza's direction. At the moment, she was engaged in a quadrille with Lord Braxton, the gentleman who had been showing interest in Lady Caroline, and he allowed himself to feel a hint of relief.

Had he thought about his little indiscretion with Eliza from time to time? Yes. But he had not allowed himself to reminisce excessively over William's sister, knowing where such a thing could lead. Now, though, he tried to recall the details. The feel of her hair as he slid his fingers around her head to hold her immobile. The breath of an anxious sigh as his mouth closed over hers. The trembling lips that were unbearably soft . . .

He hadn't cared as much then, so it had been easier to walk away. But now his sense of control was quickly vanishing. He loved Ashworth like a brother, but Lord help him, Thomas knew he wasn't going to be able to stop until he had claimed the man's sister. He could *feel* it.

His black mood made it feel as if a thundercloud had rolled into the ballroom, and Evanston scowled while he sought his partner for the penultimate dance of the evening. He'd almost reached the girl when he spied Sir James approaching Eliza yet one more time. The disapproving glances from the matrons nearby told him he was not the only person to notice Landry's lack of good manners, and Thomas didn't think. He didn't breathe. He couldn't even remember crossing the room, but it must have happened quickly for he suddenly found himself facing Eliza, her green eyes wide and startled as a doe's.

"M-my lord?"

He said nothing, ignoring everyone, including Sir James who had stalked forwards, his face twisted equally in astonishment and outrage. He simply reached out and grasped her by the wrist before pulling her onto the dance floor and swinging her around until she was, at last, wrapped securely in his arms for the upcoming waltz. A noticeable hush came over the guests at the scene they had just witnessed, and he caught sight of Caroline's grim and knowing visage from her distant position in the room. Every last one of them could go to hell, especially Landry.

At first, Eliza subtly attempted to defy his movements. But his authoritative lead, driven primarily by the strongest jealousy he had ever experienced, left her little choice in whether she participated or not.

"Thomas," Eliza hissed under her breath as they twirled in unison. "What in heaven's name are you doing?"

"I am protecting you from Landry's poor judgment."

"It seems that you have traded one brand of poor judgment for another instead."

"Is that how you feel?" he asked, tightening his hold around her possessively, relishing the feel of holding her. "I wonder what Sir James thinks, if indeed he thinks at all."

Her eyes flared, but this silenced her for a while. The orchestra played, Landry seethed, the crowd stared, and he danced with Eliza as if none of it mattered. He had forgotten how well they danced together. As he remembered, they always had.

Thomas saw her frowning, her eyes seemingly affixed to his chest. Silently admonishing himself for allowing his gaze to wander further, Evanston could not help but notice the snug fit of her bodice, the low cut of her décolletage, the mounds of her breasts. Eliza's teeth worried at her bottom lip, and he suddenly wished they were somewhere private, a place where he could taste her lips for himself as he had once before. Except this time, he would not stop at her lips. He would taste her everywhere.

Her voice intruded on his contemplations.

"Thomas, you broke your word. You told me . . . you *promised* . . . that you wouldn't ask me to dance."

He tipped his head down to whisper in her ear. "As you'll recall, I didn't ask."

Her tiny intake of breath was all he required. She was angry with him, but had she been mortally offended she would have shoved him away by now. He knew her well enough to say that with certainty.

Resigned now to finishing the dance, she floated, graceful and light, in his arms. It was a stark contrast to the discontent he knew she must be feeling. Still, he could detect the same hint of surrender she had shown him at the theater, a tendency to soften and dissolve into his embrace. It was a curious reaction, to be sure, one he could envision playing out in a number of scenarios. And it would, by God, if he had anything to do with it.

The pervading sense of defeat he had felt for most of the

night was gone, banished by his own need, and the curve of her waist beneath his hand. No woman here or anywhere could ever match her exquisite beauty or her intelligent nature. He inhaled hungrily, eager to memorize her smell. An alluring hint of jasmine drifted upward from the warm skin at the base of her throat, and fire filled every cell of his being. Sweet Jesus, how did Landry manage to look so staid and dignified in her presence, when every instinct *he* possessed screamed for more of her . . . here . . . now.

"Have I told you how lovely you look, Eliza?" he murmured huskily, the words escaping his mouth before he'd realized what he'd said.

She blinked up at him in shock. Her feet faltered and she missed a step, but his agile hands guided her, compensating for the slip.

"I—"

She pressed her lips together, glancing towards the unhappy Sir James before coming back to meet his sultry gaze with uncertainty in her eyes. Her mouth parted to finish her reply, but the words were stolen by the final notes of the song, straining out across the floor. Trying to disregard the disappointment that flooded through him, he released Eliza to bow deeply and she lowered into a curtsy, staring up at him with what appeared to be confusion. Good. He would rather see confusion than the determination to be set against him entirely. He held out an arm. After a brief hesitation, she accepted it and he escorted her off the dance floor.

A fresh wash of color suffused her skin as they arrived beside her friends. She turned to take her place by Caroline, who was staring at him in undisguised indignation. Lord Braxton stood nearby with a look of bemusement on his face, while Landry nearly spat in fury. Evanston tipped a haughty nod in the man's direction, then directed his searing gaze at Eliza.

"My lady, it was a pleasure."

And without further conversation, he strode from the ballroom.

"What have you not told me?"

The carriage door had only just shut behind them when Caroline started asking questions. Sudden panic constricted Eliza's throat, and she cleared it demurely, feigning ignorance.

"I'm not sure what you mean."

Caroline leaned forwards to take Eliza's hand in her own.

"I mean it appears Lord Evanston had an emotional response to seeing you monopolized by Landry. I wish to know why." Her friend eyed her warily. "What has happened between you two of which I am not aware?"

Eliza shifted uncomfortably. "Could it not have simply been the defensive reaction of a friend?"

"No, it could not. Or are you conveniently forgetting his promise not to interfere with your suitors?" she asked acidly.

A thrill raced through Eliza at Caroline's assertion, but was immediately vanquished by the realization that she was going to have to explain herself, explain everything, confess the truth after years of concealing it. She lifted her gaze in dread.

"I can't—"

Her friend tipped her head in warning. "You'd better—"

With a sigh, she ripped her hand from Caroline's grasp to throw herself back against the seat.

"Fine. Thomas has kissed me once before."

Silence filled the vehicle, louder than any reproach could have been. Eliza glanced hesitantly in Caroline's direction. Her stunned expression was half-concealed in shadows amidst the gloomy interior of the carriage. Finally, she spoke. Loudly.

"*When?*"

Eliza's face grew hot with shame. "I—it was back before I married Reginald. On the night of our engagement party . . ."

Now it was Caroline's turn to throw herself back against the seat. "The night of your engagement party?" She paused, her eyes darting, parsing together recollections of the past. "Oh Eliza, what a scoundrel." A notch formed between her auburn brows. "Why didn't you tell me?"

Eliza's voice wavered. "Well, I knew you did not like him and—"

"Wrong," she said, shaking her head. "There is a vast difference between liking a person and approving a match. I like Thomas well enough, even if he is a disreputable pleasure seeker."

"See! Why would I tell you?"

"But why conceal it from me if there was no scandal and you ended up marrying Reginald anyway? You didn't tell me about his call to your town house either, but I could have tried to help you . . . or at least tried to make sure you wouldn't be at any of the same parties."

The carriage jostled across the uneven roads and Eliza fidgeted with the edge of her shawl. "I didn't think it would be this much of a problem. And I also didn't think that he . . . was interested in me. Although I might have been wrong about that."

Caroline's eyes blazed. "Oh, you were *definitely* wrong about that. You should have seen him tonight when he snatched you away from Landry. He looked positively feral." Eliza couldn't help but feel a dark thrill at that, and it was possible that Caroline noticed, for she continued, weighing her words carefully. "And because I can see how you . . . feel . . . about him, I think the last thing you need when seeking a husband is to have the complication of a man who is . . . not the ideal choice."

While Eliza couldn't disagree, as she'd been telling herself the same thing, she didn't like hearing it from someone else, even a well-meaning friend whose only wish was to protect her. She compressed her lips in displeasure but tipped a reluctant nod of agreement, turning her head to stare out the window.

The rest of the ride passed in silence, and soon the carriage lurched to a stop in front of Caroline's residence. Her friend gathered her items in the discomfiting quiet, then moved closer to the door, a small, sad smile lurking at the corner of her mouth.

"You'll see, Eliza. You'll feel differently tomorrow."

Caroline leaned in to kiss her lightly on the cheek. The carriage door was opened, and with a last glance at Eliza, her friend stepped out of the vehicle.

Eliza's driver resumed the voyage home, and she sulked quietly in the darkness until slowly, clearly, a new idea formed in her mind. An idea that filled her with certainty, and no small amount of trepidation.

Yes, I shall feel differently tomorrow, she thought, *for I will speak to Evanston tonight.*

Chapter Six

Before she could reconsider, Eliza leaned forwards to rap against the roof. The carriage slowed immediately and she could see Linton rotating on his bench to peer through the window at the front of her enclosure.

"Yes, my lady?" he called out.

"Lord Evanston's residence, please." At the driver's disbelieving stare, she added, "I am aware of the hour. Now make haste."

His mouth clamped shut instantly, a bow of deference signaling his compliance. Then he efficiently turned back around and snapped the reins. One sharp lurch and they were off, leaving Eliza to wonder, heart leaping in her chest, if she had finally managed to go stark raving mad. She supposed she could allow this transgression to go unanswered this evening, but something inside of her—perhaps her pride—demanded an explanation from the viscount while the injury was still fresh.

Eliza had known Thomas for all of her life, and William had seen some of his more sordid behavior firsthand. He'd even alluded to it in his repeated attempts to convince her that the viscount was not marriage material. Likewise, Eliza was not deaf to the rumors of his dalliances with certain married women—and widows—of the *ton*, and neither, she was sure, were their husbands, likely off having discreet affairs of their own. While such behavior was considered quietly acceptable within London's elite, each new tale of his prowess, whispered in hushed giggles by the glittering women at after-dinner card tables during various soirées, had caused her blood to heat ever so slightly. The hold he'd unknowingly had over her for years had only tightened since her arrival in London, and she knew she must resist or risk making the wrong choice.

It also reminded her of their kiss on that warm summer day when she'd been just sixteen years old, and then how he had walked out of that room, never to speak of it again. Oh, he would flirt with her, to be sure. Even bed her, if he was bored and should the opportunity arise. But would it mean something to him?

No, and it never would.

Still, the image of him angrily—for it *had* been angrily—striding over to grasp her wrist and tug her onto the dance floor had stayed with her since then, a shock of warmth blooming deep inside her belly each time she recalled the event. She should have refused him, made some attempt to gracefully exit his hold before reaching the dance floor . . . if not to preserve her own sense of dignity, then on behalf of her intended dance partner. But she'd chosen to do no such thing. Evanston had claimed her before the *ton*, and even in front of Sir Landry himself.

Had it been the element of surprise, or the pull of her own indecent desires, long held in check, that permitted him to do so? While it was impossible to comprehend the viscount's feelings and motives behind such a move, one thing was for certain.

She had enjoyed it.

Fury flared through Eliza's chest, white-hot and undeniable. Who was Lord Evanston to invade the London season, *her* season, and interfere with her efforts at finding a proper husband?

The detour was brief, and they arrived at Evanston's doorstep within a matter of minutes. She accepted Linton's proffered assistance down the steps of the vehicle, hazardous considering the length and breadth of her formal dress with its abundance of petticoats and skirts. Sweeping them aside with her right hand, Linton steadied her on the left until she reached solid ground, then did his best to appear inconspicuous. He finally elected to return to the carriage, deciding wisely to avert his eyes. She couldn't blame him for his discomfort. It was unseemly for her to be climbing the stairs of the viscount's town house in the middle of the night, and she cast a quick look at her surroundings before clearing her throat and using the brass knocker to rap loudly three times against the door.

Eliza pulled her shawl tighter around her shoulders. Two minutes passed in silence, and with each dragging second her cheeks burned in mortification. This had been a mistake, but she had already made her presence known and was committed to the act. Once more, she raised her fingers to utilize the brass knocker, the noise a stark disruption in the surrounding stillness. The street remained thankfully empty of gawking passersby, but still her embarrassment rose. With a humiliated sigh, she turned to go back to the carriage just as the door to Evanston's residence flew open behind her. Spinning back around, she lifted her chin in anticipation of an awkward conversation with his butler, but no words left her lips in the stunned silence that ensued.

It was not a manservant, but Lord Evanston who stood before her in the gloom, holding a candle. Eliza, only mildly comforted by the fact that he too had been caught unawares, met his equally surprised gaze before realizing the compromised state of his attire. The formal clothing from earlier—his jacket, waistcoat and cravat—were missing. His shirt was unbuttoned much farther than would normally be considered appropriate. She had interrupted him in the midst of his repose, which made sense at this hour. An image of him resting in his study, eyes drifting closed, leaning back in a comfortably worn leather chair, glass of brandy in his long-fingered hand, entered her mind.

Her eyes wandered further down to the strong column of his neck, the sleek contours of his collarbones, the slight dip where they came together. She saw the hint of crisp dark hair that adorned his chest. An unwelcome surge of need, swift and hot, flowed through her body and before she could censor her traitorous brain, another image emerged. One where he was occupying the same study, the same chair, but was not alone. This time she was with him, removing the brandy from his grasp to set it firmly on the desk before shifting her heavy skirts to sit astride his lap, the hard feel of his body beneath hers as he leaned back with a muted groan . . .

His low voice interrupted her illicit reveries.

"You should not be here," he said, the edge of his words softened by drink.

Eliza dragged her focus upward to his face, partially illuminated in the unreliable glow of his candle. He appeared tired now, with dark smudges beneath his eyes, but before she could allow herself to feel pity for the man, she registered cool resentment behind the hypnotic blue gaze. Lord Evanston was angry with her for some reason. Which served to remind her . . . she was angry with him as well. She summoned all the indignant fury she possessed.

"*You* owe me an explanation, Thomas. And an apology."

Evanston stared at her for a moment, unimpressed. "You will receive neither from me, however, so I will bid you good night." He took a step backwards, swinging the door closed as he did.

Without thinking, Eliza placed her foot in the doorway, her formal slipper doing little to impede the momentum of the heavy wooden door. At her pained cry, Evanston jerked the door back open, concern stamped plainly upon his face.

"Eliza . . ."

As upset as she had been with him just a moment before, her humiliation now outweighed any other competing emotion. Suddenly, all she wanted was the privacy and relative comfort of her own home. She cast a wretched look at her carriage, hoping Linton might come and assist her. But her driver was far enough away that he remained studiously unaware of Eliza's predicament.

She tried standing on the injured foot and her next words were cut short by a sharp hiss of pain. He muttered an oath and set the candle holder on the table in the foyer.

"I—I'll be fine. I just need to—"

Before she could finish speaking he sighed and bent forwards to gather her in his powerful arms, one supporting her back with the other sliding under to cradle her legs and mass of skirts. Lifting gently, Lord Evanston compressed her against the warm, solid span of his chest, and she gasped again but for a different reason entirely. Her head spun in dizzy circles. How had this happened? Eliza was dangerously close in proximity to that sculpted neck she'd admired mere moments ago. She tried to stifle her cries, but her agony won out and she turned her face towards his shoulder, unable to prevent the flow of her tears from seeping into the fine linen of his shirt.

Were she not in so much misery, she might be able to enjoy the fact that Lord Evanston was holding her now, pressing her against his chest. With Eliza in his arms, Evanston took a cursory glance up and down the street, then brought her inside, kicking the door shut behind them.

He wronged you tonight. Don't forget why you came here.

She knew part of her wanted to forget, though. Wanted him to stride past the drawing room and continue up the staircase. Make her forget the intense throbbing in her foot with other, intensely pleasurable sensations. In this moment, it didn't matter that he would never love her, or that he wasn't suitable, or that he would never ever be faithful . . .

Her distant and ludicrous hope of being ravished was dashed as Evanston turned to enter the drawing room, carefully navigating the darkened surroundings. Eliza was barely able to register her disappointment, for by the time he set her down on the settee her teeth were chattering from discomfort.

"Truly, Thomas, I'm f—fine—"

Ignoring her, he strode to the hallway to fetch his abandoned candle holder, the golden glow illuminating his familiar chiseled face upon his return. Placing it on the table beside them, he knelt before her and sighed.

"Yes, I'm certain you are, but I'd like to have a look all the same to be sure."

His hands stretched out to encircle her ankle and she twitched her foot back beneath her skirts.

"I think not, my lord. You may consider me easy prey, but you are mistaken," she said, not truly feeling the certainty of her declaration, but needing to say something to keep him from touching her now.

Evanston jerked his eyes up to meet hers, cocking an eyebrow and leaning back on his haunches. "Have I ever treated you like easy prey?"

"I don't know," she snapped, her nerves on fire. "What do you call it when you take advantage of a young girl?"

He stared at her, and she was surprised to see a flicker of remorse behind his eyes.

"I'm sorry if it felt that way to you," he said. Then, bracing his hands upon his muscular thighs, he leaned closer, and her lungs stopped working. "But I don't remember you objecting until the kiss was finished. Do you still think it fair to lay the blame solely at my feet?"

Eliza's embarrassment worked its way up her neck to flood her cheeks, and she sighed. "No," she admitted, chastened by his serious tone.

"Then all physical charms of your ankles aside, do you mind if I ensure that your foot isn't broken before allowing you to travel home? Besides," he added gruffly, "you act as if I've never seen your ankles before."

She gaped at him in offense until he clarified.

"The oak tree, remember?"

In an instant, Eliza did. She only wondered at his remembrance of the event. Often, growing up, she and her brothers would traverse the countryside that lay between Lawton Park and the Dower House, and Thomas was regularly with them. There was a hill that signified the halfway point between the houses, and one time when she was no older than fourteen, the boys—men really, as they were home on holiday from Oxford—took turns climbing first the knoll, then the singular great oak tree atop it.

Each boy conquered the tree handily, waving down at her from the pinnacle. She had glowered at each one in envy for she could not follow, burdened as she was by the skirts of her walking dress. One by one, Lucas, William and Thomas jumped down from their respective perches to resume their course down the hill. But she couldn't resist trying, at least once, to emulate their victory.

She'd fought her way up to the first set of branches, a rush of triumph accompanying her clasp around a wooden limb, swiftly replaced by fear as her fingers lost their hold to send her crashing to the ground below. Her right ankle had bent wickedly beneath the force of her fall, and she had yelled in pain, hoping beyond hope that someone was still close enough to hear her.

Clutching her sprained ankle in mounting desperation, she'd nearly given up thinking any of the boys would come back to find her. Thomas had been the one who'd returned.

He'd hushed her cries and had examined her ankle with care, causing her cheeks to burn crimson in adolescent mortification. Then he had scooped her up, much as he'd done tonight, and taken her to William and Lucas. Recalling it now, she realized he had never once reprimanded her efforts to climb the oak as her brothers had. Thomas had refrained from judgment, seemingly acknowledging the fact that until Eliza had made the ascent herself, even were she to fail, she could not possibly be satisfied.

Evanston had helped her before, and he wanted to help her now. Nodding stiffly, Eliza extended her leg back into view. She jumped with excitement as his hands slid around her ankle, lifting it so he could remove her slipper. He began his examination by caressing her lightly, running his fingers over her stockinged foot.

"Does this hurt?" he murmured.

She wished it did. Maybe then her thoughts wouldn't be running wild with ideas of what could happen if his fingers continued their incendiary pathway up her leg.

"No," she managed.

He flexed her ankle, and when she gave no reaction he gently moved her toes. The play of candlelight within the varied layers of his ebony hair was mesmerizing, but she forced herself to focus on the task at hand. Eliza had very nearly forgotten about her injury by the time Thomas found the sensitive place where the door had struck the outer edge of her foot, and she issued a distressed cry, pulling it away from his hold.

"Ouch," she yelped, trying not to sound pathetic.

Evanston winced and tilted his head in thought. "I'm no physician, but I don't believe your foot is broken or there would likely be more swelling. You should rest now, though, to minimize your discomfort."

She watched as he stretched his long torso across the settee to retrieve a cylindrical pillow, then raised her ankle carefully to place it beneath. When he was finished the room had gone strangely quiet, and Eliza almost believed she could still feel the warmth of his hand on her leg. With a start, she realized he had never removed it.

"This may hinder your ability to dance for a few days," he stated with what sounded like regret. "Although I could probably manage to still lead effectively regardless of your infirmity. Something your other suitors are likely not up to—"

Her gaze snapped over to his, and he fell silent. She stared at him in remonstration, then suddenly remembered her reason for coming here this evening.

"Why did you humiliate me at the ball, Thomas?"

Evanston's brow furrowed. "That was not my intention."

"And yet it happened. So, what was your intention?"

His hand slipped away from her ankle and she felt an internal tremor of remorse. Discarding the annoying reaction, she stared expectantly at the viscount. After all, she had come here seeking an explanation and she wasn't leaving until she had one.

Thomas rose to stand in one fluid motion and began pacing the carpeted floor, hands restlessly clenching and unclenching. "I'm not sure I had one. It was simply a reaction."

"That is a not an excuse. I don't suppose you know how it felt to be embarrassed in such a way."

"And I don't suppose you know how it feels to watch that arrogant little man dance with you over and over," he snapped.

She rolled her eyes. "Thomas, he can hardly be held responsible for the fact that you tower over every man in London—"

His pacing paused. "You've managed to miss my point entirely."

Eliza shifted to glare up at him, elbows digging into the plush settee on either side of her.

"Oh, I think I understand. What I fail to grasp, however, is how I'm meant to accept jealousy as an excuse for your poor behavior, based on the fact that you've *never shown an interest in me*. Please explain."

Evanston's eyes searched hers, but he said nothing.

"Besides, how many women would eagerly warm your bed?" She was both emboldened and mortified by her own audacity. "Ten? A hundred? Widows? Debutantes? Does it even matter . . ."

"It does matter," he ground out. "I want you in my bed, Eliza."

Her defiance evaporated in an instant and the breath whooshed out of her. When she managed to regain her voice, it was barely more than a croak.

"What did you say?" she whispered.

"I said that I want you," he repeated, dropping down to kneel beside her. His eyes grew brighter as his hand traced along the bare length of her arm. "In my bed."

Eliza stared at him in shock, shaking her head. "I—I don't understand. The moment I venture away from my brother's estate, you suddenly decide that I am worth your attention?"

Thomas stroked her palm with his thumb and his eyes flicked up to capture hers. "Perhaps I've come to realize that you were always worth my attention." He raised her hand to drag his mouth across the sensitive flesh of her inner wrist. "And perhaps I stole you away from Landry tonight because I couldn't bear the sight of you with someone else."

A fiery need coiled inside her, low and hot, while her heart hammered in panic. She had every intention of shoving him away. But the sight of him looming beside her in the candlelit dark . . . powerful and masculine and longing for her . . . was the manifestation of countless fantasies, now spectacularly come to life. She might not have protested when he'd kissed her before, but she needed to now. Eliza knew what would happen if she did not.

"Thomas . . . you shouldn't. We're only meant to be friends—"

"And could we not be something more?" His eyes closed

as the sculpted softness of his mouth brushed against her skin. In a barely perceptible voice he added, "Are we not already?"

Rotating her hand, he guided it to rest lightly against the square line of his jaw. Although he had clearly shaven before the ball, she could feel the new, rough growth of his beard beneath her fingertips. He turned his face to bury it into her palm and Eliza remained frozen, driven to exquisite madness by his lips. Many, many times she had imagined such a scenario. His mouth . . . her skin . . .

Eliza watched in both fear and excitement while his kisses coasted steadily farther up the length of her arm. A surge of adrenaline brought her back to reality, and she pulled away just enough to break the contact between her skin and his mouth.

"We can't—"

Evanston allowed her to retreat, then countered by leaning over her to place both hands on the settee, bringing himself even closer until their faces nearly touched. His gaze snared hers, then dropped to her lips, causing her heart to stutter. He bent forwards and lightly, so lightly, brushed his lips against the corner of her mouth.

"Can't we?"

As her years of celibacy could attest, she was not a widow given to casual lovemaking. But the question, posed by this particular man in a voice unsteady with longing, was nearly impossible to resist. Her earlier wish to have him ravish her in his bedchamber was rapidly replaced by the very real possibility of being taken right here in the drawing room instead.

Loneliness had been a wretched companion in the years since her husband's death . . . She knew that losing herself in Evanston's arms would be infinitely more pleasing . . .

Thomas hesitated at her silence, then kissed the delicate outer shell of her ear, the whispered current of his breath laying waste to her plans of resistance. A soft groan escaped him, and his hands wound around her bodice. She felt his long fingers curling into her waist as the force of his desire increased, and the possessive clasp unleashed a wave of lust that sent an accompanying jolt of pleasure racing between her thighs. Grasping for anything to pull her out of the sensual fog that was rapidly clouding her judgment, she thought of her family.

Reginald. Father. Lucas. William. Men, both departed and alive, who had held Lord Evanston in high esteem but still would have taken great issue with Evanston for presuming to approach her. William could still thrash him, and probably would, should he ever discover the truth.

His kisses strayed dangerously to her collarbone and her head fell back, mind whirling at all the things Thomas could accomplish with her lying on his settee. She felt the scrape of his cheek, and then he turned to blaze openmouthed kisses over her chest, down to the swells of her breasts, displayed as they were by the restraining fit of her satin bodice. Eliza let out a shaky moan, her traitorous body quivering in anticipation while her mind was still feebly attempting to remind her of why this was a dangerous endeavor. She was drunk off the feel of him, the heat, the smell. Starched linen, soap, brandy, mingled with his own powerful, aroused scent. In a daze, Eliza wondered how he would taste.

Rosa. Her daughter, who cared for Thomas, but would never understand when he would probably disappear for days at a time, or why he'd perhaps become bored with her mother. If not for herself, she owed it to both Reginald and Rosa to choose a husband with an established history of managed appetites, not one of indulged vices.

She wanted him, yes. He knew it, and here they were. But she could not allow herself to be seduced by him now.

Thomas leaned over her, his eyes kindling with desire. "Kiss me, Eliza."

It was impossible to tell if he was making a plea or a demand, but regardless, she found herself wanting to submit. To this and any other request he might make of her.

"I can't," she said desperately, squeezing her eyes shut and trying to steel herself against his scorching advances.

He came closer, the tip of his nose softly brushing hers. "Kiss me now."

Eliza could imagine William's fury at discovering them like this. But here in Lord Evanston's drawing room, she found herself contemplating the extent of the fallout that would occur if she permitted this one night's indulgence . . .

Her eyes flew open and she brought her hands up against his shoulders to give him a shove.

"I can't!"

Evanston finally recognized her urgency and jerked back to gaze at her, hurt evident within the shadowed planes of his handsome face. She guessed it could have been the only time he'd ever encountered such a reaction from a woman. The emotion vanished and he stood quickly, the angled planes of his face shadowed in the flickering light. Eliza watched in trepidation as he worked to master himself before speaking to her, his broad chest heaving. Finally, he turned to face her.

"You don't trust me," he rasped.

"No, Thomas. I don't. And I can't believe I have to remind you of this, but I came to London in search of a husband—"

"—not a man like me," he muttered under his breath.

"Yes!" she exclaimed. "I cannot be just another one of your widows, and it's selfish of you to expect it."

He shook his head in bitter acceptance. "So you wish to save yourself for Landry."

"The notion of marriage has never been approached by Sir James," she said, blinking. "But if I did accept his proposal, then yes. I feel I would owe that to him."

The muscles of his jaw flexed as he retrieved the candlestick from the table and strode to the doorway. "I understand. This was a mistake—" His teeth squeezed shut at the end of his sentence, and he cleared his throat to speak once more. "You are injured. Pray, don't trouble yourself. I will fetch my infernally lazy butler and he will escort you to your carriage, since any contact with me is so apparently odious to you."

Her mouth fell open to make a reply in her defense, but he had already ventured down the hallway, taking the light with him and plunging her into darkness.

Chapter Seven

Eliza was unsure how things had changed between her and Evanston after her reckless visitation, but feared they were not for the better. His absence at various social engagements and, therefore, his silence on the matter did not ease her nervous suppositions that their friendship had been broken to an irreparable degree. She had already sent two missives to his residence, letters intended to be friendly inquiries, both of which had gone unanswered. Despite her best efforts at diverting her attention, the looming distraction of having lost Evanston's regard bothered her more than she cared to admit.

Caroline had been understandably concerned upon learning of her detour to the viscount after the ball. Eliza recounted some of what had occurred, omitting, of course, any allusions to words or deeds of a more intimate nature, because while she appreciated Caroline's confidence, she also knew that acknowledging her physical weakness for Thomas would only cause her friend to question her motives. Eliza had gone to his home seeking answers, but someone might wonder if her desire for Lord Evanston, accompanied by the thrill of seeing him late at night within his own domain, might have influenced her choice.

Which of course it had. Any woman with a modicum of intelligence would know better than to venture into his territory that way. Or at the very least, would know what to expect once she got there. Despite her unwillingness to outwardly admit this, she knew it to be true. But one thing she had not expected, one thing that had taken her quite by surprise, was the unmistakable flash of hurt that had darkened his features when she had rejected him. Could it have simply been the product of his wounded pride? Perhaps. But she'd always held the impression that he viewed his affairs with less feeling, not more. That his liaisons, while intimate in nature, never ventured anywhere near his heart.

Eliza considered the women in his life. Yes, there were his London amusements, but family? He had one close female relation she knew of—his mother, Gertrude Dornham, the Viscountess Evanston.

Lady Evanston had lived in relative seclusion on his estate since the death of her husband some ten years before. There were no other children, and Thomas had been born the solitary heir to his father's title and lands. Eliza had been just eleven years old at the time of the elder viscount's passing, but she remembered the man vividly. He had been tall and handsome, as was his son, with the same unruly black hair. His eyes had been blue as well, but were more muted in tone, not electric and striking like the ones Thomas possessed. She wasn't certain where he had acquired those, as she'd always known his mother's eyes to be cold, black orbs staring out from a sharply featured and unforgiving face.

As severe as his mother was, his father had been quite the opposite. Time had shown the passage of his more agreeable traits down to Thomas, and perhaps this was why Lady Evanston despised them both. Her husband had made no secret of his affairs with other women, and while his wife had eventually sought dalliances of her own, she harbored no small amount of resentment for the man's lack of devotion, nor for her son's tendency to emulate him. In fact, Eliza would have been hard pressed to recall ever hearing a kind word from Gertrude Dornham to her son. Was it any mystery, then, that the man had such difficulty in matters concerning love?

The very thought created a melancholy awareness of him that she could not shake.

Still, if that night had accomplished anything, it had eliminated any doubt that he would readily have her, were she willing. Her greatest challenge had been trying not to seem as willing as she really was. And try as she might, she could not forget his compliment to her at the ball . . . could still feel the dark tendrils of fire that had spun out of control upon hearing his words.

Have I told you how lovely you look, Eliza?

All this came as a surprise. Not simply that he viewed her as desirable after years of treating her akin to a relation, but that he might willingly jeopardize his relationship with William to have her. Surely Thomas knew the potential consequences, so why was he doing it when the cost could possibly be no less than losing his best friend?

These questions plagued her. And on this particular day, she did not feel like prancing through Hyde Park, paying calls or writing letters. Rather, she tucked herself away in the drawing room, curled up in an armchair, drinking tea. She was reading over her most recent correspondence from Rosa when a quiet knock intruded on her solitude.

"Yes?" Eliza called, not raising her eyes from the letter in her hands.

The door opened, and the familiar sound of her butler's voice broke her troubled reverie. "Pardon me, my lady. Sir James is here to see you."

The paper leaves wilted in her hands. She glanced up at Roberts in surprise.

"Is he?" She stowed the letter safely into her pocket, untucked her legs from beneath her skirts, then commenced struggling to straighten her appearance. "Please show him in."

Eliza neatly smoothed a few errant strands of hair, taking an extra moment to pinch her cheeks for color, before discerning the sound of approaching footsteps. She straightened her posture in preparation to receive her guest.

Sir James entered with considerable pageantry, extending a formal bow in her direction before advancing to address her personally.

"Lady Eliza, I apologize for the spontaneity of my call,

but I was beset by the need to see you following your absence in the park this morning." She stared while he grasped her hand and pressed a kiss upon her bare knuckles, his perfectly coiffed moustache tickling against her skin.

"My apologies, Sir James. I certainly did not intend to cause you distress," she replied with a smile, gesturing to the settee. "Will you stay for tea?"

He shook his head despondently. "Alas, I cannot. I am in the process of acquiring new horseflesh and must be off to Tattersall's shortly."

"I recall you mentioning the venture when last we spoke. I trust you are nearer to concluding your search for a trustworthy steed?"

"Indeed, I am close," he replied solemnly. "Although I feel I'd be closer if your friend, the viscount, had not recently seen fit to interfere."

The room suddenly seemed to shrink, as did the capacity of her lungs.

"I beg your pardon?" she inquired weakly.

"It appears I have surprised you," Landry said, evaluating her closely. "Forgive me, dear lady, I thought perhaps you may have heard of it from Lord Evanston himself."

"I have not been in correspondence with him for the past two weeks, since the ball." Eliza felt a stab of guilt. She had seen him after that, of course. "And I can assure you that if I had any knowledge of his intention to disrupt your purchase—"

"No, no," said Landry, rising to a stand. "I did not mean to imply you played a part in his scheme." He paced back and forth, much as Evanston had done that evening she had called on him, although she couldn't help but notice that Sir James did not possess the untamed grace that came so naturally to Thomas.

"Tell me what happened, sir."

At this request, Landry looked slightly abashed. "Well, I suppose I don't have any concrete evidence of wrongdoing on his part. Only, it seems too much of a coincidence that he would create such a scene at the ball, then simply happen to buy the very animal in which I'd shown a strong interest."

She felt her face grow warm and tried very hard not to let a laugh slip out. Knowing Thomas the way she did, it had been no coincidence and was a deliberate action meant to aggravate Sir James. An inappropriate spark of delight raced through her. Evanston had thus far refused to return her correspondence, but could he be using these circumstances with Landry to exert his frustrations? If so, it would mean that he still cared enough to cause trouble—a notion that, although it should irritate her, pleased her as well.

Eliza evaluated her current facial expression, found it incongruous with Landry's complaints, and censored herself into an attitude of supportive concern instead.

"Sir James, despite his conduct at the ball, it is entirely possible this could all be coincidence." She fidgeted nervously before adding, "If you would like, I can make inquiries on your behalf?"

His pacing halted. "Good heavens, no," he replied with

distaste. "The deed is done, and I would rather he remain ignorant of my displeasure, if possible."

She shook her head. "But why? Perhaps I can assist in resolving what may be a misunderstanding—"

"I care nothing for the viscount's good opinion . . . only of yours. I have reason to believe our growing acquaintance offends him."

Knowing it was true, she asked anyway. "Why would the particulars of our acquaintance offend Lord Evanston?"

Sir James shot a shadowy glance in her direction. "Because for once, he cannot have what he wants."

Her mouth went conspicuously dry. "What makes you think he wants me?"

"He's made it obvious," he replied, tugging sharply down on his jacket. "And it takes quite a lot of nerve, if you ask me. Evanston seems set on humiliating me at every turn."

Eliza's brow furrowed. "Apart from the ball and buying the horse, what exactly has the viscount done to affront you, sir? Does it worry you that we are friends? Because after a lifetime, that is not going to change, even if he does misbehave on occasion."

His hands slowly lowered to his sides. "Well, no. It's not that exactly—"

"And if you are concerned that he is courting me, let me put your mind at ease on that account. Had he chosen to court me, though, would it not be his right? Without a proposal from another party, he may do as he likes."

Landry's mouth twitched. "Yes, certainly. I only meant

that perhaps it serves him right that you would not have him, since he is known for his licentious behavior with women—"

Eliza stood abruptly. "He has been a loyal friend throughout my family's time of great need."

Landry stopped talking and stared at her. In a panic, Eliza realized that she had just placed the courtship of one man in jeopardy, in favor of loyalty to another whom she had already seen fit to reject, and with good reason. Still, she could not stand idly by while Sir James listed the faults of a man who had only ever been kind to her family, scoundrel that he was. She assessed him with a sigh.

"Forgive me, Sir James, but I cannot understand why you would be so anxious where Lord Evanston is concerned. True, he is flawed," she confessed with a tug at her heart. "I only wish you were not so quick to judge, for if there has been a man created without imperfection, I have yet to meet him."

Sir James's mouth opened to say something, then closed mutely. Finally, it opened again.

"I can see I have upset you. Forgive my pride and lack of judgment in this matter." He came forwards to clasp her hand, pressing a kiss against it once more. "I—I hope you will permit me to call again soon."

Eliza felt a small twinge of remorse as Landry bowed, turned on his heel and made a hasty exit from her drawing room. Her head hurt, and she pressed her hand against it to ward off the pain, sinking back down into her favorite armchair.

She could only imagine how different her season could have been without the added complication of Evanston.

Hating him was impossible, loving him even more so. But one thing was absolutely certain as she reflected on the situation with Landry's "stolen" horse, her lips reluctantly curving into a grin.

He was certainly entertaining.

Eliza arrived at Caroline's town house as daylight gave way to dusk. She wondered if Caroline might find amusement in the retelling of Evanston's latest disturbance, or whether she, like her suitor, might find cause for upset. The truest reason for her friend's dismay would likely stem from Eliza's argument with Landry. No, better to leave that part out.

Anticipating a quiet dinner with Caroline and her aunt, she relinquished her shawl to the butler and followed him into the residence. Upon being escorted into the empty drawing room, however, she had the unmistakable sense that something was wrong. Rarely did her friend keep her waiting. The apprehensive countenance of the butler as he rushed about to bring refreshments did not quell her uneasy feelings. Yet there was no need for anxiety tonight—not for a routine evening spent among friends.

She sat waiting for nearly a quarter of an hour when the muffled sound of yelling from upstairs nearly caused her to drop her china teacup. Eliza set it down on the side table with a disharmonious *clank* and rushed out the doors to the foot of the staircase. Meg, Caroline's now wide-eyed housemaid, stood sentry between her and the steps beyond.

"Excuse me, please," said Eliza in a low voice.

The girl trembled before her. "Begging your pardon, my lady, but Lady Caroline requested that no one be allowed—"

She narrowed her eyes.

"I'd like to check on my friend. Move aside."

With less fight than anticipated, the maid hopped to the side. Eliza lifted her skirts and began a harried course up the stairs to stop at the door to Lady Frances's bedchamber. A tumult of noise—objects falling, panicked yells and Caroline's hushed pleas—was audible through the wooden portal. She rapped sharply on the door.

"Yes, come in, Meggie. I need your help," came the desperate reply.

Eliza twisted the metal knob and pushed open the door. She saw Caroline, her hair mussed and bodice crooked, with frantic eyes that grew huge in recognition. Her friend threw her hands outward, beseeching.

"No, Eliza. Stop there. Please—" she cried, her voice choked with emotion.

Too shocked to stop, Eliza allowed the door to fall open, revealing the source of Caroline's alarm. Her friend's elderly aunt, a woman who was normally the very example of polished refinement, was running madly across her bed, gray hair flying, clad in only her chemise.

"*The rabbits have escaped their hutch!*" she yelled. Latching onto Eliza's surprised gaze, she lurched forwards on the bed, lowering her voice into a harsh whisper. "Quickly, you must get Father!"

A tear trailed down Caroline's cheek and she huffed in frustration. "I've told you, Auntie, we have no rabbits."

"Liar!"

Lady Frances reached over to her bedside table and hurled a candlestick across the room, and Caroline raced to the bed to wrap her aunt in her arms. Eliza guessed the gesture was both meant to restrain and comfort. She stood dumbfounded for another second, watching the pair struggle with each other, trying to make sense of what was happening. Lady Frances was in a confused and agitated frame of mind, and upon watching her friend's practiced attempts to soothe the elderly woman, it became clear this was not the first episode. Indeed, it might explain Caroline's abstaining from certain social gatherings in weeks prior.

Suddenly, an idea came to her.

"Oh!" she exclaimed, staring beneath the bench at the foot of the four-poster bed. Eliza dropped down and made a scooping motion with her hands to retrieve a small pillow, most likely flung during the lady's fit of rage. "I've found one!"

The motion on the mattress stilled. She glanced up to see both sets of gray eyes staring at her, one set shining and hopeful, the other faded and wary.

"Show me," came the demand.

Making a display of cradling the pillow, Eliza rose and approached the bed.

"You must be careful."

Gently, she passed the cushion to Lady Frances, who skeptically examined the object even as she accepted it into her arms. Eliza's eyes flitted to her friend's, both women holding their breath in expectation of the older woman's temper. To their surprise, though, the lady cooed softly and sank back into a jumbled mass of blankets.

"There, there. You're safe now, little Tipper," sang Frances. She raised her eyes imploringly. "Girls, quickly. You must find the others."

It took Caroline a moment to realize what needed to be done, jumping off the bed a moment later to join Eliza in the rabbit hunt. They were unsure how many rabbits would be required, but thankfully Lady Frances possessed multiple pillows and had hurled them all to various corners of the room. After the pillows had been collected, they sheepishly presented their offerings to Caroline's aunt, who scrutinized each one in turn.

"Yes, I see Crumpet, you naughty boy . . . and Digger . . ." Her voice trailed off and she suddenly glanced at Caroline in offense. "Wait, what's this? We've only got three rabbits—"

Before her agitation could rise once more, Caroline tossed the extra cushion out of sight and reached out to stroke the woman's shoulder. "Auntie, I'm so glad we found them. Do you want us to put the rabbits back in the hutch? Or would you like to hold them a little while longer?"

Lady Frances greedily hugged the pillows to her chest. "I'd like to comfort them a bit more," she said in a breathy tone of voice.

"Why don't we get you settled too?" asked Eliza. She and Caroline helped ease Frances back into the bed, tucking the coverlet snugly around her hips while the lady quietly soothed her imaginary pets. Caroline cleared her throat.

"I'll ring for some tea. You just relax."

The women tiptoed out of the room, terrified that one misstep might alert Caroline's aunt to the false pretense to which she had succumbed, and gently clicked the door shut behind them. They stared at one another until a sob escaped Caroline's lips and she slapped a hand over her mouth to stifle it. Her weeping began in earnest once Eliza pulled her into her arms, hugging her tightly.

"Oh, Caroline. Why did you not tell me?"

Sniffling, her friend raised her red-rimmed eyes to meet Eliza's. "I was hoping it would pass," she admitted tearfully. "But the episodes have become more frequent, and . . . more intense."

Eliza's thoughts went immediately to Thomas. William would have been willing to help, but he was back in Kent with Clara and Rosa. It didn't make sense to impose on him when his best friend, the man who had come to her aid countless times—the one she had defended to Sir James this very afternoon—was right here in London.

Even if she was no longer certain Lord Evanston would help her.

She gave Caroline a reassuring squeeze before releasing her to step backwards. "I'll make some discreet inquiries, my dear. It may be that returning to Hampshire is in both your and your aunt's best interest."

Caroline nodded, sending a crystalline teardrop sailing off the tip of her nose. She sighed dismally. "I suppose it is ironic that the one time I find an interesting man in London, my season is to be cut short. Lord Braxton will surely move on once I return home."

"Not at all. The season is nearly over as it is, and I will speak to my brother about inviting him for the house party he is planning." She smiled in reassurance. "I'll work out the logistics of getting you and Lady Frances back to Hampshire, but it may take a few days. In the meantime, you must try to act normally." She paused. "It might mean requesting a bit of help from Thomas. Would that be amenable to you?"

Caroline gasped quietly. "Oh no, Eliza. Don't place yourself in such an awkward position."

Eliza waved off her protests. "Nonsense. Evanston and I know where we stand with each other."

Her friend easily discerned the falsehood and frowned while retrieving a handkerchief from her pocket to dab at her nose. "That is categorically untrue and you know it. How could I forgive myself if he used the situation as an excuse to—"

"Honestly, Caroline. If he hasn't already taken advantage of me by now, I think it's safe to say he is immune to my attractions."

Although he certainly had not acted immune while I was on his settee . . .

She dismissed the intruding remembrance before it could make her blush. In fact, it was probably best to change the subject. Catching sight of Meggie peering from around the wooden banister, Eliza quickly waved her over and bade three dinner trays be prepared and brought up to Lady Frances's bedchamber. As the maid hurried off to carry out the request, Caroline wrapped her arms around Eliza in a fierce embrace.

"You are so kind," she whispered. "Thank you."

Eliza pulled back to kiss Caroline on the forehead. "You are very welcome. I wouldn't want Lady Frances to be alone tonight."

Outwardly she ventured a smile, but inwardly she was already steeling herself for a thorough rejection from Evanston who, by this point in time, likely wanted nothing more to do with her.

"A letter for you, my lord."

Thomas glanced up from the soft refuge of his pillow, vision clouded after a night of cards and heavy drinking, then shut his eyes against the intruding butler and lowered his head once more.

"Not now, Burton. I'm busy," he mumbled.

It was both a blessing and a curse that he was a member of all the fashionable gentlemen's clubs. Brooks's, White's and the slightly less savory Putnam's were places to which he could easily escape—something he'd desperately needed as of late.

He much preferred the skillful machinations of cards in the clubs to the dice games in the gambling hells, where the player's success relied solely on luck. Luck would always be part of any game, but as it turned out, his improved dramatically when playing whist. Thomas played to win, but in what some would deem an uncharacteristic break, he refused to "play deep," acting on advice his own father had delivered shortly before his death:

There is excitement in the challenge, but no thrill to be had once you've lost it all.

This was advice that could have easily applied to his relationship with Eliza too except he hadn't had the good sense to follow it with her. Normally, he might be waking next to some delightful minx he'd met the night before, sated and carefree. But his current condition—head pounding from an excess of brandy, lying askew on his bed in last night's clothing—was a worrying reminder of how things had changed. That the one woman he longed for during his moments of ecstasy would never be there, and the imposters in his bed would serve as paltry imitations. He didn't think he could cope with the inevitable disappointment that would follow, so he drank instead. Especially when tormented by the memory of Eliza's scowl as she had shoved him away from her.

It took him half a minute to realize that Burton had still not retreated. Rather, the butler remained standing beside him, nearly concealed in the poor lighting of the bedchamber, a gleaming silver salver held steadily in his gloved hand. Thomas stared up at him in bleary disbelief.

"Can I help you? Or would you rather find employment elsewhere?" he snapped.

Burton's spine stiffened at that. "No, my lord. But this is a letter from Lady Eliza."

The air was suddenly heavy with the weight of her name lingering, and Thomas sat up to glare at the man. "I instructed you to dispose of any incoming correspondence from her."

"Yes, my lord. However, seeing as this is her third letter to you in fewer than as many weeks, I thought you might make an exception." Burton executed a small bow. "Just this once."

Evanston clenched his teeth. "You mean you want me to make an exception."

"It is not my place, of course, to have an opinion one way or the other." Stepping closer, the man extended the silver tray, burdened only by the singular ivory envelope upon it. "I only thought you might consider it."

Despite Burton's insolence and his own increasing annoyance, Thomas squinted in the gloom to stare at the letter, mocking him from its seat on the platter. After reaching out to snatch it quickly, he squeezed the parchment in his fist.

"Fine, I've taken it. Now leave me."

Burton acquiesced with a bow, then lighted a lamp beside the bed for easier reading. "I'll send your valet up to help you dress, my lord," he said, leaving the room before his master could curse at him.

With the door safely closed, Thomas let out the breath he had not known he'd been holding and glanced at the missive in his hand. A trace of fragrance, barely detectable, filtered across the still air of the room. Jasmine. Her scent.

The smell was indistinct, too faint to have been spritzed onto the stationary deliberately. It had likely been absorbed by simple contact with her.

Contact with her. His jaw tightened at the remembrance of the last time they had touched. His lips, her skin, his hands on her, the smell of her hair . . .

Evanston examined the pretty style of her penmanship in the flickering golden light. He'd been trying to forget about her. Truly, he had. Even dealing with Ashworth's blasted cotton mills was preferable to torturing himself over the man's sister. But her refusal had grated on him like nothing ever had, and the idea of her marrying another was troubling. He could imagine Landry or some other stuffy aristocrat trying to manage the vivacious Eliza and her spirited daughter, expecting them to comply in all manners of propriety. Unlike other, more suitable men, he rather liked them the way they were.

At this point, he longed to move on. If he could not have her himself, it was the most he could ask for. But how was he supposed to move on when she persisted in sending him these damned letters?

It could be an apology. An invitation.

But he knew better, didn't he?

He glanced down to find the missive a crumpled mass in his palm. Before he could give it additional thought, Thomas unfurled the envelope and tore the letter to pieces, tossing the remnants out across the dim expanse of his room.

Chapter Eight

The day's post brought nothing from Evanston. Still nothing came the following day, and as the hours wore on, Eliza found herself theorizing about the potential reasons for the delay of his reply. She was sure to exclude the most sensible explanation, of course, which was that he did not wish to speak to her. The disappointment associated with that idea overtook her mood each time it breached her consciousness. This was a setback she could not afford, especially when trying to maintain normalcy for both Caroline and her aunt during this sensitive time.

Adding to her gloomy disposition was the disclosure of some information, albeit innocently imparted to her, by her friend that afternoon. Caroline, taking advantage of an upturn in her aunt's condition, had dressed Lady Frances in her finest day dress and took the carriage to Bond Street for some shopping. It was there she observed Thomas departing from a shop, having purchased what appeared to be a gift of some kind. He had exchanged brief words with the ladies, then disappeared into his awaiting carriage.

It was none of Eliza's business, but her active imagination couldn't help but ponder the possibilities, conjuring images of a delighted female recipient. Perhaps even one with dark hair and a ruby-red dress.

Eliza could only attend this evening's party at the Fitzwilliam residence as a means of both adhering to routine and preventing her attention from straying relentlessly towards Thomas. After much debate, she decided on a luminous gown of pale lavender. Amethysts adorned her earlobes and throat, and her fair hair was swept up into a sophisticated mass of curls. Patterson had exhaled in admiration when securing the clasp of her necklace, and Eliza had to admit that she too was pleased with the overall effect.

At least she felt confident she looked her best, especially since she was journeying alone this evening. As a widow, she enjoyed the ability to attend gatherings without the necessity of a chaperone, but tonight she longed for company. Caroline had felt it best to stay home, as her aunt's difficulties often presented in the evening hours, and since Eliza was not overly familiar with the host and hostess of the night, she found herself in a melancholy state of mind.

From what she did know, the Fitzwilliams were a fashionable couple of the landed gentry who enjoyed throwing soirées when they were not busy attending them. Despite their children being grown and married, the couple still participated in the season with enthusiasm. Eliza could only presume this showy display of their vast wealth was to cement their position of relevance within the aristocrats of the *ton*, for the expense must have been considerable.

After a lengthy wait in the receiving line to meet her hosts, she sought out the cloak-room to divest herself of her shawl. Sparkling crystal chandeliers caught her eye on her way, and she paused to admire the gilded paneling along the walls and the ornately designed Axminster carpets beneath her slippers. Eliza was examining the intricate pattern woven into the sage hall runner when she suddenly had the distinct impression she was being observed. She raised her eyes to find the same raven-haired beauty who had previously accompanied Thomas to the theater, wearing yet another dress in the same daring shade of red.

Their eyes held one another's, and Eliza's heart plummeted. At best, she could hope for an awkward interaction. At worst—well, at worst . . .

Lord Evanston stepped into view, his arm extended in the woman's direction. He did not yet see Eliza, and with a slight tug on his arm his companion ensured that, at least for now, he would not. The lady expertly steered him into the drawing room, breaking the gaze between herself and Eliza with the smallest of smiles.

She stood frozen in the hallway, her mind waging a panicked battle between the need to observe etiquette, and her overwhelming desire to bolt from the house. Eliza was aware of the need for propriety, but the all-consuming thought at this moment was that perhaps no one would notice if she simply kept her shawl and called her carriage back around.

The only thing worse than being shunned by Thomas in person was the idea of also being disdained by the woman he had most certainly selected to warm his bed in her stead. The same one he'd likely been out buying gifts for on Bond Street.

Eliza knew she could not loiter in the hallway for long. More guests were arriving every moment. She needed to speak to Thomas about Lady Frances, and although this evening's party was not the best place or time, his lack of response left her little choice in the matter. The only course available now was to approach him with a friendly countenance and hope for the best.

She placed her hand on her abdomen and took a shaky breath, replacing her terror with a poise and coolness that was not genuine. Deciding to leave her shawl with an attendant at last, she made her way down the final length of the hallway to enter the drawing room, instantly catching the attention of its occupants, including a surprised Baron Latimer.

"Lady Eliza! What a surprise," he effused while raising her hand for a kiss. "Sir James will be sorry to have missed you tonight, but rest assured I will tell him how very well you look." This last statement was punctuated with a mischievous wink.

Eliza laughed graciously at the flattery, highly aware that the man in the periphery to her right was Lord Evanston.

"No need for that, my lord," she replied diffidently. "Only tell me how the season has treated you thus far."

The gentleman launched into a lengthy description of

his various pursuits, but Eliza wasn't listening. Her energy was directed instead at attempting to discern snippets of Thomas's conversation with his paramour, but there was precious little discourse to be heard. Risking a glance to the side, she discovered his companion had redirected him to the opposite side of the room.

Frustration welled inside of her, but what could she have reasonably expected? For him to casually turn her way and join in the conversation? For the woman he was with to allow it?

This will certainly be more difficult than that.

"Perhaps you can tell me," voiced Latimer loudly, "the whereabouts of our friend, Lady Caroline? I have not seen her for some time now, and I know her parents are quite anxious for a match this year."

Eliza tore her gaze away from Evanston at the abrupt change in subject. "I understand she was taken abed with a headache this evening. I will be happy to convey your regards when I see her, though."

He harrumphed in dissatisfaction. "Yes, I thank you. Although she might be best served with a reminder of the fickle nature of love," he said, nodding his graying head towards the rear of the drawing room. "She is set to lose the only suitor she has ever managed to entertain."

Her eyes widened and she turned to find the amiable Lord Braxton paying quite a lot of attention to a pretty young debutante, the girl's hopeful mother standing nearby. A bitter swell of anger rose inside her on behalf of her friend. If Lord Braxton's regard could so easily be gained and lost, then perhaps he was not worth having. Still, it was best not to address the issue with Caroline while she was so occupied with her aunt's well-being.

Eliza swiveled back around to make a reply to the baron, but stopped to notice that Thomas had also discerned Braxton's flirtations from across the room. His neutral countenance gave nothing away, but his bright eyes flicked over to Eliza for the briefest of moments before returning once again to his beautiful companion.

He'd glanced her way. She was unsettled to discover that this tiny gesture could provide her with such comfort. It betrayed an interest, and if there was still interest, perhaps she could use it to gain his notice long enough for a conversation. She owed it to Caroline, who was likely about to lose everything she had worked for this season.

She aimed an insincere smile at Baron Latimer.

"Yes, of course I will remind Lady Caroline, my lord."

And with a small curtsy, she left the man to cross nearer to the hostess, who was in the process of lining guests up for dinner.

Thomas stared through the swirling brandy depths of his snifter, cursing his luck. Or lack thereof, as it would seem. Presently, Eliza was out of his sight, but it had taken every trace of willpower he possessed not to marvel at her loveliness throughout the entire course of dinner. She had also not failed to impress the men seated on either side of her, much to his chagrin.

Normally he would have found relief in Landry's absence, but tonight it turned out to be of little consequence. Landry's attentions had easily been replaced by new admirers, and if given enough time, Thomas was sure such interests could transform into pursuits of their own. Remembering it now, the men staring a bit too long, overtly concentrating on her every word, caused a heady blaze of envy to spread through his chest.

He would have given anything to be seated next to her, conversing easily—but it was not to be. She had not come to London in search of a man like him, and had most recently, literally shoved him away. William had warned him away too so Thomas knew he was a fool to continue after Eliza, and yet he could think of no other. Not even his old paramour, Victoria Varnham, had been able to attract his notice as she once had, and she had tried. Repeatedly and with enthusiasm.

But since seeing Eliza that first night in Belgravia, he'd found himself utterly bewitched. And to his surprise, the idea of lying with another woman after that seemed pathetic and unsatisfying, a waste of his time. He was not even remotely interested. When confronted by Victoria regarding his indifference to her advances, he'd merely shrugged. Of course, the woman was naturally competitive, and it was this side of her personality that took his loss the hardest. He knew she had no real feelings of substance for him, and had always seen fit to entertain herself with multiple men, but it had taken a while for her to make peace with the situation as it was. In the end, he valued her as an old friend, and she valued going to the theater and socializing among the *ton*. Anything else was pure illusion at this point, created solely to inspire Eliza's own jealousy. Much like with Landry's horse . . . even if nothing changed, at least it gave him a tiny bit of vindictive satisfaction. Although, should something change—

A strong slap on the back jarred him to awareness, and with a glance at the gentlemen at the table, he realized he'd just spent the majority of his time after dinner in contemplation of his best friend's sister.

"You there, old chap?" joked Lord Braxton, puffing on a cigar. "What have you been wool-gathering about?"

Mr. Fitzwilliam smiled slyly. "Probably a woman."

"Since when have I been known to *wool-gather* about a woman?" he muttered, not pleased at being discovered.

This resulted in hearty laughter round the table. "True enough," said Fitzwilliam. "You are known to be a man of action with regard to the fairer sex. Although if there was one lady worthy of imaginative fancy, I'd say Lady Eliza Cartwick might tempt me."

Murmurs of agreement circulated among the male guests, along with a wave of fresh cigar smoke. One of the gentlemen who had admired her excessively during the meal spoke up across from him.

"Indeed! What a beauty. Enchanting in every single way."

Fitzwilliam appeared thoughtful. "I would be shocked if she were to receive no less than five offers of marriage prior to her departure from London." He tipped a glance at Baron Latimer. "We know about your boy, Sir James. He has been fairly active in his pursuit. But I would wager that there are more suitors waiting silently for their chance to offer for the loveliest lady to grace London in a long while."

Thomas sighed, ignoring the turn of conversation as best he could. London used to be a place to forget himself and his cares. A sanctuary to indulge his less respectable appetites. But now he knew why Eliza had avoided the city for as long as she had. Why each of her captivating smiles bore a lonely longing for home just beneath the surface. There was simply no pleasure to being picked apart by the gossips of high society, particularly with one's heart on the line.

Thankfully Fitzwilliam let the matter rest, the subject naturally easing into something less obtrusive and flirtatious. In time, the men snuffed their cigars and stood, quaffing what remained of their drinks and moving to join the ladies for some card games in the parlor. Thomas felt the cold weight of dread settling in his stomach. He wasn't certain he could handle seeing Eliza again.

But he inevitably made his way to the door of the parlor, evaluating how best to reach the far side of the room while avoiding her position, about midway through the tables. In line with his current run of misfortune, she spotted him immediately, rotating in her chair to physically capture his gaze. He took in the intricate arrangement of her golden hair and thrilled at the way her eyes shined brighter than the jewels at her throat. His glance dipped down unwittingly to take in the lilac silk of her dress, how it enveloped her voluptuous curves. Recalling the sweet taste of her skin, he shook his head as if in a dream.

Does she do this to torment me?

No, he would not flatter himself. She was always the most beautiful woman in the room regardless of who was in attendance.

He was snared. But like a madman, Evanston still attempted to pass without engaging her. The cause was lost when she rose to stand before him, effectively blocking his path. She cast him a pleasant smile, but he noted her eyes were filled with unease.

"Good evening, my lord."

Desperately focusing on the tables beyond her, he tipped her a cursory nod.

"Eliza," he murmured softly.

She paused in surprise at his use of her first name in such a setting, and truthfully, he didn't know what had made him utter it. Before anything else could be said, he tried to brush past her, but rather than letting him, she reached down to touch his hand. The soft glide of her fingers against his caused his pulse to accelerate considerably.

"Please. I must speak to you . . . It's important," she whispered.

He jerked his hand away. "What could possibly be so important that you would subject yourself to my presence? I think we have established that you would really rather not."

She winced at his cutting tone. "Thomas, you know I—" Eliza paused, glancing around the room, taking in the curious onlookers. "May we speak in the hallway? Then I promise not to disturb you further, if that is what you wish."

Not seeing an alternative, he sighed, then nodded crisply

and allowed her to pass. Before turning to follow her, he caught sight of Victoria, fuming, at the distant card table.

They stepped out of the stuffy confines of the parlor, venturing down the hallway in search of privacy. Eliza came to stop beneath a large window that overlooked the rear gardens, now blackened by night, and reached up to touch her coiffure with her fingertips as she was wont to do when anxious. He stared down at her, waiting, and at last she met his gaze.

"Did you receive my letters?" she inquired.

"I did."

Clearly not knowing what to do with her hands, she seemed to finally settle on clasping them before her bell-shaped skirts. "Did you read them?"

"I did not."

An unmistakable flicker of hurt crossed her face. Thomas found himself regretting his candor, but then Eliza straightened and tipped up her chin. The tiny movement, a motion that displayed a small fraction of her strength and bravery, made him want to pull her against him. Lay waste to her elaborate farce of indifference. Free her from the confines of how she believed a proper widow should act. He fought the urge back down into submission, knowing she would scorn him if he did not.

"Had you read my first two letters," she began, her voice shaking, "you would know I am sorry that things have grown so complicated between us."

"I believe I already know that."

"And," she continued, "had you read my final letter, you would know that someone dear to me is in trouble."

Thomas froze in alarm, his eyes locking onto hers.

"Rosa?" he asked hoarsely, edging closer to panic.

Now it was Eliza's turn to go still. "I—well, no. It's not Rosa. Rosa is fine."

He took a shuddering breath and glanced away. "Who is it, then?" he managed.

Still evaluating him closely, she stepped closer and lowered her voice. "My friend Caroline needs to return home immediately. Her aunt is . . . unwell."

"Lady Frances?" he asked, pausing in thought. "And you trust me to help?"

Her disbelief appeased his wounded ego only slightly. "Why would you ask me such a thing? Of course, I trust you to help."

Eliza's eyes shone up at him, and his gaze dropped to her mouth. It would take no effort at all to slide his arms around her and claim those lips for himself. He wondered if she would pretend to struggle at first, as she had at the ball, or if she would melt against his chest and kiss him back with all the fiery passion he knew she possessed.

Gritting his teeth, Thomas tamped down the fantasy, looking away instead to study the patterned wallpaper. She would not trust him nearly so much were she aware of the sudden turn of his thoughts.

"What seems to be the issue?" he ground out.

"It seems . . ." Eliza paused and looked away, uncomfortable. "It seems that Lady Frances has been misremembering things as of late. She has episodes of confusion that can turn rather violent. I bore witness to one such event, and it is why

I have come to ask for your assistance." Her gloved fingers twisted together. "Anything you could do to facilitate their speedy and inconspicuous exit from London would be most appreciated."

"You do realize that if Caroline leaves London now, her chances with Lord Braxton are all but extinguished," he said with a sigh. "I assume you have seen the toll her absence has already taken on his affections?"

She stiffened at his observation. "I'm sure Caroline is aware of the possibility, my lord, but I would ask that any particulars be kept from her for now. The last thing she needs while caring for Lady Frances is to be torn apart by Braxton's changeable regard."

Looking at her now, color heightened and breath quickened in defense of her friend, Thomas grudgingly admitted to himself that this was one of Eliza's many fine qualities. Loyalty. Regardless of the fact that he repelled her to some degree, he had an idea that were someone to attack him, she would leap to his defense.

Evanston gazed at her thoughtfully. "Caroline is fortunate to have your friendship."

"You have my friendship as well, you know," she answered softly.

He decided to ignore that and considered her request in silence. At last he shook his head, knowing he would never deny Eliza what she needed under normal circumstances, and certainly not under ones as dire as these.

"Fine," he sighed. "Yes, I will help them leave London and ensure they are settled safely back in Hampshire."

Eliza's eyes widened in gratitude. "Thank you. Oh, thank you, Thomas," she breathed, coming forwards to embrace him. Her palms grazed his chest before he took a swift step away. The incendiary contact was enough to drive him backwards with considerable speed.

"Don't."

She jerked her hands away, humiliation overcoming her. "Forgive me. I—"

"I do have one condition, if I am to do this for you," he said quickly in an abrupt change of subject.

Eliza blinked at him, lifting her brow in dismay. She shook her head slightly to send her glowing purple earbobs swaying from side to side.

"You do?"

The innocence with which she asked the question nearly made him reconsider, as his charity had never come attached with the strings of obligation before. While he hated that current circumstances necessitated the change, a vision of her, lying in his bed wearing only her amethyst jewels, intruded on his thoughts. Ruinous wretch that he was, he could not give up on that version of reality quite yet—a reality where Eliza Cartwick would willingly choose him above all others.

This would be a gamble unlike any other he had taken before.

A means to an end . . .

"Yes, I do," said Evanston with a tug on his cravat. "I require that you defer responding to any and all requests of marriage you may receive. That is, until you have returned to the country."

Silence was his answer. He held her stunned gaze, realizing that, should she refuse his terms, it would be ungentlemanly of him to fulfill his threat and walk away during her time of need. And with Eliza, he always *tried* to be a gentleman. Thomas held his breath as she scanned his face.

"Why?" she asked in astonishment.

"I'll leave you to draw your own conclusions."

Her expression closed, and her hands dropped into fists at her side. "And what if I say no?"

He stepped closer to her, near enough almost to touch. Eliza's eyes grew large but she did not retreat, and he watched her resolve fade away as their bodies joined in smoldering, silent communication. He leaned down to whisper in her ear, her golden curls tickling his cheek.

"Will you?"

Eliza stared at his chest and said nothing.

Evanston lingered for a moment, absorbing her scent and her heat, memorizing the feel of having her body so close to his, then straightened. "Have Caroline and her aunt prepare for departure tomorrow. We will leave early the following morning, while it's still dark."

She glanced up quickly. "I wish to come too. To be of some assistance."

"No," he snapped. Then lowering his voice, said, "You must remain here until the end of the season."

Again, pain flickered across her features. "Thomas, why?"

He ran a hand over his face. "I need to do this without any added . . . distractions," he answered, knowing she would be a distraction of the most tempting kind.

She stared at him then, breathing coming in shallow fits and starts, color heightening in her anger. "After all of this, I have to wonder," Eliza fumed, her eyes darting furtively down the hall to ensure they were not being heard. "if your singular goal in coming to London was to interfere with my finding a husband."

It certainly hadn't been when he'd arrived. But now . . .

Taking her hand in his, Thomas raised it to his lips and lowered his voice.

"Would it make a difference?" he asked, brushing a kiss across the back of her knuckles.

Eliza stared at him in stunned silence as he released her and returned to the party . . . back to the crowded drawing room, back to the whist tables and back to the eagerly awaiting stares of the *ton*'s most ferocious gossips.

Chapter Nine

Lady Frances snored softly amidst the flickering shadows of the drawing room, while Eliza and Caroline conversed quietly between themselves. The servants had disappeared belowstairs to preserve their energy for the precipitous departure of their mistresses, and Eliza found herself covering a yawn with her fingertips and glancing at the grandfather clock as it sounded the hour. It was three o'clock in the morning and Thomas still had yet to arrive, although this was most likely by design. Many balls and events ran into the small hours of the morning and she knew, in an effort to be inconspicuous, that he would time his arrival when most of the carriages had already returned home.

She wondered at how he might react to her presence tonight, given that he had issued her a strict command not to be there. Still, Eliza found herself anticipating his arrival, as she always did. Finding a proper husband would have been such an easier task without the constant knowledge that Evanston was never far from her, in actuality and in her thoughts. But the seemingly determined viscount had no interest in making things easy. Quite the contrary, in fact. His request that she consider no offers of marriage until returning to Kent was both infuriating and exhilarating, and briefly she had wondered if he would hold her to such a condition. Would he truly withdraw his assistance should she refuse his terms? It was not a chance she could reasonably take when her friend's well-being was on the line.

And she could not place her difficulties squarely at his feet. Not when elation coursed through her at the very notion that he still held an interest in her. No. Her feelings for him had been, and always would be, her single most inconvenient obstacle when attempting to settle on a husband. Landry was a gentleman—all of the men so far had been gentlemen—but when compared to Thomas, she found they were simply lacking. Regardless of his illicit reputation, and of the other women whose very existence felt like a dagger to her heart . . . Eliza wanted him still.

Absently, she toyed with the lace that edged her sleeve at the wrist, preoccupied with her longing. A question posed by Caroline rapidly brought her out of her stupor.

"So, you have not told me what Thomas required of you."

Eliza blinked up at her friend. "For what?"

"For assisting us."

She glanced away. "He has never required anything of me before."

The corner of Caroline's mouth twitched. "And yet, something tells me that this time was different."

Eliza stared at her friend, knowing that to argue or to conceal the truth would be a pointless exercise. Besides, she had already been less than honest with Caroline on multiple occasions. Quite frankly, she deserved better.

"Yes," she murmured, and resumed plucking at her sleeve. "This time was different."

Caroline pulled herself into an upright posture, her gray eyes instantly alert. "What did he want, Eliza?"

"Nothing, really. He only wanted—"

The sudden rapping of the brass knocker caused both women to jump. Eliza rose to a stand and smoothed her dark, granite-colored skirts.

"Evanston is here," she said. "I will let him inside."

But her progress was impeded by Caroline's grip on her wrist, pulling her back down onto the settee. "Not before you tell me what agreement has been struck."

Eliza glanced worriedly in the direction of the front door. "Certainly nothing as sordid as what you're likely imagining," she answered. "He only asked that I delay considering any offers of marriage until returning to the country."

Caroline released her and stared in surprise. Eliza took advantage of the moment and stood once more to cross the room.

"He's buying himself time," came her friend's abrupt statement.

Eliza paused before entering the hallway and turned to regard her. "For what?"

"To seduce you, of course."

The thrilling bloom of heat in her belly was in direct contrast to the grim aspect of Caroline's face. Eliza exulted in the excitement but was chilled by the familiar shade of guilt a moment later. Her friend thought she was a good and moral woman. Her father had believed the same. But she couldn't deny being enticed by the notion of being compromised by Thomas, and at the very great expense of her ability to land a proper husband. Part of her was only shocked that she'd managed to resist him for this long, but if he were to keep trying? She could not say how much longer it would be.

The staccato rhythm of the knocker could once again be heard, and Eliza decided against answering the door herself, even though every part of her ached to go to him, be near him. Instead she reached over to tug on the bellpull and seated herself once more beside Caroline, hoping her friend had not observed her indecision. Within moments, the butler appeared and admitted their guest, whose deep voice could be heard immediately issuing instructions.

Eliza had often recognized this as one of Evanston's fortes, especially during the past few years. He was an efficient leader in times of trouble. She could recall countless instances of his willingness to help and his effectiveness once called upon, not to mention the compassion which he could not quite disguise as something less meaningful.

The viscount strode into the drawing room, his large frame and dark hair unmistakable even in the dim light, and she snapped to attention. Frantically, she willed the furious blush that crept up her neck to dissipate. He tipped his head to Caroline in greeting, then stopped short at the sight of Eliza. His brilliant gaze focused on her with displeasure.

"Why are you here?" he asked brusquely. The timbre of his voice resonated through the still of the room and startled the dozing Lady Frances awake.

"Good heavens! There is a man—"

Eliza and her friend rose from the settee, with Caroline quickly rushing to Frances's side.

"Remember, Auntie?" she asked, soothing the elderly woman with gentle strokes upon her arm. "This is Lord Evanston. He has come to escort us safely back to Hampshire."

Lady Frances cast her cloudy eyes at the man in question, who regarded her politely and bowed in her direction.

"Forgive me, my lady, for the rude awakening. I am here to help if you will allow it."

Even with his initial irritation at her, Eliza felt herself warm at his words. He was, despite everything, here at her request. She crossed to stand near him, placing her hand upon his arm and trying not to notice how he stiffened beneath her touch.

"You have met him before, Lady Frances. At Lawton Park, where my brother resides."

Caroline's aunt smiled girlishly beneath the gray wisps of hair that swept across her forehead. "Of course, I remember the viscount. I just wasn't expecting such a handsome man in my drawing room at this late hour."

This elicited a modest chuckle from Evanston. The noise of trunks being moved behind them diverted Caroline and

Frances, who ventured into the hallway to supervise the efforts of the servants, and Eliza took advantage of the opportunity to gain his attention. She gazed up at him, his face half-illuminated in the poor lighting, and felt her pulse race as he returned her glance.

"Thank you for doing this."

"You weren't supposed to be here," he replied under his breath.

She smiled innocently. "I agreed to remain in London until the end of the season. And here I am . . . in London."

His eyes held hers fast, then shifted down to where her hand lay upon his arm. "Very clever. Now if you would step away, I'd appreciate it."

For a fraction of a second, she considered tightening her grip in defiance. Contemplated running her fingers over the fine broadcloth of his coat to feel the hard musculature beneath. Instead she backed away, but not before earning a curious glance from Thomas, who seemed to sense a conflict of some kind happening within her.

"Certainly, my lord. My only aim is to help." She raised her hands to tuck an errant lock of hair back into place, noticing how he followed the movement. "I do have a question, though."

He met her eyes. "Which is?"

"What could you possibly stand to gain by interfering with my suitors?"

"And I could ask what you hoped to gain by visiting my town house late at night," he replied.

"Answers," she said smoothly, regardless of the blood that heated her face. "Of which you seem to have precious few."

Thomas scoffed and glanced towards the ceiling. "Fine. What do you wish to know?"

She took a steadying breath. "There are only two possible reasons for you to keep imposing yourself on me in this way. So, which is it?"

"What are my choices again?"

Coming closer, she stopped just shy of their bodies touching, and Eliza could see the moment when his azure gaze turned hazy with desire. It was a dizzying revelation that she held such power over him. She moistened her lips, suddenly nervous.

"I'd like to know—do you wish to bed me, or to wed me?"

For once, he didn't have something witty to say. No clever retort, no snappy comeback, no inappropriate comment that would make her blush. He merely stared at her, mouth slightly open, looking very much taken by surprise.

"Surely you must know what you are after, and all the reasons why I can't possibly agree to either one." Rising high on her tiptoes, Eliza placed her fingertips on his chest to brush a kiss against his cheek, watching the dark sweep of his lashes as his eyes fell closed. "But I do thank you very much for your help," she whispered.

And with that she left the room, leaving Evanston alone to contemplate his own reasons in silence.

The noise of Patterson tugging the curtains aside stirred Eliza from her slumber, but it was the stream of yellow light lancing across her face which truly woke her. With a sleepy groan, she burrowed beneath her coverlet, seeking refuge from the assault to her senses.

"Patterson!"

A muffled chuckle could be heard through the protective layers above. "Begging your pardon, my lady, but it's nearly three o'clock in the afternoon."

Eliza sat bolt upright in disbelief, her blankets falling away. "Three o'clock?"

Her lady's maid approached to seat herself on the edge of the bed, nimble fingers instantly set on the task of undoing Eliza's plait.

"I let you sleep as long as I could, given your arrival at such an early hour this morning." Patterson eyed her with sympathy. "Was Lady Frances's departure a success?"

"It was," replied Eliza, stretching her arms and yawning. "But I am exhausted. I can only imagine how they must feel, as their travels will last at least two full days before reaching Willowford House. I am hopeful that Caroline and her aunt are able to sleep during the ride. I, myself, am never able to sleep . . ." Her voice trailed off in melancholy remembrance of the passing of her loved ones, taken violently from her in a carriage accident.

With Eliza's hair finally released from its confines, Patterson slid her fingers through the thick tresses to massage her sensitive scalp. "No," she said softly. "Of course, you can't." She reached towards the bedside table and retrieved a silver hairbrush. Gently, she skimmed it over her hair, made wavy by the braid, and steered the conversation in a different direction. "Do you know if they will stop for lodging? Or were they riding through?"

"Evanston's only planned stops were to change horses and find refreshment. He felt that lingering any longer might invite unwanted questions."

The maid nodded. "In that, I am sure he's correct." She paused. "How was the viscount last night?"

"Annoyed at seeing me!" said Eliza with a laugh.

Patterson grinned. "Turnabout is fair play, my lady."

"Yes," she agreed. "I think I managed to irritate him a great deal, and yet, he still managed to annoy me."

"A talent of his. Although when performing such a selfless task, I suppose he can be allowed an indulgence?"

"Yes," Eliza admitted. "I suppose."

"Well, I am glad things went smoothly. Now we must get you dressed and ready. You have a good many things that need tending to."

She furrowed her brow. "Like what?"

Patterson walked across the room to return the hairbrush to its resting place on Eliza's vanity. "Like the flowers and cards that have arrived for you this morning."

"Flowers? From whom?"

"A great many men, apparently. And one woman."

Although Eliza's interest was piqued, the maid would say no more. So she hurried to get dressed, certain that Patterson must have been exaggerating or mistaken. Upon the pair of them arriving downstairs, however, she found that the foyer was indeed crowded with bouquets. Oddly, one single perfect ruby-red rose stood defiantly in its own tiny fluted vase against the showy backdrop of comparative extravagance.

"Oh Patterson, this is beyond belief!" she exclaimed, admiring a bouquet here, leaning in to inhale the rich fragrance of another there. Yet her eyes kept straying to the rose. Something just didn't seem right, and hadn't Patterson mentioned that she'd received flowers from a woman?

Eliza plucked the card from the base of the vase. There was no message, as with the others. Only a name:

Mrs. Victoria Varnham

Stunned, she dropped the card.

"What is it?" asked Patterson in concern.

Eliza shook her head, her eyes wide. "I—I think this rose is from one of Lord Evanston's mistresses," she answered faintly.

Her maid came forwards to examine the card, then shook her head in dismay.

"Why would his mistress send you a rose?" she asked, suspicion setting her mouth into a grim line.

A knock on the front door interrupted their queries, and Patterson quickly shooed Eliza into the drawing room. Seating herself on the settee, she tried to still her shaking hands while straining to hear any fragments of the conversation at the front door. While she could not make out the details, one thing was clear.

The visitor was female.

Anxiety surged through her and thwarted her attempts to remain calm. She inhaled deeply in an effort to regain control of her emotions, and when the door slowly opened, Patterson's troubled gaze was all that was required for her to confirm the identity of her guest.

"It is Mrs. Varnham." She evaluated Eliza's uneasy reaction to the news. "Shall I tell her you are not at home?"

"And open myself up to future visitations? No, absolutely not," she declared. "If she wishes to seek me out, then she shall find me, and we will end this speedily."

Patterson frowned and nodded. "As you wish, my lady."

Eliza stood and clasped her hands, awaiting the arrival of the unwelcome visitor. The woman swept into the drawing room, clad in a day dress that was an unsurprising shade of scarlet, her ebony ringlets half concealed by the hat that covered her head. Eliza lowered into a polite curtsy, attempting to smile despite the bitterness that rose in her throat.

"I don't believe we've been properly introduced, but I welcome you to my home. My name is—"

"I know who you are, Lady Eliza," she interrupted with a bored glance in her direction. "My name is Victoria Varnham. I believe you received my gift."

The woman was a contradiction, and Eliza steeled herself for the uncomfortable conversation that was to come.

"Yes, I did. Which leads me to the question of why you would send anything at all, particularly when you insist upon being rude."

Mrs. Varnham seated herself in an armchair, taking her time arranging her skirts before raising her eyes to meet Eliza's. "Because it is the only thing you will receive where Lord Evanston is concerned, this season, or ever."

Interesting. Eliza sank back down onto the settee. Apparently, this woman saw her as a threat.

"What makes you think that I expect anything regarding Lord Evanston?"

Her guest uttered a sharp bark of laughter and stared at her incredulously. "It is quite plain to see, my lady. It's in your actions, when you abscond with him from our theater box . . . when you usher him away from the whist tables . . . and in every one of your stolen glances while you are in his company."

Rather than argue against what was clearly factual information, Eliza remained silent and held the woman's hostile gaze. She was vaguely aware that her palms were sweating, but resisted the urge to dry them on her skirts lest she betray her nervousness. Instead, she straightened her back and tipped her head slightly.

"Why are you here?"

"It's quite simple, really," Mrs. Varnham replied, extending her arm to examine the fingers of her pristine gloves. "I want to clear up this little misunderstanding. This idea you seem to have that Thomas has some interest in you." She smiled broadly. "I can assure you that I hold his interest very well indeed. Particularly in, shall we say, *private* chambers. I can only imagine that perhaps one of the many men who have sent you flowers here today might be able to comfort you in this time of loss."

Eliza reeled in jealousy. This woman's only purpose was

to assert her claim over Thomas, and regardless of whether or not her claims were actually true, she felt certain that he might take issue with any woman foolish enough to do such a thing.

"I understand completely," she said with a nod. "In fact, I will pay you a courtesy. I will write to him at my earliest opportunity. I want him to know that I have been apprised of the situation."

At this, the woman's dark eyes grew large, then narrowed into slits. Fury twisted her features. "You are not the woman he wants," Mrs. Varnham seethed. "You are not the *widow* he wants."

"Let us assume this is true," Eliza said, cursing the tremor in her voice. "If you were truly so secure in your relationship with Evanston, why would you go to such lengths to explain it to me?"

The woman rose abruptly and brushed her skirts back behind her. "He is mine. We each have our separate flirtations, but this recent behavior is intolerable. Whether you agree or not is unimportant, but you will abstain from seeing him in the future."

Eliza stood as well, shrugging noncommittally. "I will make no promises."

"We will see about that."

With one last haughty glare, Victoria Varnham stormed into the hallway and, without waiting for assistance, threw open the front door and left the house. A moment later, Patterson poked her head into the drawing room.

"Are you well, my lady?"

"I am," she replied, resting her hand on the back of a chair for support.

Patterson approached and wrapped her arms around Eliza in a warm embrace. "It sounded like you gave as good as you got."

"Did it?" she asked, resting her chin on the maid's shoulder. "I certainly hope so. Although I'm not sure how I'll be able to face Thomas after this. The idea of him being intimate with that woman, and so recently—"

"I'm not sure Mrs. Varnham can be believed. But even if she could . . ." Patterson hesitated. "Does it matter? I was under the impression you wanted a different kind of man."

Eliza's head drooped sadly.

"I'm not sure I know what I want anymore." She sighed.

Thomas assisted the footmen in unloading the final trunks from Caroline's vehicle after ensuring the ladies were made comfortable inside the residence. Upon arriving at Willowford House, Lady Frances had immediately been ushered upstairs to rest and regain her strength—a necessity as the trip had taxed the elderly woman. Although he'd followed the pair in the privacy of his own carriage, Caroline had hinted to him that there were difficulties along the way. One only need observe the strain on her face to grasp the verity of her claims.

After briefing the household staff on her aunt's fragile state, Caroline joined him downstairs in the dining room for an impromptu dinner consisting mostly of sliced meats and roasted vegetables. Simple fare, made more delicious by their famished state. The two of them ate in companionable silence, their hunger overriding any outward motivation to be polite, with both parties fully aware there was no offense intended.

Her pangs seemingly assuaged, Caroline breathed a sigh and took a long swallow of wine. She glanced over at Thomas, who was absently twirling the stem of his glass between his fingers, unseeingly focused on the light that tricked off the rim.

"Thank you for helping us, my lord."

He blinked up at her. "You are quite welcome, although Eliza is more deserving of thanks. Had she not seen fit to make inquiries on your behalf, you would likely still remain in London."

"I have thanked her many times over. Especially since I know a bargain was struck to secure your assistance."

Evanston's gaze sharpened. "I'm certain that's none of your business."

"Hmm. Yes and no." She raised her wineglass for another sip, then held his eyes as she replaced it on the snowy linen tablecloth. "While she is welcome to conduct her own private affairs, if a dear friend finds herself distressed on my behalf, I consider that my business."

"Distressed?" He eyed her incredulously. "I've never placed her in a position where—"

"Did you not kiss her on the night of her engagement?"

He paused, then conceded with a nod. "I see she finally told you about that."

"And do you not believe that might cause a young woman some distress?"

"I doubt distress is what it caused," he said sarcastically. "Clearly you and I have never kissed."

She eyed him critically. "You hide behind your bravado when the questions get tough. Don't think I hadn't noticed."

Thomas tossed his napkin beside his plate. "And don't think for one second that my request of Eliza has caused her any sort of sacrifice. She agreed to the terms, after all."

"Eliza is a grown woman and can do what she pleases. But I disagree with your point about sacrifice. I think expecting her to postpone replying to any impending offers of marriage is quite a sacrifice indeed. And to what purpose, my lord?"

Thomas could feel his anger rising. "To whatever purpose I wish," he enunciated slowly.

"And if she should lose suitors because of it?"

"Then they never deserved her to begin with."

"Oh," she seethed, leaning forwards. "And you do?"

The legs of his chair scraped loudly as he stood to scowl down at her. "*No,*" he ground out. "But damn it, *I have to try.*"

Thomas had said it without thinking, and only the dropping of Caroline's jaw hauled him back to reality. He stared at her, nonplussed, while the truth of what he'd just spoken resonated in the stillness of the dining room. He ran a hand over his face.

Christ . . .

He took a breath, and then another. When he finally opened his eyes, Caroline was staring at him silently, her dark gray eyes round and shining. Thomas forced himself to speak.

"I am tired after the journey. Excuse me."

She dipped her chin into a nod, her wide eyes never leaving his face. And as he turned on his heel to make a swift exit, one thing was abundantly clear.

They were both now painfully aware that he was in love with Eliza.

Eliza squinted across the expanse of Hyde Park. Lifting up her white silk parasol, she snapped it open, then settled back against the wooden bench with a weary sigh. She had nearly stayed at home on this final morning before returning to Kent, especially since Caroline and her aunt were already safely back to Hampshire and she would have nobody to accompany her to the park.

But a last-minute prompting from Patterson had urged her forth in the midst of her melancholy mood. Her loyal lady's maid had insisted that the fresh air and sunshine would do her some good, and now that she was here, Eliza couldn't deny it was refreshing. But still she was troubled. While she was relieved that her friends had successfully completed their journey, she felt the loss of their company most keenly. The palpable absence of the black-haired viscount who had helped them was felt more keenly still.

Much of her time the past week had been occupied by various callers—including multiple suitors—some who had already taken the leap and proposed, with others merely alluding to the possibility of such a thing taking place. The pace of these visitations had picked up at this late point in the season, and the frenzy was enough to make her head swirl.

Really, it was quite bothersome, each proposal presenting Eliza with perpetual reminders of Thomas, and the comparisons between them all. Her relationship with Evanston had lately been strained, but she could not help but be affected by his willingness to assist her friends. Similarly, his request that she defer choosing a husband until later caused her blood to stir, her mind dwelling feverishly upon the possible reasons why.

A cluster of wood pigeons pecked at the ground across the pathway. Eliza watched as a large male broke away, puffing its chest out proudly to bow and coo at a nearby female. Twirling round in an elaborate dance of courtship, he followed the feathered maiden as she ignored him, set on finding her repast among the grass. It reminded her of the season and all the posturing she had seen over the past summer. Not by Thomas, of course. Had this particular pigeon possessed an ounce of that man's charm, Eliza was certain every female in the group would be regarding him with wide eyes and rapt, hopeful attention . . .

The birds scattered suddenly, their wings clapping noisily behind their backs as a horse trotted to a stop near her bench. She blinked and gazed up at the rider, tipping her parasol to block the sun so she could see.

"Ah, Lady Eliza, I was hoping I might see you here. Rumor has it you are leaving later today."

Sir James dismounted swiftly to make his bow and she rose to greet him.

"The level of interest the *ton* pays to my movements never fails to astonish me," she answered with a laugh. "And yes, my trunks are packed. I will be leaving this afternoon."

He gripped the reins of his horse and tucked his riding crop beneath an arm. "I am only thankful to still find you in London. After all, it seems your friends have already departed for the country without so much as a farewell."

She smiled and waved the comment off. "Pressing matters called them home."

"And the viscount?"

The question had been asked lightly enough, but she knew it surely carried more weight than he was letting on. Eliza raised her eyebrows in a show of indifference.

"Why, I'm not certain what has caused Lord Evanston to leave London. Although, if I had to guess, I'd say it might be some business negotiations with my brother."

His forehead creased and his gloved fingers reached up to smooth one side of his moustache. "So, he could be in Kent upon your arrival?"

"I suppose that is a possibility." She shifted on her feet and twirled her parasol with a shrug to convey a general attitude of inconsequence, but her heart had begun thundering like a steam engine. She was getting the feeling he was preparing to say something important . . . and soon. Perhaps before he believed Thomas could seize the opportunity himself.

Landry sighed and glanced off to the side, staring at the gentlemen astride their horses on the boulevard and the ladies who rode beside them. As if in the midst of an internal debate, he muttered beneath his breath then shook his head to gaze at her once again.

"I told myself I would wait until the time was right—"

Eliza found herself growing rigid in alarm. A curious reaction, since she'd always thought to welcome his approach, particularly with thoughts to marriage.

"By all means, one should always ensure the time is right," she interrupted with a nod, as if to confirm that his timing couldn't be more wrong. Inwardly, she berated herself, even as her whole body seized at the thought of him continuing.

What on earth are you doing?

"But I find I cannot wait any—"

Eliza turned away with a tiny gasp. "My goodness, it has suddenly become warm," she effused with a fanning motion of her hand. It wasn't a lie. Suddenly she was burning up in excess of some unidentifiable emotion.

He paused to glance upwards at the light-dappled canopy of oak trees. "Er, why yes, I suppose the temperature has increased since earlier this morning. Regardless—" he continued.

She was not listening now, instead casting her gaze out to the fashionable men and women, searching for someone, anyone she might know. Her reprieve came from an unexpected source.

"Lady Eliza!"

Eliza waved at Baron Latimer, who cantered lazily towards them upon his own steed. She lowered into a curtsy and Landry doffed his hat politely, although the expression on his face was anything but.

"Baron Latimer," he muttered, casting an anxious look at Eliza, who did her best to conceal the extent of her gratitude.

"Forgive me, I cannot stay long. I only saw you from across the way and wished to inquire about Lady Caroline," he shouted down from his horse. He shook his graying head. "It looks like she's managed to foul up another season's chances. Where is the girl, anyway?"

Eliza felt her temper flare in defense. The chances of this conversation ending without her saying something regrettable had just become very slim.

"*That girl* is my friend, and the daughter of the Duke of Pemberton. And you may rest assured that if she felt the need to return home, then there was an actual need to do so." Her eyes flicked between the two men, who were now both regarding her with wary fascination.

"I—I see," stammered the baron. "Well, I thought I would just inquire since I received a letter from the duke just the other day . . ."

Gripping her skirts, Eliza swished them behind her. "It's funny how all his letters to you have not yet altered the outcome of her seasons. Why, I suppose if he were truly so concerned, he might come speak to his daughter himself. Although he would need to return home to do so, and I know how much he enjoys his travels." She dipped into an obligatory curtsy and risked a brief look at Landry. "Sir James, it's been a pleasure. Perhaps we will see each other soon."

Landry's posture deflated at the sudden and abrupt shift of events. He started forwards as if to impede her withdrawal, then thought better of it, his hand snapping back down to his side. "I, yes, of course, my lady. I will count the days."

With a sharp turn, she retreated along the path she had come, blindly dodging riders and walkers alike. She was enraged at Caroline's family, but she was also confused, kicking herself, and filled with dread. Eliza knew that, at this moment, the only thing giving her more relief than avoiding Landry's attempted proposal was the thought of returning to Lawton Park for the chance of seeing Evanston once more.

And that, she knew, was not good.

Chapter Ten

"Mama!"

The excited squeal came barely a second before the little girl hurtled through the open door of the carriage, her soft cloth dolly clutched tightly in one hand. Quickly, Eliza opened her arms to receive her daughter's embrace. Rosa's infectious laughter mingled with her own cries of joy, and soon they were both wiping away the happy tears that were streaming down their faces.

"I missed you so much," she said with a sniff, giving Rosa a tight squeeze. "Did you have such fun with your Aunt Clara and Uncle William?"

Rosa's green eyes shone. "Oh, yes. But I missed you a lot too," she admitted sadly.

Eliza stroked a golden curl away from Rosa's eyes and tutted in sympathy. She planted a kiss on an irresistibly chubby cheek.

"I am back now, my sweet, and I can't wait to hear about all of your adventures."

A soft knocking near the open door diverted her attention, and she peered around Rosa's head to see her brother, the Earl of Ashworth, smiling into the vehicle.

"Your journey must have been long, Eliza, and yet you don't seem to want to leave the carriage." He leaned in further to glance at the interior, appearing to admire the cushioned seats and gleaming lacquer of his own vehicle. "It is really rather nice, if I do say so myself," he added with a wink.

"William," said Eliza with a teasing swat on his arm, "you are ridiculous!"

The change in her brother's demeanor since marrying Clara was marked and profound. Gone were the days of self-imposed solitude and misery. William had saved Clara, and she, in turn, had saved him. Lawton Park was once more filled with the laughter and light that had been missing in the years since the accident, and while it gladdened her heart to see it so, Eliza couldn't help but be reminded of her own precarious circumstances. As of yet, there was no resolution to be found for her and Rosa.

He grinned and withdrew, extending his hand at the door to assist them both as they disembarked. Unable to wait a moment longer, Clara rushed forwards to pull her close for an affectionate embrace.

"Oh, Eliza, it is so good to have you home again."

"It is good to be home," replied Eliza wearily. "Appeasing the *ton* can be so tiresome. And I'm not altogether certain I provided the entertainment they were hoping for. After all, not every woman is willing to pose as a housemaid," she said, smiling impishly.

Clara's dark eyes sparkled with mischief, and she cast an affectionate glance at William. "You may call it *willing*, but I call it *desperate*." Her hand slipped into the earl's. "There was a lot of luck involved in finding this man, both bad and good. Besides," she continued, "I thought you'd mentioned in your letter receiving several offers of marriage prior to your departure from London."

Eliza sighed, her eyes wandering restlessly around the drive. The servants were lined up, as per the usual ceremony . . .

"'Tis true, but—"

Her eyes landed on an additional person, waiting patiently to greet her. His ebony hair glinted in the sunlight, blue eyes alert and awaiting the rest of her reply.

"I, oh. Thomas!" Eliza hastily curtsied towards the viscount. "Forgive me, I didn't know you were there."

He stepped forwards to make his bow. "I did not wish to miss your homecoming," he responded politely, guardedly.

Eliza's eyes darted over to her brother. His presence served as a reminder that the events which had passed between her and Evanston were a secret, and must remain that way lest they risk jeopardizing the friendship between the two men.

Tucking an errant lock of hair back beneath her bonnet, Eliza fumbled for a reply and caught sight of Clara, whose intelligent eyes were busy searching her face for an unknown answer to a question that was not yet being asked.

"Shall we go inside to get settled?" Eliza asked a bit too cheerfully. "I'd like to take a walk with Rosa before the hour grows late."

William extended his arm towards the house. "By all means. But you should know that a 'walk with Rosa' might involve engaging in afternoon tea with the squirrels." At Eliza's look of astonishment, he added, "Not to worry, dear sister. They really are quite well-mannered, especially when supplied with Mrs. Humboldt's tarts. Their preference is raspberry."

Upon their return to the Dower House later that evening, Eliza insisted that Rosa spend the night with her in her bed-chamber. The two had lain awake spending hours catching up after a long summer spent apart, with Rosa eventually submitting to her fatigue after a particularly fanciful re-telling of a theatrical performance put on by Clara and the servants. Eliza woke the next morning and smiled to see her daughter nestled up against her, dolly safely tucked beneath an arm, a lock of Eliza's hair gently twirling between her tiny fingers.

Her joy at being reunited with Rosa was an effective distraction from her problems . . . which consisted, most notably, of Lord Evanston. His behavior on the day of her arrival had been uncharacteristically docile, and had William known to look for signs that something was amiss, he would have noticed right away. Eliza was unsure if Clara had detected the strange friction between them, but she feared that the more she and Thomas were placed together, the more obvious it would become that there was an issue.

Of course, she also worried about her impending conversation with him regarding her marriage prospects. The one where she would have to confess that, despite receiving numerous offers from men of minimal acquaintance, Landry had not proposed before departing London. Granted, she had essentially prevented him from officially making an offer, but this did not change the fact that Eliza was, as of yet, still unattached. It was a rather perilous position to be in with Thomas lying in wait, perhaps ready to seduce her at the first vulnerable moment.

She and Rosa spent the next couple of days splitting their time between the Dower House and Lawton Park. Eliza anticipated this would now be the usual way of things, as her daughter had become used to the very attentive staff members, not to mention the affectionate doting of her aunt and uncle. On the morning of her third day back home, however, Patterson knocked quietly on her bedchamber door to deliver a missive.

"A letter for you, my lady . . . from Hawthorne Manor."

Eliza's fingers paused in midair, then descended the final distance to pluck the note from the maid's awaiting hand.

A letter from Thomas.

"Thank you, Patterson," she replied hastily. "That will be all."

She closed the door then turned to lean against it, clutching the letter tightly. An infusion of dread clutched at her chest, until she could stand waiting no more. Eliza slid a finger beneath the flap to break the wax seal, then unfolded the paper to behold a brief note, written in his hand:

Dear Eliza,

Would you do me the honor of joining me this afternoon?

Yours, Evanston

She let her head fall back and groaned aloud. The thought of seeing him again, alone . . .

Eliza snapped up from her defeated posture. No, this would not do. She was an independent woman who had survived many situations, most recently a confrontation with his mistress. Surely, this could not be more difficult than that. Besides, she had yet to take him to task for that debacle.

Yes, she had a few questions of her own that required answers, although his recent assistance with Caroline and her aunt complicated things a bit. She could not begin on the offensive after he'd gone to such lengths to help her.

Eliza crossed to her vanity and safely concealed the letter inside a drawer. Then she tugged on the bellpull, taking a moment to glance at her appearance in the mirror. Having just woken up, there was much to be done.

This ordinary day, after all, had suddenly become much more interesting.

The moment her carriage arrived at Hawthorne Manor, Eliza wished she had stayed at home. Seeing Thomas standing at the ready to greet her caused her stomach to perform a series of slow and not unpleasant somersaults. He was dressed impeccably in a morning coat of dark blue, with an ivory waistcoat, and light trousers. She marveled at the way the dark blue suited him so well, working to highlight the azure shade of his eyes, and contrasting against the ivory in much the same way his jet-black hair opposed the color of his skin. Eliza gazed down at her own pale pink dress, hoping—although she knew she shouldn't—that he might find it similarly attractive on her.

Quelling her nervousness, she disembarked and approached the awaiting viscount. She glanced up at him, a small smile on her lips.

"Lord Evanston," she said with a curtsy.

Thomas made his bow, a reciprocal smile lurking at the corner of his mouth. "Lady Eliza, thank you for seeing me today. I trust you and Rosa have been able to reconnect after your long summer away?" He extended his arm.

"Yes, we have," she answered, sliding her hand around the hard curve of his bicep. The contact set off shockwaves of delight throughout her body, which she struggled to suppress. "I have not yet had the chance to thank you for safely delivering Caroline and her aunt back to Willowford House," she managed.

He glanced downward as they made their way up the front steps of the house. "Your thanks are not necessary, so long as you remembered why I performed the service."

Her happiness rapidly transformed into displeasure, and she halted where she stood, dropping her arm and forcing him to stop as well. "Oh yes, my lord, I remembered. And I honored your request . . . perhaps jeopardizing my chances at finding a match . . . because you saw fit to—"

Evanston's expression was one of utter confusion, and Eliza found she could not continue her halting speech with him looking at her in that way. His perplexity finally gave way to amusement, and an irreverent grin tugged at his lips.

"Eliza, surely you know I would have never denied you such a request. I'm not even certain I expected you to honor my condition, although I'm glad to hear you did," he added in a low voice.

Eliza stared at him, wanting to be angry, but feeling something else entirely. Thomas had meddled in her affairs, even after promising her he wouldn't. He had interfered with the men pursuing her. He had tormented and annoyed her repeatedly during the season. Yet despite all this *and* the fact that she had rejected him, he had still chosen to help her—simply because she'd asked him to.

She was suddenly aware that they were standing very close. As if detecting the uncomfortable course of her thoughts, he extended his arm once again in a gesture of casual familiarity.

"I had tea brought upstairs, if you are interested."

A few minutes later, she was seated in his drawing room, sipping the warm drink. Eliza was thankful for the plates of tiny sandwiches and biscuits, as her state of anxiety had worked to make her more than a little hungry. Soon, they were back at ease, talking as old friends would, although Eliza couldn't help but notice that the viscount had chosen brandy over tea. She pondered whether her company stirred him to the extent that his affected her.

"So, tell me," he said, leaning against the mantelpiece, taking a swallow of his drink. "How has Rosa been amusing herself? She promised to write and tell me, but alas, her busy schedule proved too demanding."

Eliza laughed and set her plate on the side table. "Well, as William mentioned the other day, she is quite taken with squirrels."

"Squirrels! Why she loves those wild rodents so much is certainly beyond me."

"Oh no, not at all. They are furry and delightful—"

"So are dogs," he replied skeptically.

"They are apparently fine companions—"

"As long as your pockets contain treats."

She surveyed him with a sigh. "Come now, Thomas. Is it any mystery how a four-year-old little girl might love a tiny woodland animal with a fluffy tail?"

"No. In fact, I believe Rosa and squirrels share many of the same fine qualities." At Eliza's amused look, he clarified, "I only mean that they are both lively and fun."

"And adorable," she added with a stern expression.

He laughed. "Yes, of course."

Eliza sipped her tea and replaced the fine china cup back gently onto its saucer. They smiled warmly at each other for a moment.

In truth, it had been many months since the two of them had been able to share a friendly exchange that had not been tainted by the unwise intimacies they had shared. At this moment, it seemed he was willing to ignore their differences, making this moment of unspoiled friendship a rare treasure.

He's buying time to seduce you.

Caroline's earlier warning sang insistently in her head. As much as Eliza wished he could be trusted, she had to admit this was still a possibility. Suddenly restless, she rose to go stand near the windows, her eyes taking in the considerable natural beauty of Lord Evanston's estate. She did not wish to ruin this moment of peace between them, but she had things to say.

Eliza cleared her throat. "I had an unusual visitor in London. An acquaintance of yours. Or rather more than an acquaintance, I suppose."

A notch formed between his brows, and she could see him mentally calculating the probabilities. Finally, he relented.

"Who was it?"

She folded her arms across her midsection in what she guessed was a protective posture. "It was Mrs. Varnham."

He had no outward response, no change of expression, but his eyes glowed more vividly in concealed emotion.

"And what was her business with you?"

Here, Eliza hesitated. To tell him the truth might serve to paint herself in a competitive light, as a woman vying for his affection. It had the potential to ignite an already inflammatory situation. Still, she'd told him too much now to go back.

"It seems she wished to clarify the nature of your relationship with her."

Thomas pushed away from the mantel to survey her closely. "Which is?"

"Apparently, quite . . . intimate," she said, stumbling nervously over her words.

Evanston approached her, pausing near the side table, where he leaned down to deposit his glass, his gaze unnaturally focused on his task. "And if I denied it . . . would you believe me?"

Her temperature was steadily rising. "I'm not certain what to believe. Not that it matters," she added.

"No," he agreed softly, finally glancing up at her, blue eyes dropping to her lips. "Not that it matters . . ."

The noise of a carriage on the drive interrupted their conversation. Thomas stepped closer to glance out the window, only to withdraw immediately, his brow lowered in irritation. "Lady Evanston has seen fit to pay a visit today."

Eliza's eyes widened. She knew of the turmoil that existed between Thomas and his mother. "Oh. Were you expecting her?"

"No, of course not," he muttered. "She only ever arrives unannounced." As if to illustrate his point, he threw open the doors of the drawing room. Loud footsteps echoed through the large, marble-floored foyer, coming closer, until at last she was revealed. The widowed viscountess, a sight to behold, sailed through the door well ahead of the apologetic butler.

Dressed in full mourning—despite the fact her husband had died many years before and she never really liked him to begin with—she was swathed in layers of voluminous black crepe. Even her wide black hat was ornamented with similarly black feathers, which swooped and bobbed with each movement of her head. It appeared Burton was still struggling to greet her, as if she had pushed past him at the front door.

Evanston waved to the butler in dismissal, then clasped his hands behind his back. "Hello, Mother. So very nice of you to stop by, although as you can see, I am busy entertaining a guest."

The lady's head twitched in Eliza's direction and sent her feathers aflutter. Combined with her sharp features, Eliza couldn't help but be reminded of a quail.

"I see Eliza Cartwick. Where is your guest?" his mother inquired, her cold eyes unflinching.

She could sense the viscount's temper from where she stood across the room.

"*Lady Eliza* is my guest, mother. I invited her here today. You, however, have arrived without notice."

Lady Evanston skewered him with a look. "I used to live here, or have *you* forgotten?"

"I have not. But lest you forget, I am the master of this estate now. Your presence here is welcome, but not at the expense of my privacy and my friends."

"Friend? Is that what we're calling her now? I'd assumed you'd taken her to bed years ago. It's what your father would have done, after all."

Eliza's face went numb with shock. She watched mutely as the viscountess proceeded to walk around to seat herself on the settee and help herself to the tea sandwiches. Eliza risked a glance at Thomas, whose eyes had grown black with rage.

"Say what you like about me," he said in a deadly tone, "Lord knows no one can stop you. But take special care to omit Eliza from your judgments. There will be consequences if you do not."

Her heart ached at his words. That he should endure such treatment from his own mother but insist on courteousness towards Eliza . . . it was nearly too much to bear.

"Oh?" replied the woman around a mouthful of cucumber sandwich. "Perhaps your revenge will be to philander while gambling away the family fortune. Ah, but no. You were doing that already."

"I have never jeopardized the health of the estate," he fumed.

"You need an heir to continue the line. A wife," she spat, glancing derisively at Eliza. "Not a paramour."

Eliza decided that she had heard quite enough.

"Stop," she demanded angrily, coming to stand before Lady Evanston, who merely regarded her with an expression of distaste. "You willfully misunderstand your son. I can only assume this is because he shares many traits with your late husband, but I knew his father as a child. He was, despite his faults, a good man. A kind man. *Thomas* is also good and kind, and I will not stand here in silence while you blacken his character."

His mother sat in offended silence, and Eliza raised her eyes to meet Evanston's stunned gaze.

"I was happy to see you today, Thomas. Perhaps next time we meet, it will be a more peaceful occasion."

With a swish of her skirts, she exited the drawing room, gaining notice of a footman who stood nearby. She was suddenly very eager to be on her way home.

Lady Evanston uttered a snort of disbelief as Eliza departed the drawing room, and Thomas stared after her retreating form in no less amazement. Surely he had misheard some portion of what she had said. If he had not, it would mean she had just displayed a measure of feeling for him he had not known she'd possessed. This would have been astonishing by itself, but to level the fierceness of her convictions at his, albeit spiteful, mother . . .

A surge of hope, however foolish, rose inside his chest. Unpleasant, scoffing noises distracted him to his right, and his eyes flicked over to the viscountess, who was so taken aback by Eliza's angry reaction that she was having trouble formulating a complete sentence.

"The . . . the *impertinence*—"

Evanston's eyes narrowed. "Tell me, is it also considered an impertinence to arrive at my home uninvited, while skulking about and casting insults?" He glared down at her in disdain. "Yes, you birthed me, however reluctantly. But I do believe I have been too polite with you."

Thomas turned and swiftly propelled himself out of the room, suddenly needing to find Eliza. He cast a meaningful glance at the footman on his way out, and with an obedient nod the man closed the doors behind him as he left. His mother could finish her sandwiches or stew in her ill temper for all he cared, but she would do it behind the privacy of those oak-paneled doors and out of his sight.

Thomas hurried to the foyer, hoping Eliza couldn't have left the premises in such a short amount of time. If indeed she had run outside and leaped into her carriage, he would just as quickly go fetch his horse and stop her on the road until he knew more. Why—if she found him as dishonorable as she claimed—had she just made a vigorous stand to defend him? Could friendship alone explain the force of her reaction?

Fortunately, her voice could be discerned from near the front door, and Evanston rounded the corner to see her addressing the butler.

"Eliza," he called urgently, "I need a word with you." Thomas quickened his pace, his footfall sounding loudly within the large enclosure.

Burton left with a bow and Eliza glanced up at Evanston briefly before turning towards the front door.

"My apologies," she said stiffly. "It was not my intent to create trouble for you—"

He reached her in that moment, hand encircling her elbow to spin her around to face him. Large green eyes, wide and hesitant, sought his, and desire surged through his chest, nearly choking him. Clenching his teeth, he focused on the question at hand.

"Did you mean it?"

Eliza paused and blinked, but the rising color in her cheeks told him that she knew what he was asking. His grip on her arm loosened but did not relent.

"I—I'm . . ."

She wet her lips with the tip of her tongue. A nervous movement to be sure, but it drove him mad all the same. He concentrated on breathing calmly, evenly, while her gaze darted everywhere but to his face. When she finally raised her eyes to meet his, a touch of lingering irritation had resurfaced.

"Yes, of course I meant it. The transgressions of your father are his alone. I don't think it's fair for Lady Evanston to hold you accountable for his sins, whatever they may have been—"

The door to the drawing room banged open loudly from around the corner. Thomas felt Eliza jump beneath his touch and he glanced over to see his head footman trailing after the viscountess on her way out. His mother's nose was tipped high in the air as she marched towards the front door, and despite her head start, the footman hurried and reached the door first to yank it open. She stopped briefly to turn and lance them with a glare.

"Ignoring me for a woman. You are *just* like your father," she spat accusingly.

With that, she stalked outside to her carriage. The footman shot his master an earnest look of apology before closing the door behind him to follow the enraged lady, and Thomas dropped his head and sighed. After a moment of silence, he raised his gaze to meet Eliza's once more.

"It is possible I am very much like my father," he conceded, his mouth twisting, "and that is why she holds me accountable to such standards."

Her eyes flashed. "It is also possible you deserve to be compared against your father's best qualities, of which he had many," came her curt reply. Eliza turned to resume her course out the front door, pulling at her arm, which was still in his grasp. "Now if you will excuse me, I should be leaving too—"

One tug was all it took to whirl her back round to face him. Thinking back, he was ashamed that their kiss long ago had been such a farce, an exercise in amusement from a jaded man who'd never known anyone worth holding dear. But as he gazed down at Eliza now, he could hardly believe he'd been so blind. This was a woman who could bring him to his knees, and for the first time in his life, he would gladly sink down.

His mouth descended on hers, and a flood of heated pleasure infused his veins. A moment of shock, a tiny noise of surprise, and then she responded beneath him with a passion he had hoped for but not expected. Thomas leaned into the kiss, tasting her deeply, and she responded by opening for him, moaning against his mouth and tugging on his coat to pull him closer.

Thoughts flickered through his head as he indulged in his desire. He saw himself lifting her in his arms to carry her upstairs to his bedchamber. He imagined taking her swiftly the first time, and so very slowly the next . . .

Then he thought of the consequences of such an act.

Wincing, he gently gripped her arms and eased her away. He needed to show her he had changed. That he could be a better man. As he had said to Caroline before, he had to at least *try*.

"Eliza," he said in a voice that came out no louder than a whisper. He cleared his throat and stated more formally, "Lady Eliza . . ."

Eliza stood, stunned, staring at the linen shirt covering Lord Evanston's broad chest as he broke the contact between them. Her body hummed and buzzed as it never had before, and her mind scattered frantically to make sense of what was happening.

Thomas kissed me, her brain insisted, but that couldn't be right. There was no earthly reason why he would choose to kiss her over some young debutante, unsullied by marriage and childbirth. Or one of his other worldly widows, like Victoria Varnham, who had the experience to drive him wild in ways she couldn't even imagine.

Her lips tingled, and she lifted her fingers and brushed them across her mouth in a sacred gesture. An attempt to preserve his kiss in her memory. In a daze she stared at him. Her defenses had been breached. Passion, long held in check, now simmered beneath her skin, in every cell, in every breath. Were he to kiss her again, she could not account for how she might react.

Thomas's eyes searched hers, and they were filled with dread. "Forgive me. I—I didn't mean for this to happen."

She blinked furiously to dispel the haze of longing that lingered. It had been years since a man had been intimate with her. She had tried to imagine it with Sir Landry, but to her everlasting frustration, the man of her fantasies had always transformed into Evanston—this man standing before her now, with eyes as bright as a lightning strike. The effect on her was no less overwhelming. He'd always been capable of wrecking her with his gaze, but his kiss . . . well, she was still struggling to find her wits. It had been a moment lived straight from one of her reveries and vastly different than the first time. Almost as if he believed she were the only woman in the world worth kissing.

Before he could speak another word of apology, Eliza's hands were behind his head to pull him down. This time she rose high upon her toes to meet him in her greed, mouth opening to receive him, her blood heated with lust.

Initially frozen in astonishment, his hands held her at bay for the span of a breath before he issued a low growl and hauled her up against him. With her arms twined around his neck, there was nothing to be done but surrender to the extent of his embrace, and the feel of his body against hers caused her to gasp aloud. Eliza arched into it, every wicked part of her cursing her blasted corset for hindering the delicious friction between them.

The velvet slide of Evanston's mouth against hers assailed her over and over until she could feel herself shaking, and his hands skimmed dangerously over the small of her back, then paused. He broke the kiss, just barely, his lips hovering inches above her own.

"Eliza," he said huskily as he fought to catch his breath, shaking his head in regret. "You should not have come here today."

She frowned in confusion, swaying unsteadily on her feet. "But you invited me here."

The viscount released a soft, mirthless laugh. "Obviously, an invitation is no guarantee of civility. I would devour you utterly, despite my best intentions."

Her heart thudded hard, then seemed to stop altogether. His eyes held hers just as his hand, warm and strong, remained possessively in its position, low on her back. The temperature in the air seemed to increase exponentially but she suspected it was only her, flushing pink at his words. Evanston had meant them as a warning, and she supposed the fact he was warning her at all meant something important.

But in as many ways as the viscount was appealing—his masculine good looks, easygoing sense of humor and abundance of seductive charm—he was now infinitely more attractive through this show of simple consideration for her. And after years of suppressing her greatest wishes, with her desire for him now no longer a secret, the thought of him devouring her was not the deterrent he might have thought it was.

His breathing labored, he struggled to get out his next words. "You should leave before this goes too far."

She frowned again, sliding her hands down from around his neck to curl her fingers around the fabric of his lapel. He was right, of course. To continue this insanity would be a hideous mistake. He was not the stable father figure she required for Rosa. And she couldn't forget that William would never allow such a thing even were she to yield. In fact, the discovery of any involvement between Eliza and Evanston would mean the end of William's long-standing friendship with the viscount . . . a thought that grieved her to no end.

And what would become of their friendship? Would she sacrifice it all merely to appease this blood-heated frenzy that had seen fit to plague her since before she'd been married?

Eliza inventoried her senses, deliriously taking stock of how he affected her. His nearness. How solid he was beneath her fingertips. His crisp, clean, masculine smell. The lingering taste of him.

The tortured look on his face. His eyes begging her to ignore his advice . . .

Helpless to do otherwise, she lunged forwards for another ravenous kiss. Evanston muttered in protest, but the effort was unintelligible and halfhearted at best before she parted her lips to welcome the slick thrust of his tongue. He advanced on her, sending them colliding into the nearest wall. An ancient vase, possibly quite valuable, went toppling off its pedestal to crash onto the unforgiving floor beneath, shattering into a thousand tiny pieces around their feet.

Eliza broke away to twist worriedly in his arms, glancing down at the damage.

"Oh—"

Evanston was indifferent to the loss, sinking his long fingers into her elegant coiffure to maneuver her head, exposing the side of her throat to his mouth. She writhed against him with a cry as the viscount worked his way back up with scorching kisses and light nips of his teeth along her neck until she eagerly reclaimed his mouth with her own, winding her fingers through his thick hair.

"Eliza," he whispered against her mouth in between fiery, openmouthed kisses. His hands rose up to squeeze the mounds of her breasts. Then his fingers hooked over the edge of her bodice, as if he were a hairsbreadth away from tugging it down and baring her to his eyes. "My God—"

Her head was reeling. She couldn't gasp or cry out. She couldn't even breathe. She only wanted to be his, wanted his hands all over her, wanted his mouth on her, wanted him inside her.

The sound of the front door opening alerted them to the reentry of Burton. Evanston's head rose sharply and he moved his body to shield Eliza from view. Of course, Burton would not be expecting to see the familiar Lady Eliza caught in an embrace with the lord of Hawthorne Manor. And he certainly wouldn't have anticipated seeing them amidst a mess of ceramic pieces strewn over the usually spotless marble floor. She saw inevitable recognition dawn in the man's eyes, but to his credit he quickly checked himself, adopting an appropriate and docile demeanor more befitting of his station.

"I will fetch a housemaid to clean this mess, my lord. Also, Lady Eliza's carriage is ready for her whenever she has need of it." He gave a perfunctory bow. "Is there anything else you require of me?"

"Your absence, Burton," Thomas said, working to control his breathing. "Please."

"Yes, my lord."

The butler disappeared quite rapidly for a man his size. Evanston turned back to her, and in one smooth motion, he leaned down to scoop her into his arms. It seemed he was done playing games in the foyer of his own house. Eliza was immediately reminded of the night he'd carried her, injured, into his London town house, except now his movements were filled entirely with carnal purpose. There was no doubt where this would lead.

"Thomas—" she gasped. She pressed her hand against the wide breadth of his chest, her gaze wildly searching his.

Rather than argue with her as he had done in the past, he kissed her. Hard. He kissed her until the panicked tension in her limbs melted away, until her resistance transformed back into eager submission. Then he tore his mouth away and resumed his course up the stairs.

His arms were rock-solid and steady around her, and his pace was resolute. Evanston was not going to change his mind. He was not going to slow down or stop. He would continue forwards until she was lying beneath him on his bed, driven senseless with the pleasure of being taken by him at last.

Eliza couldn't let it get that far, she reminded herself, although her feeble efforts to resist him up until now did not bode well in that regard. She supposed she should wriggle out of his arms but found herself tugging on his cravat to loosen the knot instead. Unthinkingly, she shifted in his hold to press her mouth against the newly exposed length of his neck, and his ensuing groan of need caused her body to quiver in anxious reply.

The slam of the bedchamber door behind them jarred her senses, and panic took hold once more as he dropped her upon his bed, then held her gaze as he stepped back to rip his cravat aside and toss it to the floor. Eliza was rendered motionless by fear, desire, and the greedy need to have him all for herself. Her heart raced like the wings of a frightened bird, eyes mesmerized, following the movements of his fingers as they lowered to open his shirt. She envisioned those same fingers unfastening his trousers. Could imagine them hastily raising her skirts . . .

He could take her right now to be his wife . . . his mistress . . . his lover . . .

I would say yes to it all. Whatever he wanted.

He's buying time to seduce you.

Caroline's words repeated in her head. Eliza scrabbled into an upright position and pushed herself backwards off the mattress, rising swiftly to regard him wide-eyed from the opposite side of the room. He froze, then glanced down at his discarded cravat.

"I can put that back on, if you'd prefer," he said slowly.

His attempt at humor nearly made her laugh. "Stop it, Thomas—" She covered her eyes with both hands. "Please, just stop."

There was silence for a moment, then a concerned inquiry.

"Eliza, what's wrong?"

Her voice was shaking. "I cannot be your next conquest." She straightened her spine. "I will not be just another widow in your bed."

"You are the *only* woman I want," he said quietly. "Widow or not."

God, how she wanted to believe him. But she would be risking everything on a hope . . . a wish. Even worse, she'd be taking a chance on her daughter's life, too.

She felt her head shaking before she was aware of doing it. "I need to leave."

Regret creased his forehead, and he took a small step in her direction, his hand outstretched. "Eliza—"

"Please, Thomas. Don't." Backing away, she leveled her gaze at him, taking in the shock that flickered across his handsome features. More than handsome. Beautiful. Gorgeous. Her heart ached at the sight of him. "I need a husband, my daughter needs a father, and you are just not suited to playing either of those roles. I am certain this would be no different . . . even if you've somehow fooled yourself into believing it would be."

Although he stared at her, his expression wounded, there was an unmistakable hint of injured resignation that he could not conceal. It pained her to see it, and before he could say something to change her mind, Eliza gathered her skirts and hurried past him to throw open the bedchamber door. She careened blindly down the staircase and out through the foyer, holding her stinging breath until a harsh gasp finally escaped as the slam of the carriage door shut out the world. A world that included Viscount Evanston with shirt disheveled and cravat missing, standing solemnly on the steps of his home while he watched her carriage drive away.

Chapter Eleven

Evanston's pen scratched against the parchment as he signed his name, and he leaned back in his chair, scanning the letter to ensure it had struck the proper tone. He wanted his anger to seethe out from the pages unquestionably, but most of all, he wanted the woman receiving it to know things were irrevocably broken between them. Done. Finished.

Satisfied at last, he twisted the red wax above the flame, watching as it melted and dripped down onto the envelope. He pressed his seal against it, then stared at an errant smudge of ink on his hand. His brow drew down and he rubbed at the spot in annoyance, yet still it remained, a black mark upon him. His head started to ache . . .

Giving up, Thomas jerked his sleeve down in irritation to cover it. He glanced at the sideboard, to the amber-filled bottles that winked at him in the late morning sunlight. Losing himself in the bottom of a crystal decanter had been easy before, but now not even brandy could numb him enough to ignore the fact that Eliza found him strategically lacking when compared to her other suitors. When compared to the lukewarm *Landry*, for God's sake.

And no amount of alcohol could compete with the unadulterated intoxication of feeling her respond in his arms, or the sight of her, supple and wanting, on his bed. How he yearned to be drunk on Eliza again. If only he could find a way to forget . . .

A brief knock sounded just before the door to his study flew open.

"Pardon, my lord, but you will be late for your meeting with the earl."

Burton regarded the viscount from the doorway, his face contorted into a mask of worry. Thomas focused his thoughts back to the task at hand, flipping the envelope over in his hands to quickly address the parchment, then standing to face the butler.

"You worry too much, Burton. I am riding on horseback and can easily make up the lost time. Besides, this is important." Coming closer, Thomas handed him the missive. "Please ensure this letter is included in the next post. I'd like Mrs. Varnham to receive it as soon as possible. It contains a few choice words I've reserved just for her."

"Mrs. Varnham?" asked the butler in an inquisitive tone. "Certainly, my lord." Burton crossed back towards the door, but paused before leaving, clearly debating whether he dare say more. Evanston's gaze flicked up, the dark arches of his brows lifting as he reached for his riding jacket.

"Out with it, man."

Burton jumped a little at being caught, the silver filaments in his hair catching the late morning light from the windows. "It is of no purpose, my lord. Only, I wanted to say how very . . . *ahem* . . . nice it was to see Lady Eliza here yesterday." Thomas slid his arms into the sleeves of his coat, his movements slowing in evaluative contemplation while the man struggled to continue. "I mean, there had been a time in London where you were not . . . *ahem* . . . responding to her entreaties. And it's, well, I was glad to see—"

"You saw rather more than you bargained for," recalled Thomas sardonically with a sharp tug on his jacket.

The butler glanced down at the letter he carried, his cheeks turning red. "Yes, well, I suppose I did. I must say, however, that I've always liked Lady Eliza."

"As have I, Burton. However, she is currently deliberating over multiple marriage proposals, one from a man whom she will likely accept," he added, hardening his tone of voice to prevent any emotion from creeping in. "She would never have me."

"It looked very much to me as if she could be convinced to consider it."

Thomas threw a disapproving glance in the man's direction. "As a master concerned for the state of your employment, I'd like to recommend you not look too closely next time. Besides, appearances can be deceiving."

"Yes, my lord," said Burton quickly. "My point is simply that one has heard . . . not that one listens, of course, but one has heard that she has been remarkably selective since the death of Mr. Cartwick. One might say to the point of exclusion. Until yesterday. With you."

Evanston snorted and retrieved his riding crop from the leather chair where he had tossed it earlier. This was a dangerous line of thought to entertain. The fact that his butler was the one belaboring the point did make the matter mildly amusing.

"She was courted by others in London. Yesterday was one hint of an indiscretion," he stated dismissively, her objections echoing painfully through his mind. "A mere moment of weakness on her part."

"Now *you* are making assumptions, my lord."

Thomas pierced him with a dark look. "I don't remember asking for your opinion on any of this."

"You'll forgive me, my lord, but I find I care, despite my best efforts. And while I know of no love that truly follows the confines of reason or logic, I have to think that your chances would substantially increase were you to make a proposal of your own." Burton lowered his head a bit after speaking, almost as if expecting a rebuke for his brazenness.

Evanston froze and stared at his butler. Then he raised a hand to point at the letter. "Next post. Make sure of it. Now step aside, please," he muttered, brushing past Burton on his way out of the room. "I'm late for my meeting."

Despite the lateness of his departure, Thomas made excellent time to Ashworth's estate. His recently acquired chestnut performed admirably on the winding country roads, as it had upon the cobbled streets of London. It had been the least he could do, parading Landry's near-purchase before him. Still, it would bring only minimal comfort should the blasted man succeed in winning Eliza's heart—or at the very least, her acceptance of his marriage proposal.

The day was warm, and the dry, musty smell of hay and horses filtered through the air inside the stables. He handed the reins to the stableboy, then proceeded swiftly towards the house, anticipation coursing through him with every step. Evanston shook his head in annoyance. He was incredibly anxious at the idea of seeing Eliza again, especially so soon after their unexpected encounter. His blood heated at his thousandth remembrance of carrying her off to his bedchamber, and he struggled to wrestle his thoughts back to the business of the day. Here, Thomas felt more than justified in blaming his meddlesome butler for at least some of his trouble.

He had come to Lawton Park to discuss the acquisition of a site for Lord Ashworth's cotton mill in Manchester. Although many of his evenings in London had been spent pursuing Eliza, he had also spent a good number of daytime hours in meetings with various land agents and men connected within the northern textile industry.

Yet, none of this interested him at the moment. Evanston hoped he could disguise the fact that the only thing that did interest him currently was the earl's own sister. The sumptuous glide of Eliza's hand behind his head in an effort to kiss him more thoroughly. The thrill of her body pressed tightly against his. How she had loosened his cravat then scorched his neck with her lips, her tongue. He groaned out loud inadvertently.

Thomas scowled in self-remonstration. He needed to gather his thoughts, hide the ones about Eliza in some faraway place, and bring Manchester cotton mills into unyielding focus. If he could not, he ran the risk of William discerning the truth of the situation. Or worse, nurturing the idea that he wished to somehow corrupt his widowed sister against his own very specific instructions. While Thomas normally took great delight in ignoring orders, what had happened in London had been somewhat accidental and entirely out of his control.

Once Matthew admitted him inside, Evanston made his way to the study. He couldn't prevent himself from glancing around the interior, expecting to perhaps spot an errant child running through the hallways, or a lovely mother chasing just behind. Thankfully, he saw neither of these things, so his head remained relatively clear when he raised his fist to rap sharply upon the door.

"Come in."

Thomas entered the room in his carefree manner, dropping down into his usual seat opposite the earl, a mahogany chair covered with rich Moroccan leather. He stared at his friend, who gathered the papers on his desk, tapping them evenly on the surface before setting them aside to give the viscount his undivided attention. William's mouth hitched up in a smile.

"Firstly, I want to thank you for taking care of business in London while I was otherwise occupied here at home."

"You are quite welcome," replied Thomas, attempting to suppress a grin and failing. "I would not want to interfere with you becoming better acquainted with your beautiful new wife."

The earl raised his eyebrows in response. "Yes, well, I'm sure you were likewise able to take advantage of all the season had to offer. Within reason, of course."

Evanston tried to ignore the ensuing jolt of guilt. Better to change the subject entirely. "I was. In fact, I found Mr. Petry, the land agent, to be quite charming in his own way."

Ashworth eyed him carefully, then chuckled. "Tell me."

"Well," began Thomas with a sigh, "I informed him that, although there are easier, cheaper methods of starting a cotton mill in Manchester, you were committed to the most difficult and expensive one."

William leaned back in his seat to fold his hands across his abdomen. His golden head tilted in displeasure. "The whole point of this endeavor is to crush that man, Scanlan, financially—"

"And here I thought it was to make a sound investment," muttered Evanston under his breath.

"Why would I buy out his mills and put money in his pocket right at the start?"

"Well, one reason might be that there is an existing framework to build upon," Thomas said pointedly. "That your purchase price is a finite amount, not the potentially boundless income provided by a thriving business. That even the threat of opening a large mill in close proximity to his smaller ones might be enough to force him to consider your predictably meager offer. Unless, of course, his grudge runs as deep as yours."

"No. Absolutely not. Not until we have run him aground and he comes begging to sell."

"Fine. I knew you'd say that," said Thomas in resignation. "Which is why I had Petry locate a building along the canal that is currently available. It's large enough for the operation you have in mind, although it will require some major alterations."

William surveyed him with cautious optimism. "I trust your judgment in this. Will the site be sufficient for a mill the scale of which we discussed?"

"Petry and I both agree that it should serve well. We will need your eyes on it to be sure, of course, prior to finalizing the deal."

Ashworth scooped up the sheaf of papers lying on his desk and handed them to Thomas. "Yes, of course. I have architects and laborers lined up for the work required. Will you inform Mr. Petry of my decision and arrange a time for us to meet in London? Perhaps from there, he and I can take the train north together."

"I'll send a letter this afternoon."

William regarded his friend thoughtfully, his hazel-green eyes unsettling and astute. "You were rather productive in London, Thomas. It seems you did behave after all, although I would have thought the temptations of the *ton* and the lure of your clubs too much to resist."

Not sure how to respond to Ashworth's baiting, Thomas merely shrugged. "I like to surprise you every now and then."

He winced subtly, reflexively. What would surprise the earl most would be Evanston's unprecedented and determined pursuit of his beloved only sister. Thomas's conscience often reminded him that this man, his friend, would consider him a menace were he to discover the truth.

The clamor of Rosa running through the house brought both men out of their conversation, and Eliza and Clara could be heard laughing quietly behind the rambunctious little girl. Evanston's head snapped towards the door, his heartbeat doubling its pace in an instant. He stoically affected nonchalance despite his racing heart.

"Were they at home this whole time?" he inquired innocently.

William stood and grinned, his serious expression giving way to something resembling joy. "No. The ladies took Rosa down to the village for a bit of shopping this morning." He crossed to the sideboard and poured two glasses of brandy. "Undoubtedly, Clara and my sister spent an inordinate amount of time discussing the house party I will be hosting next month." His eyes fluttered closed in reluctant acceptance of the situation. "It will require opening up the west wing, of all things, but Mrs. Malone seems eager for the challenge."

Thomas rose to join him and accepted the drink Ashworth offered. "I think that sounds excellent. It will be good to liven up the house again." He swirled his brandy, eyeing it closely on its circular course around the glass. "Will I be receiving an invitation? Or has my presence finally lost its novelty?"

To his relief, Ashworth evaluated him with shock. "Oh, you'll be there," he said, raising his glass for a drink, then lowering it to issue a pleasant hiss from the burn of the alcohol. "You can't leave me alone as sole matchmaker for Eliza."

The amber liquid in Evanston's glass came to a sudden standstill.

"What do you mean?" Thomas asked in a rusty-sounding voice. "Did she not receive numerous offers before leaving London?"

"Well," said William, tossing back the rest of his drink and placing his glass down on the sideboard, "she did, actually. But she confided in Clara that when the gentleman widely considered to be her most marriageable candidate approached her to propose . . . she demurred."

Thomas glanced away, unsurprised. Eliza had simply been following his request.

"You mean she postponed making an answer."

"I didn't say that," replied Ashworth succinctly. "More like she balked, and prevented the proposal from ever fully taking place. Hence, Clara has now set out to invite the man to the house party to see if he can't finish what was begun."

Evanston stared at his friend, mute. He assessed the timeline of this situation. William would likely be gone for the better part of a month on his business trip to Manchester. Upon his return, the house party would commence, and Sir James would arrive to formally offer for Eliza's hand. Time was running out.

But more importantly, Eliza was exhibiting reservations towards Landry.

Why?

Thomas cleared his throat. "I see." Blindly, he set his glass, still full, down on the sideboard.

The earl frowned down at the undrunk liquor, then shrugged and turned to leave. "Shall we find out what sorts of mischief those women have been up to?"

Evanston's conscience asserted itself once more. Shaking off the bothersome guilt, he smiled politely.

"After you."

Thomas followed the earl into the hallway, then glanced around. It was empty and silent. He looked to William in bemusement.

"Did they come inside and go . . . back outside?"

Rather than give him an immediate answer, Ashworth strode swiftly to the drawing room, only to find it vacant. Evanston trailed after him as he walked to the dining room, also found to be deserted. There William paused, his eyes falling closed and head dipping forwards, a broad smile spreading across his face.

"I know where they are," he murmured with a huff of quiet laughter.

Wordlessly, he crossed to the green baize door off the dining room. The supposed rarely crossed boundary between upstairs and downstairs, between the elite set and the servants.

Of course, William had never been much of a stickler for social etiquette, particularly after the loss of his family members, which left him essentially alone here at Lawton Park. However, nothing could have stopped him from crossing those restrictive peripheries once he'd fallen in love with his servant.

Clara had made many friends in her time belowstairs, and she returned to them often. Likewise, Rosa had also come to adore the various personalities of the people who lived and worked at Lawton Park, and traversed the door freely whenever she wished.

The earl pulled open the door, the sounds of laughter and conversation drifting upward to float freely around the two men, who carefully started their descent of the stairway. Mrs. Malone crossed below them in the hallway, paused in dismay, then lowered down into a troubled curtsy before the earl and the viscount. She cast a furtive glance in the direction of the servants' hall, where Rosa's chortle could be heard amongst the voices.

"Forgive me, my lord," she pleaded, "but no matter how hard I try—"

"It's fine, Mrs. Malone. You need to accept that there are some things beyond your control." William took the final step into the hallway, his eyes sliding towards the direction of the tumult. "This would be one of them."

The housekeeper pursed her lips in discontent. "Yes, my lord," she said, before abruptly resuming her path to the kitchen. Her massive keychain jangled loudly with the strength of her righteousness.

The men shared an amused glance.

"You see what I must deal with, Evanston?"

Thomas fought the urge to laugh. The pair proceeded towards the servants' hall, where the boisterous intonations of Mrs. Humboldt, the cook, could be heard.

"Now this one here is made with an almond paste, Miss Rosa. And over here, is a biscuit topped with black currant jelly . . ."

The words died on the woman's lips, her already ruddy cheeks flaring crimson at the unexpected appearance of both the Earl of Ashworth and Viscount Evanston in the doorway. Hastily, she stepped backwards to perform an awkward curtsy, her eyes darting anxiously at the people occupying the long table beside her.

"My lords—"

The harsh sounds of a dozen chairs scraping backwards filled the air with noise as the gathered servants rushed to pay their respects. Clara came forwards to wrap her arms around her husband in an outward display of affection that, in another household, would have been considered quite scandalous. Here, however, the earl simply beamed down at his wife.

"Mrs. Malone seems well on her way towards having some kind of nervous fit. I'd say you are the cause, Lady Ashworth."

Clara's dark eyes went wide. "Oh, but not at all! We were only sampling Mrs. Humboldt's newest creations."

At this proclamation, the child in question came bounding forwards to thoroughly wrap herself around Ashworth's legs.

"They're for the squirrels too, Uncah!"

He reached down to smooth his hand over her small blond head. "But of course they are. I would expect no less." William looked over the selections on the plate. "Now tell me, which is your favorite?"

Rosa pulled eagerly on Ashworth's hand, towing him

behind her, and Clara turned to smile at Thomas. He dipped his head in friendly acknowledgment, then casually directed his attention to the swarm of people surrounding the table, selfishly seeking a glimpse of Eliza. Finally, he spied her. Wearing a day dress of lightest yellow, she had tucked herself in between her brother and Mrs. Humboldt as if trying to conceal herself from view. He was reminded of a ray of sun slipping discreetly behind a mass of clouds. Almost as if she could feel his gaze, Eliza glanced his way, blushed, then looked down at her hands.

His body stirred warmly at her nearness. Were she not still affected by what had passed between them yesterday, he felt she would not take such care to avoid his gaze now.

God forgive me, I wish to affect her again.

The pulsing rush of desire flooded through him, and he curled his fists in white-knuckled fortitude. Needing a distraction, Evanston stepped forwards to take part in the conversation.

"What's the verdict, Ashworth? Almond or currant?" he asked, feeling foolish.

William was chewing, a thoughtful look upon his face. Finally, he swallowed and said, "Neither. Naturally, they are all delicious," he added, with a wink to the cook, "but I do believe I prefer these hazelnut biscuits."

"I like those too!" exclaimed Rosa, who seized two of the favored cookies off the plate and approached Thomas. By the time she reached him, only one cookie remained, the other having been stuffed into her mouth without ceremony.

"*Tie un,*" came her muffled and barely intelligible request.

He glanced around awkwardly before dropping down to one knee and accepting the offering. After consuming the biscuit, he raised his eyebrows in what he hoped was a show of enthusiasm.

"I quite agree," he said, staring into the adorably diminutive version of her mother's clear green gaze. "But what will the squirrels think?"

Her eyes lit up. "We should let them try!"

The arrival of Mrs. Malone, who was apparently unwilling to relinquish the control required for a squirrel biscuit-tasting, sent the servants into bows and curtsies as they politely excused themselves from the hall.

Thomas pushed up into a stand. "Would not a dog be less trouble?" he whispered loudly to Ashworth.

Eliza heard his reference to their previous conversation, her hint of a smile from behind the golden curls near her face the only acknowledgment he required.

Rosa seized the plate of treats and led the charge towards the rear door of the kitchen, dodging people as she went, her mother following closely. William and Clara trailed after at a leisurely pace, leaving Thomas a brief opportunity to speak with Eliza. She glanced uneasily over her shoulder as he increased his speed to catch up to her.

"Thomas," she murmured. "You shouldn't."

They exited the house, a shock of bright August sun causing them both to squint. Rosa barreled up ahead, heedless of the light or the heat, and Evanston leaned down a bit closer.

"We have been known to speak before. It would seem stranger, perhaps, if we were to stop speaking altogether."

She cast another furtive glance over her shoulder, then turned back after ensuring her brother to be too far behind to detect the nature of their discourse. "There is some truth to that, I suppose. But that was before we . . . well, that was before yesterday," she forced out. "Which is why you and I should not be speaking right now."

"So you think conversation is the greatest risk at this point?"

Her fair skin paled further at his remark. "It is conversation that can lead elsewhere, as you well know," she quipped. "Simply being in your company might be enough to—"

"Really?" he asked, unable to prevent a smile from curving his lips.

She stared up at him, apparently aware that she had said too much, then directed her gaze forwards once more. "I didn't mean that."

"Then tell me, what did you mean?" Thomas inquired. "It sounded as if you were saying you have difficulty controlling yourself in my presence—"

"I told you we shouldn't be speaking." She set her jaw.

Color crept across her chest, along her cheekbones, all the way up to the tips of her ears. Eliza may have been outwardly repelling him, but her blush betrayed her. Obviously, she wanted him. He just wasn't certain if her desire was attached to any emotions of a stronger nature. Up to this point he had not come right out and declared his love for her, but felt that given their conversations both in London and in Kent, she could probably guess his affection for her was genuine. This could either weaken her defenses against him or drive her away entirely.

He needed to change his tack. Inspiring her jealousy during the season had gotten her attention, but she'd been surrounded by suitors at the time. It had been necessary. Here at home, there was no need to resort to such methods. And while his natural inclination was to tease her, he knew that in this moment it would not lend itself to her pursuit.

She was feeling sensitive. Defenseless. Sharing something of himself might help ease her discomfort. The very thought of it caused a sheen of perspiration to break out across his brow. He cast his gaze uncomfortably out to the treetops.

"Despite how I behaved in London, Eliza—"

"Stop!" she hissed, her eyes blazing with alarm.

"—I need you to know that . . . I want more."

Eliza's footsteps halted along the flagstones beside him. Her fingers grazed his sleeve as if to catch her balance, then jerked suddenly away. Thomas slowed his pace at her hesitation, then resumed normal speed once she compelled herself to continue walking. Farther ahead on the lawn, Rosa cried with glee at the sight of a squirrel.

"More of what?" she asked weakly.

Christ.

This was harder than he'd thought it would be. He couldn't help but reflect on how easy it was to seduce a woman versus convincing one to fall in love with you, especially a bright woman like Eliza. But things had changed with his realization in Hampshire. His desire for her was still inextricably bound to his feelings, but rather than simply seeking his pleasure, now he found he couldn't imagine settling for something less than absolutely every single part of her. Every last emotion. Every beat of her heart.

The need to possess a woman in this way, completely, wholly, and without reservation was unfamiliar territory. Her candid question caused him to choke on his own honesty.

"More of everything," he finally managed.

Eliza's stride continued unabated. "That's not true."

Now it was his turn to stare at her incredulously.

"Excuse me?"

"Thomas, just yesterday you hauled me up to your bedchamber without a thought for what it would mean. Trust me, I know what you are after . . . and I would know if that had changed."

They neared Rosa, who was crouched, huddled in the grass, observing a red squirrel scamper about the plate she had set carefully on the ground. The creature sniffed at the assorted cookies, flicking its tail in excitement. Before they were close enough to be heard, he placed his hand gently on her arm and leaned down near her ear. Eliza shook her head from side to side, but she did pause ever so briefly.

"No, Eliza. You would not," he whispered fiercely. "In fact, I would conceal the truth of it, even from myself, until I could conceal it no longer."

She blinked, confusion and awareness lighting her eyes from behind, only a second before William came forwards to clap Thomas magnanimously on the back before passing him to join Rosa near the trees. He clenched his teeth while a fresh wave of guilt consumed him.

Clara approached the pair to regard Eliza with an abundance of cheer. "Come, dear sister. Let us see what the squirrels have decreed!"

"Yes," murmured Eliza in a tone that sounded like relief. "Let's."

Lady Ashworth curtsied politely to Evanston, then casually looped her arm through Eliza's to steal her away. But not before capturing his gaze with her own slightly twinkling, and very knowing glance.

Chapter Twelve

Eliza was not happy that William was leaving on a business trip that was expected to take the better part of a month, especially once Clara had informed her that Lord Evanston would be coming to stay at Lawton Park during his absence.

She had attempted to convince her brother that the best course of action was his remaining in Kent, to no avail. William could not be dissuaded, and while he would be back in time for the house party, now she was preparing to endure nearly a month of dealing with Evanston in the best way she knew how . . . by trying to ignore him. This had been made substantially more difficult by his shocking admission on the lawn, and she couldn't deny that the thought of the viscount having deeper feelings for her caused her heart to ache in fretful longing. But it was no matter. She just had to maintain until Landry had a chance to finalize things with her, and this time she was determined to let him. No doubt

Thomas would find another lady to assuage his wounded pride, and would forget about her as quickly as he'd forgotten about their first kiss.

The idea of accepting Sir James was still a bittersweet notion, but she was convinced this was the wisest resolution for both her and Rosa. Eliza knew there was a part of her that despaired over losing the viscount forever, although again she reminded herself, regardless of their friendship and whatever intimacy they had shared recently, he was not hers. And the only thing she could ever truly hope to share with Thomas was the pleasure of a physical union. Delicious as she knew it would be, he just wasn't a man designed for anything else, and she couldn't allow desire to be the sole criterion when selecting her husband.

On this resplendent day, Eliza and Clara were sharing a pot of tea out on the back patio, being pleasantly warmed by the sunlight slanting over the northern side of the house. It felt lovely and decadent at the moment, but Eliza knew that by midafternoon the heat would likely be sweltering. Thankfully, she could enjoy this moment of privacy with Lady Ashworth prior to Evanston's arrival at the house later. The very thought of seeing him again caused her heart to flutter painfully.

Inhaling a soothing breath, she admired the splendor around her. Lawton Park was awash in full glorious color, a sight that Eliza would never find tiresome. The pale blooms of blush noisette roses arched and crept gracefully along the stately stone wall surrounding the courtyard. Mossy green ground cover wove its way through the flagstones, and an abundance of her favorite cerise peonies perfumed the air while black-and-yellow-striped bumblebees trundled and buzzed heavily between the brightly colored offerings.

Rosa ran through the gardens singing, her little legs pumping beneath the tea length hem of her skirt, the gleaming white ribbon in her hair trailing aloft behind her as she sprinted. Her favorite dolly in its faded pink dress was clutched tightly in her fist.

"My goodness, look at the little darling. How wonderfully she entertains herself," gushed Clara, beaming with affection. A happy shriek from the little girl punctuated the observation. "Now," she continued, switching topics, "for the house party, if the weather is still warm enough, I was thinking . . ."

Clara discussed her plans, but Eliza found herself unable to follow the thread of the conversation. Her mind kept wandering while she sat watching her daughter, who reminded her so much of herself as a child, racing through the bushes with hair flying wild like a heathen. She fondly recalled chases with William and Thomas through these same gardens, musing that perhaps since the boys were so much older than she, they had participated in many youthful activities simply for her sake.

This was something that, in retrospect, she was very thankful for. Eliza wasn't certain she had ever fully acknowledged the level of kindness they had shown to her. Especially from Evanston, who was not even a relation but simply a friend of the family. A friend who had no preference for children to begin with. It was a jarring realization that perhaps maybe the viscount was much kinder than he was inclined to let on. Now, many years later, she reflected on that kindness, and thought about the ways it had manifested towards her daughter as well, albeit awkwardly and often at a distance.

"Eliza?"

She glanced at Clara with a start. "Hmm?"

"You seem distracted. Have you heard anything I've been saying?"

"Oh yes. You've been discussing your outdoor plans for the house party," she said, guessing hastily.

The comment may have been vague, but it also must have hit the mark to some degree, for Clara nodded in agreement. "Yes, right. So the invitations were sent last week, and . . ."

Her mind unwittingly evoked her recent visit to Hawthorne Manor, recalling with unsettling clarity the sounds of Evanston's groans and the brandied taste of his lips. The feel of his hands sliding possessively over her back . . . the hard surface of his chest raking against her breasts through the unyielding fabric of her bodice . . . the way he had swept her into his arms . . .

I want more.

More of everything.

It was hard to believe. Especially since she had been the one who'd wanted him for years—since that budding moment of self-awareness. With the awe he had inspired within her as an impressive specimen of the masculine sex. She had matured and changed considerably since the first sparks of desire for him had started to smolder and knew his need for her did not go back nearly that far. But now she was curious. When had it begun? Had it all happened during the course of the season?

And had he actually been trying to tell her that his feelings had evolved into something resembling . . . love?

Eliza's head began to ache. She squeezed her eyes shut against the morning sun, slowly reopening them as Clara's hand slid gently over her own.

"Are you well?" Clara asked softly, her dark eyes full of concern.

"Yes, forgive me," she replied. "You were speaking of—"

"Eliza." The countess eyed her insistently, raising her eyebrows for emphasis. "Is something wrong?"

Eliza gazed out at the courtyard, where Rosa had seen fit to lie on her stomach, her chin propped up in her hands. Amidst the music of birdsong, she could hear her daughter conversing with the various creatures crawling among the moss.

"Rosa!" she called out, rising from her wrought-iron chair. "Your dress will get filthy!"

A hushed chuckle was her daughter's only reply. No doubt the insect now crawling across the girl's hand was receiving an earful regarding Rosa's thoughts on overbearing mothers.

Clara laughed and took a sip from her china cup. "No harm done. I'm sure you did worse to your dresses as a child."

"Oh yes. I know it," said Eliza, sinking back down into her seat, immensely relieved at the benign turn in conversation. "I climbed trees in my dresses."

"You didn't!"

"I did, actually," she asserted with an amused grin. "With both William and Thomas for playmates, how can you doubt me?"

"Point taken," Clara replied, her eyes dancing. There was a slight pause. "And how is Thomas's faring?"

Something in Clara's tone made Eliza think the inquiry stemmed from some kind of suspicion.

"I believe he is well. Why do you ask?"

"No reason, really," answered Clara, shielding her eyes and searching the garden for Rosa, who had concealed herself behind a hedge. "Although, and I might be mistaken in this, things did seem a bit tense between you two the other day."

"Did they?" managed Eliza with a barely convincing laugh. "Well, you know Evanston. He does like to tease, and after twenty years of it I suppose I may just be reaching my limit."

Clara's gaze slid over to settle heavily on Eliza, her expression inscrutable. "Yes, I understand," she agreed. "It's as if he is unable to tell when he should stop."

Uncomfortable with the direction of the conversation, Eliza simply nodded and occupied herself by taking a long sip of her tea. Clara surprised her with another question.

"I assume you have rejected your other offers of marriage by now?"

Eliza set her cup down on its saucer much harder than intended, resulting in a noisy *clank*. The entire subject—and Evanston's involvement, of course—still caused her agitation.

"Yes, of course I've sent letters," she said, staring down at her hands. "I was only shocked that I had managed to garner such attention with Landry having shown such outward interest throughout the season."

Lady Ashworth chuckled. "I, however, am not surprised at all." She leaned forwards, her dark eyes shining. "Tell me of Sir James. Is he a hopeless romantic?"

"Oh yes. In fact, he caused quite a stir at a ball by paying an immoderate amount of attention to me." Eliza laughed in reflection, then paused, also recalling Evanston's fury and what it had prompted him to do before the watchful faces gathered there.

Sir James was certainly romantic in the traditional sense. He was affable and polite, enraptured in her presence, made certain she received a steady stream of letters and flowers, and had even tried—and failed, because of her—to declare himself. Evanston was not a romantic, not in the truest sense of the word anyway, and yet there was something strangely tender about him. A dark magnetism that tugged her back each time she thought she might have broken free.

The minute tilt of Clara's head caused Eliza to fumble for words. "Sir James is lovely. He took me to the theater, we danced together often, and we took a great many walks through Hyde Park. He comes from a very well-respected family," she rushed to add. "I met many acquaintances of his who all agreed that he is a stable and trustworthy sort of man."

Clara's lips twitched and she leaned back in her chair. "He does sound lovely. I look forward to meeting him here at Lawton Park." Her gaze moved out across the courtyard to where Rosa still played, seeming to consider something, and Eliza feared she had suspected the truth of the matter. That although Landry could create a stir in a ballroom, he could not quite cause Eliza's blood to stir the way Thomas did so effortlessly. She'd seen the countess watching them both since their return from London.

Eliza had sometimes wondered if Evanston's only motivation in delaying the response to her suitors was to pay her back for her rejection of him during the season . . . a move that might have been more in line with his character before. But a lot had happened over the summer, and now something about this idea didn't ring true. The only answer that did ring true time and time again was that he, against all odds, wanted her for himself. Her search for a husband would have been more than enough to force his hand, were he to actually feel affection for her.

In fact, now that she thought about it, Lord Evanston *was* the one acting like a hopeless romantic . . .

Both ladies straightened up at the sudden appearance of the head footman. Clara smiled at him.

"Yes, Matthew?"

"Pardon the interruption, my lady, but Lord Evanston approaches the drive."

"Ah, lovely," said Clara. "Thank you, Matthew. We will meet him out front. Rosa!" She called out towards the garden. A cherubic face peered out from behind a cluster of rose bushes. "Thomas has arrived!"

"Hooray!"

The ladies proceeded to the drive from around the side

of the house. They emerged out front just as his carriage was pulling up, and Eliza spied the viscount behind the vehicle, seated astride his chestnut horse. She knew he preferred riding whenever possible, and had to admit it was somewhat humorous he had elected to bring the animal he'd managed to snatch out of Landry's grasp. Once she had torn her eyes away from the distracting cling of his riding breeches, she met his azure gaze and lowered into a curtsy alongside Clara and Rosa.

"Greetings, my lord." She examined him with a wry look. "I would congratulate you on your fine steed, but I happen to know the circumstances behind its acquisition."

Clara's eyebrows shot upward and she grinned in anticipation. "Do tell, Eliza. Thomas excels at causing scandals, but I long to know how he managed to generate one through the purchase of a horse."

Evanston swung out of the saddle with agile grace to land on the gravel drive, a flash of surprise preceding a warning glance directed at Eliza.

"It was nothing. Only a minor coincidence, and not even truly scandalous."

At his censorious demeanor, Eliza realized her error. In referring to the viscount's purchase of this horse, an animal which Sir James had shown great interest in at the time, she was close to outwardly accusing him of trying to vex her most promising suitor. And William would be enraged to discover that Thomas's time in London had been spent trying to influence the men pursuing her. It could absolutely destroy their relationship.

She glanced at Thomas in panicked understanding just a moment before Rosa rushed forwards to hug his legs.

"Hello!" she chirruped, beaming up at him.

Relief flooded through Eliza at her daughter's fortuitous interruption. Knocked slightly off balance, Evanston rocked back on his feet then lowered himself to one knee.

"Greetings, Miss Rosa." He chuckled softly, casting a sideways glance at the worn doll clutched lovingly in her hand. "I brought something for you, but you will need to wait until my trunks are unpacked to receive it."

Rosa's eyes widened to nearly comical proportions. "Really?"

"Really," Thomas assured her. "But you will have to wait," he repeated with a wink.

Rosa groaned theatrically and threw her arms around his neck in a forlorn hug, and Thomas's hands remained suspended in midair for a moment before coming to rest gently around the little girl. Clara smiled down at the pair, then glanced towards Matthew and Charles, who stood in nearby silent attendance with the rest of the servants. They immediately jumped forwards to unload the carriage, and Evanston rose to a stand.

"Let us give the viscount a chance to be settled," Clara said, taking Rosa's small hand in her own before turning to approach the front door. "Although, I will not forget to ask about the horse, Thomas. Do not think you have escaped me on that score," she teased over her shoulder.

He nodded dutifully in Clara's direction, then slid a chiding glance at Eliza. "Duly noted, my lady. I shall relate the boring particulars at your earliest request."

The countess and Rosa made their way into the house, and Eliza felt an unseemly rush of excitement when Thomas leaned down to add under his breath, "And you had better learn to exert more caution, Eliza. That is, unless, you wish to create chaos."

The irony of his words proved too much for her to ignore. "Haven't you managed to do that already?" she bit back.

"Have I?" Evanston raised his dark brow and paused, silently evaluating her, his gaze running a leisurely pathway across her face.

Eliza could only stare at him mutely in response to his scrutiny. Then, with an excess of civility, he extended his arm. She scowled at it, knowing that to refuse his gentlemanly gesture before the remaining servants on the drive would only succeed in creating gossip—speculation that all was not well between the earl's sister and his friend. Since she had no choice, Eliza accepted his offer and the pair started off to join Clara and Rosa.

"You are lucky there are witnesses," she grumbled.

By the time Evanston finally came downstairs, the late afternoon light had turned into an amber glow, filtering hazily through the south-facing windows of the drawing room. Being an uncommonly warm day, he had elected not to retain his coat and waistcoat, and given his intimate acquaintance with the family, he knew that formality would not be required. He could see immediately that both ladies were of a similar mind. They had changed into their lightest gowns. Even then, he noted in sympathy, they remained encumbered by layers of skirts.

Eliza looked miserably hot, the curve of her cheek tinged pink from the overbearing heat. Thomas remembered the discreet glimmer of perspiration on her face that evening in Belgravia, the night Landry had followed her into the garden. Then he recalled how she had retrieved a handkerchief to blot at the moisture, freeing his calling card from the confines of her reticule to flutter down amidst the mossy flagstones.

Evanston often wondered . . . had she destroyed the slip of paper that had served to bring her embarrassment, or did she still carry it out of sentiment?

Clara and Eliza stood to greet him, and he ceased his musings to bow politely in return. Rosa grinned impishly, bouncing on the powder-blue couch cushions, her dolly flopping about beside her. A turn of the head and an outstretched hand from her mother was all that was required to bring the child into standing, curtseying politeness.

Thomas couldn't help but be entertained by the ever present mischievous twinkle in Rosa's eyes. It reminded him of himself as a child, although on this specific occasion he knew the reason for her excitement. He slowly brought forth a box he'd been holding at his side and lowered himself next to the countess as she seated herself once again.

"It is my understanding, Miss Rosa, that you were exceptionally well behaved while your mother was away in London." His eyes flicked over to Clara. "Is this true?"

Lady Ashworth smiled knowingly and folded her hands primly upon her lap. "Indeed, my lord. A finer example of youthful refinement I've yet to behold."

Across from them, Eliza seated herself as well, but he detected a thoughtfulness to her movements, her gaze intensely focused on the box in his hands. It was a reaction that appeared to originate from something other than the expected anticipation of a gift. Her response stirred his curiosity.

Meanwhile, Rosa was literally quivering with anticipation. She left her dolly with her mother and came forwards to meet him.

"I tried to be good," she whispered earnestly, twisting her fingers before her skirts.

Her seriousness caused him to laugh. "I know you did. Which is why you have earned this." Thomas relinquished the gift box, wrapped in a wide, vibrant green ribbon, the color chosen as a tribute to the eyes of its recipient.

Those very eyes widened with delight, and he felt a pleasure so sharp and so different from any he'd ever felt that it caused his breath to halt in his throat. His gaze immediately sought Eliza, whose slender fingers were touching her lips in intrigued observation. Her eyes met his, but her expression was still frozen in contemplation, unsmiling. By way of contrast, Clara was beaming broadly.

"Open it, Rosa! What did he bring you?" she exclaimed.

The little girl tugged on the ribbon, then gripped the lid and raised it to reveal a china doll, wearing a soft ivory dress interwoven with golden thread. The doll did not have molded porcelain hair as many other dolls did, but was rather covered in an intricate blond wig. The wig was arranged in the fashionable style of Queen Victoria, parted in the middle with plaited sides that wound around the ears to meet atop the head in a knot. Rosa's gasp could be discerned throughout the still of the drawing room, and she stared reverently at the blushing doll face, glazed and gleaming beneath her tiny fingers.

"This is a fancy dolly," Rosa declared in awe.

Clara leaned over for a better view. "Oh, it's lovely, Thomas. Where did you find such an exquisite gift?"

"There is a little shop on Bond Street that I frequent from time to time," he replied with a smile.

Rosa gently scooped the doll from the padded confines of the box and held it as if it were a baby, causing Clara to chuckle softly. "You had better not be cleaning floors with that doll, Miss Rosa."

"Oh, no," replied the little girl. "I'll be so careful." She approached Thomas then, and he froze as Rosa's eyes raised to his, filled with brimming appreciation. Leaning in, she placed a kiss squarely on his cheek. "Thank you."

A little discomfited, yet gratified, by the sincere show of affection, Evanston bowed his head and smiled. "You're very welcome."

It was only upon glancing at Eliza that he saw she was not well. Her cheeks were now fully flushed, lungs working with the effort to take a normal breath. He regarded her in alarm.

"Eliza? What is—"

She rose abruptly, swaying slightly in her haste. "I beg your pardon . . . I need some air."

Clara placed an arm around Rosa. "By all means, it's dreadfully hot in here. I'll watch after Rosa."

Briefly waving her thanks, Eliza hurried from the room. Rosa's eyes grew large as she regarded Clara.

"Is Mama sick?"

"No, no, my dearest. She is just so very sensitive to the heat." Clara's gaze shifted to Thomas, who had risen from his seat and was already halfway to the door. "But perhaps you could go check on her in a moment, my lord. To be certain."

Eliza sank down onto the stone retaining wall near the garden, her breath hitching in her throat. Her eyes fell closed, and she pressed the heels of her palms against them until bright spots illuminated the darkness. She felt ridiculous for reacting in such a way, particularly in front of Thomas. But in the end, it had been her own foolish assumptions that had set her up for such a shock.

She'd been so certain Thomas had been at Bond Street seeking a gift for his mistress that day he'd been spotted by Caroline and her aunt. He'd built himself a dubious reputation upon the adoration of many women. So who would have guessed . . . who would have even believed . . . that the notorious libertine, Lord Evanston, would be seen in Bond Street buying a gift for a little girl? Her little girl, no less.

It meant disaster for her heart. If he cared for Rosa, it was more difficult to ignore his continued assertions that this time, it was different. That against all odds, he really did want more with Eliza. More than a flirtation. More than a few hours of pleasure. More than he'd experienced with any other woman.

With a groan of frustration, she buried her face in her hands. Thomas was a good person, but in William's eyes, and perhaps even hers, he was fatally flawed. Her brother had seen him at his worst, in school and beyond, when Thomas hadn't cared one whit for the good opinion of others. And as much as he held her family in high esteem, he'd betrayed them too on the night of her engagement. His greedy kiss in the name of *insatiable curiosity* was all it had taken for her to understand that, to him, loyalty was a flexible notion—one that could be bent and manipulated based on whichever desire tempted him most. Nor was that the only time he'd shown such selfishness. Even Rosa's birth had apparently been an opportunity for him to indulge his bad habits, for he'd been discovered by Mrs. Malone the following morning, insensible with drink, lying haphazardly on the staircase.

Regardless of the tales, Eliza had to admit that Thomas must have felt very alone after the elder viscount's death. She was sure the bitter insults he received regularly from his mother had served as a painful reminder of his father's love, now lost forever. Perhaps this alone explained his gravitation to William and her family. Perhaps it explained why he had ventured to their house so often. Perhaps it explained his reckless, wild behavior.

And perhaps somewhere along the way, he had changed.

Reaching down, she gripped her skirts, balling her hands

into fists and crushing the fragile muslin beneath her fingers. William would never be swayed, and she would be risking Rosa's well-being on a hope. A wish. What kind of mother was she, anyway, to consider such a match? To allow her own feelings to cloud her judgment? Feelings that were unsettling, and more confusing each and every day . . .

She stiffened at the sound of approaching steps. It was the footfall of a man, and Evanston appeared seconds later, his eyes glowing bright with concern despite the fading light and the shadows cast within the garden.

"Eliza?" he asked urgently, lowering himself down next to her on the wall. She turned away.

"I'm fine," she said, annoyed, blotting at her heated face. "Thomas. I just—"

The gentle pressure of his fingers along the curve of her jaw quelled her remaining thoughts. He guided her head around until his eyes held hers fast within their turquoise depths, darting over the mottled surface of her cheeks.

"You're not fine. You're upset." A notch formed between his brows as he released her. "Why?"

Because of you.

"No, truly I'm fine. It was just the heat . . ."

His low laugh surprised her, and he leaned back to regard her in confusion. "Eliza, given the traumas you have endured these past years, I would never have guessed you to be so vulnerable to a mere increase in temperature. Yet it seems to be your undoing, both here and in London." Evanston shrugged. "Who knew?"

Eliza felt her mouth curve into a smile, even as her eyes

narrowed at him. "You can go back inside if you insist on teasing me. I didn't ask you to come out here."

"And yet, I felt compelled," he replied with a sigh. "Now be honest. I'm sure Caroline must have told you about my visit to Bond Street, so why did my gift seem like such a monumental discovery to you today?"

Her mouth opened in reply but the words died on her lips. How honest could she really be?

"Fine," she relented. "I knew you had purchased a gift on Bond Street the day Caroline and Lady Frances saw you. I just thought . . . that it was for . . . someone else."

Evanston's gaze became alert. "How could you possibly surmise who it was intended for?"

"I suppose the fact you are often in female company has escaped your remembrance? Or that Mrs. Varnham had accompanied you around London?" she asked acidly.

A pause. Silence.

"I have not *truly* shared female company since before seeing you at the party in Belgravia," he clarified.

The first time they'd met during the season. The night she'd met Landry, when Evanston had followed them out into the garden. Eliza stared at him, inordinately aware of the sounds of their breathing and the luscious fragrance of the peonies fanning out from behind them.

This would mean that he hadn't been with a woman in *months*.

"I don't understand . . ."

His head lowered. "I think you do."

Pressing her lips tightly together, Eliza tried to ignore

the surge of adrenaline racing through her veins. If she could not, she worried her next action would be the gripping of his white linen shirt as she pulled him close.

"But Mrs. Varnham said—"

"Mrs. Varnham was lying."

She stared at him, desperately grasping for something to say. "Even so, you have never liked children," she pointed out. "What would lead me to believe you would go out of your way to buy her a gift?"

Thomas looked taken aback. "I have always cared for Rosa."

"Perhaps, although I remember a day when you spoke of never wanting children of your own."

His face turned serious. "Yes, because I can't imagine worrying about them. It seems it would be a terrifying burden. But there is no denying that Rosa is like family to me." He shook his head and glanced away, then rose to a stand. "I should be heading back—"

Her hand shot out to grasp his. The move surprised them both, and she stared at her hand as if it belonged to someone else.

"I'm sorry, Thomas," she said before she could lose her courage. "You've always been kind to Rosa . . . despite what you may have said before."

Evanston stood there for a moment, his fingers warm and strong around her own. Then, with a soft tug, he pulled her upward to face him. They were standing much too close, the heat from his body scorching her own, and she could detect a hint of his masculine scent . . . spicy, almost woodsy . . . as a wayward breeze stirred the air around them. Eliza felt herself tilting in his direction, could perfectly recall the sublime sensuality of his kiss. Knew that, were he to lean down, she would willingly be lost once again.

"Don't kiss me," she whispered, panicking. "Please."

His eyes held hers fast as they wandered over her in sultry evaluation.

"The next time we kiss, Eliza," he stated quietly, "it will be at your behest."

She folded her arms across her chest and raised her eyebrows defiantly, while inside she feared it was the truth. It took every ounce of restraint she possessed not to beg him for it now. Feebly, she made an attempt at anger.

"Caroline warned me, you know," she said accusingly. "She said you were buying time to seduce me."

He evaluated her sternly before making his reply. "Lady Caroline knows better."

To that Eliza had no reply, angry or otherwise, and she could only watch him mutely as he turned on his heel and strode back into the house.

CHAPTER THIRTEEN

May I request the honor of this dance?"

Sir James Landry led Eliza to the dance floor, his gloved hand lightly touching hers, and she turned to face him with a swirl of her skirts, assuming a proper starting position.

The music began and they were off, his lead effective and reserved, blue eyes smiling down at her throughout the turns and steps. She couldn't help but feel a tiny bit disappointed. For what, she knew not.

The lilting cadence of the waltz echoed through the ballroom. This had been what she'd wanted, to be courted by him. Such a respectable man would surely make a fine father for Rosa. His hand tightened upon her waist and he spun her faster, making her dizzy. It wasn't an entirely unpleasant feeling, so she allowed her eyes to drift closed, enjoying the feeling of floating across the dance floor, wrapped safely in the arms of the man she would marry.

They twirled around and around. He pulled her closer against him, but he felt different somehow. Larger. More impressive. Enticing. Distantly, she noticed that the music was playing faster, much faster than was required. She felt Landry lean forwards, his breath hot against the side of her neck.

"Have I told you how lovely you look, Eliza?"

Her nerves sparked with fiery awareness. With eyes still closed, she felt her lips curve into a smile.

"You never speak that way to me."

Another dizzying turn.

"You just never listen."

She frowned. Something wasn't right. Her eyes snapped open, and to her utter dismay, she found herself in the arms of Lord Evanston.

The music played even faster.

Eliza needed to find Sir James, although truly, she had no desire to leave. The viscount's eyes were not the disappointment they'd been with Landry, but electric blue. His arms were warm and solid. She ached for him to bring her closer, could feel the strength of his own longing.

"I don't understand," she protested weakly as they swooped together into another turn. Eliza wasn't just dizzy now. She was no longer even able to tell floor from ceiling.

Abruptly, the song ended. The spinning stopped. Evanston finally pulled her closer, and she stopped breathing.

"I think you do," he whispered.

Eliza jerked awake with a gasp, her frenzied pants sounding strange within the solitary interior of her bedchamber.

Her heart drummed wildly in her chest. Moonlight streamed in through the gauzy curtains, and she could discern the sheets upon her bed twisted wildly around her feet.

Gingerly, she plucked her sweaty nightgown away from her body. After rolling off the mattress to a stand, she stripped off the soaked fabric, then wandered naked, stubbing her toe on her mother's armoire in a blind search for a new covering. Eliza squeaked in pain and leaned down to grasp the affected foot. Perhaps that was her mother admonishing her from beyond the grave for being so foolish.

At the very least, it seemed even her sleeping mind knew that Thomas posed a serious threat to her sanity. At most, he threatened everything she had worked towards during the season. She'd often yearned for the mother she'd never had, but it was now, when she could use some motherly advice, that she ached for her most.

The pain in her toe soon abated, and she worked up the courage to continue her quest for clothing. She found a fresh nightgown and slid it over her head, then stood shivering in the dark, considering what she should do. At last, she had an idea. Lighting a candle, she opened her door to creep quietly downstairs to the library.

She was going to write a letter requesting some much needed reinforcements.

Two weeks later, and Thomas knew with certainty that Eliza was avoiding him. Her visits to Lawton Park dwindled, becoming less and less frequent. Clara took the carriage to the Dower House each morning, but more often than not, it was only Rosa who accompanied her back on the return.

He had plenty of regrets about Eliza, and nearly as many about her brother. Thomas knew he had gone about this the wrong way—gone about everything the wrong way—and that William would be well within his rights to cast Thomas out of their lives for good should he ever learn the truth.

His pursuit of Eliza would not be easily forgiven, especially when one had been warned off in the first place. Thomas could only imagine the extent of his friend's rage had he actually been successful, and now, was it any wonder Eliza stayed away? Would it be any surprise when William despised him for this betrayal of his trust?

On this morning, he sat in the breakfast room, brooding sullenly over his coffee. He had attempted, and failed, to eat—his plate sitting before him, the food long gone cold. Clara entered quietly, looked in his direction, then retrieved her own coffee from the sideboard. She seated herself across the table to observe him thoughtfully.

"Thomas."

He glanced up from his cup. "Hmm?"

"You should speak to her."

Evanston stared at her, motionless, trying to decide how much she knew and how he should respond to such a suggestion. He cleared his throat.

"I beg your pardon . . . speak to whom?"

The countess rolled her eyes, took a sip of coffee, then set the cup back on its saucer to assail him with a look. "You think I have not seen the way you look at Eliza?" she asked boldly.

His back straightened. "These are matters that don't concern you, Lady Ashworth," he replied with a scowl.

"I'm trying to help. Don't you see?" she said, her tone softening. "Unless my assumptions are incorrect, it certainly seems you could use some help."

"You are the last person on earth who should help me right now. Do not involve yourself."

"Why?"

"Because William . . . he does not approve. He would shun me entirely if he knew how I'd pursued—" He broke off and swore to the side.

Her eyebrows rose. "So you have actually been courting her?"

Evanston stood and crossed to the windows, staring stonily at the spot where he'd last spoken to Eliza.

"You could call it something like that," he answered, gazing into the garden.

He heard her rise from her chair and come to a stand beside him. She placed a hand on his arm, looking up at him with earnest dark eyes.

"Then you should talk to William too."

Thomas scoffed, a harsh sound in the quiet of the room. "It's far too late for that. Had I been able to exert some semblance of control, I might have spoken to him *before* nearly seducing his sister."

Her hand slid from his arm. "You what?"

"You heard me."

"And she . . . refused you?"

"She did."

She blinked. "Yet you are still pursuing her?"

"I suppose I am," he said with an annoyed jerk of his head.

"Well, this certainly explains a few things." Clara surveyed him with a sigh. "Thomas, you must speak to William. Soon. Immediately upon his return. In the meantime, talk to Eliza."

"William and I have already spoken. He pulled me aside the night before Eliza left for London and told me to keep my distance."

"He did?" Clara's eyes widened.

"He did," Thomas said. "But I tried to earn her affection anyway, like an idiot. And now I'm sure to lose them both."

"Oh, I'm so sorry," she said, her voice rich with sympathy. "But you can't stop trying now."

He eyed her warily. "Aren't you even going to ask if I love her?" he asked offhandedly, as if using a casual tone might temper the seriousness of his words.

She patted his arm as if he were a young child and regarded him with compassion.

"No, I'm not. I'm afraid it's already very much apparent that you do."

Eliza set out immediately after Clara's brief visit to retrieve Rosa. She hated not seeing her daughter during the day, but accompanying her to Lawton Park would place her within arm's reach of Lord Evanston, and she knew full well what he could accomplish in that distance. In the interim, she had been plagued by her dreams, and by the terrifying yet exhilarating prospect of their next kiss, which was inconvenient given Landry's imminent arrival at the estate.

The morning air was warm, with an accompanying breeze that was still brisk. Eliza inhaled deeply, enjoying the fact that she *could* inhale deeply. She had disregarded every decent notion, namely her corset, to venture out into the fields in her buckskin breeches. She often wore them beneath her riding habit, it was never permissible to wear them alone. They were a luxury she had indulged only in the privacy of her Hampshire estate. She had also chosen a button-up blouse more appropriate for a woman in the wild frontiers of America than the rolling meadows of England, but today she had no one to please, and after months spent trying to impress the *ton*, the freedom was simply irresistible. Besides, a corset and dress would certainly keep her from what she so desperately wished to do.

The dew clinging to the long grass was knocked asunder by the pathway of her boots as she walked steadily ahead, her destination clear in her mind. With any luck, Caroline would be arriving today, well ahead of the rest of the houseguests. She'd felt comfortable making the request since her friend's last correspondence, in which she had informed Eliza of Lady Frances's improvement at home. Caroline was planning carefully and surrounding her aunt with familiar people, trusted servants and friends, before leaving for Lawton Park. As Caroline had never been anything but suspicious of Lord Evanston and his motives, Eliza was certain her friend would be able to provide the support she so greatly needed.

The oak tree rose before her on the hill, its branches stretched towards the sky, proud and stately, just as it had always been. It had occurred to her this morning as she lay abed, that despite her brave attempt when she was younger, she had never actually conquered climbing the tree. William and Lucas had done it. Thomas had done it. She had tried and failed, spraining her ankle in the process, but she'd been much younger and burdened by her skirts. Well, today she was wearing pants, and she was going to climb this tree.

Eliza acknowledged that her sudden desire to scale the tree didn't make much sense, but nevertheless, she continued. Her hands clutched the rough bark and she aligned her boot with a depression in the trunk. Reaching above her, she gripped the lowest branch and pulled herself up while pushing off with her foot. It would take some work to reach a branch thick enough to support her weight entirely. She repeated the process . . . grip, dig, pull, push . . . until finally she'd made enough progress to stretch towards an ideal branch, one she could stand on.

She resisted the urge to glance down, knowing that to do so would likely throw her off balance. Instead, she looked towards her goal, continuing to work her way up into the thick of the tree. A wisp of hair slipped from the mass at the back of her head, and she twitched her head to displace the offending lock from her eyes. Slow and steady, she extended her leg to rest her left foot on the branch. Eliza tested it hesitantly, then transferred her weight.

The wood snapped and gave way beneath her.

Swiftly, she plunged towards the ground, but before she had time to think, she threw her arm out and latched onto a neighboring branch. Eliza pulled with all her might and felt the satisfying way her body swung over to safety, and then quickly she resumed climbing.

. . . grip, dig, pull, push . . . grip, dig, pull, push . . .

Twigs scraped her flesh and pulled at her hair, but she was so close now. So very close.

Soon, Eliza had made it as far as was safe to go, nestled up amidst the leafy foliage of the old oak tree. She gazed out at the vista surrounding her and shook in excitement.

"*Ha!*" she screamed at no one in particular.

Exhausted, she sank down to a seated position on the branch. It wasn't until she brushed her hair away from her face that she realized she'd been crying. She wasn't surprised. It seemed that lately her emotions were always at war, and sometimes she felt so very tired of being strong and stoic. The torment of loving one man while aiming to marry another was an ever present shadow upon her, and it felt good to take charge for a change. Even if she were only asserting herself over a tree.

Eliza sighed, resting her head against the trunk. How had things spun to such out-of-control proportions? Reflecting on her life, she realized it had never truly been in her control to begin with. She'd lost her mother at birth, something that would always weigh heavily. Eliza did not pity herself, for she had been fortunate to have the devoted affection of her remaining family and friends who had served to shield her from some of the uglier aspects of being a motherless daughter in high society. The *ton* was not kind, after all, their smiles tainted with judgment and their malicious hunger for gossip never entirely quenched.

William, having been traumatized by the carriage accident that had killed most of his family, had endured sufferings too. The deaths of their father, brother and Reginald had inextricably linked Eliza and William in their grief. Only recently had he been capable of wading out of the mire, thanks in large part to his loving new wife.

Now Eliza sought her own way out. Her goal was to defend Rosa, just as she herself had been defended. Reginald had been a good husband. A kind husband. It had been strange, giving herself to a man she'd barely known, but at the time she'd seen it as her obligation, and he had proven himself worthy. Here she stood at duty's door again, moodily wondering why the best choice for Rosa couldn't somehow be her best choice as well. Because Thomas was not that man, no matter how much she had tried to convince herself it could be otherwise. No matter how much she longed for it to be true.

Ridding herself of the bothersome thoughts, she impatiently wiped away her tears, now mingled with sweat. Once her breathing had normalized, she began her descent carefully, and when she reached the final branch, she lengthened her body and hung there for a moment before allowing herself to drop from the leafy canopy.

To find Lord Evanston beside his horse, jaw slackened, evaluating her in disbelief.

"What the *hell* are you doing?" he asked, then caught sight of her breeches. "And what the hell are you wearing?" he added, almost thoughtfully.

A jolt shook her frame. It had been weeks since she'd seen him, but of course Thomas would choose now to seek her out. He'd had plenty of time to ride his horse the short distance to the Dower House for a visit, but he had found her in this precise moment, clad in indecent clothing and filthy from her climb. Eliza felt herself turn crimson, but the last thing she wanted was for him to sense her embarrassment.

"If you must know, Thomas," she intoned haughtily, clapping the dirt from her hands, "I was climbing this tree."

He stared at her, unnerved. "Yes, I saw that. Although it was more like vaulting than climbing."

Eliza smiled despite herself. "Really?"

"I've never seen anything like it." He shook his head. "I had to come closer for a better look, and imagine my surprise when it was not some unruly trespassing boy, but—"

"A boy?"

"It was the breeches," he said, smirking. "From a distance." Evanston's appreciative gaze slid over her hips, probably noting all the ways she was so very different from a boy, and when her blush deepened it appeared he elected to not elaborate. "I didn't want to interfere, but you had difficulty with the dismount, as I recall."

She stared at him, speechless, unsure what to say. He had known well enough to leave her alone, but cared enough to stay in case she'd needed him.

A million reasons she shouldn't let her guard down flew

through her head. After all, he'd nearly taken her . . . more than once.

"I, well, thank you," she stammered. "As you can see, though, I'm fine. And I really should be returning home."

She started down the hill, intent on not slowing her pace until she was far away from Thomas.

"Eliza—"

Something in his tone caused her to pause. A quiet desperation. A plea. Grimly, she swiveled around to face him, knowing that every second spent in his presence was another second closer to her probable surrender. Every moment with him was an opportunity for her to disregard logical thought.

"Yes?"

A shadow of a frown crossed his face. "I wish you wouldn't stay away because of me."

She shook her head. "I can't be near you right now. There is too much at stake and you will do and say whatever pleases you, Thomas. You always have."

And I'm afraid that what pleases you might please me too . . .

"Is that really what you think?" he asked, the notch between his brows growing deeper.

"It is."

He came closer, and she found herself staring at the strong breadth of his chest, wishing she were raking her fingers across that hard surface right now. With a blink, she raised her eyes to meet his and found a surprising level of emotion in those blue depths. She even spied what appeared to be sincerity. It was an unsettling realization. It was much easier to discount the things he said if she could think of him as a scoundrel.

"While I won't deny that I often speak before considering the consequences, I cannot agree that I act without care."

"What about our kiss in the drawing room . . . on the night of my engagement, no less?"

His eyes glinted. "Fine, yes. That night I did as I wished."

"And the time you caused a scene at the ball? Stealing me away from Landry?"

"I would argue that Landry had already caused a scene by monopolizing your time."

"And when you tried to seduce me later that night?" she asked, leaning forwards in challenge.

"I stopped when you asked."

That was true. She huffed in frustration. "And during my visit to Hawthorne Manor—did you not almost take me in your bedchamber?"

His eyes grew brighter. "I did. Although if I'd been acting without a care, there would have been no *almost* about it."

"See?" she exclaimed, feeling vindicated at having cornered him at last. "You are without shame."

Thomas stepped nearer, his long fingers sliding along the line of her jaw. It silenced her celebration immediately. "That, my lady, is false. My biggest shame will always be that you still think this is about seduction when it is not."

Eliza stared up at him, suddenly aware of the sound of her breathing, which seemed to have paused for the moment.

"It's not?" she asked in a small voice.

He shook his head.

"But, anything else doesn't . . . make sense."

"Why?" he asked, his gaze traveling across her features. "Because William doesn't believe me capable?"

She pulled away. "No. Because *I* don't believe you capable."

Spinning around, she resumed her course down the hill. There was really no other choice. Staying would mean watching the hurt kindle to life behind his eyes and feeling the corresponding stab in her own chest. Had he actually forsaken all of his flirtations in the hopes of somehow winning Eliza's hand? Just because it had never happened before didn't mean that it couldn't . . .

Thomas caught up with her swiftly, sliding his hands around her waist and rotating his body in front of her, placing one well-polished boot ahead to stop her progress. "Please, listen—"

"Stop," she snapped, the rate of her pulse increasing. "Landry will be here soon, and I can't marry you."

He sank to one knee before her in the tall grass, and her heart stuttered then stopped altogether.

"Marry me anyway, Eliza. Landry be damned."

Paralyzed, she stared at him. Surely she'd heard him wrong, but the abrupt tilt of the world beneath her feet told her that she'd heard him just fine. There were no words she could say. All she could do was keep shaking her head, lost to the dream of being loved by him even as she gripped his shoulders to push him away.

"Thomas—" she choked. "I don't . . . I can't . . ."

She needed to actually refuse him or this would not end

with the arrival of Sir James. But the word *no* was stubbornly unwilling to leave her mouth.

Taking her hand in his, he brought it to his lips and stood in one fluid motion that was catlike in its grace. He took her breath away, as he always had, and now he was staring down at her—large and looming and enticing—in expectation of an answer she could not give.

"Don't answer this moment," he said, planting small endearing kisses across the back of her hand. "I don't care how much time you need as long as you—"

"No," she whispered at last, cutting him off. "The answer is no."

Evanston stared at her, stricken, for what seemed like forever. Finally, he dropped her hand.

"Why not?" he rasped. "Am I not deserving of even a chance?"

Eliza wanted to respond, but her attempts were futile. She could only shake her head, wordlessly begging him for forgiveness.

The muscle in his jaw jumped as he clenched his teeth, and his wrecked gaze began to shoot angry sparks. "Here I believed I would at least merit an answer. Your father and William have certainly made their wishes known. They feel I am unworthy, and I will certainly not argue with that," Thomas said, his voice cracking with emotion. He leveled a finger at her. "But *you*—"

Without thought, she threw herself into his arms, wrapping herself around his torso fiercely as if the pressure could somehow relieve the hurt she had wrought. His hands raised into the air, almost as if he couldn't bear the thought of touching her, and he stepped backwards to free himself from her grasp.

"Let go of me—" he choked.

Tears rose in her eyes and she squeezed them shut, holding him tighter, her arms locked in a vise-like grip around his rib cage. She couldn't bear it, seeing him like that, and she buried her face in his chest so there was no way she could look. Her own chest felt like it was cracking open. Eliza held on tightly, and she waited.

His struggles weakened, and the livid racing of his heart calmed into a more normal tempo. Soon, she felt his hands slide around to encircle her too and they held each other in silence, knowing when they walked away from here today it would be all over between them. This moment would be nothing more than a memory.

The heat from his body enveloped her and she knew she should leave. But she found herself lingering, eyes closed, her cheek pressed flush against the hard muscle beneath his shirt. Regardless of all the reasons they could never be together, she was disgusted at herself for having been the one to cause him pain. Even with his faults, Thomas had always been a friend to her.

The melodious call of a blackbird sounded across the hill, and it weakened her trance. His grip loosened to coast around her waist. She pulled back just enough to gaze up at him, but his hands held fast.

"We shouldn't—" she began.

He leaned down to brush his lips against her forehead.

Eliza could feel his hands moving now, one sliding up to her neck with the other pressing on her back to pull her closer. "No, we shouldn't."

She gasped eagerly at the feel of him, the world spinning, as it had in her dream, and her eyes fell closed in bliss. She should at least make some kind of effort to break the rousing contact between their bodies, but only found herself seeking more closeness . . . more heat . . . more of him.

He dove down with a hot, openmouthed kiss to sear the fragile skin of her neck, and Eliza cried out, gripping his shoulders to arch against him. The world moved as it had before, only this time it was because he was lowering her to lie in the soft grass beneath them, gazing down at her with a reverence she'd never seen from a man. The demanding pulses of her body didn't care that she'd just rejected his offer of marriage. Her body knew the truth . . . that it would never matter how unsuitable anyone else thought he was, she would always want him with blinding force. But her mind knew better. She used every last bit of willpower to push him away.

"Thomas," she said, her breathing rapid in apprehension. "Please—"

The haze of lust cleared momentarily. "I would never hurt you, Eliza. I know you are not mine to take," he said, his fingertips tracing the edge of her face.

She was certain he did, but still he bent down to kiss her cheek. Then her eyelids . . . the tip of her nose. Her breaths came unsteadily now, the fire kindling to life once more. Eliza instinctively tilted upwards to meet him, only to have him evade her, planting soft kisses along her jawline. Desperately, she sought him again, her hunger sharpening more when his mouth closed over her earlobe, the teeth grazing her flesh.

She frowned in discontent and moaned quietly, eyelids fluttering open. Speaking the words would be a betrayal of everything she'd said today, but dear God, how she longed for him to kiss her. His hands roamed, determined to torture her, and he pulled back to gaze at her in inquiry.

"Do you want me to kiss you?" he asked, skimming one hand lightly over the unbound curve of her breast.

Eliza shook her head and pressed her lips together, unwilling to appear so weak.

There was a hint of a smile as Thomas allowed his fingers to drift across the thin fabric that stretched taut across her nipple. She arched upward in supplication, a tiny noise of pleasure escaping her lips. Slowly, he unfastened the top buttons of her shirt, then eased his hand inside to touch her breast, gently kneading in a way that caused her head to spin. His need was increasingly evident in the strained pattern of his breathing, and his fingers circled the aching tip, then pinched it gently, making her gasp.

"Christ, Eliza. Tell me to kiss you," he demanded huskily. "I need to hear you say it."

Still she resisted the words, so he moved the fabric aside and leaned over her, his gaze locked with hers as his head lowered. She couldn't say what would end up happening if his mouth met her flesh . . . a kiss would be safer . . .

"Kiss me, Thomas," she breathed. "Please—"

He paused, his color heightening in recognition of her

words. Then his head dipped down anyway and his mouth closed over her breast.

Eliza released a strangled cry, then arched off the ground in wanton response, her fingers winding through his thick ebony locks as she pulled him tighter against her. He teased her mercilessly, alternating between wicked flicks of his tongue and a devilish suction that caused her to lift up even higher. Her head lashed the ground from side to side, and she tried to speak, struggling for coherency.

"N—no. Kiss me, please—"

Thomas stopped and levered himself above her, his chest heaving with desire. "Does that not count as a kiss?" he managed.

She stared at him, supposing it did, then tugged him down greedily to seal her mouth against his. There was no pause of surprise. He was ready for her and responded with excited impatience, his mouth teasing and tasting hers in the way she'd dreamed of for weeks.

Evanston's low groan of greedy animalistic desire excited her beyond measure. She let her hands roam free over his body, exploring the hard revelation of his muscles, the planes of his back, the strong angle of his jaw. With a last squeeze he released her breast, sending his hand on a new course down her stomach, across her pelvis, to slide eagerly between her thighs. His long fingers set to stroking that sensitive place through the thin layer of her breeches, and Eliza cried out in surprise, nails digging mercilessly into his arms as pleasure flooded her limbs.

"God, Eliza . . . *yes,*" he growled against her lips, his pace quickening, sending new delightful currents of sensation coursing through her.

It was all too much—the sight of him above her, the feel of his body against hers, the skillful weaving of ecstasy at his hands. The sensations layered on top of one another until she was nearly overwhelmed. She turned her head to the side and gasped.

"Oh, Thomas—"

Take me now.

The gravity of what she was about to do, and with whom, came crashing down with the force of a falling anvil. She was close again, incredibly close, to disregarding everything for the sake of losing herself in his arms. As if it were that easy. As if there were no other considerations, like Rosa, or William . . . her father, and Reginald.

Her head was awhirl. She was living her nightmare.

Mortified, Eliza twisted out from beneath him with a small cry and bolted up to a stand, immediately setting to right her unkempt appearance. He released her, but not before the same anguished look from earlier returned to darken his brilliant blue eyes.

The reality of her situation was an unwelcome burden. One she could not simply escape by pretending Lord Evanston's faults did not exist, no matter how her heart sang when he was near. Landry would be here soon, and as was expected, she would accept him. Caroline would help her stay the course.

"You know I want you," she said in a voice that was not

steady. "Please don't make this more difficult than it already is. We cannot be together."

"I have heard you, Eliza," he choked, standing to face her. "And I apologize . . . this never should have happened. But I—"

Thomas stopped to look away in sudden silence. His fingers flexed open, then curled tightly, and his broad shoulders slumped in defeat. Finally, he trained a curiously empty gaze upon her.

"I understand. I wish you and Sir James . . . every happiness."

Evanston bowed courteously before climbing up onto his horse, and as he rode down the hill towards Lawton Park, she knew she hadn't just succeeded in deterring a suitor.

She had lost her friend.

Chapter Fourteen

In Caroline's opinion, men were often unworthy.

The crumpled sheet of parchment currently seized in her fist was a perfect illustration of why. It was a letter from Lord Braxton, declining Clara's generous invitation to Lawton Park due to his sudden engagement to Miss King of Norfolk. It seemed they had met during the season and participated in what could only be described as a whirlwind romance. Of course, this was apart from his courting of Caroline prior to her departure from London, but she was certain he did not bother himself, or his new fiancée, with the inconvenient details.

The Countess of Ashworth cleared her throat discreetly from where she stood beside her.

"I am sorry to be the one to relate such unpleasant news, Lady Caroline," she said, her eyes soft with sympathy, "but I thought you should be the first to know. I understood from

Eliza that you held a preference for this man during the season."

Caroline swallowed hard, willing the rise of her tears back into submission before answering. "Thank you, my lady. I—" Abruptly, she thrust the letter back into the hands of the countess, her mortification robbing her of words. Abandoned by her parents. Replaced by her suitor. How many possible ways could she be exposed to the *ton* for its mockery? She shook her head. "I'm not surprised, really," she finally finished.

Clara's eyes widened. "Why would you say such a thing? Surely you did nothing to warrant such treatment from a man."

"No, but I did depart from London before the end of the season." Her gaze flitted about the drawing room and she lowered her voice. "My aunt is unwell. She sees things sometimes . . . hears things . . . has trouble remembering." Caroline trailed off, then met Lady Ashworth's eyes once more. "It's something I've worked to conceal these past months."

"My goodness, I'm so sorry," said Clara, seating herself beside Caroline on the settee to give her shoulders a comforting squeeze. "If you don't mind my asking, how did you manage to leave London without attracting unwanted attention?"

Caroline smiled ruefully. "In a most unexpected way. Lord Evanston provided his assistance, per Eliza's request." Seeing how Clara's expression changed, she said, "I know, my lady. I too was surprised with the arrangement, at first. But the viscount was committed to keeping our secret and proved himself to be quite the gentleman. Although," she added reluctantly, "he did impose upon Eliza one condition."

"Which was?" asked the countess, her dark eyes alight with interest.

"He asked she postpone answering any offers of marriage she should receive, before returning to Kent."

Clara leaned back against the cushions, lost in thought. "He was buying himself time," she murmured.

"Yes!" cried Caroline. "I told Eliza the very same thing."

"So you were aware of his feelings for her?"

She nibbled her lip. "I was. Although now I've been questioning the nature of those feelings."

"What do you mean?" asked Clara.

"At the start of the season, I believed Evanston would attempt to seduce Eliza, if for no other reason than his own entertainment. However, after conversing with him in Hampshire, I was led to believe that he might actually—"

"—be in love with her?"

Caroline's mouth snapped shut. She stared at Clara, nonplussed.

"Well, yes."

"Have you been able to speak with Eliza on the matter?"

"She has been unreceptive to talking about the viscount at all since my arrival. Eliza seems almost preternaturally focused on accepting Landry, yet I know she has long nurtured an affection for Evanston. For how long, I am uncertain." Caroline thoughtfully considered the point. "For years, I suppose," she finally concluded.

"I think she may hold great affection for him still, and

very little for Sir James, which poses an obvious problem," replied Clara gloomily.

Caroline's brows furrowed. "What if she is forcing herself to accept Landry when Thomas . . . I can't believe I'm about to say this—"

"When Thomas might actually be the man who suits her most?" laughed Clara. "I think it's possible. Although yes, it is a very unlikely turn of events. But what of Rosa?"

Heat spread over Caroline's cheeks and she cast her gaze guiltily to the ground. She couldn't help but remember the sweetness between Thomas and the little girl as they had danced in the hallway at Lawton Park. She also remembered keeping the truth of it from Eliza.

"Rosa loves him, I've seen it," she confessed. "What's more, he loves her too. I believe he's just inexperienced with expressing his emotions."

"Yes," Clara agreed. "Perhaps, if he'd been better at it, we would not be in this predicament, waiting for Eliza to accept an offer from the wrong man."

Caroline suddenly froze. "But what about the earl?"

The countess nervously ran a fingertip across the gleaming pearl earbob that was dangling from her earlobe. "Yes, things are indeed complicated between my husband and the viscount. I've advised Thomas to speak with him, but given the damaged state of things with Eliza, I'm not sure he'll even bother." She frowned, then nodded decisively. "Landry arrives in two days. You and I will have to help things along."

"How?" she inquired. Caroline desperately wanted to help her friend. Given the disappointing result of her own recent courtship, she would do just about anything to spare Eliza from a similar fate, or worse. She couldn't bear thinking of the smart, vibrant Eliza locking herself into marriage with a man who was all respectability simply for the sake of doing it. A man who would view her as a cold, gleaming trophy rather than the warm-blooded woman she was.

Clara rose to stand, beckoning for Caroline to follow. "It turns out I have helpful friends in many places. Belowstairs being one of them," she answered with a playful smile.

Within minutes, the two ladies were having a clandestine conversation with a few trusted servants, tucked away in the relative privacy of a west wing bedchamber. Caroline could scarcely believe Clara might attempt such a daring operation for the sake of her husband's sister. Then, she reminded herself of the woman's enterprising and dauntless acts performed on her own behalf, which had turned out quite successfully. This scheme would likely be tame when compared to a plot of that magnitude.

"Right," said Clara cursorily. "I understand this is highly unconventional. But please be assured that any action taken at my request, even one that goes against the rules, strictly speaking, shall be absolved. You are protected." She sent a meaningful glance to her faithful lady's maid, Abigail, who nodded taciturnly to her mistress in reply.

"Oh, no," said the head housemaid, Amelia, smacking a hand faintly against her forehead. "What is this about, my lady?"

Clara pointed at her and smiled. "I'm glad you asked. I am entreating your assistance with a most delicate matter.

As you may be aware, Lady Eliza is anticipating a marriage proposal this weekend by one Sir James Landry."

The dark-haired maid, Stella, glanced at Mrs. Humboldt in apprehension. The cook looked intrigued, however, leaning forwards eagerly.

"Yes, my lady. What of it?" she asked.

"Well, I would like to create an opportunity for Eliza to accept an alternative offer."

"Who is it?" Mrs. Humboldt asked, her cheeks growing rosy in scandalized excitement.

Clara paused for a moment. "It is Thomas, Lord Evanston."

A heavy silence pervaded the room before it was cut through by the cook's short bark of laughter. Soon, Mrs. Humboldt was clutching her generous bosom, lost to gasping fits of hilarity. However, at Clara's prolonged and serious evaluation of her, she eventually stifled her mirth to view the countess in shock.

"You're serious?"

"Deadly serious. I'd like to give Eliza one more chance to consider her options before Landry calls on her."

"Oh!" cried the cook, her surprise having transformed into enthusiasm. "I could serve him up a bad bit of potato. That might keep him occupied—"

"I have an idea, my lady," Abigail said suddenly. "It's not terribly complicated but will require accurate timing, for certain."

If Caroline remembered the story correctly, Abigail had been the one to help orchestrate Clara's escape from her fiancé, as well as secure her servant's position at Lawton Park.

She saw Lady Ashworth's mouth curve upward in sly contemplation of her lady's maid.

"Thank you, Abigail. I knew I could count on you."

Guests began arriving on Friday afternoon, with Landry among their numbers.

The house party would have been considered small by most lofty standards, particularly those of the London set. Still, the west wing had been opened and refreshed for the event, and the scale of the gathering felt appropriate for Lawton Park's first house party in nearly five years.

It was a shame Thomas was going to miss it.

In fact, a great many things were a shame. He thought back to the years he'd spent here, even the dark ones following the tragedies that had derailed them all. How he'd wasted his time with Eliza, allowing himself to dismiss her as simply the sister of a friend when she was the only woman with any substance to her at all. Both William and his father had considered Thomas undeserving of Eliza's heart, and to be honest, Evanston agreed. Eliza Cartwick had been through enough, and he understood why she was reluctant to open herself up to more suffering with a man who had shown himself to be unreliable. He understood, even as it tore him apart.

So here he was, at this journey's inevitable conclusion . . . a broken man. Turned inside out by the only woman who mattered enough to affect him in such a way. His priorities had shifted finally, but too late. He hadn't been able to nurture the trust necessary for her to love him, and now she was somewhere downstairs preparing to marry another. Eliza thought him fickle and unsure, when the truth of it was she was the only thing he'd ever been sure of in his life.

La douleur exquise. A French expression he'd thought to be ridiculous and trite at one time, now seemingly the only apt description of this black existence carved out before him. Literally translated as *the exquisite pain,* it described the notion of not merely unreciprocated affection, but the indescribable agony of suffering it at the hands of the one you loved.

Well, he was done with it. His trunks were packed and he was leaving tonight. He was both unwilling and unable to watch as Eliza promised herself to another man. This past week of acting as if things were fine around William had already strained his ability to pretend. He had requested that his carriage and horses be brought round in secrecy, as the situation dictated, although he was never sure how well servants could be trusted to keep a secret. Thomas had no desire to cause controversy, only to slip out discreetly so he could take refuge in London and drink himself into oblivion.

He shrugged on his coat and seized his hat. Downstairs, guests would be in the process of assembling in the drawing room prior to dinner. Men in formal black and white, and ladies in their finest gowns. He wanted to leave before he would be overtly missed—

A quiet knock sounded at his bedchamber door and his gaze locked onto it.

Inwardly, he cursed. Whoever was on the other side of

that portal could easily interfere with his departure, and once he was seen in something other than his dinner attire, word would surely make its way to William and Eliza.

"Who is it?" he snapped.

"It is Amelia, my lord," came the muffled reply.

The housemaid. He sighed in irritation, then crossed to the door and cracked it open an inch.

"What do you want?"

The redheaded girl lowered into a brief curtsy. "Forgive the intrusion, my lord, but Lady Ashworth wishes to speak with you in the library." At his narrowed glance, she added, "Just a quick word before dinner."

He shook his head in bewilderment. "Why? Is she not busy with the guests downstairs?"

"She would like to join them, my lord, just as soon as she's had a moment to speak with you."

Thomas stood there, debating in silence. If Clara had specifically requested an audience with him, it would not do for him to leave without granting it.

He slammed the door shut, muttered an oath, then reopened it again to glare at the startled housemaid.

"After you," he ground out impatiently.

Her eyes scanned his choice of attire, and then she led him briskly down the staircase, deftly avoiding going within eyeshot of the people within the drawing room. Their boisterous conversation and laughter was audible throughout the foyer, and Thomas felt his insides clench tightly in response. Before long, they would all take to celebrating the joyous occasion of Eliza's engagement to Sir James, but he would be gone by then. The moonlight was plentiful tonight, and he would ride that bloody chestnut horse as fast as it could take him away from this place.

Upon their approach, he observed one of Ashworth's other maids, the dark-haired one, exiting the library. She tipped a brief glance in their direction, then scurried off down the hall in the opposite way.

It was curious. However, given Clara's busy schedule this evening, the maid could simply be delivering some news of import regarding a guest or the impending meal. He slid a look over at Amelia, whose no-nonsense demeanor gave nothing away.

They reached the library door and she pulled it open for him, standing aside as he entered. It was only when the door closed tightly behind him that he realized something was definitely amiss. A woman's slight intake of breath from the library's interior confirmed it . . . a woman who was certainly not Lady Ashworth . . .

. . . because it was Eliza, standing near a shelf, looking over her shoulder at him, every bit as shocked as he felt.

She whirled around to face him more fully, the candlelight from the wall sconces catching the sapphire blue of her satin dress and the golden luster of her hair. It went without saying that she was achingly beautiful although increasingly distraught, as they surveyed each other in absolute astonishment.

"I—I'm not certain what has happened," she stammered, "but I was summoned by Stella the maid, to meet with Lady Caroline—"

Her words were drowned out by the amazement of his own realization, one that had come too late.

Dear God, we've been set up.

Privately, he kicked himself for confiding in women he should have known would take it upon themselves to meddle. He forced himself to meet Eliza's wide green eyes.

"I believe Lady Ashworth and Lady Caroline have had a hand in this supposed mix-up. No matter. I'll just be on my way . . ."

"Why are you not dressed for dinner?" she asked, her voice wavering.

He clenched his teeth, gripping his hat hard in a white-knuckled grip.

There's no way to avoid some kind of a scene now, is there?

"As I said," he forced out. "I am leaving. Tonight."

The pained look on her face might have been gratifying under any other circumstance, but in this moment, he couldn't bear it. He pivoted swiftly on his heel and twisted the doorknob, but her softly spoken plea gave him pause.

"Don't go."

Evanston turned back with a stare. "Or what? You won't agree to marry Landry? My faults will somehow become tolerable? Your brother will suddenly step aside to allow our union? Come now, Eliza. This was never going to end well for me, and I, for one, would rather not see just how bad it will be. Now, excuse me." He turned back to the door.

Her skirts rustled loudly as she rushed over to hook her fingers around his arm, her wounded expression only serving to increase his resentment. "Thomas, I—"

"Don't touch me, Eliza," he countered, twitching away from her grasp. "Not now . . . not ever again. I cannot take it." He jerked the door open.

She reached for him once more. "Please, don't leave—"

Thomas spun around, dropping his hat to the floor to take her shoulders in both hands. All logical thought vanished as he walked her backwards into the library, pressed her against the nearest bookshelf, and kissed her for one very last time.

It was a mistake. The sweet taste of her mouth was yet another reminder of what he would never have. Her pleasured cry when his teeth caught at her bottom lip was a plea that would forever go unanswered. Still he pulled her closer, knowing that each passing second with Eliza was a sacrifice to his sanity. A sacrifice he was somehow still willing to make.

Had he been seeking to punish her somehow? *What a fool.* He matched her passion, kiss for glorious kiss, as she punished him instead . . .

The earl's voice came from the open doorway, low and deadly.

"Step away from my sister, you bastard."

Immediately they froze, both of them highly aware of what William had just witnessed. When Thomas released Eliza to turn and face him, the fury that greeted him was anything but a surprise. He raised his hands in surrender.

"William, what you saw . . . was not precisely as it appeared."

The earl's eyes were blazing. "Really? How many ways can it appear, I wonder?"

"No, of course it was how it appeared, but not for the reason—"

His words were cut short when Ashworth took a swing at him. Thomas stepped swiftly to the side and ducked, narrowly dodging the earl's fist.

"No!" yelled Eliza, reaching out to stay her brother's aggression.

The earl shook her off and advanced on Thomas, hands trembling with rage. "Tell me the reason, then," he fumed. "Have you grown tired of your hordes of women? Did the mood just strike you? Or did you do it simply to ruin her chances with a respectable man?"

"It was none of those things," Evanston replied cautiously, his hands still hovering in capitulation. "And I know I haven't been forthright with you . . . regarding my intentions—"

"Oh," said the earl menacingly, taking a step closer. "And what exactly are those?"

"Stop!" cried Eliza, placing herself in between the earl and Thomas. "This was my doing too!"

Evanston swept her to the side with a stern shake of his head. "No. I don't want you to get hurt—"

Predictably, the moment Eliza was out of the way, Ashworth charged forwards at Thomas, grabbing him to slam him against the wall. Evanston had roughly three inches on William's height, but the force of the man's anger contributed to his strength. That, and Thomas was not willing to engage in violence in an attempt to reason with his friend. William had legitimate grievances that were founded on a sordid past, and he'd just walked in on a scene that would surely upset any protective brother.

William's teeth were clenched, his hands wound tightly around the fabric of Evanston's coat. He gave him a shake. "Explain yourself!"

Clara dashed into the room. She stopped abruptly to assess the situation in horror, then came closer to place a comforting arm around Eliza.

"William! He means your sister no harm."

But Ashworth was not able to hear her. Not yet. Thomas weighed his words carefully under the resentful stare of his best friend, soon to be lost forever, he was sure.

"I made a mistake back in London," he admitted hoarsely. "I pursued . . . your sister."

The earl released him with a visible jolt of astonishment, turning to stare wide-eyed at Eliza before his rage came back to settle on Thomas.

"You did *what?*"

Thomas sighed and tried to speak past the claws of regret that were digging into his throat. "I interfered in her London season. I shouldn't have, I know," he said, stepping away from the wall. "Or at the very least, I should have spoken to you of my feelings for your sister first."

"Your feelings?" William asked harshly.

Thomas felt his hands clenching and he fought against the impulse, uncurling his fingers one by one. "Your sister is worthy of great admiration. Is it any wonder she could evoke the sentiment in anyone, even a sinner like me?"

Ashworth glared at him and stood his ground. "I beg your pardon," he spat caustically. "I didn't realize you were given to simply *admiring* my sister, or any woman, for that matter. With your ironclad sense of morality and your weakness for—"

"I've had numerous failings, it's true," Thomas interrupted angrily, his old faults coming back to haunt him one more time. "And Eliza sees them all, believe me. I'm sure you'll be relieved to know that my proposal was not a success." He paused to glance wretchedly in her direction. "She refused me on the spot."

Evanston found himself distracted by the seriousness of her gaze, by the subtle dread with which she surveyed him now. His attention was torn away once more when William shoved him back against the shelves, knocking the meticulously organized books to the floor, which earned Ashworth a sharp rebuke from his wife.

"When did you propose?"

He grunted against the iron pressure of William's arm against his chest. "Earlier this week."

"Trying to beat Landry to it?"

Thomas shifted beneath his friend's tightening hold. "Obviously."

"Then tell me this. If my sister refused you earlier this week, why did I find you accosting her in my library tonight?" Ashworth fumed, his face flushed.

Thomas found his own patience was nearing an end. He'd only wanted to leave, spare himself the misery of seeing Eliza's engagement play out before him like some farcical theater production he couldn't help but watch. Instead, his suffering had somehow become the production, complete with an audience. The women stared at him now in horrified attention.

He shook away William's arm. Drawing himself up to his full height, he glowered darkly at the earl. "I wasn't accosting her, for God's sake, I was saying good-bye."

"Oh, I should have known." William laughed but there was no mirth, the sound rattling indignantly up his throat. "You're probably incapable of bidding farewell without your lips all over some unwilling woman—"

Infuriated at the unfairness of his charge, Thomas stepped closer, trying to swallow his own temper. "Hold your tongue, Ashworth," he growled. "I have never forced myself on a woman."

His words had an immediate effect, as he had known they would.

Evanston had less room to move this time when William lunged at him, driving his shoulder into his chest and knocking him against the wall, where both men slid down to the floor. The earl reared back and struck again, but Thomas still managed to avoid the man's fist, twisting violently beneath him amidst Eliza's and Clara's cries to stop.

"I thought you wanted the truth," Thomas struggled to say, his breathing labored as he grappled with William, rolling across the carpet. His leg inadvertently swung out and kicked a shelf, sending another cascade of leather-bound tomes scattering around them. "But it does not seem to sit well with you."

Thomas used the momentum from a lurching turn to pin William against the floor. He knew it would not hold for long; he had to say what was necessary, and quickly. Leaning over the earl, he lowered his voice to a whisper.

"Yes, I have been refused by your sister. And yes, she even rejected my advances in London." This earned him a foul curse from his friend, but he continued undeterred. "But I returned to Kent after the season, hoping to somehow win her hand at last before Landry could succeed. I only wish I'd have realized sooner . . . had more time to convince her—"

His words trailed off and he let go of Ashworth, whose golden-green eyes were alight with pure venom. Thomas rose up on his haunches, propelling himself to a stand, and turned to regard Eliza. She stood between both Clara and Caroline, who must have joined them at some point during the melee. He held her shimmery gaze and swallowed hard to prevent that same rise of emotion within him.

The earl grabbed Evanston's shoulder from behind, then spun him around to unleash a powerful right hook, sending stars through his vision and rocking his head painfully to the side. The ladies gasped in unison. Eliza rushed forwards to pull her brother away.

"Stop it!" she yelled.

William shrugged her off and stalked towards Thomas, who stumbled backwards in a daze. "I know what I saw . . . what you've told me. What could you possibly say now that would make any kind of difference—"

"I love your sister!" Evanston shouted hoarsely, lashing

out blindly, the words booming forth from some primal place deep within him. He shoved the earl away while holding his dumbfounded gaze as best he could with the blood that was flowing into his eye. "No, I didn't know it, at first. And yes, I went about it all wrong. But I would have followed her anywhere . . . done anything to show her . . ." His throat squeezed shut, but he shook his head and persisted. "Risked any friendship for just a *chance*—"

He heard Eliza from the corner. "Thomas—"

With a sharp turn of his head, he silenced her with a bleak stare. "I know the opinions of your family matter greatly to you when weighing matters of love . . . perhaps even more than love itself." He stepped closer to address her in the sudden hush of the library. "You will have the comfort of knowing your family approved your choice when Sir James has no idea how special you really are. That, try as he might, he will never know the real value of having you and Rosa in his life."

Thomas shut his eyes against the way she blinked at him, how it had sent a lone tear to tumble down her cheek, and turned wearily to face Ashworth. He was tired of this. It was time to receive his judgment.

"We are friends no longer," William said stonily, his finger shooting outward to point at the door. "Get out."

He stood staring at the man he'd called friend since they were both too young to recall. Registered the hostility behind his eyes, and the finality of his words. Bending down at the waist, he snatched his hat up from the carpet, shoved it onto his head, and straightened to utter a humorless laugh.

"So, this is the price of honesty," he said bitterly, glancing around at the solemn gathering for a moment longer. "Well, I'm not sorry."

With that, he turned and strode from the library. But deep inside, he knew how sorry he really was.

Chapter Fifteen

Eliza stared listlessly at the exquisite offering before her, saddened that she had no appetite with which to enjoy the food. Rather, she pushed the delicate slice of pheasant drizzled in mandarin sauce about her plate with the tines of her fork, before laying the silverware down to retrieve her wineglass for a long swallow.

Clara had outdone herself with the dinner party, so it was made all the more unfortunate that she, the earl, Caroline and Eliza could not manage to enjoy it. Candles shone and gleamed from high silver candelabras stationed at intervals along the table, framed by tasteful floral arrangements that perfectly highlighted the fiery colors of autumn. Crystal glasses sparkled elegantly in the light, similarly to their chandelier counterparts, which hung, glittering, above the assembled guests. Polite conversation took place between bites of the course, and while Landry was seated directly across from

Eliza, she had managed to partially conceal herself behind the flower centerpiece on the table in an effort to discourage conversation. Instead, she stared at the place Evanston would have occupied that evening. It had been surreptitiously disguised by the swift removal of his setting and chair before the meal, and the expansion of the seating arrangements on either side.

She felt the stinging rise of tears and reached for her wineglass again. Risking a glance towards her brother at the head of the table, she saw that he too endured the meal in unsmiling determination, attempting to affect interest in the discourse that floated around him. William's eyes darted up to hers for one moment to regard her, his gaze troubled, then returned to the woman beside him, who was prattling on about a recent holiday she had taken in Bath.

Why didn't you tell me he was courting you? I could have put an end to this sooner.

He had asked her this question in the brief moment they'd had in the library before being summoned to dinner, and she wasn't sure her answer had succeeded in convincing him.

I wasn't certain he was truly courting me . . . I don't think he even knew.

But the truth was, she hadn't wanted William to stop him. *I enjoyed the chase*. Had reveled in it, even. How could she possibly confess her shame—not that she might find Evanston attractive, for many women did—but that she longed to accept him. As a friend, as a suitor, and yes, as a husband.

Eliza knew his proposal had been sincere; had felt its honesty before fully believing it. Likewise, she knew the potential for upheaval between the two men had only amplified given the passage of time and the strength of the viscount's pursuit. The more things had grown between her and Thomas, physically and otherwise, the more there had been to conceal from William.

And after years of doubt, she was no longer certain Thomas was stubbornly opposed to being a father to Rosa. In fact, Eliza realized she was altogether unsure how Landry felt about children. For all her concern on the matter, given their staged encounters with one another, it had never been approached in conversation with the man, although she knew he was familiar with her circumstances. The entire *ton* knew everything about her. But in retrospect, she supposed she had assumed the best about Sir James, and the worst about Lord Evanston. Setting her fork aside, Eliza pressed the backs of her fingers against her mouth as a tide of nausea threatened to choke her.

Taking a breath, she peered over the centerpiece to evaluate Landry. He instantly caught her gaze, as if he'd been seeking it throughout the course of the entire dinner, which he probably had, and smiled. Eliza tipped him a hesitant smile in return, then lowered back down and looked to her left, where Caroline and Clara surveyed the scene with melancholy eyes.

At long last, dinner concluded. The women departed for their card games while the men remained where they were, with Matthew and Charles bringing cigars and port. Eliza could not maintain the facade, however, and leaned over to touch Clara's elbow prior to entering the drawing room. Caroline paused beside them in the hallway, her auburn brow creasing in concern, taking a moment to gently close the doors so their conversation would not be overheard.

"Please, may I return home for the evening?" whispered Eliza. "Just to recover enough for a chance to behave better tomorrow? I just—" She broke off, her lip quivering beneath the weight of her somber mood. "I just need some time."

Clara pulled her aside, casting a miserable look at Caroline. "Eliza, I'm so sorry . . ."

"It would have come out eventually," said Eliza with a sniff. "I know I ought to be relieved now that there will be no distractions where Landry is concerned. But the one thing that keeps running through my mind is . . . the look on Evanston's face . . . when . . ." Her breath hitched and she shook her head despondently. "When he said he loved me." She sighed.

Eliza dissolved into quiet tears, and Clara pulled her into her arms, stroking her head and shushing softly.

"I know how much he means to you, Eliza. You care for him greatly, as does he for you."

"He *loved* me. That's what he said." She pulled back to gaze at her friends. "Do you think he was telling the truth?"

Clara stroked her cheek and smiled sadly. "I do."

She looked to Caroline, who nodded solemnly in reply.

"I need to go." She eased away to wipe away her tears and straighten her dress. "If anyone should ask, I will return tomorrow afternoon." Eliza leaned forwards to kiss Clara on the cheek. "Thank you," she whispered, in a less stalwart tone of voice.

She embraced Caroline hurriedly, then rushed away before she could be seen by the other guests. Eliza was desperate to avoid Sir James, knowing his proposal was likely to come soon, and that he would require an answer. As of this moment, she couldn't even bear to think about it.

Clara sat in her chemise, Abigail having assisted in divesting her already, sliding a pin from her hair when William entered the bedchamber. She avoided meeting his gaze as he closed the door heavily behind him, leaned against it and sighed.

"What has been going on?" he asked with no small amount of irritation. "And why do I have the feeling you've known about this for longer than I have?"

She winced at his accusation and at the truth behind it, but rotated in her chair at the vanity to face him.

"I only discovered some of the details upon Eliza's return from London, but I have always suspected Evanston's partiality for your sister. I suspect you have, as well," she added wryly, "since he was not especially skilled at hiding it."

William scoffed and pushed away from the door to strip off his formal dinner jacket. He slung it heedlessly over a chair and seated himself upon the edge of the bed. "It has always been my firm belief that Thomas is partial to every woman he meets, in varying degrees. His interest in Eliza was an annoyance that I discouraged, and I unequivocally instructed her to look elsewhere for love—"

"You instructed Eliza in matters of love? Unequivocally, even?"

Her sardonic tone gave him pause. "Well, yes. Why wouldn't I?" he replied. "I instructed Thomas too. I am the acting patriarch of the family and her older brother, after all."

"Who found *his* love with a housemaid!" she exclaimed in disbelief.

His mouth twisted sheepishly. "You weren't truly a housemaid . . ."

Facing the mirror once more, she removed the final pin from her coiffure to send the heavy sable waves cascading down her back. William's admiration was plainly visible from the reflection in the mirror and she smiled to herself, the familiar ache of her attraction for the earl awakening at the sight.

"You will permit me some skepticism, I hope, given that your choice of wife was so highly unconventional," she stated succinctly, sinking her fingers into her hair to loosen the curls. "As you know, even Clara Mayfield was considered a prohibitive choice in terms of the *ton's* version of respectability. And let us not forget that, technically, Thomas is quite a catch."

She could see William behind her, removing his white waistcoat with a scowl. "I cannot abide the fact that he was pursuing Eliza without my knowledge or permission. In fact, I had actually *told him to stay away.* And let us also not forget that he is a changeable, dishonorable, disreputable rake who seeks pleasure where he can find it most easily," he bit back.

"I know he has been these things in the past," she responded thoughtfully, "but I have neither seen nor heard of it in his interactions with your sister, and certainly not since they have returned to Kent. Honestly, how many women do you think he has proposed to during his time as a reprobate? How many have been the recipient of his professed love? Are these not notable enough occurrences for you to give them due consideration?"

William fumbled for an answer. "I—"

"I would like to point out too that I am not the only one who believes Evanston's love for your sister is genuine," Clara continued. "Lady Caroline is also convinced, and she was not a defender of his before this London season." She rose from her seat and approached him, taking his face in her hands. The barely detectable roughness of his beard growth scratched against her palms, and his eyes fell closed with a sigh. She gazed down at him with brimming affection. "Come now, my darling. You chose a woman who had ruined herself in the eyes of society. Are you really unwilling to grant some latitude to your own sister, who so obviously is in love with Lord Evanston, degenerate that he is?"

William stilled beneath her hands, his eyes snapping open. "What makes you think Eliza loves Thomas?"

"The same thing that prompted her to defer Landry's proposal when they were in London. She longs to please you, and your deceased father, for that matter. But she cannot escape her feelings for a man whom you have both forbidden." Clara shook her head and stroked his cheek tenderly. "What a sad predicament for her. After every sorrow she has suffered, has she not earned the right to make her own choice? It seems as if she already has."

He sat pondering her words with a dawning expression of dread. "If this is all true . . . if he has indeed changed . . ."

"Then you have made a terrible mistake by casting Evanston out. And you have not only insulted your friend, you have injured him as well." She lowered herself beside him on the bed, taking his hand in hers. "As the acting patriarch, and soon to be literal patriarch, of this family, you must remedy this. With both of them."

William nodded. "I will speak to Eliza in the morning—" The earl ceased talking, his eyes widening. "Wait. What do you mean, 'soon to be literal patriarch'?"

Holding his tremulous gaze, she moved his hand to shift it over her belly.

"Why, I suppose it means you will be a father in roughly eight months' time."

He stayed frozen in position, bound by his own incredulity, then suddenly hauled her up and onto his lap with a rough gasp of joy.

"Gentle!" she laughed, a second before he claimed her with an ecstatic kiss. He continued to beset her until her limbs had loosened, and her need had been stoked to a nearly unbearable degree. His hands caressed her through the filmy fabric of her chemise, and he pulled away to gaze at her in adoration.

"Truly?" he asked, unable to prevent himself from leaning in to nip feverishly at her neck.

Clara squirmed in delight. "Truly," she finally managed.

With an unspoken promise between them to rectify things with Eliza and Thomas in the morning, the Earl of

Ashworth and his countess unceremoniously tabled the subject for the remainder of the night.

Eliza sat, gazing despondently through her window at the beauty of the morning. The glow of golden sunlight wove through the trees to illuminate the garden below, and she sighed, her chin sinking further into the palm of her hand. She'd sat in this very spot for most of the night, unable to sleep at the thought of Thomas's tortured confessions, and at the notion of accepting Landry's proposal simply because she felt she must.

A soft *plunk* alerted her to the drop of an errant teardrop onto the sill, and she passed a hand across her face, her gaze never straying from a gray-and-orange robin that kept watch in a tree, carefully seeking its breakfast in the grass. The bird suddenly dove down at a wriggling worm, clamped it with its beak and plucked it neatly from the soil.

A barely discernible knock at her bedchamber door roused her attention from the scene below.

"Come in."

Patterson cracked open the door to hesitantly reveal herself. "My lady?" she inquired, her brown eyes round with concern. "May I speak with you?"

Eliza shifted on her seat by the window to pull her shawl more tightly across her shoulders. A lethargic nod was her only reply.

Her lady's maid entered and shut the door behind her, coming forwards to survey her mistress with a sympathetic mixture of affection and concern. "You wouldn't speak of it last night, but I'd like to know what has upset you so very much. If there is some way I can be of assistance to you."

"That's very kind of you, Patterson, but I'm not sure there's anything to be done." She turned back towards the window. "Landry will propose tonight, and Thomas is gone, perhaps forever. He and William had a . . . disagreement, of sorts."

Patterson's eyes widened. "A disagreement about what, my lady?"

"About me. After William found us embracing in the library."

The maid's jaw dropped, then snapped closed. "Oh . . . I see." She cleared her throat awkwardly and directed her attention to the floor. "Was this the first time such an, ahem, event, has taken place?"

Eliza shook her head, watching as the robin took flight to land in a nearby tree, dropping its prize in the process. The bird sat motionless on a branch as if coming to terms with its loss.

"Do you think he wished to seduce you?"

"He told William he loved me," she responded, closing her eyes.

Patterson came closer to grasp Eliza's cool hand in her warm one. "Do you think he was telling the truth?"

A tear slid out from between her eyelids. She nodded.

"He would have no other reason to say such a thing to my brother. It could only succeed in damaging their relationship. Or ending it, as the case may be."

Her lady's maid sank down onto the bench beside her. "And do you love him, as well?"

Eliza sobbed loudly, unexpectedly, and she clamped her free hand over her mouth. "Landry will be proposing this evening," she whispered, as a way of negating her feelings on the matter. "Do you know, I'm not even certain how he feels about Rosa?" she added bitterly.

"Surely, he knows of your daughter."

"Oh, he knows. But it's only now, in the final hours of my search for a husband, that I realize I'm uncertain what kind of parent he will be." Eliza shook her head in disgust. "Rosa was my primary concern, and I always worried that Thomas lacked stability. Yet, I find myself here, no closer to an answer with the man whom I believed held the solution."

Patterson considered her thoughtfully. "Did you sleep at all last night, my lady?"

The dark circles beneath her eyes were an obvious answer to the maid's query.

"Well, let's get about setting you to rights, in any case. What time are you due at Lawton Park?"

"I was planning to arrive by one o'clock."

Patterson nodded crisply. "That's more than enough time."

After a leisurely soak in a warm bath, Eliza felt more like herself, and a couple hours after their conversation in her room, she was almost fully restored. Rosa came downstairs to join Eliza for a light repast of tea, bread and jam, but not before seating her two dollies at the table. Her daughter's natural exuberance cheered her immediately, and before long the pair of them were making funny faces at each other and snickering into their teacups. The appearance of the butler interrupted their games.

"I beg your pardon, my lady," Roberts said, "but you have a visitor."

Her eyes darted up in surprise. "Really? Who is it?"

"Sir James Landry, my lady. I've already summoned Florence," he said with a bow, glancing surreptitiously at Rosa. "For your convenience."

Once she'd recovered from the shock of her unforeseen guest, and his likely purpose for visiting her, she had an idea. Rising slowly from her seat, she stared down at her daughter, the girl's abundance of golden curls only partially restrained with a green ribbon. It looked suspiciously similar to the ribbon Thomas had affixed to her gift.

"Actually, no," she replied slowly. "I'd like Rosa to stay with me."

Roberts looked as if he'd been physically slapped. "My lady," he breathed in a tone that hinted of impending scandal. "I don't believe your guest would appreciate the intrusion—"

"Well, he had better," Eliza snapped testily. Instantly, she regretted the outburst. "Forgive me, Roberts. Just show him to the drawing room."

The butler departed in haste. Rosa stood to join her, retrieving her dolls from their seats and skipping ahead of Eliza through the hallways to disappear around a corner.

"Rosa!" she called. "Wait for me—"

She heard the audible gasp of a man before rounding the

corner to see Landry himself, standing stock-still in the hallway, faced with her equally motionless daughter.

"Hello," said Rosa shyly.

Landry cast his gaze beyond the tiny girl to seek out Eliza, confusion stamped indelibly across his features. His eyes darted about as if seeking a missing person.

"Greetings, Lady Eliza. Where is this young girl's nursemaid?" he asked, indicating Rosa with a cursory sweep of his hand.

In an effort to give him the benefit of the doubt, Eliza worked to remain calm. She approached to place both hands squarely upon Rosa's shoulders.

"This young girl," she stated, ignoring his question, "is my daughter, Miss Rosa Cartwick." At the lift of the man's eyebrows, she extended her arm to the side. "Shall we proceed to the drawing room?"

He nodded stiffly and followed. Roberts waited near the door with pursed lips, while Patterson stood by silently with a poor attempt at hiding her smile.

Rosa seated herself on the floor by the fireplace. This particular morning, for all its beauty, lacked the warmth of summer as they now gradually ebbed into autumn. The radiating heat from the blaze was a welcome comfort. Eliza and Sir James seated themselves in armchairs, separated by a small round table between. Landry opened his mouth to speak, but was interrupted when Roberts returned briefly to provide tea service, then subsided to close the doors upon his exit. Eliza turned to her guest at last, watching him as he took his teacup in hand.

"This is a surprise, Sir James. I was not anticipating your company again until this afternoon."

Landry seemed to find the soft sounds of Rosa's play behind them to be excessively distracting, but he took a sip of his drink and smiled faintly. "Yes. Well, truth be told, your departure last night, however irregular, provided me with an opportunity for privacy today I would not otherwise have been afforded."

He returned his cup and saucer to the table, folding his hands into position on his lap. Rosa's dolls were having a grand time of things, by the sounds of it, and Eliza watched the ticking of his minute facial expressions with great interest.

"I've come here today . . . that is, if you will permit me, I—" Sir James winced, casting a disapproving look over his shoulder, then leaned closer. "Tell me, though, my lady. Do you, in fact, employ a nursemaid?"

"I do, sir." Eliza felt her face growing hot.

His gaze turned speculative. "And is she not home, at present?"

"She is."

Rosa's enthusiasm grew, and she stood suddenly to race around the couch with both her dolls, although Eliza noticed she was still exceedingly careful with her ceramic one. She finally halted to land extravagantly on the couch, her tiny feet flailing in the air before falling to rest on the carpet. Rosa looked to her mother and grinned with a sigh. Eliza chuckled in reply, then started at the feel of Landry's hand sliding over her own. She turned to evaluate him in dismay.

"I can see the difficulties you must face as a widow, my lady," he said in a low voice. Sir James smiled comfortingly. "Finding good help can be a trying complication of running a household without a man to oversee." To her mortification, he patted her hand and leaned closer. "Rest assured, if you were to accept me as your husband, these irritations would trouble you no longer."

Eliza was rendered speechless by his words. She couldn't help but glance over to her daughter, who was now sitting up quite properly on the couch cushions, paying close attention to their conversation, her dolls forgotten on either side of her.

She knew that Landry had intended no offense. Granted, in typical high-society fashion, children were often stowed away in the nursery with a capable maid, not to be seen except at specific points during the day, and then only briefly. She and William had not been raised that way, nor had Eliza perpetrated that parental method upon Rosa once she'd been born. The little girl was free to express herself in their presence, and Eliza had to admit that Landry's resistance to engaging her daughter in this way posed . . . a significant problem.

She slid her hand out from under his and cleared her throat demurely.

"Am I to consider that an offer of marriage?"

Now Rosa's eyes had grown huge. Her large green orbs studied Eliza closely from the nearby velvet-cushioned couch.

Landry's back straightened and he smoothed a hand over his cravat. He allowed himself a small smile.

"Surely you cannot be surprised, as I have made my intentions known throughout the course of the season," he offered, covering her hand once again. "But, yes. Lady Eliza, I wish to have you for my wife. I can think of nothing that would please me more."

His words grated on her. It was impossible not to notice the differences between Evanston's repeated heartfelt pleas, and Landry's calculated bid for her hand. In fact, mere feet away, Rosa sat observing this interaction, yet might as well have been absent altogether. Sir James paid her no mind, and Eliza knew that, while they could perhaps grow closer over the years, it was more likely that he would continue as he had begun—by viewing her daughter as somewhat of an annoyance.

Three light taps upon her right shoulder brought her out of her troubled thoughts, and she turned to find Rosa standing beside her, her diminutive hands curled tightly around her new china doll. Eliza leaned over to receive her quiet whisper in her ear.

"But Mama, what about Thomas?"

She jerked back in surprise, but Rosa's concerned gaze did not waver. Her uncharacteristic seriousness alerted Eliza to the extent of her anxiety. She was young, to be sure, but she was also highly intuitive. To make this decision without, at the very minimum, consulting with her daughter, would not be giving her the credit she was due. After all, Eliza's next husband would be acting as Rosa's father.

Eliza tipped a meaningful look at Rosa, hoping to silence her for now on the subject. Then, again, slid her hand out from beneath Landry's insistent grasp. She met his eyes.

"I would like some time to consider, please."

Sir James appeared shocked. He opened his mouth to speak multiple times, before finally organizing his thoughts into a stuttering reply.

"I—well, of course. Certainly. But . . . have you not had sufficient time to consider the . . . *possibility* . . . of my proposal already? Am I somehow lacking?"

She rose from her seat and took Rosa's hand in her own. "No, Sir James. You are an admirable man. It's simply that I have not yet properly weighed certain aspects of the situation. As such, I am unable to provide my answer this very moment."

Landry rose from his chair, a pensive expression creasing his brow. "Perhaps I can help alleviate your apprehension by answering whatever questions still trouble you."

Eliza crossed to tug on the bellpull with Rosa in tow, who managed to lunge towards the couch to claim her cloth moppet on the way. "I believe you already have, sir, but I thank you for your understanding." She smiled gently. "I will not prolong the delay . . . you shall have my answer by tonight."

Roberts opened the drawing room doors, leaving Landry little choice but to perform a stunned bow and make his exit. She shut the door, then turned to lean against it, staring down at her daughter.

"Talk to me, little one."

"Are you going to marry him?" Rosa asked.

"I'd been considering it." Eliza paused. "What do you think?"

"I thought you were going to marry Thomas."

She lowered down to one knee to place both hands on Rosa's shoulders. "And why did you think that?"

The little girl's eyes dropped. "So it's not true?"

Eliza sternly checked herself at the excitement that bloomed at the mere thought of marrying Lord Evanston. To hear it suggested by her daughter made the possibility feel all the more real.

"Right now, I haven't agreed to marry anyone."

Rosa's eyes raised, shining with happiness. "Good. You can marry Thomas, then. I don't like that other man."

Eliza chuckled in amusement at the finality with which Rosa declared her opinion. However, she sobered quickly at the remembrance of what had recently passed between her brother and Thomas. Their relationship was severed; all trust between the men was broken. If marrying Evanston had been out of the question before, it wasn't even a recognized possibility now.

The thought of the viscount, alone, after the harsh assessment of his character by a man whom he'd considered to be his friend, caused her vision to blur with tears. Knowing she had added to his misery gave her no end of shame. He could be cursing her name at this very moment.

A soft knock upon the door caused Eliza to stand, and she heaved an irritated sigh. How many unwelcome interruptions could there be in one day? She swiped a sleeve at her eyes.

"Yes?"

Roberts's salt-and-pepper head appeared once more with

a salver balanced neatly in his hand. "A letter from Lawton Park, my lady."

She hoped to find a brief note from Clara but soon her heart sank, for resting upon the tray was a missive addressed to her in a familiar hand.

It was a summons from her brother, William, the Earl of Ashworth.

Thomas stumbled, drunk and bleary, from the rear exit of Putnam's gaming club. He was far too intoxicated to feel his legs, or control them, for that matter. Luckily, there was a woman tucked under each of his arms, laughing loudly as they hauled him into the street, their hands straying greedily across the linen covering his chest.

His eyes fell closed, distantly wishing it were Eliza touching him now and not these cackling pale things who preyed on wealthy drunken lords. There had been a time where he might not have cared whether these women followed him back home. But even in his current state of grief, he found himself solidly under Eliza's spell. He attempted to shrug them off, only managing to stumble across the uneven ground instead.

"Easy there, love!" exclaimed the one on his left. "Don't want ye missing the curb—"

His boot slipped on the grimy edge, and he dropped heavily, grunting as he hit the cobblestone. The women who'd been supporting him had not been very supportive at all, having fallen off to the side to lie in skirted heaps beside him, gasping noiselessly at the hilarity of the situation. He tried to push himself into a respectable seated position.

Who am I trying to fool?

No one, not even his friends, and certainly not Eliza Cartwick, thought of him as respectable. How many times could they say it, and in how many ways, before he finally believed them? Before he relinquished this folly of somehow deserving Eliza's love?

He finally righted himself to a slouching seated position, knees pulled up, arms resting on top of them. Thomas had overindulged as a way of forgetting what had taken place, not to dwell on it sadly, sitting amidst the muck of a London street. How was he to even find his way home? He'd made the trip from here a hundred times, yet he couldn't remember ever having been so compromised by drink.

"Yer in your cups now, m'lord," said the other woman, who was clearly, likewise, in her cups. Her friend hooted in mirth. Their presence was an irritation. He hadn't asked for their company, anyway. He tried to moisten his numb lips with his tongue.

"Leave," he slurred.

The noise of a man's shoes crunching against the grit of the road alerted him to another presence. He did not wish to be seen in his present state, but dimly acknowledged that it could probably not be avoided at this point. Oddly, the women who'd been accompanying him seemed to have vanished, and Thomas cast his blurry gaze upward to survey the newcomer. A bare hand stretched out to meet him.

"Looks like you could use a lift," said a gravelly voice.

Too drunk to care about the man's identity, and whether or not this was a good idea, he reached forwards to accept the offered hand. He was immediately pulled upward into a swaying, standing position. With his left eye swollen over from his skirmish with William, his vision was worse than it might normally be after a hard bout of drinking. He could only make out that the man was wearing a cap.

"Thank you," he said, breathing harshly, certain he stunk of good brandy. Honestly, he was grateful for the assistance. The past few days, in particular, had not been kind to him. "What is your name, sir?"

"That's not especially important," came the reply, the man still gripping his hand like a vise. "But Mrs. Varnham sends her regards."

A sudden sense of alarm flooded through him and he lurched clumsily away, but not before feeling the burning sear of the knife as it slid into his side. Evanston heard his own sharp intake of breath before his knees buckled, and his assailant spoke to him again from what now seemed like another world.

"She only asked that I rough ye up a bit, but I reckon I like to do things my own way."

The man carelessly wiped the bloody blade across his pants, and Thomas, his senses sobered by the pain, listened to his attacker's hasty retreat echoing between the buildings until the ground rushed up at him, the darkness finally pulling him under.

Chapter Sixteen

Matthew escorted Eliza through the hallway, the house curiously devoid of guests at the moment. She glanced cautiously in every direction, not wishing to encounter Sir James prior to her planned meeting with William.

"Where has everyone gone?" she inquired.

Glancing at her politely, the footman responded with a nod. "Lord Ashworth returned early from the shooting party, so the rest of the men are still outside. And since the weather is fine, the countess elected to take the ladies for a turn through the gardens."

He stopped at the polished oak door of the study and rapped quietly. They waited patiently for her brother's answer, but none came. Just as Matthew raised his hand again, the portal swung open before them to reveal the earl, golden hair casually ruffled from his excursion outside, still clad in his tan shooting attire and boots. The footman stepped back, and William's brief smile in his direction prompted a bow and a precipitous retreat. He then focused upon her.

"Please," he said, gesturing openly to the interior of the room. "I'd like to speak with you, if you will allow it."

Eliza's gaze dipped to the floor, her nervousness making it difficult to meet his eyes directly. She gathered her skirts and brushed past him as she entered.

"Indeed, I'd be a fool to come here at your request only to not allow it."

She seated herself in one of the two chairs that stood facing his desk to await him. Her brother let out a soft huff of amusement.

"Fair enough," he stated amicably, closing the door behind them. Rather than sitting in his usual place across the desk, William lowered down into the seat next to hers, rotating to rest his arm across the top of the worn brown leather so he could view her more comfortably. He was silent for a moment.

"Are you in love with Lord Evanston?" he asked suddenly. At her startled, wide-eyed silence, he raised a hand. "No. Let me rephrase that. How long have you been in love with Lord Evanston?"

He knows.

A sort of terrified relief filtered through her limbs at being discovered. Then a jolt wracked her body at the clarity provided by her very own admission, an idea she had never allowed herself to seriously consider. Infatuation had been much easier to discount.

I am in love with Lord Evanston.

Eliza promptly burst into tears.

She dug furiously through her reticule in an effort to find her handkerchief, too busy to observe the emotions traversing the earl's face. Dragging it from the silk purse, she dabbed at her eyes for a few moments and finally raised her gaze to meet his.

"How did you know?" she sniffed.

"Well, if I hadn't, your reaction now certainly would have confirmed it." He shook his head. "Eliza, if only you'd been more open with me—"

Her eyes flared. "Don't patronize me, William. I was more than honest with Father, if you'll recall, and you certainly didn't hold back when it came to voicing your own opinions."

William stiffened, then had the grace to appear ashamed. "I suppose that is true. But I hope you know that our decisions were made with only your best interests at heart."

"I am aware."

"So then you are also aware that the Thomas of five years ago does not appear to be the same man who was with you in London. Nor is he the man who proposed to you earlier this week. In fact, he bears less resemblance, still, to the man who insisted how much he loved and admired you—despite knowing of my prejudices against him." He raised his arm off the back of the chair to lean forwards, resting his elbows upon his knees, eyes locked onto hers. "Father had good reason to warn you away from him when he did."

"And now?" she asked, twisting the handkerchief through her fingers.

Her brother sighed. "Clara has convinced me of the seriousness of his affection for you, plus there was the surprising attestation of your friend, Caroline. What's more, I think he would be a good father to Rosa. I've seen his concern for her on more than one occasion. And I must admit to being swayed by the sincerity of his declaration, even if I still pummeled him for it." William slapped the arm of the chair in exasperation. "But damn it, how am I supposed to know better if you never speak to me of the situation? If *he* never tells me of his desire to change, to become worthy of earning you somehow? The man proposed and never mentioned it to me . . . not even once!"

Eliza shook her head. "It was all very surprising."

"Yes," said William, rising to a stand and extending his hand to her. "I agree with that assessment, and it seems like Evanston may have been more surprised than anyone. For being such a renowned lover, the man is woefully inexperienced in matters of actual love. Which brings me to my next point."

She gripped his hand and allowed him to pull her out of her chair, raising her eyes to his.

"Which is?"

He leaned close to place a soft kiss upon her cheek, then smiled.

"If you are willing, dear sister, then perhaps it's time for you to make a proposal of your own."

To say Eliza was feeling elated might have been overstating things a bit, as there was still a considerable amount of trepidation. She departed the study feeling warmly for her brother, who had come to see things as they truly were, accepted them and bade her go forth to find Evanston.

She wondered how the viscount would react. Would he tell her to go to hell? Or would his defenses crumble in light of her pleas? Eliza was filled with nervous energy, eager to convince Thomas that he should give her another chance . . . just one more chance . . . to prove herself to him. She told herself she would do whatever was necessary, all the while knowing that it could already be too late.

Still, she felt a persistent smile tugging at her lips. Eliza hoped she would be able to suppress it sufficiently to give Landry a proper amount of respect when she refused his proposal. William had given her his blessing, but after all this time, she finally realized she'd never required it. She had needed *her own* permission to love Evanston—flawed, imperfect, glorious man that he was. Now that she had it, the very idea of settling on Sir James caused her stomach to roil unhappily, as did his aristocratic notion of how to parent her daughter.

She could see now how Thomas adored Rosa, the ways he'd allowed his guard to lower, ever so slightly, in her presence; how he'd adored them all until they had cruelly ground him beneath the boot of their family's judgment. The smile that she'd worn a moment before fell unceremoniously from her face.

Eliza glanced anxiously around the empty halls, peering into the vacant rooms, wishing the guests had already returned from their outings. The need to be with Evanston had become nearly overwhelming, but she had a few things to take care of before her departure. An errant drift of female voices echoed through the house, and she hurried towards the front door to greet Clara and Caroline. Their expressions brightened with cautious optimism at her smile, the restraint dropping away altogether when Eliza pulled them in for an exuberant hug. The rest of the group tittered awkwardly behind the trio, unsure of what had provoked such an affectionate scene.

"I'm leaving to find Thomas," she whispered to her friends. "To ask if he will be my husband."

Clara uttered a happy cry, and Caroline's eyes danced with laughter. They squeezed her more tightly into their circle.

"Have you given Landry your answer?" asked Caroline.

Eliza shook her head. "Not yet. I'd been hoping to see him before leaving, but I'd rather not wait for long. Rosa—"

"—will be cared for," interrupted Clara. "I will send my carriage to retrieve both her and her nursemaid."

Eliza's shoulders dropped with relief and she hugged her friends with gratitude.

"Thank you, so much, for everything. I can only assume you two were responsible for my surprise encounter with Thomas in the library?"

Caroline looked appropriately shocked, but Clara was beyond affecting pretense, owning the plot with a sly grin.

"After the way I ruined your ball by being kidnapped, I figured it only fair to provide you with a chance to indulge in a little scandal at my house party."

After one final laughing embrace, Clara called Matthew to request the carriage be brought around. Eliza stood on the steps of the house where she'd been raised, the sunlight warming her skin, ready to make a new beginning—a life of her choosing. A deep breath of fresh air renewed her sense of purpose as the clatter of horse hooves struck loudly against the drive.

"Eliza!" came William's voice from behind. "One moment!"

She turned to face her brother, and he pressed a sealed letter into her hand, the red wax still tacky and warm to the touch.

"Please give this to Evanston, when you see him." A shadow of guilt passed across his features. "Although, I'm not certain he will want to read it."

Eliza ran her fingers thoughtfully over the parchment. "He's ignored my letters in the past too." She smiled. "I'll do my best."

"Knowing now how he feels about you, I doubt your best will even be remotely required." His gaze flicked up over her shoulder, and he nodded at the approaching group of men. "Good timing. Now you can conclude things here, before setting them right with Thomas."

Landry caught her gaze almost immediately, the guarded expression her first clue that he was not necessarily anticipating her acceptance. William trotted down the stairs ahead of her.

"Gentlemen! I trust you would not be averse to joining me for brandy on the back terrace after your morning of sport?"

A collective round of approbations erupted from the group, which he expertly diverted around the side of the house and away from Eliza and Landry, who stood facing each other at the bottom of the steps. He tipped his chin down to survey the gravel beneath his boots and shoved his hands into his pockets. She supposed it was the most casually he had ever addressed her.

"My lady."

Eliza descended two more steps to face him more fully. "Sir James."

"I assume you have considered my offer?"

She wrapped her fingers tightly around her reticule, wishing she were anywhere else at this very moment. "I have, and while any woman would be fortunate to have you, I find I cannot agree to such an arrangement."

He grimaced at her reply, his eyes shifting to the side. "Does Lord Evanston have anything to do with your decision?"

"No," she stated emphatically, a little surprised that he would even mention the viscount. "I am refusing you based solely on my perception of our incompatibility."

"I suspect a proposal will be forthcoming from him, nonetheless," he retorted sharply. "Unless he merely wishes to amuse himself at your expense."

Eliza evaluated him with compassion, knowing her rejection had stung. Still, he was making this considerably easier than it had been at the start.

"With all due respect, Sir James, I don't believe you know him."

I certainly don't believe you know me.

She curtsied in polite farewell. "I wish you the best. Truly."

"Likewise," he said grudgingly with a bow, then stalked past her up the front stairs of the house, apparently not in the mood to join the others for brandy.

The days had become noticeably shorter even with the russet leaves still clinging to the trees, so Eliza did not wish to waste one minute of time. Once she had made a brief stop by the Dower House to inform Rosa of her plans—which had been greeted with such excitement as to leave no doubt she had chosen correctly for her daughter—she'd packed a small trunk and left directly for Hawthorne Manor. In the time between her residence and Evanston's, she'd worked through every potential outcome in her head. Failure, success, outrage, rapture . . . every scenario was experienced thoroughly in her mind's eye to prepare her for any possibility.

So it had come as a shock to find Hawthorne Manor absent its owner. The housekeeper had answered her knock and informed her that Evanston had departed for his London residence, and she was unsure when he would be returning. With a tight smile, she thanked the woman and climbed back into her carriage, weighed down beneath an overwhelming sense of foreboding.

Now she rode through dark of night to seek him in

London, her head resting against the unforgiving lacquered wood of the vehicle's interior to survey the shadows as they sped by. The previous night had been filled with sleepless recollections of Thomas. This night would undoubtedly be occupied by bleak memories of carriage accidents and lost and injured loved ones. Of carriages bent and twisted beyond repair, utterly incapable of protecting their inhabitants.

Since the night of the accident, she'd lost the ability to sleep while traveling, so it was unsurprising that she found no respite now. Eliza's head jostled against the panel and she blinked wearily, attempting to discern the shapes outside. Then she finally tugged the curtains closed with an irritated sigh. She tried to work through the proposal scenarios in her head, as she had earlier in the day, but now there was only one situation that reappeared with stubborn insistence.

It was success. Success, at any cost.

Anything else was just not acceptable. The notion that she had rejected his love, squandered it ungratefully when he had offered it, ruined things between them beyond repair . . . these were ideas that could not be borne. And yet, she feared it was all true. Every last part of it.

Her eyes burned and she closed them. She tried to think of something else . . . *anything* else. Eliza listened closely to the pattern of the hoofbeats upon the hardened dirt road. She tried to distinguish whether the different horses produced beats at different rates. But regardless of how many hoofbeats she counted, she could not escape the anticipation of her failure.

Hours passed, long after she'd reached the point of exhaustion, leaving her slumped against the seat cushions, staring idly into space. The sun rose to hover in the sky, gazing down upon the world with cosmic indifference. At last the roads beneath her changed, and the familiar noisy echo of cobblestone roused her from her wearied stupor. Before long, her driver pulled the carriage to a stop before Evanston's London residence, and Eliza rushed to refasten her falling hair with its pins. She wiped at her eyes, then pinched her cheeks, hoping to revive some of their color.

Her arrival at Evanston's home renewed her sense of steadfast determination. She had allowed herself to wallow during the black vacuum of night, but no more. He was inside this building, so close, and she was going to do whatever it took to win back his heart. Eliza needed him to trust that the love he'd been brave enough to extend to her would never again be slapped away. It would be reciprocated in abundance, and reinforced by the veneration of a little girl who had indisputably chosen him for her father.

Shedding her mantle of defeat, she gathered the tiered layers of her rose muslin skirts and stepped down from her vehicle to ascend the front stairs of his town house. After seizing the brass knocker in her gloved fingertips, she rapped sharply three times, then waited, her heart thundering in her ears. The last time she'd come knocking at his doorstep, he had carried her inside like a bride. The memory of his closeness sent searing trails of fire chasing over her skin.

Burton, the butler, answered the door, as she expected. What she had not expected, however, were the surprising expressions of worry and concern that were so plainly etched on the man's face. He reached forwards abruptly to take her hand, the strict rules of servants' etiquette cast aside in his urgency.

"Lady Eliza, thank God," he exclaimed, pulling her hastily into the dwelling. Eliza found herself acquiescing before having a chance to contemplate the strangeness of it all.

She gazed up at him in increasing alarm. "Burton, what has happened?"

He continued to guide her towards the staircase. "It's Lord Evanston, my lady—" The butler trailed off in the midst of his distress, and it was only when Eliza yanked her hand from his grasp that he blinked and assessed her with anything remotely resembling clarity.

"What's wrong?" she repeated slowly, with forced patience.

"I beg your forgiveness. We have all been rather distraught since the viscount was found outside Putnam's in the street. He'd been attacked—"

Eliza reached out to grip his sleeve, her panic rising. "Is he in his bedchamber?"

The servant nodded mutely and she pushed past him to bolt up the stairs. Unsure of the precise location of his bedchamber, she had already decided to try every door. As it was, she found him on her first try.

Pushing open the heavy oak door, which thudded loudly against the wall, she discovered his chambers in darkened disarray. A housemaid yelped in surprise and dropped the stack of fresh sheets she'd been carrying, nearly knocking over a candle in the process.

"Begging your pardon, my lady—"

Eliza did not care. The only thing she did care about in that moment was seeing Evanston. She had to tell him, *needed* to tell him, how much he meant to her . . . that there was no other man she would marry . . .

The steel-blue curtains on his grand four-post bed had been tied aside. She approached, desperately forcing her eyes to adjust to the dim light and finally discerned his shape, half covered by sheets and head turned away as if sleeping. Her initial reaction was one of surprised admiration, and she swallowed at the sight of his broad chest, the unreliable light playing against the hard contours of his muscles and the appealing dark hair that covered it.

Given the circumstances, it wasn't the appropriate reaction, so she suppressed it quickly and scanned him for injuries. She observed the blackened perimeter of his eye, acquired at the hands of her enraged brother, and a heavy sadness washed through her. But she moved on to the cloth bandage tied tightly against his midsection. The maid stepped closer.

"It's on the far side, my lady, where he was stabbed."

Cool fingers of dread clutched at Eliza's heart and her breathing paused in her throat. She stared numbly at the woman, then returned her attention to Thomas who lay in the bed, still as a marble statue, and just as pale. Leaning across him, she slid her hands gently around his rib cage, her fingertips encountering the edge of a poultice. That was good. Reassuring, even. He had been receiving some sort of care.

He stirred beneath her touch, and she shifted up the bed to slide a hand along the strong column of his neck. His skin was warm. Too warm.

"Thomas, can you hear me?" she asked softly.

His head swiveled slowly at the sound of her voice, eyelids languidly opening to reveal impossibly fever-bright eyes. Evanston recoiled in what appeared to be disgust.

"Get away from me," he growled, before turning his head and falling insensible against the pillow once more.

"It's the laudanum," Dr. Brown reassured her an hour later in the hallway. The physician closed the viscount's door quietly behind him. "Small pupils, rapid heart rate, profuse sweating, hallucinations. I'm quite certain he believed you were somebody else."

Eliza was not as certain. According to Burton, in the past day he had only revived once, and it had been to the sound of her voice. The fact that his reaction had not been agreeable gave her cause for concern on a personal level, but as long as he continued to heal, that would always be the priority, regardless of whether or not he had decided he was finished with her.

Her chest clenched at the thought. She cleared her throat and folded her arms around her waist. "What can I do to help?" she asked. "I will stay for however long it takes." Burton's sigh of relief was audible from his position behind her.

"That will certainly be a boon for his lordship," replied the elderly physician with a nod of approval. "Well, then. His sheets will need changing regularly. The poultice must be refreshed and his wound examined every few hours. I stitched it closed yesterday, but there is a good chance it will fester." The man's faded eyes glanced towards the ceiling, as if marking boxes on a mental checklist. "Do not expose him to night air, but do try to air out the room once a day, at a minimum."

Eliza frowned. "With the factories and the smell of the Thames, isn't daytime air just as dangerous, if not more so?"

The physician shrugged. "I'll admit, London air is not ideal, but you must do your best. In his current state, transporting him to the country would be problematic, and the journey might end him altogether. Try draping a wet sheet over the open window to catch the worst of the pollutants."

She tipped him a nod of uneasy assent. "What of medicines?" she inquired. "Is it necessary for him to be on such a heavy dose of laudanum?"

"At this time, I would like to keep him sedated enough to prevent the reopening of his wound. Lord Evanston was fortunate that the blade missed his internal organs, but I do not wish to impede healing by allowing him to thrash about." The man began to shuffle his way towards the staircase, black leather satchel in hand. "I have left you a plentiful quantity of herbs for the poultices. Only be certain to apply it over a layer of lard or oil to prevent adhesion to the wound."

Eliza followed the snowy-haired man down to the foyer. "And if the wound should fester?" she asked worriedly.

Dr. Brown donned his black hat, then turned to regard her seriously. "Let us hope it does not. Leeches, though, if it does."

An icy chill tripped up her spine. She thanked the man,

and Burton closed the door behind him. Then she glanced sadly at Thomas before burying her face in her hands. Hot tears blazed against her palms, and the butler stepped closer to clasp her shoulders. Wearily, Eliza dropped her hands to stare up at him.

"I know not what occurred between Lord Evanston and yourself this past week. What I do know is that you are here now, ready to help him." He shook his head, glints of gray hair amongst the black catching the last light of dusk that fought its way through the windows. "This could have happened to Lord Evanston on any number of days, any number of ways, and for no reason at all. I've watched him for years, and I'm only shocked it wasn't sooner."

Eliza sighed hopelessly. "He doesn't even want me near him. How am I supposed to help when he does nothing but snarl at my presence?"

"By insisting upon it, my lady. Frankly, at this point in time, he simply doesn't have a choice." Burton slid her a confident gaze. "And I can assure you, he most certainly wants you near him. Right now, you are the thing he needs most—" he paused, remembering his position, "—in my own humble opinion."

She stared at him, registering both his sincerity and kindness. Eliza pulled away, wiped at her eyes, then smiled sadly.

"Thank you, Burton."

Burton's eyes crinkled with warmth only a moment before bending forwards into a polite bow. "I am at your service, my lady."

Eliza nodded succinctly. "Then let's get to it."

Thomas drifted in and out of an uneasy sleep that did not really seem like sleep at all. The black abyss that had engulfed him on that stinking London street had only grown stronger, the current tugging him down whenever he flailed nearer to the surface. It was frustrating, but at least it was painless in these cool depths. For that, he was thankful. The blazing agony in his side had abated, for the time being.

A quiet cadence of voices drifted around him, receded, came again. None of it mattered. He was content to drift in the void.

"Thomas. Can you hear me?"

The current tugged him upward. It was Eliza, and yet, it couldn't be. He had felt the weight of her gaze on his back as he'd strode from the library on that fateful day, whenever it had been. Time had very little meaning in this place—he couldn't remember if it had been two days ago or two years ago. It didn't matter.

Still, he swam towards the voice. He couldn't resist, he knew that by now. Any chance to glimpse her again, to touch her, to hear her laugh. Wrestling through the dark, it took every ounce of fortitude he possessed to pry open his eyelids and turn his head.

Victoria Varnham reclined lazily beside him on the bed.

Mrs. Varnham sends her regards.

Her ebony curls coiled around her shoulders like the hissing snakes of Medusa. In her hand, she held a knife, the silver blade flashing in the gloom.

"Get away from me," he ground out in horror.

The bleak waves overtook him, and he gratefully sank down into their lightless protection once more.

Hours passed. Perhaps days? Years? There was no way to be sure, but the voices returned often. Sometimes, he was aware of a bitter trickle of liquid streaming down his throat, which drove away the voices and everything else for a short while.

It was lonely here in the abyss, but it was safe. He surrendered to its pull, to its absence of everything.

"Surely we can ease off on the laudanum now? See how he does?"

She was here again. His dream-Eliza. Had she ever left? Was she even here to begin with? Thomas struggled upward again, could feel his eyes rolling uselessly in his head.

"—Liza," he muttered. He thought he felt his right hand flop to the side.

Soft hands graced either side of his face, their cool slide prompting the stubborn current to guide him upward.

"Darling. I am here."

Anger bloomed in his chest, and he turned his face away to slide back down deep. This could not be her. His Eliza did not love him—she had let him leave. She had broken his heart. This dream-Eliza was a pretender. Where she truly was, he didn't know, but it was not here. Thomas would not submit to this siren's call . . . he'd had enough of crashing upon the rocks. He would pay the pretender no mind.

The abyss became stifling, his swirling black sanctuary transforming into a muggy pit of discomfort. Thomas lashed out against it, but the searing pain in his side had returned.

Slowly, at first, then swiftly, strongly. The depths grew warmer. Hotter. They were not the cool respite he'd found them to be earlier. He heard a man cry out hollowly in the silence, then realized from afar that the man could have been him.

"No, Thomas. Be calm." The light stroke of a woman's hand passed over his head, and he couldn't help but turn his face to the caress.

She sounded like Eliza . . . she even smelled like her.

Now that he hovered closer to the surface, this all seemed rather humorous. Unable to win her in life, now to be tormented by her in death, or in whatever hellish purgatory this was. He could have her voice, her touch, but never her. Never her.

He wanted to scream with either laughter or tears. Either would suffice, but he could do nothing. He could hardly even breathe with this molten vise around his ribs. If only it would . . . just . . . let up . . . so he could take a breath . . .

Eliza watched over him, observing in terror as Thomas's relative restful ease changed into a state of pained agitation. She rose hurriedly, tugged on the bellpull, then crossed to the door and threw it open.

"Burton, call for the doctor," she yelled into the hallway, abhorring the panic in her voice. "Something is wrong!"

She detected reciprocal anxiety in the butler's shouted reply. "Yes, my lady!"

Returning to Evanston's side, she leaned over the edge of

the bed to clasp his fingers tightly with her own. She couldn't bear to look at him, but listening to his rapid breathing was almost just as difficult. The minutes passed by, and finally Burton came upstairs to join her, his heavy tread marking the butler's rushed journey up the staircase and final entry into the bedchamber. He stared at his master, wide-eyed, then focused on Eliza.

"Help me turn him," she instructed, "so we can check on his wound."

The viscount was a large man, and her lack of sleep and the direness of the situation rendered her hands clumsier than usual. It took all of Eliza's strength and most of Burton's to sufficiently move him so the bandages could be navigated, and the poultice peeled back. Evanston cried out at the rough handling, and briefly she reached over to stroke his head. Eliza could not bear to see him suffering.

At last, the wound was revealed. She stared at it in disbelief, her eyes raising to meet Burton's, his gaze no less haunted than her own.

The laceration had festered.

"But . . . how?" she asked in shock. "We changed it every three hours. We took such care . . ."

The quiet *thunk* of Dr. Brown's satchel in the doorway diverted her desperate musings.

"I am sorry, my lady, but caring for the ill can be a paradox," said the physician, adjusting his spectacles upon the bridge of his nose to view her with empathy. "Even when everything is right, it can still all go terribly wrong."

Chapter Seventeen

Eliza sat, a surreal sense of dread overtaking her, viewing the doctor's examination from a chair in the corner of the room. It was ridiculous, but part of her almost believed she had brought this on or earned it somehow. She had allowed herself to hope after those first days had passed. His wound had been healing well, and he'd been handling the effects of the laudanum as best as could be expected.

Now, however, Thomas writhed restlessly among the bedclothes, muttering incoherencies, lost in the grip of the fever that was consuming him. While it was true that infections could, and often were, overcome during the course of the healing process, she found herself fearing the worst: that she had raced to London to stand helplessly by, while the man she loved died in his own darkened bedchamber.

Since a few days had passed, she had finally thought to write to Clara and William, advising them of the situation and providing an explanation for her sudden lack of communication. Likewise, she had sent a missive to Lady Evanston, Thomas's mother, although she was unsure whether to expect any reply from that woman at all.

Since she had not truly slept in days, her only reprieve was found in stolen moments of drowsing in her cushioned armchair, or slumped over the edge of the bed near Thomas. Burton had cared for her as best he was able, pulling her out of the room periodically for a sip of tea or a bite of toast. She submitted to the butler's pleas because she knew she must. While she was not hungry in the slightest, it would do no good for her to fall ill at Evanston's bedside.

Eliza was, oddly, too exhausted to cry, although her spirit grieved unflaggingly at the sight of his agony. It was a feeling she had not experienced since the massive loss of life her family had been dealt just two years before. Back then, it had been too late for most of them. There had been no prayers for help or mercy for the dead; those entreaties had already been denied. But she had kept vigil at William's bedside until he had awoken from his injuries, much as she was doing now for Thomas. Eliza had nearly sworn off her God in those dark times. But now, here in this room, she found her prayers again.

Please . . . just give me a chance to love this man.

Her heart sank at the thought that she had already shunned her chances many times over.

The doctor finished his inspection, then tugged the sheets back up to Evanston's chest. Proceeding to Eliza's location in the corner to address her, the old man sighed wearily.

"I'd like to check back on him in a day's time. If he worsens considerably, I think leeches, or even bloodletting, are viable options for treatment." At Eliza's despondent expression, he added in a low voice, "The viscount is a strong man. There is every reason to believe that he will overcome this infection. That said, I can make no guarantee."

She nodded numbly. "I understand."

Eliza would never allow him to bleed Thomas. It was how her mother had died, with an overly copious bloodletting following an afterbirth infection. The physician had insisted it was the infection that ended up taking her, though her family knew better. That practice would never be repeated. Not while she had anything to do with it.

Dr. Brown withdrew four jars and one glass bottle from his leather satchel, then turned to hand them to Burton, who stood nearby.

"Here is a renewed supply of laudanum, herbs for the poultice and fever-mixture. You are to administer two tablespoonfuls of the mixture, three times a day as the fever persists. If you have not been applying laudanum to the poultice as well, I suggest you start. This will help alleviate some of his pain."

Her eyes flicked over to catch Burton's gaze. Privately, she believed they both worried about the overuse of such a potent drug.

"He has been out of his wits on laudanum thus far. Is there not an increased risk in using both the oral and the topical administration?" she asked, unable to help herself.

The doctor appeared mildly offended. "Certainly, there

can be increased risk," he answered gruffly. "There is also an increased risk once a patient is infected. We treat them as we must."

"I understand," she said, hoping her annoyance was sufficiently disguised. She rose from her seat. "We will send word if anything changes. Thank you for your assistance."

Dr. Brown closed his satchel with a snap and bowed. "My lady."

Once the door had closed on the physician, she released the sigh she had been holding. She crossed over to Evanston's bed to sit beside him, sliding her fingers across his hand, now clenched in his discomfort.

"My lady," murmured the butler. "You should get some rest yourself. I'd venture to say you have not slept in days. I will watch over his lordship until your return."

Eliza shook her head, gripping Thomas's hand tighter. "No, Burton, I'm not leaving him. But if you could help with his medicine before you leave, I would appreciate it."

Between the two of them, they managed to coerce the semiconscious viscount into taking his medicines, even forcing a bit of water down his throat for good measure. A fresh poultice was applied to his wound, then secured with Burton holding Evanston upright while Eliza wrapped the cloth bandage around his ribs. He did not struggle against them, as he had done previously, but hung limp against his butler, pale and waxen with flags of red upon his cheeks.

The hours passed, and evening came. Eliza snapped awake with a jerk, realizing her exhaustion had overtaken her at some point. She lifted her head off the bed to survey

Evanston's face, noting that his breathing had become rapid and shallow. He squirmed and groaned in misery on the mattress. Gingerly, afraid of what she would find, Eliza laid her palm against his forehead. The skin there scorched her . . . he was so much hotter than he had been before. He was burning up.

"No—"

She lunged for the bellpull, and Burton appeared within moments. Likely noting her expression of panic, he stood silently with large eyes.

"We need cool water in a bowl. A-and a sponge."

The butler nodded tersely and left the room while she returned to Thomas. Until this point, she had been almost afraid to speak overmuch in his presence. She'd worried that, rather than finding her voice soothing, it would only serve to upset him further given the awful nature of their last meeting. His angry reaction to her on the first day had only reinforced this notion. Now though, she worried that he would succumb to his injuries, never having heard her near him. Never knowing how much she truly cared.

"Thomas," she said forcefully, running her hand along the curve of his cheek, roughened with dark stubble. "This is Eliza. Can you hear me?"

Her words prompted a reaction although his eyes remained tightly shut, his breath hitching for a moment before he squinted, as if in pain. Remorse flooded through her at the distressed response, but she persevered anyway.

"You are in London, and you are ill. You were hurt."

His face twisted into a grimace, his dark brow pulling down. ". . . Sends her regards . . ." he muttered through chapped lips.

Eliza wasn't certain what to make of his words. The butler appeared with the requested items, setting them down on the table next to the bed. With a word of thanks, she retrieved the sponge and squeezed it partially out over the ceramic bowl. The rest she squeezed over Evanston's dark hair, eliciting a sigh and a shiver from him.

"I am here, my love," she said, her throat constricting in despair. She hitched her hip upward to seat herself next to him on the mattress. "I will stay as long as you need." Eliza moved the sponge in a cool swipe against his forehead, then leaned over to rest her head against his. "Forever, if you'll let me," she whispered.

Raising her head, she stifled her sadness. She would not cave in now, not when he needed her so badly. She dipped a fingertip into the bowl and brought a hovering drop of water to his lips to quench the skin. He did not respond, having fallen unconscious once more.

Burton approached with the viscount's next dose of medication, which they both worked to administer.

"Would you like to air out the room now, my lady?"

Eliza shook her head. "No, I prefer to do it in the early morning hours, after the air has had a chance to settle." She leaned back in her chair. "Let us change the bedclothes, though. I think a set of clean linens would do him some good."

Calling upon the other servants to assist, the group managed to maneuver Thomas's large frame while stripping the mattress to replace the sheets. Evanston shivered and groaned but looked relatively peaceful once the operation had been completed.

They passed through the dark of night much as they had entered it, with her caring for him while his fever persisted. He suffered mightily, but he did not sweat, and she knew he would not until his fever finally broke. If it ever did.

She continuously sponged cool water over him, allowing her hands to comfort him, letting them roam across his head, his shoulders, his chest. Had circumstances been otherwise, she would have thrilled with the act, but now she only sought to make a connection with him. To make sure he felt her presence and knew she would be waiting for him when he awoke.

Eliza told him stories, she sang to him, she even regaled him with tales of his own audacity. She confided that, although his antics during the London season had enraged her at the time, they had also secretly pleased her. His shows of attention—each stolen glance, every verbal sparring match—had meant the world to her, and she had cherished every moment they had been able to share together despite her best attempts at pretending otherwise.

Retrieving the letter from her reticule to place it nearby on the bedside table, she told Thomas that when he was feeling better, he could read the contents. She told him of her meeting with William, and how her brother had seen the error of his judgments. Eliza spoke of how the earl had urged her swiftly away from Lawton Park to seek out the viscount in the hopes of winning him back.

Finally, Eliza declared that he had been chosen by Rosa herself. She relayed how, in no uncertain terms, her daughter had made it clear that Thomas had been the only real candidate. With a quivering voice, she told him that both she and her little girl would be honored to build a family with him.

And should he not desire such an arrangement after all she'd put him through? That was understandable. She just wanted him to come back.

The first gray light of dawn broke weakly through the curtains. Evanston mumbled beneath his breath, nothing she could reasonably discern, then reached out to wrap a mound of sheets around his fist. Eliza eyed him worriedly, then crossed to the curtains and drew them aside to fling open the casements. A reviving breeze, cool and brisk, flowed through the opening. She wanted to refresh the room before settling in for the day's sickroom routine.

Energy-drained and filled with melancholy, she leaned against the window to view Evanston's immaculate garden. Gardens in town were generally small due to their space limitations, and this one was no different. Yet its layout gave the illusion of something more. Larger than what could be perceived with the eye. Distantly, in some alternate version of this reality, she could envision Rosa dancing amidst the carefully potted ferns and azaleas. Eliza and Thomas would be following behind her, with hands entwined—

"Reginald . . . she's screaming."

The blood turned to ice water in her veins. The low voice had been so faint, the statement so weakly delivered, she was uncertain whether it had even happened at all. Her eyes flicked over to find the viscount, lying prone upon the bed. Motionless. It was unusual given the agitation he'd exhibited throughout the night.

She searched the shadowed corners of the room in a frantic bid to ascertain whether someone had crept in while she'd been distracted at the window. Finding nothing, she came closer to the bed, spooked. Evanston's lips were indeed moving, with small whispers slipping out. Afraid of what she might hear, she leaned towards him anyway. His eyes moved incessantly beneath their lids, and he grimaced and clenched his teeth.

"Help her, she's screaming."

This could be an effect of the fever, some delirious scene his mind had conjured, simply because the conditions allowed it. Something told her, though, that there was an element of truth to this hallucination. A truth she dreaded to hear, but needed to know.

"Thomas," she said, reaching out to stroke his pale cheek. "No one is screaming. All is well—"

He wrenched violently away from her touch. His features drew down into a scowl.

"She can't be left in there with just a midwife."

Eliza froze. Then she jerked suddenly backwards, eyes round at the realization of what he was saying. Thomas's voice was feeble as he continued, but still somehow full of angry determination.

"You go in with her, or I will."

Men were absolutely not allowed in the birthing room. It simply wasn't done, not even with husbands. Yet, Reginald had joined her at some point during her difficult and lengthy labor. His presence had been a comfort she hadn't known she could request.

A remembrance of something William had told her long ago surfaced in her mind. How Lord Evanston had been found on the staircase the morning following Rosa's birth, passed out with drink. Mrs. Malone had thought badly of him for it. But now, Eliza struggled to comprehend the truth.

What if the sounds of her suffering had driven him past his capacity to bear?

Could he have loved her, even then . . . perhaps before he knew it himself?

My God . . .

She launched herself onto the bed, gripping his colorless face tightly between shaking hands.

"Thomas, I'm here!" she said, her words dissolving into barely intelligible sobs. "I am here! You're not alone!"

Wrapping her arms around his chest, she buried her face against the fever-warmth of his neck. She kissed him. Then she kissed him again, up the length of his jaw, along the hot scrape of his cheek, across the dry surface of his lips, which were still silently moving in his pleas to her dead husband, locked in the retelling of a tale now four years past.

"*Not alone*," he repeated thinly, his breathing swift and furious.

Eliza kissed the bruised skin around his eye and he sighed. She soothed him with gentle caresses. Gradually, he became calmer until at last he fell silent. Reaching backwards to the table, she found the sponge in its bowl, squeezed it, then brought it across to dampen his warm brow.

"I love you, Thomas," she whispered, pausing to wipe her sleeve across her streaming eyes. "Do you hear me? *I love you.* You will wake up soon." She nodded, more to herself, she supposed, than anyone else. "You will wake up."

For his sake, she took care to sound surer than she felt.

A gentle hand on her shoulder roused Eliza from an onslaught of fitful dreams. As she always did now upon discovering she had fallen asleep, she bolted upright to find Burton standing above her. Her mortification at being discovered lying in bed alongside Thomas was eclipsed by the excited expression on the butler's face. His finger was pressed against his lips, which he then turned to point at Lord Evanston.

Eagerly, she turned to see that his normal color had revived. His cheeks were flooded with healthy color, and his breathing had returned to normal, with none of the feverish panting that had served to tire him earlier. He was also drenched with sweat. For that matter, so was she, having been sleeping so closely to him.

Eliza yelped with delight, and nearly fell out of the bed in her haste to pull Burton in for an unconventional but much needed celebratory embrace. Quickly returning to the task at hand, the pair rang for more assistance, then set to work changing Thomas's poultice, administering his medicine and stripping the bed in exchange for fresh linens. A large bowl full of soapy hot water was brought in. Burton treated his still as yet unconscious master to a refreshing sponge bath. She excused herself at this point, suddenly feeling like an intruder. As pleased as she was about Evanston's recovery, the likelihood of his waking at any moment had increased her anxiety in other ways.

So she busied herself, filling the next few days ensuring the viscount's household would be in proper working order and ready for him when he was again able to conduct his own affairs. She and Burton delegated tasks to available servants, Eliza ran errands of her own and Burton fell into a routine of caring for his master, now without her assistance. There were times when their paths crossed in the hallway or the foyer, when she could detect a curious sideways glance from the butler. But she was sure to keep her own gaze straight ahead, pretending that her abrupt shift in behavior was simply a normal adjustment to the change in circumstances and not her avoiding Thomas out of fear.

Often, she would stop by Thomas's door, wary and unsure. Eliza would touch the cool metal of the doorknob, wishing that she had the courage to face him. But her mind would make its excuses, and after all, it would be a shame for her to disturb him in the midst of his healing repose. Each time her fingers would drop heavily away, and she would hurry down the stairs into the library, either to distract herself with a book or to write additional letters updating their loved ones on the current status of the situation.

One evening, there was a soft rap on Evanston's front door. Surprised, Eliza glanced up from her correspondence and waited to see if there was a servant nearby to answer. She knew Burton was likely busy upstairs with the viscount, as she had removed herself from that situation. Now the least she could do was open the front door to greet whoever was knocking.

She set the missive aside and rose from her armchair to walk swiftly out of the drawing room. Eliza threw open the front door to find, not a relation or acquaintance waiting upon the doorstep, but a rather scruffy-looking boy. He was small in stature, not altogether clean, and gazed up at her with uncertainty in his large blue eyes, a black smudge of soot marking his pale cheek.

"Beggin' your pardon ma'am, but is the master of the house in?"

She regarded him in shock. A rush of cool evening air swirled around them both, smelling faintly of coal smoke and the Thames.

"Viscount Evanston is unavailable to visitors for the time being. May I help you instead?"

He shuffled his feet in their worn and ill-fitting brown shoes, hands plunging deep into his pockets. "No, ma'am. Only I was sent to ask after his condition by a lady, and wouldn't want to return empty-handed, if I could help it."

Something wretched clutched at her heart, and she looked upon him with newfound seriousness. "Who is this lady, may I ask?"

"You can ask for sure, ma'am, but I don't even know. She didn't tell me nuffin' other than to find out about the master who lives here." He blinked at her earnestly.

"I see. Well, Lord Evanston is indisposed," she replied grimly. Sliding her hand into the pocket of her skirt, she retrieved a small purse. Eliza removed a crown from the interior and placed the coin into his hand. He stared down at it with wide eyes, then glanced back up at her mutely. She reached out to curl his fingers closed over the gleaming silver currency.

"But—but what's this for, ma'am?"

She smiled. "That is to thank you for your visit. Now you'd best be off to report back to your mistress."

He nodded and attempted a bow, still too flummoxed by her payment to fully observe etiquette, before dashing off into the shadows. Quickly, she retrieved her cloak and slid it around her shoulders, pulling the hood over her head before also entering the darkened streets. Eliza was intent on following the urchin to discover the identity of the woman who had sent him here. She had formulated a guess already, and if proven correct, knew this would not be their first meeting with one another.

Sweeping into the night, she pursued the visitor across the uneven cobblestone streets, being careful to stay concealed. When he ducked into a nearby alleyway, she pressed against the closest building and slowed her pace, inching along and straining to hear any semblance of conversation. After a few moments, her efforts were rewarded.

"That's it?" a woman's voice seethed in displeasure. "I wanted to know how the man fares, not simply that he is *indisposed*."

"I'm sorry, me lady," came the tremulous voice of the lad, "but she offered no other information."

The woman issued an unladylike growl. "Well, that tells me nothing, boy. Begone."

Eliza heard the boy scamper off down the alleyway, then

stepped forwards into view, enjoying the expression of astonishment that overcame Mrs. Varnham's attractive features, partially concealed by her own cloak.

"You should have paid the viscount the courtesy of asking yourself," she said quietly. "I wouldn't have turned away a well-wisher. Not even you."

The woman forced her face into an attitude of concern that did not seem altogether natural. "Is it true? I have . . . heard . . . that Lord Evanston was attacked by a criminal. I only wish to know whether or not—"

"—he will live?" finished Eliza. "Do you truly care? And if so, why send an errand boy to inquire on your behalf? You've never been shy about confrontation before."

A shadow of guilt passed over her face. She glanced to the side and chewed on her lip, which got Eliza to thinking. Frantically she searched her memories, grasping at the words Thomas had uttered in the midst of his fevered state.

. . . sends her regards . . .

Her eyes widened.

"You did it!" she cried. "You sent a man after Evanston!"

The woman flinched at Eliza's accusation, still unable to meet her gaze. Her shifty discomfort confirmed her role in the whole affair.

"Now that is jumping to conclusions—"

"Why?" Eliza's gaze narrowed dangerously.

Heaving a sigh, Mrs. Varnham finally raised her eyes to meet Eliza's. "He'd moved on," she rasped. "I never thought he would. You must believe me . . . the man wasn't supposed to have a knife."

Eliza turned to ice. Gooseflesh erupted across every inch of her skin and her fingers clenched into hardened fists. "But he was supposed to hurt him." She saw the large satchel resting on the ground next to Mrs. Varnham's skirts. "And it appears you are ready to leave town? A wise choice. You should do that before I am able to summon the magistrate. I think you should leave and never come back," she said coldly.

Needing no additional motivation, Evanston's former mistress only nodded and grasped the handle of her bag. Eliza watched as the woman hurried away, the sound of her departing footsteps echoing within the alley until finally fading into nothingness.

Nearly five days later, Eliza found most of the household business had been addressed and all the required communications had been sent. Taking advantage of the opportunity, she slipped out discreetly for a warm bath in Evanston's slipper tub. She submerged her tresses beneath the water, then sank until her face gazed upward through the shimmering lens of the liquid, wishing she could wash away her cares. She knew she must brace herself for the possibility that even after all they had been through together, and after caring for him at his bedside, Thomas might have already closed his heart to her.

Sputtering for breath, she emerged from the depths of the tub to grasp distractedly for her towel. There was nothing to be done, save for convincing him of her sincerity and, failing that . . . returning home alone. Her mood was subdued at the idea. She dried herself and donned a loose muslin dress in dismal contemplation, pinning her thick golden hair into a messy chignon. Patterson would have been horrified by the lazy attempt, but Eliza was too sullen to care.

Later that evening, the declining autumn sunlight sparkled at her from the edge of the crystal brandy decanter on the sideboard in the library. The doctor had come and gone yet again. Eliza had inquired with the maids regarding Thomas's welfare, then returned to her refuge downstairs. She had long since finished her day's letters and sent them off with the post, but still she sat alone in the empty library. Her aversion to facing the viscount was not necessarily a reasonable reaction, but she was feeling it, nonetheless. If the two of them never spoke, he could never reject her, as she had done to him before. She sought to preserve the distance that prevented such a thing from happening.

The echo of Burton's footsteps in the foyer alerted her to his presence mere seconds before he entered the library after a brief, perfunctory knock.

"Lord Evanston is awake, my lady. He has been awake and sitting up for the past four days."

She flashed a smile. "That's lovely, Burton. The doctor has told me." Her glance dropped to her hands. "How does he feel?"

"A bit tired perhaps . . . restless . . . Dr. Brown says he has the fortitude of an ox." The butler frowned as he viewed her askance. "Honestly, my lady, you would already know, were you to see him yourself."

"Yes, of course," she admitted, wincing at his subtle censure. "I plan on it, just as soon as I—"

"How about now?" he offered a little too pleasantly, taking a step back and gesturing towards the doorway.

At her hesitation, Burton paused, closed the library door, then approached her with a kindly expression.

"He loves you," stated the man in a hushed tone, "but you lose your nerve *after* he's declared himself? That is something I do not understand."

"No," she responded hotly, "you don't. You haven't seen how I've rejected him. How he's been hurt by both me and my family—"

"You're wrong," Burton interrupted. "I have seen him. I've seen him after your spurnings and rejections." He leaned closer. "And what I've also seen, for the first time since I've known him, is that he persisted . . . regardless of his mounting failures, because of that love you would not give him credit for."

I love your sister! he had shouted at William. *I would have followed her anywhere . . . done anything to show her . . . risked any friendship for just a chance . . .*

She hung her head in shame. Even now, when she had come to terms with her own love for him, she was unable to give him the credit he was due. This was Thomas, the man who had stood up for her on the night of Rosa's birth. Who had teased and annoyed her in London until she could think of no other man. Who had laid his own heart at her feet . . .

A moment later, she found herself faced with his bedchamber door once more. Inhaling a deep breath, she rapped her knuckles softly against the oaken surface. When no answer was forthcoming, she cracked the door open for a peek.

Evanston was reclining against a mound of pillows, asleep. Once she had closed the door behind her, she allowed her gaze to travel across him in the way she had not permitted herself to while he was sick. The first thing she noticed was that his shirtless state was not the benign, medical necessity it had once been. Now, the sight of him, recovering and at rest, healthier than she'd seen him in days, stirred something dark and carnal inside of her.

Eliza came closer to notice that his sleek black hair had been washed and combed, his stubble shaven meticulously away. She longed to stroke his chin with her fingers, to feel its smoothness for herself, but stayed the inclination. He was only just recovered and she was still unsure of his feelings towards her.

Yet, she recalled how good it had felt to kiss him, despite the sorrow that had prompted her to do so. It had not been so long ago, yet if felt like ages had already passed. To kiss him now felt forbidden. The fear that had kept her away caused her to linger again, unmoving and inactive. She clenched her teeth in determination and approached to seat herself on the bed beside him.

"Thomas. Can you hear me?"

The last time she'd spoken those words, he had not reacted well. This time, his head rolled slowly in her direction, and he awoke. He stared at her, his eyes a cool blue flame.

"Hello, Eliza." His voice sounded rusty and unused.

She pressed on, hopeful. "How are you feeling?"

A ghost of a smile lifted at the corner of his mouth. "Like I've been hit by a steam engine," he said, his eyes drifting closed briefly, then opening again to view her. "Burton says you've been here for days. I didn't believe him."

"Why not?"

Thomas winced in pain and shifted himself higher up on his pillows. "Well, for one thing, you wouldn't show yourself. And when last we parted—"

"Stop, please," she said quickly with a stab of guilt.

Rather than attempting to continue, he fell silent and evaluated her curiously.

"I heard you from my place in the darkness, you know."

Her eyes widened. "You did?"

He nodded. "You said the nicest things, which was how I knew I must have been dreaming." A tiny gleam in his eyes told her he might have been teasing, but she wasn't certain.

"I'm sorry, Thomas," she murmured, eyes focused on the hands fidgeting in her lap. "I've been so awful to you."

Thomas considered this a while before answering. "I think you were doing what you believed was the right thing to do," he replied carefully.

She raised her eyes to meet his. "What if I told you that I refused Landry's proposal, and I believe it was the right thing to do?"

He opened his mouth to reply, then closed it. He glanced away.

Eliza leaned closer to him on the bed, sliding her fingertips across his chin as she had longed to do earlier. The skin-to-skin contact caused him to freeze, even as he submitted to her touch.

"What if I left for London immediately after, in the

barest hope you might forgive me despite everything I've put you through? That I believed it was the right thing to do?"

His mouth twisted. "Eliza, don't."

"What if Rosa believed it was the right thing to do? And William?"

Thomas's gaze snapped over to meet hers, but he said nothing.

Terrified but resolute, she continued. "What if," she said, her hand straying down towards the hard, muscular planes of his chest to cover his heart, "I've wanted you since before my marriage to Reginald, and loved you nearly as long?"

His gaze sharpened. "That's a lie."

"What if it's not?"

Even with his resistance, she felt his temperature increase at her words. Could see his pupils dilate, the black pools spreading in a sea of blue. She let her fingers trail through the dark hair on his chest, feeling her own response to his nearness. Drifting closer, her lips passed over the sharp angle of his cheekbone. Evanston's eyes fell closed.

"What if you became the worthiest suitor by far, and I was just too blind to see it?"

"*Worthiest* might be an exaggeration," he said quietly.

She silenced him by pressing her lips against his, gently at first, then more insistently. Rather than shove her away, as she had feared he might, his hands slid up to cradle her head, pulling her closer so he could deepen the kiss. His tongue slowly stroked hers, and she accepted his invitation, darting to meet and match his movements. Evanston's breathing hastened and a low groan issued from his throat.

Reluctantly, Eliza broke the kiss to pull back and gazed down at him. Hope lightened her expression, but the worry remained.

"Thomas," she breathed, pleading, "I've been so foolish and I cannot bear to lose you. Please say you'll marry me. A life without you doesn't seem like much of a life at all."

Despite his impassioned state, he did his best to appear uninterested, turning his head away with a bored glance and a mischievous smile.

"Perhaps. But not until after I've made you suffer sufficiently for such torment," he teased.

The veil of doubt that had burdened her for years finally lifted and a thrill blossomed inside her heart. "Are you going to make me beg?" she asked hopefully.

"I'd consider myself a failure if I didn't."

She brushed her lips against the tip of his nose. "I think I'll make you beg, instead."

"Oh, you do?" he scoffed.

He pulled her down again, savoring her lips, tasting her deeply, only to ease her away when her kisses became too eager. She gave a soft cry of complaint, then decided to take charge, shifting across the bed to climb over and straddle him. He uttered a soft laugh at her impatience, but his amusement subsided quickly when she lowered down against him. Eliza could feel the large shape of his manhood pushing through her skirts and she writhed insistently on his lap, excited to feel how well they fit together. But no . . . she was unwilling to rush their lovemaking. Not after years of dreaming about being with him.

Evanston tried to seem indifferent in an attempt to tease her and failed with a groan, flexing his hips up to meet hers, his eager hands coasting upwards to squeeze the heavy weight of her breasts. The thin fabric of her dress did very little to mask the sensation of contact and Eliza could not conceal the intensity of her reaction. With a moan she moved on top of him while he gasped and kneaded her flesh through the muslin.

"I'm sure this is against all doctor's orders," he managed to say, "yet I can't seem to care."

Tugging the front of her bodice sharply down, he exposed the naked curves of her breasts to his greedy gaze. The abruptness of the motion caused her to gasp in breathless surprise.

"Dear God, how I've dreamed of you," he said, his voice roughened with what remained of his restraint. His thumbs caressed the tips of her breasts and he leaned forward, letting his lips drift across her shoulder, over her collarbone. "You are . . . beyond gorgeous," he whispered. "You're perfect."

He slid his hand around the supple curve of one breast, then took her nipple into the warm depths of his mouth. Suckling until she cried out, he then teased the tip with soft flicks of his tongue and pulled away. Evanston gently squeezed the moistened peak with his fingertips before moving to the other side to torment her there as well.

She wanted to make some reply. To tell him how very happy he had made her. That despite the advice of everyone around her and her own best laid plans, he'd always been the only man for her. But she could only call out his name and rake her fingers through his thick black hair, arching forward to bring him even closer.

Although still sapped from his recent illness, he possessed every ounce of his usual male virility as his body responded beneath her. Reaching down, she slid her hand beneath the sheet and exhaled softly in appreciation at the extent of his arousal. She started to caress him, tearing a hoarse gasp from his throat, and she realized how grateful she was for the chance to discover him in this way after nearly losing him.

"I need you, Thomas," she sighed. "I've needed you for so long."

Evanston made a low noise back in his throat and removed her hands with a devilish glance. "You touch me like that and this will be over before it's started," he whispered against her neck. "There's no need to rush . . ."

Disappearing beneath her skirts, his fingers slid between her parted thighs, causing her entire body to jump at the intimate contact.

"I—oh . . ." she breathed faintly, suddenly short of breath.

He began a leisurely and erotic exploration, his fingertips softly toying with her. Eliza wriggled and moaned, the tension building with each tiny circular motion of his fingers. Then he slid them even further to penetrate her. She felt her body eagerly tighten around them, kindling excitedly within seconds. It would not take much effort from him at all for her to find her release. She cried out and he slipped an arm around her waist to clutch her tighter.

"God," he rasped, a thin sheen of sweat already glistening

on his brow. His restraint was dissolving before her very eyes, and the speed of his hand was hastening. "I want to hear it when you—"

Eliza shook her head, sending golden strands of hair tickling her face as they fell from their pins. "No," she managed to say through the waves of delirium-inducing sensation. Placing her hands on his chest to lever her body upwards, she forced herself away from his touch. "Not yet."

She knew how much more powerful it would feel if they were joined when the moment arrived, and she refused to be robbed of that perfect bliss. Not this time . . . not when the viscount was about to be hers at last. Impulsively, Eliza pulled away the sheet; the only barrier that remained between them.

Rising up onto her knees, she ravished his mouth with a hungry kiss, and he seized her plump bottom lip between his teeth in response. An unbridled jolt of need coursed through her and she could feel herself melting in wicked anticipation.

"Are you sure?"

Oh, she was sure. Eliza had burned for him for *years*, the sensual cycle of desire and denial repeating itself on a merciless loop, and her patience was now at its end. With a lightly mocking glance, she lowered down to rest upon him—flesh against flesh, the slick heat of her softness gliding over the impossibly hard length of his swollen shaft.

Evanston choked in surprise, his eyes half-closed in delight, and she tipped her hips back and forth, deliberate and slow, forcing herself to wait just a little longer before actually having him at last. Her fingers dug into his bare shoulders and with a little moan, she allowed their bodies to convey what their words no longer could . . . anxious to solve the sensual mystery that only their physical union could answer.

"I need to be inside you." Thomas leaned forward for another tantalizing taste of her breasts, then shuddered with a trembling breath. "I only wish I was recovered enough to do you honor, my love."

"Mmm," she murmured with another tilt of her hips. "The doctor said you have the fortitude of an ox," she replied with a lazy smile, her pleasure steadily building, her body making ever-increasing demands.

"Is that all?" he asked, attempting nonchalance, causing her to laugh in the middle of their embrace.

She wanted to admonish him for his audacity but found it difficult through her giggles. "Thomas, you are—"

A sudden flex of his hips caused her to say his name for another reason entirely. The amusement faded from her lips and her breathing became heavy and labored, matching the shift in his own.

"Can you tell me . . . is it true?"

His question roused her from her trance, surprising her. She blinked foggily at him.

"Is what true?" she asked.

He rocked upward again and she sucked in her breath, enslaved by the way he was pressed so intimately against her sex. She had no idea how he expected her to answer his question or think at all when he insisted on doing that.

"What you said about the others."

In a moment of clarity, she understood. He needed to hear it again after being hurt so many times before. Ignoring the insistent pulses of her body, she gripped his face in her hands to address him earnestly, the hint of fear in his eyes tugging sharply on her heart.

"Everything was true, Thomas," Eliza whispered. "All of it. They love you, and they want you to come home." Her head fell forwards to rest against his. "I love you, and I want you to come home."

"Eliza," he said huskily, his voice full of emotion. "How long I've waited to hear that."

Her need for him driving her now, she kissed him furiously while they both worked to tug her dress up over her head. It was not a feat that would have been typically achieved, had she not dressed herself so carelessly in such a simple gown. Without the rows of buttons normally dictated by fashion, the garment was soon hastily cast to the floor, followed by her chemise.

She exhaled slowly, taking in the glorious sight of his body, ready for her. Eliza slid her hand up the thick length of him, loving the satiny-hard feel of his manhood against her palm. His breath caught and he leaned back further against the pillows, trembling as she touched him, shaking his head.

"There are so many things I want to do. I've yearned for you . . . for so long." He broke off into a hiss at the glide of her hand over his excited flesh.

"And you will. Right now, though, you must preserve your strength." She kissed him hotly then smiled. "Let me take you instead."

His brows raised a moment before she sank down onto him, no longer willing to wait, unleashing a desire that had long been refuted and fulfilling countless fantasies in the process. Thomas's voice rang out, drowning the echo of her own moans as he entered and filled her, stretching her to capacity. She struggled to take him all in, wriggling to accommodate the snugness of their fit, but did not halt her descent until he was buried to the hilt, and there she had to pause. The satisfaction of having him inside her was already nearly enough to push her into climax.

"Oh . . ." she keened softly, her thoughts whirling while she tried to suppress her body's response. Eliza could sense his anxiety rising in the way his head rolled on his shoulders and his eyelids fluttered.

"Please, don't stop," he managed.

"But I need to wait a moment—"

He cursed softly. She placed her hands against his chest and rocked against him experimentally. Ecstasy shot through her core and she froze once more.

"Sweet Jesus, yes," he ground out. "Eliza, keep going."

He seized her waist and brought her down to meet his swift upward thrust, and she knew that this would not take long for either of them. With her sounds of pleasure mirroring his own, she momentarily worried about his overexertion. But all rational thought was lost as her control dissolved, and Eliza rose up above him to fall down, her body eagerly crashing home on top of his.

Again they met. And again, until gradually they found each other's rhythm, desperately reaching towards the pinnacle that was promised. The drive of their hips became an instinctual tempo that they couldn't help but follow, and Eliza could feel the dizzying pressure mounting. Although she would have loved to prolong their union, she simply didn't have the self-control required to wait. It felt as if they'd already waited forever for one another. They would have a lifetime to take it slowly.

Their fervor grew, their pace increasing, and before long they were careening off the precipice together, lost in the throes of their union. An incendiary heat flowed through her body as his fingers dug into her hips and he shoved upwards in a last hard thrust, a rough cry erupting from his lips. Her body came alight with blazing sensation and she threw her head back with a gasp, catapulted into the heavens and taking Thomas along with her, each equally senseless until they both found themselves shaky and trembling, lying exhausted beside each other.

Slowly, Eliza regained awareness, tiny shivers of pleasure still racing through her sated limbs, and she rose to meet his heavy-lidded gaze. Smiling, she claimed him for another kiss, then collapsed next to his good side while being mindful of his injury. They lay there together, enjoying the minutes comfortably with one another, both working to catch their breath. Finally, she gazed at him in admiring amusement.

"You did quite well for being infirm, my lord, although I was not able to make you beg as I would have liked."

He shook his head, breathing still slightly ragged with the recent expenditure of effort. "I will remind you that I've nearly been begging for months," he said mischievously. One of his arms wrapped around her to pull her close, and he pressed his face into her hair to inhale deeply. "More than once, I had to convince myself that you were truly there and that I had not fallen prey to another torturous, although quite welcome, fever-induced hallucination."

She buried her face against his shoulder in silence, happier than she'd felt in many years. They would marry soon, and she would become his wife. The only thought that brought her more peace was the fact that he would also take on the role of a much-needed and much-loved father to Rosa. Relief flooded through her at having made her choice at last, and what was more, having made the *right* choice.

Gradually, his breathing eased, hitching slightly when she felt him twist around to survey the bedside table. A slight grunt of pain was his only indication of his healing wound and the fact that it still bothered him, which was miraculous given his condition just a week before.

Eliza pushed herself upward to view him with concern.

"I've aggravated your injury," she said guiltily. "Do you need more medicine?"

He twitched his head. "No. I only just saw that envelope on the table."

"Oh yes." Eliza retrieved the sheet from the foot of the bed to wrap it around them modestly, then reached over to pick the missive off the table and hand it to Thomas. She curled up next to him again, savoring the warmth of his body next to hers, the irresistible tickle of his chest hair against the sensitive tips of her breasts. "I'd totally forgotten. It's from William."

Evanston's eyes widened but he accepted the parchment, broke the wax seal with his fingers and unfolded the letter. A scrap of paper fluttered down onto the sheets beside him, but for the moment, he paid it no mind, his eyes busily scanning the scrawled passages. Eliza watched him mutely until her curiosity won.

"What does he say?" she asked.

Thomas's eyes were shining, as if he were battling off some kind of strong emotion. He cleared his throat and glanced sideways at her.

"He says, and I'm quoting him, that 'even the high and mighty Earl of Ashworth has been known to be an ass from time to time.'"

A laugh bubbled up from her lips. "Well, surely that was common knowledge to some of us," she said, giggling. "What else does William say?"

Evanston swallowed hard before speaking. "He told me he hopes that I will consider your offer of marriage, as it would serve to officially make us brothers. He also says he can think of no better man for both you and Rosa."

His eyes returned to the page then dropped down to the sheets, his hand searching until it closed around the piece of paper that had fallen. "There is a postscript, as well, where he again requests my cooperation, 'for any woman who carries your calling card in her reticule, is nothing short of completely besotted.'"

Thomas glanced down at the small card with a grin, then flipped it around in his fingers so she could see it for herself, the name imprinted in black ink, the top left corner folded over.

Viscount Evanston

Eliza's mouth fell open, her cheeks turning pink.

"What? I, but no, that couldn't be—"

His eyes gleamed wickedly. "It wouldn't be the first time you've been caught carrying my card, dear lady."

Hadn't she cast that thing into the fire? No, she realized with a warm rush of embarrassment, she had returned it safely into her purse, like some selfish magpie who refused to relinquish its treasure.

Eliza thought back to her last encounter with William, in the study at Lawton Park. She'd been crying, had rummaged through her reticule for a handkerchief, and then . . .

She gazed up in panic to meet his eyes. Thomas burst out laughing, pausing to wince slightly at the ensuing pain.

"Fine," she conceded in irritation. "Yes, I carried it with me, all through London and back to Kent. And do you know what?" Eliza pushed up on her knees to pluck the white card from between Evanston's fingers. "I want it back."

Eliza tried to roll off the bed but Thomas was surprisingly quick, grasping her around the waist to jerk her back against him. She shrieked in outrage but ceased struggling at the strong feel of his arms around her and the slide of his naked skin against her own. His mouth drifted hotly against her ear, making her squirm.

"Keep the damn card, if you like," he whispered huskily, "but I can't let you leave until I've been able to reward you for such loyalty."

And given the limitations of his injured state, he did everything he could to show her how very grateful he could be.

Chapter Eighteen

Evanston's carriage wheeled up the drive of Hawthorne Manor, his country estate. Burton could be seen standing proudly upon the top stair. Once they had stopped completely, footmen would jump into action, unloading trunks and conveying their belongings inside for unpacking. Another glossy black carriage sharing the Evanston family seal was conspicuously parked to one side, the coachman tending to the horses as they whickered restlessly. Thomas's eyes widened at the sight, then hung his head and sighed.

"My mother, unannounced, as ever. I suppose I must subject myself to her presence now that I have healed." His eyes shifted to Eliza accusingly. "Unless you knew about this already?"

She laughed and raised her hands in capitulation. "My only crime was updating the viscountess on your progress, and perhaps . . . er . . . providing her with the date of our return to Kent."

He stared at her mutely, then addressed her in a low voice. "You did what?"

As the vehicle bounced to a halt, she clasped his fingers gently between her own.

"Forgive me, darling. I felt that even your mother, such as she is, deserved to know the welfare of her only child. Surely you would not deny her the chance to see your recovered state for herself." Eliza raised his hand to her lips, then lowered it to gaze at him fondly. "And in my defense, I received no reply, so could not readily anticipate her being here today. Not for certain."

Evanston stared at her, still annoyed, but relaxing a bit. "You, of all people, should know what that woman is capable of." He slumped backwards against the cushions of the vehicle's interior. "I'd willingly slide back into unconsciousness to avoid her company."

She tsked chidingly and leaned in to kiss the corner of his downturned mouth. "Come now, Thomas. That isn't being very charitable. While it's true she's said some awful things in the past—"

"I can't remember a time when she's said something nice," he muttered under his breath.

"—I feel that if she is willing to finally show some concern for your well-being, that perhaps you could let her try?"

Her brilliant green eyes held his gaze in steady contemplation, and while he knew she was trying to convince him of the validity of her point, he could see empathy there too.

Eliza sighed softly. "Although, if you truly wish her to leave, I do understand. Since I informed her of our imminent arrival, I will go speak with her myself and ask her to depart."

She had provided him with a means of avoiding his mother, but if it would make Eliza happy for him to walk in there and speak to the woman, then, by God, he would make an attempt. Besides, no one said the conversation had to be lengthy.

With a grunt of assent, he leaned over to kiss her on the cheek. "You may owe me for this later." Her complexion glowed at his words. Clearly it was a price she was willing to pay.

He descended off the metal steps and Thomas handed her safely down off the carriage.

"Burton," called Eliza. "Please have tea brought to the drawing room."

The butler, who clearly held her in high regard, snapped into action with a nod of assent. "Yes, my lady," he replied smartly. "And might I just add, my lord," he said meeting the viscount's eyes, "it is so good to have you *both* at home." He smiled surreptitiously at Eliza before disappearing into the house.

Thomas gave Eliza an amused look. "It appears you've already gained the admiration of my staff," he teased.

Before she could reply, the soft beat of footsteps caused the pair to turn. Lady Evanston had emerged from inside Hawthorne Manor and stood now upon the front stairs, her demeanor hesitant and unsure for perhaps the first time in her life. Rather than the harsh black mourning dress she had insisted on wearing in the time since his father's death, she had tempered her choice of clothing, wearing the rich purples and violets of half-mourning instead. Her hat was a rather understated affair in muted gray, not the sharp black feathered things that normally protruded from her head. He felt his brows lift in amazement.

"Hello, Mother," he said slowly.

Eliza stood silently beside him, her hand wrapping securely around his own. She nodded at the woman and dipped into a curtsy.

"My lady."

Lady Evanston's black gaze flitted between the two of them, finally coming to rest on her son. The corner of her thin lips twitched in what could have resembled a smile.

"Greetings. Thomas, you must be much improved," she stated, her eyes scanning over him to appraise his condition. "Lady Eliza informed me of the dire nature of your injury, but I am still uncertain how you came to acquire it in the first place."

Christ. Here we go . . .

He would not coat the truth with sugar merely to appease his judgmental mother, but still did not happily anticipate her reaction. A light squeeze of Eliza's fingers gave him the extra motivation he required.

Evanston cleared his throat. "You will appreciate the irony, I am sure, of my former mistress hiring a thug to attack me. It seemed my love for Eliza brought out her more sinister side."

His mother's eyelids lowered to skewer him with a

hooded stare. "Tarrying with the wrong sort of woman? Perhaps it served you right." He then registered her gaze flicking over to Eliza, who was likely directing her own glare at the viscountess. A slight mien of remorse passed over her face and the older woman's lips twisted in censure. "What I mean to say is, I'm glad you're all right." She tipped her nose slightly higher in the air. "Am I to understand this criminal was never apprehended?"

Thomas shook his head. "No, although I did receive a vague letter of apology from Mrs. Varnham, just prior to her seemingly disappearing into thin air. Apparently, she didn't wish to murder me at all, but only wanted to express her strong displeasure over being slighted." He slid his arm around Eliza and shook his head. "It doesn't matter any longer."

"No," agreed the elder woman, taking a step closer to stand next to them on the drive. "I suppose it doesn't." Lady Evanston laced her gloved hands together before her. "And am I also to understand that you two are to be married?"

He pressed a kiss to the side of Eliza's head, who smiled happily in return.

"You are," he replied, his heart swelling with joy, still in wonder at the sudden turn his life had taken. After such an uphill fight, his heart still sometimes struggled to believe that the battle had finally been won.

"Well then, I would like to offer a gift." The lady glanced over her shoulder towards her carriage, and her footman appeared suddenly as if on cue, a small decorative box in his hands. He gave the box to Lady Evanston who stared solemnly at it before raising her eyes to Eliza. She extended it towards her.

"This is for you, if you would like it."

Thomas watched as Eliza opened the gilded box to reveal a large emerald ring, glowing incandescently in the cloud-filtered sunlight that shone from above. He could detect her soft intake of breath as she removed it from its cushioned seat reverently to behold it aloft. The vibrant green center stone twinkled amidst the halo of pale, sparkling diamonds that surrounded it.

Given his recent injury and convalescence, Thomas had not yet had an opportunity to find a ring for Eliza, a situation he had intended to remedy immediately. He jerked his gaze up to meet his mother's eyes, his head tipped in inquiry.

"This is not your wedding ring."

Lady Evanston scoffed and evaluated him in something akin to horror. "I would not dream of cursing your bride with a token of such a contentious marriage," she admitted openly. "However, my mother enjoyed a happy arrangement with my father, and this was hers."

"Did you know," said Eliza, her words stilted and overcome with emotion, "the emerald is my birthstone?"

Thomas knew birthstones were commonly used in engagement rings, although he couldn't imagine his mother had actively planned such a fortunate coincidence.

"I did not," the viscountess said quietly, "but I believe that bodes well."

Hesitantly, with great care and respect, Eliza slid the ring onto her finger. The fit was perfect, and she glanced up at Thomas in delight. He raised his eyebrows and smiled.

"It suits you, my love," he murmured softly, his joy at seeing her pleased expression causing his heart to constrict.

Thomas stepped closer to his mother and she stiffened at his approach, years of reinforced barriers between them conditioning her response one more time. He paused, waiting for her to be at ease, finally leaning down to place a soft kiss upon her cheek when she was. Despite her prickly exterior, Lady Evanston's eyes fell briefly closed at the gesture of affection. He straightened to look at her, viewing the woman as if she were some new variant of deep sea creature, never before having been discovered or seen.

"Thank you, Mother," he said gruffly, glancing uncomfortably away. "Whatever my faults may be, I admire you for ignoring them in appreciation of my bride-to-be, who has none."

Eliza snorted lightly in reproach and pushed at his arm.

Lady Evanston's amused glance shifted from Eliza back to Thomas. "Whatever your faults, Thomas, and I think we know you have more than a few, I can see you are marrying a woman who is entirely capable of standing up for herself. It's a more valuable quality than perhaps you know, one I only acquired after my husband's passing. Besides," she said, "you seem newly open to the idea of reform, and I hope to know my new granddaughter—perhaps better than I've permitted myself to know my son." She cast a sheepish glance in Eliza's direction.

"I think Rosa would like to know you, as well," Eliza replied, her gaze suddenly turning uncertain. "Although, you should be aware that she is a rather unconventional child . . ."

With a firm shake of her head, the viscountess silenced Eliza on the subject. "I have known your venerated family for decades, Lady Eliza. Do you really think I would expect anything less?" She leaned closer with a conspiratorial glance to each side, then spoke in a hushed tone. "I used to love *playing in the mud*. It drove both my mother and the laundry maid to distraction."

Eliza's mouth fell open a second before she erupted into laughter. "Well, then, I can see you two getting along quite well," she answered warmly.

Eliza was here with him, conversing easily with his mother, wearing his family's ring on her finger, standing on the drive of the estate that they would soon share together. It was hard to believe after everything that had transpired this past year, and he felt he was close to bursting with happiness.

Thomas could feel his temperature increasing, and the urge to find himself alone with Eliza had suddenly become unbearable. Tamping down the inconvenient rise of his desire for her, he forced himself to address his mother and gestured to the house.

"Would you care to join us for some tea?" he inquired politely amidst a haze of indecent thoughts about his soon-to-be wife.

Lady Evanston laughed dismissively and brushed past them, making her way towards her awaiting vehicle. "Good heavens, no. I've no intention of overstaying my welcome so soon. Besides, you've only just arrived back home. I'm sure you wish to rest after your taxing journey."

"Rest," he echoed in eager relief, not thinking of rest at all. "Yes, absolutely."

He slid a hand around Eliza's waist, and with a snap of the reins, his mother's carriage lurched away back down the drive, the gravel crunching beneath the wheels as it went. Thomas and Eliza waved until the gleaming black shape could no longer be discerned along the pathway. Then he tugged her unceremoniously against him, his hand imprisoning the delicate line of her jaw so he could lower his mouth greedily to hers. She uttered a tiny noise of surprise before readily submitting to his hunger, then thought better of it, shoving firmly at his chest to cast an uneasy glance at their surroundings. Likely not by coincidence, the scene had become curiously devoid of servants.

"Not here, Thomas," she whispered fervently. Her eyes darted around in thought. "Upstairs?"

Desperate now, he gripped Eliza's elbow as he strode to the house. Exhilaration flooded through his body, ready and eager to claim her. For the thousandth time since winning her heart, he felt like the luckiest man alive.

"Perhaps the library," he replied as they started up the stone stairway to the front door. Upstairs seemed so far away. Turning, he could see her evaluative gaze of his aroused state, not missing the way her peridot eyes glowed in appreciation. Wholly unable to resist, he jerked Eliza against him for another heady kiss. Then he forced himself to withdraw in an effort to resume their route into the manor.

"And if you continue to look at me like that, my lady, we will never even make it inside," he muttered, pulling her behind him.

They only made it as far as the drawing room, which wasn't very far at all but would serve given his need. Thomas closed the door securely behind them, then turned to slide his hands around her neck, cradling her there and nipping at her mouth. She moaned softly in heated excitement.

"Do you remember the last time we were in this room?"

Eliza's dark eyelashes fluttered open to gaze at their surroundings. Her lips curved just before meeting his for another soul-stealing kiss.

"Mmm . . . I do. Tea and sandwiches and . . ." she broke off as he squeezed her breast through her dress ". . . your angry mother." She laughed breathlessly.

He tugged her bodice down just enough to expose one swollen nipple. He squeezed the bud into rosy distention with his fingers, then lowered his head to moisten it with his mouth. She arched against him with a tiny cry, gripping the rigid curves of his shoulders to pull him closer.

"I was rather remembering you," he whispered against the soft curve of her breast. He rose up to kiss her again, his hand sliding along her collarbone while his mouth laid claim to hers. "That pink dress of yours . . . and how you were unfathomably nice after a long season of shunning me." He pressed her against the door. "It was pure torment, but it made me think that all might not be lost."

"I nearly gave in to you that day," she murmured, her

glassy eyes drifting closed as he curled his fingers around her skirts. "I've never wanted anyone as much as I want you."

Thomas raised the fall of skirts to expose the shapely length of her stocking-clad legs. He ravished her again with a kiss, then leaned in to press his hips forward, wanting her to feel the magnitude of his arousal. Eliza's gasp only excited him more.

"Then you shall have me. And this time, I'll be sure to leave on my cravat. Hold these."

Her soft laugh faded as he guided her to clasp the bunched mass of her skirts. Then he moved one hand behind her waist while the other slipped intimately between her thighs. Dear God, she was ready for him, and Eliza's face flushed as she cried out, her breathing turning rapid as his fingers slid into her.

"Oh, Thomas," she moaned.

An audible knock sounded on the door, and they both froze.

"Yes?" she forced out.

"You requested tea, my lady?"

It was Burton, efficient as ever. Evanston grinned wickedly and resumed his attentions, pressing her harder against the very door that separated their lovemaking from the butler. His fingers worked cleverly beneath her dress, and Eliza's eyes widened as she attempted to construct a logical response while dealing with such a distraction.

"I—yes . . ." she stammered, clearly struggling. "Take it . . . to the library . . . please . . . *oh*."

Thomas smiled at the tiny moan that punctuated the end of her sentence. Thankfully, Burton was steadfast in his efforts to ignore their mischief.

"Right away, my lady," he replied succinctly.

"Thank y—"

Evanston silenced her with another kiss. Burton could be heard moving away, the jingling noise of the tea set marking his progress, and Eliza's hips jerked forwards in helpless response to his caresses.

"You are unkind, my lord," she pouted breathlessly, tearing her mouth away from his.

"On the contrary," he answered slyly, his rhythm picking up speed, "I am *very* kind."

Her cries grew louder, lovely eyes falling closed in near rapture. Thomas would never tire of seeing her submit wantonly to his touch, could finish this right now if he wanted, but it was not nearly enough.

His fingers withdrew and Eliza's glassy green eyes flew open. They were confused, slightly accusatory, right until they widened in surprise when he dropped to his knees before her. His hands found her again and he circled his thumb over the sweet secretive place that drove her wild, being driven to madness himself by the way she writhed above him.

"Shall I kiss you here?" he asked, his voice thick and husky with longing. He brushed his lips against the vulnerable skin of her thigh, then turned his face to exhale warmly against the most sensitive part of her. Eliza's breathing quickened eagerly.

"Oh yes—"

He nudged her legs further apart, then plundered her with soft sweeps of his mouth. Her head fell backwards against the polished wood of the door and she stifled a pleading moan, her fingers clutching restlessly at her skirts as his tongue slid and flicked across the overly sensitized flesh. When her hips bucked forward to meet him, he closed his mouth over that one deliciously tender place, kissing and suckling relentlessly until she was no longer able to resist.

The sounds of Eliza finding her pleasure drove him wild with anticipation, and when she had quieted at last, he propelled himself to a stand and unfastened his trousers. She leaned against the oak panel to catch her breath, watching him through a haze of satisfaction and desire, and when he was freed, Thomas gripped the round curve of her bottom to raise her up against the door.

"Welcome home, my love," he murmured against her lips, just before welcoming her home in the most enjoyable way he knew.

It was the following afternoon when Eliza and Evanston arrived at Lawton Park. Rosa broke away from the housekeeper's hold to burst out the front doors and hurtle towards her mother with the force of a steam engine. With a laugh and steadying hand on her shoulder from Thomas, Eliza righted her balance and kneeled down to reciprocate her daughter's affectionate embrace. She nodded at the harried Mrs. Malone, who curtsied and withdrew to allow them space for their reunion, then cinched her arms tightly around her little girl.

"Mama! I didn't think you'd be here until tonight!" Rosa shifted her dolls in her arms. "We were upstairs and I saw your carriage through the window!"

Eliza buried her face in Rosa's shining golden ringlets, then pulled back to gaze at her. "We decided to surprise you, my darling. Tell me, have you been a good girl for your aunt and uncle?"

"Yes, Mama," Rosa declared, followed by a moment of silence. She glanced shyly up at Thomas, her green eyes flitting back to her mother in inquiry.

Acknowledging the silent question with a tip of her head and a soft smile, Eliza reached out to clasp the little girl's tiny hand.

"Would it please you to know that Thomas and I are soon to be wed?"

Rosa's large eyes grew even larger. They darted back and forth between both Eliza and Thomas in increasing excitement.

"Really?"

The viscount dropped to one knee, laughing at her exuberance while she threw herself into his arms for a hug. Her dolls collided with his head in the process, but he only chuckled and squeezed her tighter, innumerable emotions passing across his face as he did. Thomas kissed the girl soundly on the cheek, tucking a loose tendril of hair behind her ear to evaluate her seriously.

"I've heard you are to thank, at least in part, for talking some sense into your mother." He winked slyly at Rosa, who grinned brightly in return. She leaned in to make her reply.

"I don't know what she was thinking," she whispered.

Evanston laughed loudly. Eliza could not help but giggle herself at the sight of her child gazing at Thomas with such obvious admiration. Rosa leaned in yet again.

"I've never had a papa before," she said softly, as if confessing a great secret.

Thomas stared at her in surprise, then directed his gaze to Eliza, whose own eyes had filled with tears. Eliza parted her lips to speak, but Evanston turned back to address Rosa before she could.

"You have, my sweet, although you do not recall. But one thing *I* remember is how much he loved you," he answered, smoothing her hair. "I love both you and your mother, and I can promise I'll be the very best papa I can be."

Rosa blinked at him, and a smile spread slowly across her face. She threw her arms around his neck, hugging him once more, and Eliza inclined her head to brush a kiss against his temple. Evanston's eyes fluttered closed, his handsome features relaxing with a contentment she'd never thought to see upon his face.

When the trio finally rose to a stand they found Clara smiling from the front steps of the manor. Even the usually stern Mrs. Malone could not help but be moved by the scene that had just played out before her, and Lady Ashworth came forwards to rest an affectionate hand on the housekeeper's arm.

"Mrs. Malone, are their rooms prepared? I know they are a bit early."

With a huff of pride and a dab at her eyes, Mrs. Malone

addressed her mistress. "I always plan for every contingency, my lady, including early arrivals."

Clara smiled knowingly. "Yes, I should have known better than to ask." She reached a hand out to Eliza and Evanston. "Please come inside and be settled. You can see what has prevented William from greeting you himself."

Rosa bounded ahead of the group and raced up the stairs, her chortles resonating behind to echo throughout the foyer. Eliza slipped her fingers into the warm clasp of Thomas's hand, a seemingly small act that she could not imagine would ever cease to delight her. He caught her gaze, squeezed her fingers, and brought her knuckles to his lips for a kiss.

His brilliant eyes were softened with an affection that she'd not seen outwardly expressed from him during their years of prior acquaintance. Thomas had spent years hiding his emotions behind his flirtations, while she had similarly found comfort in thinking of him as an irredeemable devil. Now, with all those pretenses aside, they could both stop pretending and simply be together, in love.

The group followed Clara into the upstairs gallery where they found William, dressed immaculately in his finest aristocratic garb, standing poised upon a wooden step that had been draped in ruby velvet. A wide area had been covered with a drop cloth, and an artist was positioned at his easel, creating a worthy portrait of the fifth Earl of Ashworth.

Determinedly, her brother held his pose, with fingers tightly gripping the lapel of his crisp blue jacket, although Eliza detected William's eyes flicking over to her and Evanston. His mouth curved into a slightly embarrassed grin.

"I find the timing of your arrival exceedingly unfair, as I cannot even properly greet you two."

The artist pursed his lips, causing his dark moustache to twitch, and gave a small sigh of exasperation. "If you could refrain from speaking, my lord, that would be most helpful."

William rolled his eyes. "Indeed, I cannot even speak."

Eliza laughed. "I am so happy to see this!" she exclaimed, coming forwards to survey the varying colors and brushstrokes used by the artist to compose a handsome likeness of her brother. Eliza glanced at Clara in grateful approbation. "It is high past time for a commissioned portrait."

Lady Ashworth stepped closer to Eliza and smiled, her eyes darting between the painting and her beloved. "I agree," she said, winking at her husband.

Clara squeezed her arm. Eliza turned to meet her gaze. Then her eyes dipped downward. Having an instinctive reaction at seeing the way Clara's other hand was resting gently upon her abdomen, she froze, unsure, staring at her sister-in-law.

"I thought it especially important to mark William's place in history now," admitted the countess, "as it turns out the earl will soon be a father."

Eliza shouted with joy and threw herself into Clara's arms for a tight embrace, who laughed and returned the hug. She dashed her happy tears away with impatient swipes of her hand. "What happy news for us all."

Rosa stopped playing in the corner and glanced up excitedly. "Auntie Clara is having a *baby?*"

Before Eliza could reply, Thomas strode past her into the

middle of the room to approach William. The portrait artist rose testily from his seat to peer over the easel in irritation.

"Pardon me, my lord, but it is quite difficult to—"

In true Evanston fashion, he raised his hand to silence the man, intent on addressing his friend. Eliza could discern William's posture tighten slightly in apprehension, then he stepped down from his perch and reached out to strongly grip the hand Thomas had extended in his direction. The men shook heartily, staring at one another with profound respect.

"Congratulations, friend," said Thomas sincerely.

Still clenching Evanston's hand in his own, William pulled him closer.

"Likewise, brother."

The gallery was silent for a moment as Thomas struggled not to lose his composure. The earl took mercy on him and tugged him once more to pull him close, his other hand clapping him loudly on the back, before retreating again to look at the viscount.

"Although just to be clear, if you make my sister unhappy, I will kill you," he added with a lopsided smirk.

"*William!*" exclaimed both women in unison.

Thomas laughed good-naturedly and raised his hands. "Fair enough." He gazed tenderly at Eliza. "But there will never be a need."

Rosa was now standing in the middle of the adults, clinging to her dolls, eyes bulging in her search for answers.

"*Auntie Clara is having a baby?*" she asked again.

Eliza lowered to a knee and kissed her little girl on the

cheek. "Yes, sweetheart. Auntie Clara and Uncle William will be having a baby."

Rosa's face transformed, much as it had upon the news of her mother's impending wedding. She ran across the drop cloth, tripping over the gathered material, to land in Clara's arms. William crossed over to join the embrace.

"Will the baby want to play with me right away?" she asked, concerned. "I can help Mrs. Humboldt bake the tastiest things, and we can have tea, and—"

"Easy, my darling," replied William with a smile. "Babies simply like to drink milk and sleep for a while before they are strong enough to play. Although surely once the baby is able to crawl, you two will have all sorts of fun together."

Rosa grinned, then directed her gaze towards Eliza and Thomas. "Will you have another baby, Mama?"

Far from being a jealous question, she was quite obviously thrilled at the prospect of being surrounded by a plethora of tiny playmates. Eliza felt her face turn red and she awkwardly looked up at Evanston, who grinned like a reprobate.

"I, well, um—" she stammered.

William leaned over to Clara with a roll of his eyes, almost certainly to deliver a sarcastic remark on how Thomas would waste no time in the endeavor. The earl was stopped in his tracks by a narrowed glance from his wife, tempered by a mischievous quirk of her lips.

"Don't say it," she warned, catching sight of the ring on Eliza's finger and gasping aloud. "Oh, that is lovely, Thomas. I wouldn't have thought you'd have time for formalizing the arrangement with jewelry, given your lengthy recovery."

A faint smile played about his mouth. "Actually, my mother took the task upon herself." He raised Eliza's hand so all could see the twinkling emerald in its bed of diamonds, and Rosa's greatly exaggerated *ooh* of appreciation caused Clara to chuckle. Lord Evanston's deep voice softly rang among the group.

"This belonged to my grandmother, and now it belongs to Eliza." He lifted her hand to his lips, holding her eyes with his own as he did so.

The rest of the room dissolved away for a moment, and it was only her brother's abrupt clearing of his throat that brought the pair back into the present. Blushing deeply, Eliza realized they would need to work on concealing their outward affection for one another a little better when out in public.

"Now, dear sister, I have a question for you," William said, stifling a laugh. "How soon will it be before we can get you out of the Dower House?"

Epilogue

The Dower House, Lawton Park
Kent, England
January 1847

Eliza pressed her back against the coolness of the stone wall, hiding behind it to catch her breath. Her exhalations puffed white in the frozen air, and a giggle escaped her lips at the sounds of Rosa's happy shrieks bouncing through the courtyard. Most certainly, her daughter had hit her target, and that target was most definitely Lord Evanston. Eliza craned her neck upward to hear the ensuing good-natured growl of her husband, followed by more of Rosa's exclamations as she scampered away from him once again.

Despite the chill of the weather, she was sweating beneath the heavy layers of her dress and cloak. She had not planned on participating in the snowball fight this afternoon, but the fun had been too much to resist once William, Clara and Caroline had joined in as well. Her brother was protective of his wife, observing that she took care not to overexert herself given her increasing condition. No one present was truly comfortable firing snowballs at the countess, who was seated safely upon a stone bench. But in a bold show of Machiavellian ruthlessness, this did not prevent Lady Ashworth from launching an excess of her own projectiles. William had viewed her behavior in pretend shock while Thomas's rich laugh of hilarity showed his appreciation of her strategy.

Eliza took a moment to peer over the wall at her viscount. Currently, he was giving Rosa a ride upon his back, racing a circuit along the frozen flagstones while she pelted the others with snowy missiles. Caroline and William cried gamely in dismay upon being struck, then elected to flee when Thomas circled back for another round. Rosa cackled in triumph from beneath her thick felt bonnet, while Clara continued her own assault on the viscount from her seat upon the bench.

Eliza grew warmer at the sight of her husband's powerful frame. He was every last bit the mischievous rake he'd always been, but now his exploits were strictly limited to her, every longing glance intended only for his wife. Eliza knew better than to be surprised by his enthusiasm in bed, but the extent of his happiness, both in the bedchamber and throughout the course of their daily life, was still something she marveled at.

His eyes flicked over and found her, never failing to send that familiar jolt of electricity through her core. She ducked down immediately, eyeing the wall that concealed her before choosing to slide down a bit further. The protection it offered was limited at best, and she wondered if he would rally the group together before advancing, or if he would stalk her by himself.

She hoped it was the latter.

The gritty crunch of snow signified an approach on her position. She froze in place and listened. The footfall was too heavy to be Caroline's, and she could discern her brother's voice in the distance. It would seem that Lord Evanston was making a move.

Crouching down, she sank her gloved fingers into the downy white snow, working to prepare her arsenal in the short time she had before being discovered. Eliza quickly fashioned three respectable snowballs, then jumped upward and fired them over the top of the wall. The only thing more satisfying than hitting Thomas squarely in the chest was his incredulous expression of surprise.

"*Ha!*" she cried out. "*I got you!*"

Eliza should have known she was in trouble by the wolfish grin that spread across his face. Before she could turn and run, Thomas had hurtled forwards around the wall in a show of agile grace that stole her breath. He seized her wrist to jerk her up against him.

"Why no, Lady Evanston," he murmured. "I've got you."

She opened her mouth to make a reply worthy of such a comment, but her husband swooped down to take her lips with his own. Even though they were in full view of the courtyard, she found herself acquiescing in his arms, with the liquid heat of his mouth causing her to forget any objections she might have had. When the kiss ended at last, she was gratified to see he appeared similarly affected, his gaze softened by a thick haze of arousal.

"You looked lonely over here, watching me from behind the wall," he said. She could hear the smile in his voice.

Eliza shot him an innocent glance, enjoying the feel of him against her. "What makes you think I was watching you, my lord?" she teased.

Evanston swiftly pulled her aside, shifting them both behind a nearby tree so they could not be seen by their companions in the courtyard. His hands curled around her hips and he pressed closer, his mouth finding her neck.

"Hmm." The vibration of his response against her skin caused her to tense in anticipation. "If you were not, then perhaps I should work harder to get your attention."

Eliza's lips curved with a satisfied sigh. He did so enjoy getting her attention . . .

Thomas nipped at her earlobe, then stroked the tender place with his tongue. She sucked in a sharp breath.

"The rumors were right. You *are* a troublemaker."

He laughed darkly. "The rumors weren't even close, as you well know." He leaned close to brush his lips against her ear. "Or have you forgotten our wedding night?"

Indeed, Lord Evanston had proven his prowess to be far beyond the scope of the *ton's* rumormongering. But he had also shown himself to be vastly generous, both in the bedchamber and out of it. At this moment, his hands were of a singular purpose, roaming over her velvet bodice in an effort to remind her. He must have been joking, for there was no earthly way she could forget their wedding night . . . and every night since . . . and most days, for that matter.

The wedding itself had been a glorious and family-filled affair at Lawton Park, small and private and perfect. Her dress too had been lovely—champagne-colored satin with ivory lace accents and modest layers of petticoats and skirts. Thomas said that the simplicity of its design was what he liked about it most—the way it complemented her natural beauty rather than concealing it beneath mounds of ruffles and fripperies. Eliza's mother's beloved pearl necklace had gleamed around her throat, while the Evanston family ring had likewise sparkled from its place upon her finger.

Rosa's tea length dress had been a soft shade of rose-pink satin, edged in lace, and a perfect match to her dollies, clutched tightly in her fists in their own pink finery throughout the duration of the ceremony.

But Lord Evanston, in his dove-gray coat, ivory waistcoat, breeches, and cravat . . .

The sight of him awaiting her approach had caused heart palpitations not unlike the ones she'd felt as a young woman, newly discovering the awe of his potent masculinity. But the look in his eyes had caused her heart to flutter the most, knowing the sultry intent behind his stare. Knowing they would be alone in a few short hours.

Eliza thought back to that night, remembering the secure feeling of his limbs wrapped around her own. The sounds of their breathing as they lay on the bed, energy utterly spent, until their arousal rose yet again. How the sheets had been wrapped haphazardly around their bodies after their lovemaking. Most of all, she remembered his words to her then:

No other woman had been worth waiting for. Worth pursuing.

Worth loving for the rest of his life.

Her eyes dropped closed and she slid her hands beneath the heavy layers of his cloak, unwilling to stand idly by while he touched her.

"Eliza," he whispered, breaking away just long enough to speak before diving down to take her lips again. "My love—"

Dimly, she heard voices approaching from beyond the wall. Thomas pulled back. She could see him working to quickly dispel his desire, his eyes becoming sharp and focused once again.

"It would not do, to be discovered like this," he stated with regret, stealing a final kiss.

She laughed. "No. It would not."

As if proving the verity of her statement, Rosa rounded the tree, immediately followed by William, Clara and Caroline. Her brother's eyebrow arched comically at seeing them standing so closely together.

"Did we interrupt something, Evanston?"

Thomas glowered at his prodding, then smiled grudgingly. "I wouldn't tell you if you did, Ashworth."

Caroline demurely covered her laugh with gloved fingertips, and Eliza kneeled down to regard Rosa and change the subject.

"Tell me, who won the fierce snowball battle?"

"I did!" she exclaimed, before suddenly dashing off

to follow the tinkling call of a goldfinch, flitting hurriedly through the stark landscape of leafless trees. Thomas uttered a dramatic sigh.

"If only the rest of us could be as fascinating as a bird or a squirrel."

Evanston and Rosa had become fast friends, dreaming up new and mischievous ways to have fun. He had assured her that, although the squirrels were scarcely about this time of year at Hawthorne Manor, they would be out in numbers come the warm breath of springtime. Rosa had also sampled the skilled offerings of his cook, finding them to be both delicious and worthy of her discriminating forest companions. This was her very highest form of culinary praise, and the viscount advised the mortified cook to receive the compliment with gratitude, lest he attempt to poach the affable Mrs. Humboldt from Lord Ashworth's estate.

Eliza gazed wistfully at the Dower House that had served her and Rosa well this past year. "The removers have been finished for a while, Thomas. We should be leaving, especially because you know Burton will be waiting for us with a blazing hearth." She was teasing, but the comment was likely true. No butler in history could possibly be as excited as the one expecting their arrival at Hawthorne Manor.

Evanston chuckled. "Yes, dear Lord, I don't want to keep Burton waiting. The man has been beside himself making preparations for you and Rosa. I suppose his preference for you will be something I'll get used to in time."

"Ah yes, that reminds me . . . you won't be needing Roberts any longer, will you?" asked William.

Clara cried out in delight beside him. "Oh, please tell me you'll bring him to Lawton Park! Poor Mrs. Malone has been so overworked as of late—"

"You should take him with you," enthused Eliza. "He is a wonderful butler."

"Fine, yes," William assented. "It seems like the right thing to do." Ashworth slid an arm affectionately around his wife's waist and pulled her close. "I must let Clara have her way on occasion."

Obviously, that was a joke, as Eliza knew her brother did everything possible to please his wife. Clara smiled in knowing satisfaction, and stifling a giggle, Eliza turned to eye Caroline good-naturedly.

"And what awaits you back in Hampshire? Have you heard from the new master of Greystone Hall?"

Her auburn-haired friend wrinkled her petite nose in disdain. "Not yet, but I have certainly heard from the man's land steward. Apparently, the border fence along the northwest edge of my property is placed significantly over his property line."

"Ah, yes. That was a known discrepancy," Eliza sighed. "But let me guess . . . he would like you to adjust the boundaries?"

"I believe he would," Caroline replied, shrugging noncommittally with a small smile.

Eliza's brows raised. "I can't imagine you submitting peacefully to such a request."

"I can't imagine that either," her friend agreed grumpily.

With a shake of her head, Eliza kissed Caroline on the cheek before pulling away to gaze fondly at her. "Take care."

Thomas leaned forwards to kiss Caroline on the cheek as well. "Never change."

"I wouldn't dream of it," she said with a laugh. "And thank you for your assistance during the season."

"We are but a letter away," he said seriously. "Send word if you need us."

The conversation was interrupted by the sudden appearance of Rosa, her tiny body jittering with excitement against her mother's heavy cobalt skirts. Eliza glanced down at her.

"Are you quite alright?"

"Look!" she exclaimed, pointing skyward. "It's snowing!"

The descent of glittering, crystalline flakes could barely be seen, they were so tiny. Yet, there they were. She turned to look up at Evanston.

"It will be snowing for our journey today," she said anxiously.

Thomas encircled her in his arms. "You've nothing to fear. I've instructed the driver to proceed cautiously, given the cold weather, and it is not such a long trip." He looked towards Caroline. "If there is any doubt about the roads to Hampshire, you come stay with us instead."

Her friend shook her head and tightly laced her thick scarlet cloak around her neck. "Thank you, but I'm sure it will be fine. The way is well-traveled."

After one last round of farewells and a promise to visit soon, the Earl and Countess of Ashworth boarded their vehicle and departed for home. Lady Caroline, likewise, took her leave, and Eliza soon found herself nestled within the cozy interior of Lord Evanston's carriage, her husband's strong form on her right and her daughter's diminutive one to her left.

Normally, the fit might have been too tight for her liking. But on this day, she found herself reveling in the way their warmth surrounded her. She snuggled more closely between them, although Rosa couldn't help but strain towards the window to watch the whitening hedgerows beyond. Eliza sighed serenely.

"Mmm, what a day. I feel so tired suddenly."

Her eyelids drooped in her weariness, and she rested her temple against the shoulder of Evanston's jacket, inhaling the clean, enticing scent of him. Relief coursed through her in palpable waves. An awful chapter of her life had come to an end, giving way to the happy new one that would be written with both Thomas and Rosa by her side.

It had been an exhausting journey.

Eliza felt her husband shift slightly against her. Then his fingertips skimmed along the curve of her cheek. "You should sleep if you're tired," Evanston said quietly. "We will be here when you wake."

She nodded and yawned, her eyes drifting closed. Rosa's voice grew faint as Eliza slid into a dreamless and peaceful slumber.

"Silly Papa, don't you know she never sleeps in the carriage?"

But strangely enough, this time she did.

Acknowledgments

Here we are again! I'm thrilled to have you with me at the end of another story, and I hope you had as much fun as I did. As always, I am not even close to the only person involved in making this book a reality, and I am thankful to everyone who has shown their support in different ways, big and small. You all made such a difference.

Lots of love and gratitude to Gary: my husband, friend, sounding board, tech support, and all-around amazing person. To Elise and Reid, you two are the best kids I could have ever asked for or wanted. It's not always easy sharing me with my writing, I know, but I appreciate it and love having you with me on this crazy journey.

Thank you to my parents, Dave and Dorinda, whose excitement, love, and support have meant the world to me. A big high-five to my mom, who not only reads and critiques each chapter as I write them, she also reads and re-reads every edited version of the complete manuscript, then reads the book again once it's published! Thank you to my brother, Adam, for our fun chats and your words of encouragement, and to my nephew, Connor, who is always a ray of sunshine. And thank you to my mother-in-law, Pat, for being an enthusiastic reader and cheering me on.

Thank you to my writing partner, Erika Bigelow, who helps guard against misspellings, awkward grammar, and things that sound better in my head than they actually are on paper. To Heather Bottomley and Shannon Sullivan, thank you for making "the power of the Tres" a real thing. Thanks to Rachel Whitaker and Anna Waller for your careful reads and helpful insights. Thank you to Eryn Frank and Kristi Beckley, who have been such good friends of mine for so long. Many thanks to Mary Murphy, Sakura Sutter, David O'Connell, Eduardo Cruz, and Alexandra Sipe for their friendship, advice, and support. And thank you to the members of the RWA and my local ERWA and GSRWA chapters for helping me find the inspiration to not only start writing, but to keep writing. I am lucky to know so many talented authors.

Thanks to L.E. Wilson and Samantha Saxon for showing me the ropes and for being great friends and supporters from the very beginning. Heartfelt thanks to Lenora Bell, who reached out to me during *Lady*'s debut and made everything that much brighter during our trips to Portland and Kansas City. Thank you to Lori Foster and her husband for their kindness on the road and beyond. And big thanks to Christy Carlyle and Charis Michaels for letting this baby author tag along in Denver. I can't wait to see all of you again.

Thank you to my wonderful agent, Kevan Lyon, who gave

me a chance to prove myself in this industry, and who helps me every step of the way. To Priyanka Krishnan, thank you for giving me a shot as a published author, and for being that first editorial voice to wiggle its way inside my head. Thank you to Elle Keck for being the second editorial voice to get inside my head—I look forward to many more books with you! And huge thanks to everyone at Avon/HarperCollins, including Pam Jaffee, Jes Lyons, Kayleigh Webb, Caro Perny, and Jennifer Stimson.

Finally, I couldn't do any of this without YOU. Many thanks to all of my readers, and to those of you I had the privilege of meeting this year! You're the best.

Warmly,
Marie

Don't miss Caroline's happy ever after coming next in

WAITING FOR A ROGUE

Available Winter 2019

About the Author

MARIE TREMAYNE graduated from the University of Washington with a B.A. in English Language and Literature. While there, a copy of *Pride and Prejudice* ended up changing her life. She decided to study the great books of the Regency and Victorian eras, and now enjoys writing her own tales set in the historical period she loves. Marie lives with her family in the beautiful Pacific Northwest.

www.marietremayne.com
www.facebook.com/MarieTremayneRomance
www.facebook.com/avonromance

Discover great authors, exclusive offers, and more at hc.com.